G.A. HENTY

December 8, 1832 — November 16, 1902

A Knight Of The White Cross

A Tale of The Siege of Rhodes

By G. A. Henty

ILLUSTRATED BY RALPH PEACOCK

Preston Speed Publications

Pennsylvania

A note about our name: Preston/Speed Publications
In an age where it has become fashionable to denigrate fathers,
we have decided to honor ours.   Our name is in loving memory
of Preston Louis Schmitt and Speed - Lester Herbert Maynard
("Speed" is a nickname that was earned for prowess in baseball).

This book is printed on acid-free paper, and its binding
materials have been chosen for strength and durability.

Published June 13, 1895 by
BLACKIE & SON, LONDON

Blackie & Son Title Page Date: 1896

Heirloom (hardcover) ISBN 1-887159-24-X
Popular (softcover) ISBN 1-887159-25-8
Printed in the U.S.A.

PRESTON/SPEED PUBLICATIONS
RR #4, BOX 705
MILL HALL, PENNSYLVANIA   17751
(570) 726-7844
1999
www.prestonspeed.com

INTRODUCTION:

G. A. Henty's life was filled with exciting adventure. Completing Westminster School, he attended Cambridge University. Along with a rigorous course of study, Henty participated in boxing, wrestling and rowing. The strenuous study and healthy, competitive participation in sports prepared Henty to be with the British army in Crimea, as a war correspondent witnessing Garibaldi fight in Italy, visiting Abyssinia, being present in Paris during the Franco-Prussian war, in Spain with the Carlists, at the opening of the Suez Canal, touring India with the Prince of Wales (later Edward VII) and a trip to the California gold fields. These are only a few of his exciting adventures.

G. A. Henty lived during the reign of Queen Victoria (1837-1901) and began his story telling career with his own children. After dinner, he would spend an hour or two in telling them a story that would continue the next day. Some stories took weeks! A friend was present one day and watched the spell-bound reaction of his children suggesting that he write down his stories so others could enjoy them. He did. Henty wrote approximately 144 books plus stories for magazines and was dubbed as "The Prince of Story-Tellers" and "The Boy's Own Historian." One of Mr. Henty's secretaries reported that he would quickly pace back and forth in his study dictating stories as fast as the secretary could record them.

Henty's stories revolve around a fictional boy hero during fascinating periods of history. His heroes are diligent, courageous, intelligent and dedicated to their country and cause in the face, at times, of great peril. His histories, particularly battle accounts, have been recognized by historian scholars for their accuracy. There is nothing dry in Mr. Henty's stories and thus he removes the drudgery and laborious task often associated with the study of history.

Henty's heroes fight wars, sail the seas, discover land, conquer evil empires, prospect for gold, and a host of other exciting adventures. They meet famous personages like Josephus, Titus, Hannibal, Robert the Bruce, Sir William Wallace, General Marlborough, General Gordon, General Kitchner, Robert E. Lee, Frederick the Great, the Duke of Wellington, Huguenot leader Coligny, Cortez, King Alfred, Napoleon, and Sir Francis Drake just to mention a *few*. The heroes go through the fall of Jerusalem, the Roman invasion of Britain, the Crusades, the Viking invasion of Europe, the Reformation in various countries, the Reign of Terror, etc. In short, Henty's heroes live through tumultuous historic eras meeting the leaders of that time. Understanding the culture of the time period becomes second nature as well as comparing/contrasting the society of various European and heathen cultures.

Preston/Speed Publications is delighted to offer again the works of G. A. Henty. Action-packed exciting adventure awaits adults and a whole new generation. The books have been reproduced with modern type-setting. However, the original grammar, spellings and punctuation remains the same as the original versions.

Foreword

Reading G. A. Henty's *Knight of the White Cross* took me back to my boyhood. I felt the same excitement, the eagerness to know what would happen, and the pleasure of exploring history with a master story-teller. I was interested too in Henty's choice of the time of his tale. A little later, another siege of Rhodes occurred, and, still later, the siege of Malta, one of the most dramatic events in history, a tale of heart-pounding excitement. But Henty chose an earlier time in order to depict the peoples, the conflict of cultures, and the importance of a man's character on human events. Henty was always a teacher. He dealt with the past to help prepare his readers for the future. It is no wonder that some writers and leaders of the 20th century gained direction from Henty. A couple of generations were greatly influenced by him, and the present revival of interest in Henty's books will continue that impact.

According to Henry Van Til, culture is religion externalized. It is noteworthy that this present revival of Henty is closely associated in most circles with home schools and Christian schools. In recent years, books by Henty have become, in the English world, collectors' items, some commanding high price. The new interest, in Christian educational circles, may well make Henty more influential than ever before.

It is interesting that Henty has always interested readers both young and old, so that, although intended for boys, he yearly commanded the interest of men, and also girls. There is a reason for this. Henty wrote with as much interest and concern in his subject as his children would have, if not more. He believed that Western civilization was at stake, and that a thorough knowledge and an awareness of our past were necessary ingredients to maintaining, developing, and extending our civilization. The Crusades began to protect the pilgrims to the Holy Land who were being raped, robbed, and enslaved by the Moslems. That the Crusaders were at times derelict in their conduct gives us no reason to obscure the grim facts which led to the Crusades.

The order of the Knights of St. John began with a hospital at Jerusalem but in time and out of it necessity became a military order. The first siege of Rhodes is the subject of this book.

This book is very good reading and a joy to see in print again.

Dr. Rousas John Rushdoony
June 2, 1997

"Then the Knights leapt on to the deck of the pirate."

PREFACE.

MY DEAR LADS,

The order of the Knights of St. John, which for some centuries played a very important part in the great struggle between Christianity and Mahomedanism, was, at its origin, a semi-religious body, its members being, like other monks, bound by vows of obedience, chastity, and poverty, and pledged to minister to the wants of the pilgrims who flocked to the Holy Places, to receive them at their great Hospital—or guest house—at Jerusalem, dedicated to St. John the Baptist, and to defend them on their passage to and from the sea, against attack by Moslems. In a comparatively short time the constitution of the order was changed, and the Knights Hospitallers became, like the Templars, a great military Order pledged to defend the Holy Sepulchre, and to war everywhere against the Moslems. The Hospitallers bore a leading share in the struggle which terminated in the triumph of the Moslems, and the capture by them of Jerusalem. The Knights of St. John then established themselves at Acre, but after a valiant defence of that fortress, removed to Crete, and shortly afterwards to Rhodes. There they fortified the town, and withstood two terrible sieges by the Turks. At the end of the second they obtained honourable terms from Sultan Solyman, and retiring to Malta established themselves there in an even stronger fortress than that of Rhodes, and repulsed all the efforts of the Turks to dispossess them. The Order was the great bulwark of Christendom against the invasion of the Turks, and the tale of their long struggle is one of absorbing interest, and of the many eventful episodes none is more full of incident and excitement than the first siege of Rhodes, which I have chosen for the subject of my story.

Yours truly,
G. A. Henty

CONTENTS

ILLUSTRATIONS

CHAPTER I
The King-Maker

A STATELY lady was looking out of the window of an apartment in the Royal Château of Amboise, in the month of June 1470. She was still handsome, though many years of anxiety, misfortune, and trouble, had left their traces on her face. In the room behind her, a knight was talking to a lady sitting at a tambour frame; a lad of seventeen was standing at another window stroking a hawk that sat on his wrist, while a boy of nine was seated at a table examining the pages of an illuminated missal.

"What will come of it, Eleanor?" the lady at the window said, turning suddenly and impatiently from it. "It seems past belief that I am to meet as a friend this haughty earl, who has for fifteen years been the bitterest enemy of my House. It appears almost impossible."

"'Tis strange indeed, my Queen; but so many strange things have befallen your Majesty that you should be the last to wonder at this. At any rate, as you said but yesterday, naught but good can come of it. He has done his worst against you, and one can scarce doubt that if he chooses he has power to do as much good for you, as in past times he has done you evil. 'Tis certain that his coming here shows he is in earnest, for his presence,—which is sure sooner or later to come to the ears of the Usurper,—will cause him to fall into the deepest disgrace."

"And yet it seemed," the queen said, "that by marrying his daughter to Clarence he had bound himself more firmly than ever to the side of York."

1

"Ay, madam," the knight said. "But Clarence himself is said to be alike unprincipled and ambitious, and it may well be that Warwick intended to set him up against Edward; had he not done so, such an alliance would not necessarily strengthen his position at Court."

"Methinks your supposition is the true one, Sir Thomas," the queen said. "Edward cares not sufficiently for his brother to bestow much favour upon the father of the prince's wife. Thus, he would gain but little by the marriage unless he were to place Clarence on the throne. Then he would again become the real ruler of England, as he was until Edward married Elizabeth Woodville, and the House of Rivers rose to the first place in the royal favour, and eclipsed the Star of Warwick. It is no wonder the proud Earl chafes under the ingratitude of the man who owes his throne to him, and that he is ready to dare everything so that he can but prove to him that he is not to be slighted with impunity. But why come to me, when he has Clarence as his puppet?"

"He may have convinced himself, madam, that Clarence is even less to be trusted than Edward, or he may perceive that but few of the Yorkists would follow him were he to declare against the Usurper, while assuredly your adherents would stand aloof altogether from such a struggle. Powerful as he is, Warwick could not alone withstand the united forces of all the nobles pledged to the support of the House of York. Thence, as I take it, does it happen that he has resolved to throw in his lot with Lancaster, if your Majesty will but forgive the evil he has done your House and accept him as your ally. No doubt he will have terms to make and conditions to lay down."

"He may make what conditions he chooses," Queen Margaret said passionately, "so that he does but aid me to take vengeance on that false traitor; to place my husband again on the throne; and to obtain for my son his rightful heritage."

As she spoke a trumpet sounded in the courtyard below.

"He has come," she exclaimed. "Once again, after years of misery and humiliation, I can hope."

"We had best retire, madam," Sir Thomas Tresham said. "He will speak more freely to your Majesty if there are no witnesses. Come, Gervaise, it is time that you practised your exercises." And Sir Thomas, with his wife and child, quitted the room, leaving Queen Margaret with her son to meet the man who had been the bitterest foe of her House, the author of her direst misfortunes.

For two hours the Earl of Warwick was closeted with the queen; then he took horse and rode away. As soon as he did so, a servant informed Sir Thomas and his wife that the queen desired their presence. Margaret was standing radiant when they entered.

"Congratulate me, my friends," she said. "The Star of Lancaster has risen again. Warwick has placed all his power and influence at our disposal. We have both forgiven all the past: I the countless injuries he has inflicted on my House, he the execution of his father and so many of his friends. We have both laid aside all our grievances, and we stand united by our hate for Edward. There is but one condition, and this I accepted gladly—namely, that my son should marry his daughter Anne. This will be another bond between us; and by all reports Anne is a charming young lady. Edward has gladly agreed to the match; he could make no alliance, even with the proudest princess in Europe, which would so aid him, and so strengthen his throne."

"God grant that your hopes may be fulfilled, madam," the knight said earnestly, "and that peace may be given to our distracted country! The Usurper has rendered himself unpopular by his extravagance and by the exactions of his tax-collectors, and I believe that England will gladly welcome the return of its lawful king to power. When does Warwick propose to begin?"

"He will at once get a fleet together. Louis, who has privately brought about this meeting, will of course throw no impediment in his way; but, on the other hand, the Duke of Burgundy will do all in his power to thwart the enterprise,

3

and will, as soon as he learns of it, warn Edward. I feel new life in me, Eleanor. After fretting powerless for years, I seem to be a different woman now that there is a prospect of action. I am rejoiced at the thought that at last I shall be able to reward those who have ventured and suffered so much in the cause of Lancaster."

"My hope is, madam, that this enterprise will be the final one,—that, once successful, our dear land will be no longer deluged with blood, and that never again shall I be forced to draw my sword against my countrymen."

"'Tis a good and pious wish, Sir Thomas, and heartily do I join in it. My married life has been one long round of trouble, and none more than I, have cause to wish for peace."

"There is the more hope for it, madam, that these wars have greatly diminished the number of powerful barons. It is they who are the authors of this struggle; their rivalries and their ambitions are the ruin of England. Save for their retainers there would be no armies to place in the field; the mass of people stand aloof altogether, desiring only to live in peace and quiet. 'Tis the same here in France; 'tis the powerful vassals of the king that are ever causing trouble."

"'Tis so indeed, Sir Thomas. But without his feudal lords how could a king place an army in the field, when his dominions were threatened by a powerful neighbour?"

"Then it would be the people's business to fight, madam, and I doubt not that they would do so in defence of their hearths and homes. Besides, the neighbour would no longer have the power of invasion were he also without great vassals. These great barons stand between the king and his subjects; and a monarch would be a king indeed were he able to rule without their constant dictation, and undisturbed by their rivalry and ambitions."

"That would be a good time indeed, Sir Thomas," the queen said, with a smile; "but methinks there is but little chance of its coming about, for at present it seems to me that the vassals are better able to make or unmake kings, than kings are able to deprive the great vassals of power;

and never since Norman William set foot in England were they more powerful than they are at present. What does my chance of recovering our throne rest upon? Not upon our right, but on the quarrel between Warwick and the House of Rivers. We are but puppets that the great lords play against each other. Did it depend upon my will, it should be as you say; I would crush them all at a blow. Then only should I feel really a queen. But that is but a dream that can never be carried out."

"Not in our time, madam. But perhaps it may come sooner than we expect; and this long war, which has destroyed many great families and weakened others, may greatly hasten its arrival. I presume until Warwick is ready to move naught will be done, your Majesty?"

"That is not settled yet. Warwick spoke somewhat of causing a rising in the north before he set sail, so that a portion at least of Edward's power may be up there when we make our landing."

"It would be a prudent step, madam. If we can but gain possession of London, the matter would be half finished. The citizens are ever ready to take sides with those whom they regard as likely to win, and just as they shout at present 'Long live King Edward!' so would they shout 'Long live King Henry!' did you enter the town."

"This may perhaps change the thought that you have entertained, Sir Thomas, of making your son a Knight of St. John."

"I have not thought the matter over, madam. If there were quiet in the land I should, were it not for my vow, be well content that he should settle down in peace at my old hall; but if I see that there is still trouble and bloodshed ahead, I would in any case far rather that he should enter the Order, and spend his life in fighting the infidel than in strife with Englishmen. My good friend, the Grand Prior of the Order in England, has promised that he will take him as his page, and at any rate in the House of St. John's he will pass his youth in security whatsoever fate may befall me. The child himself already bids fair to do honour to

5

our name, and to become a worthy member of the Order. He is fond of study, and under my daily tuition is making good progress in the use of his weapons."

"That is he," the prince said, speaking for the first time, "It was but yesterday in the great hall downstairs he stood up with blunted swords against young Victor de Paulliac, who is nigh three years his senior. It was amusing to see how the little knaves fought against each other; and by my faith Gervaise held his own staunchly, in spite of Victor's superior height and weight. If he join the Order, Sir Thomas, I warrant me he will cleave many an infidel's skull, and will do honour to the *langue* of England."

"I hope so, prince," the knight said gravely. "The Moslems ever gain in power, and it may well be that the Knights of St. John will be hardly pressed to hold their own. If the boy joins them it will be my wish that he shall as early as possible repair to Rhodes. I do not wish him to become one of the drones who live in sloth at their commanderies in England, and take no part in the noble struggle of the Order with the Moslem host, who have captured Constantinople and now threaten all Europe. We were childless some years after our marriage, and Eleanor and I vowed that were a son born to us he should join the Order of the White Cross, and dedicate his life to the defence of Christian Europe against the infidel. Our prayers for a son were granted, and Gervaise will enter the Order as soon as his age will permit him. That is why I rejoice at the grand prior's offer to take him as his page, for he will dwell in the hospital safely until old enough to take the first steps towards becoming a knight of the Order."

"I would that I had been born the son of a baron like yourself," the prince said earnestly, "and that I were free to choose my own career. Assuredly in that case I too would have joined the noble Order and have spent my life in fighting in so grand a cause, free from all the quarrels and disputes and enmities that rend England. Even should I some day gain a throne, surely my lot is not to be envied. Yet, as I have been born to the rank, I must try for it, and I trust to do so worthily and bravely. But who can say what the end will be? Warwick has ever been our foe, and though my royal mother may use him in order to free my father, and place him on the throne, she must know well enough that he but uses us for his own ends alone, and that he will ever stand beside the throne and be the real ruler of England."

"For a time, Edward," the queen broke in. "We have shown that we can wait, and now it seems that our great hope is likely to be fulfilled. After that, the rest will be easy. There are other nobles, well-nigh as powerful as he, who look with jealousy upon the way in which he lords it, and be assured that they will look with a still less friendly eye upon him when he stands, as you say, beside the throne, once your father is again seated there. We can afford to bide our time, and assuredly it will not be long before a party is formed against Warwick. Until then we must bear everything. Our interests are the same. If he is content to remain a prop to the throne, and not to eclipse it, the memory of the past will not stand between us, and I shall regard him as the weapon that has beaten down the House of York and restored us to our own, and shall give him my confidence and friendship. If, on the other hand, he assumes too much, and tries to lord it over us, I shall seek other support and gather a party which even he will be unable successfully to withstand. I should have thought, Edward, that you would be even more glad than I that this long time of weary waiting for action is over, and that once again the banner of Lancaster will be spread to the winds."

"I shall be that, mother. Rather would I meet death in the field than live cooped up here, a pensioner of France. But I own that I should feel more joy at the prospect if the people of England had declared in our favour, instead of its being Warwick,—whom you have always taught me to fear and hate,—who thus comes to offer to place my father again on the throne, and whose goodwill towards us is simply the result of pique and displeasure because he is no longer first in the favour of Edward. It does not seem to me that a throne won by the aid of a traitor can be a stable one."

"You are a foolish boy," the queen said angrily. "Do you not see that by marrying Warwick's daughter you will attach him firmly to us?"

"Marriages do not count for much, mother. Another of Warwick's daughters married Clarence, Edward's brother, and yet he purposes to dethrone Edward."

The queen gave an angry gesture and said,—

"You have my permission to retire, Edward. I am in no mood to listen to auguries of evil at the present moment."

The prince hesitated for a moment as if about to speak, but with an effort controlled himself, and bowing deeply, to his mother, left the room.

"Edward is in a perverse humour," the queen said in a tone of much vexation to Sir Thomas Tresham, when Gervaise had left the room. "However, I know he will bear himself well when the hour of trial comes."

"That I can warrant he will, madam; he has a noble character, frank and fearless, and yet thoughtful beyond his years. He will make, I believe, a noble king, and may well gather round him all parties in the state. But your Majesty must make excuses for his humour. Young people are strong in their likes and dislikes. He has never heard you speak aught but ill of Warwick, and he knows how much harm the Earl has done to your House. The question of expediency does not weigh with the young as with their elders. While you see how great are the benefits that will accrue from an alliance with Warwick, and are ready to lay aside the hatred of years and to forget the wrongs you have suffered, the young prince is unable so quickly to forget that enmity against the Earl that he has learnt from you."

"You are right, Sir Thomas, and I cannot blame Edward that he is unable, as I am, to forget the past. What steps would you advise that I myself should take? Shall I remain passive here, or shall I do what I can to rouse our partisans in England?"

"I should say the latter, madam. Of course it will not do to trust to letters, for were one of these to fall into the wrong hands it might cause the ruin of Warwick's expedition; but I should say that a cautious message sent by word of mouth to some of our old adherents would be of great use. I myself will, if your Majesty chooses to entrust me with the mission, undertake to carry it out. I should take ship and land in the west, and would travel in the guise of a simple country gentleman, and call upon your adherents in all the western counties. It would be needful first to make out a list of the nobles who have shown themselves devoted to your cause, and I should bid these hold themselves and their retainers in readiness to take the field suddenly. I should say no word of Warwick, but merely hint that you will not land alone, but with a powerful array, and that all the chances are in your favour."

"But it would be a dangerous mission, Sir Thomas."

"Not greatly so, madam. My own estates lie in Sussex, and there would be but little chance of my recognition, save by your own adherents, who may have seen me among the leaders of your troops in battle; and even that is improbable. At present Edward deems himself so securely seated on the throne that men can travel hither and thither through the country without being questioned, and the Lancastrians live quietly with the Yorkists. Unless I were so unfortunate as to meet a Yorkist noble who knew that I was a banished man and one who had the honour of being in your Majesty's confidence, I do not think that any danger could possibly arise. What say you, wife?"

"I cannot think that there is no danger," Lady Tresham said; "but even so I would not say a word to hinder you from doing service to the cause. I know of no one else who could perform the mission. You have left my side to go into battle before now, and I cannot think that the danger of such an expedition can be as great as that which you would undergo in the field. Therefore, my dear lord, I would say no word now to stay you."

She spoke bravely and unfalteringly, but her face had paled when Sir Thomas first made the proposal, and the colour had not yet come back to her cheeks.

"Bravely spoken, dame," the queen said warmly. "Well, Sir Thomas, I accept your offer, and trust that you will not be long separated from your wife and son, who will of course journey with me when I go to England, where doubtless you will be able to rejoin us a few days after we land. Now let us talk over the noblemen and gentlemen in the west, upon whom we can rely, if not to join our banner as soon as it is spread, at least to say no word that will betray you."

Two days later Sir Thomas Tresham started on his journey, while the queen remained at Amboise eagerly awaiting the news that Warwick had collected a fleet, and was ready to set sail. Up to this point the Duke of Clarence had sided with Warwick against his brother, and had passed over with him to France, believing, no doubt, that if the Earl should succeed in dethroning Edward, he intended to place him, his son-in-law, upon the throne. He was rudely awakened from this delusion by Charles of Burgundy, who, being in all but open rebellion against his suzerain, the King of France, kept himself intimately acquainted with all that was going on. He despatched a female emissary to Clarence to inform him of the league Warwick had made with the Lancastrians, and the intended marriage between his daughter Anne and the young prince; imploring him to be reconciled with his brother and to break off his alliance with the Earl, who was on the point of waging war against the House of York.

Clarence took the advice, and went over to England, where he made his peace with Edward, the more easily because the king, who was entirely given up to pleasure, treated with contempt the warnings the Duke of Burgundy sent him of the intended invasion by Warwick. And yet a moment's serious reflection should have shown him that his position was precarious. The crushing exactions of the tax-gatherers, in order to provide the means for Edward's lavish expenditure, had already caused very serious insurrections in various parts of the country, and his unpopularity was deep and general. In one of these risings the royal troops had suffered a crushing defeat. The Earl Rivers, the father, and Sir John Woodville, one of the brothers, of the queen had, with the Earl of Devon, been captured by the rebels, and the three had been beheaded, and the throne had only been saved by the intervention of Warwick.

Thus, then, Edward had every reason for fearing the result should the Earl appear in arms against him. He took, however, no measures whatever to prepare for the coming storm, and although the Duke of Burgundy despatched a fleet to blockade Harfleur, where Warwick was fitting out his expedition, and actually sent the name of the port at which the Earl intended to land if his fleet managed to escape from Harfleur, Edward continued carelessly to spend his time in pleasure and dissipation, bestowing his full confidence upon the Archbishop of York and the Marquis of Montague, both brothers of the Earl of Warwick.

The elements favoured his enemies, for early in September the Duke of Burgundy's Fleet, off Harfleur, was dispersed by a storm, and Warwick, as soon as the gale abated, set sail, and on the 13th landed on the Devonshire coast. His force was a considerable one, for the French king had furnished him both with money and men; on effecting his landing he found no army assembled to oppose him. A few hours after his disembarkation, he was joined by Sir Thomas Tresham, who gave him the good news that the whole of the west was ready to rise, and that in a few days all the great landowners would join him with their retainers. This turned out to be the case, and Warwick, with a great array, marched eastward. Kent had already risen, and London declared for King Henry. Warwick, therefore, instead of marching thither, moved towards

Lincolnshire, where Edward was with his army, having gone north to repress an insurrection that had broken out there at the instigation of Warwick.

Lord Montague now threw off the mask, and declared for King Henry. Most of the soldiers followed him, and Edward, finding it hopeless to oppose Warwick's force, which was now within a short march of him, took ship with a few friends who remained faithful, and sailed for Holland. Warwick returned to London, where he took King Henry from the dungeon in the Tower, into which he himself had, five years before, thrown him, and proclaimed him king.

On the day that this took place Dame Tresham arrived in London with her son. The queen had found that she could not for the present cross, as she was waiting for a large French force which was to accompany her. As it was uncertain how long the delay might last, she counselled her friend to join her husband. The revolution had been accomplished without the loss of a single life, with the exception of that of the Earl of Worcester, who was hated for his cruelty by the people. Edward's principal friends took refuge in various religious houses. The queen, her three daughters, and her mother, fled to the sanctuary at Westminster. All these were left unmolested, nor was any step taken against the other adherents of the House of York. Warwick was now virtually King of England. The king, whose intellect had always been weak, was now almost an imbecile, and Margaret of Anjou was still detained in France. Sir Thomas Tresham went down to his estates in Kent, and there lived quietly for some months. The Duke of Clarence had joined Warwick as soon as he saw that his brother's cause was lost; and as the Duke had no knowledge of his changed feelings towards him, he was heartily welcomed. An act of settlement was passed by Parliament entailing the Crown on Henry's son Edward, Prince of Wales, and in case of that prince's death without issue, on the Duke of Clarence. On the 12th of March following (1471) Edward suddenly appeared with a fleet with which he had been secretly supplied by the Duke of Burgundy, and, sailing north, landed in the Humber. He found the northern population by no means disposed to aid him, but upon his taking a solemn oath that he had no designs whatever upon the throne, but simply claimed to be restored to his rights and dignities as Duke of York, he was joined by a sufficient force to enable him to cross the Trent. As he marched south his army speedily swelled, and he was joined by many great lords.

Warwick had summoned Henry's adherents to the field, and marched north to meet him. When the armies approached each other, the Duke of Clarence, who commanded a portion of Henry's army, went over with his whole force to Edward, and Warwick, being no longer in a position to give battle, was obliged to draw off and allow Edward to march unopposed towards London. The citizens, with their usual fickleness, received him with the same outburst of enthusiasm with which, five months before, they had greeted the entry of Warwick. The unfortunate King Henry was again thrown into his dungeon in the Tower, and Edward found himself once more King of England.

Sir Thomas Tresham, as soon as he heard of the landing of Edward, had hastened up to London. In his uncertainty how matters would go, he brought his wife and son up with him, and left them in lodgings, while he marched north with Warwick. As soon as the defection of Clarence opened the road to London, he left the Earl, promising to return in a few days, and rode to town, arriving there two days before Edward's entry, and, purchasing another horse, took his wife and son down to St. Albans, where leaving them, he rejoined Warwick. In a few days the latter had gathered sufficient forces to enable him to risk the fortunes of a battle, and, marching south, he encamped with his army on the common north of Barnet. Edward had come out to meet him, and the two armies slept on Easter Eve within two miles of each other.

A KNIGHT OF THE WHITE CROSS

Late in the evening Clarence sent a messenger to the Earl, offering to mediate, but the offer was indignantly refused by Warwick.

In the darkness, neither party was aware of the other's precise position. Warwick was much stronger than the king in artillery, and had placed it on his right wing. The king, in his ignorance of the enemy's position, had placed his troops considerably more to the right than those of Warwick's army. The latter, believing that Edward's line was facing his, kept up a heavy cannonade all night upon where he supposed Edward's left to be—a cannonade which was thus entirely futile.

In the morning (April 14th) a heavy mist covered the country and prevented either force from seeing the other's dispositions. Warwick took the command of his left wing, having with him the Duke of Exeter. Somerset was in command of his centre, and Montague and Oxford of his right.

Edward placed himself in the centre of his array, the Duke of Gloucester commanded on his right, and Lord Hastings on his left.

Desirous, from his inferiority in artillery, to fight out the battle hand to hand, Edward, at six o'clock in the morning, ordered his trumpets to blow, and, after firing a few shots, advanced through the mist to attack the enemy. His misconception as to Warwick's position, which had saved his troops from the effects of the cannonade during the night, was now disadvantageous to him, for the Earl's right so greatly outflanked his left that when they came into contact Hastings found himself nearly surrounded by a vastly superior force. His wing fought valiantly, but was at length broken by Oxford's superior numbers, and driven out of the field. The mist prevented the rest of the armies from knowing what had happened on the king's left. Edward himself led the charge on Warwick's centre, and having his best troops under his command, pressed forward with such force and vehemence that he pierced Somerset's lines and threw them into confusion.

THE KING-MAKER

Just as Warwick's right had outflanked the king's left, so his own left was outflanked by Gloucester. Warwick's troops fought with great bravery, and, in spite of the disaster to his centre, were holding their ground until Oxford, returning from his pursuit of the king's left, came back through the mist. The king's emblem was a sun, that of Oxford a star with streaming rays. In the dim light this was mistaken by Warwick's men for the king's device, and believing that Oxford was far away on the right, they received him with a discharge of arrows. This was at once returned, and a conflict took place. At last the mistake was discovered, but the confusion caused was irreparable. Warwick and Oxford each suspected the other of treachery, and the king's right still pressing on, the confusion increased, and the battle, which had been so nearly won by the Earl, soon became a complete defeat, and by ten in the morning Warwick's army was in full flight.

Accounts differ as to the strength of the forces engaged, but it is probable that there was no great inequality, and that each party brought some fifteen thousand men into the field. The number of slain is also very uncertain, some historians placing the total at ten thousand, others as low as one thousand; but from the number of nobles who fell, the former computation is probably nearest to the truth. Warwick, his brother Montague, and many other nobles and gentlemen, were killed, the only great nobles on his side who escaped being the Earls of Somerset and Oxford; many were also killed on Edward's side, and the slaughter among the ordinary fighting men was greater than usual.

Hitherto in the battles that had been fought during the civil war; while the leaders taken on the field were frequently executed, the common soldiers were permitted to return to their homes, as they had only been acting under the orders of their feudal superiors, and were not considered responsible for their acts. At Barnet, however, Edward, smarting from the humiliation he had suffered by his enforced flight from England, owing to the whole country declaring for his rival, gave orders that no quarter was to be granted. It was an anxious day at St. Albans, where many ladies whose husbands were with Warwick's army had, like Dame Tresham, taken up their quarters. It was but a few miles from the field of battle. In the event of victory they could at once join their husbands, while in case of defeat they could take refuge in the sanctuary of the abbey. Messengers the night before had brought the news that the battle would begin at the dawn of day, and with intense anxiety they waited for the news.

Dame Tresham and her son attended early mass at the abbey, and had returned to their lodgings, when Sir Thomas rode up at full speed. His armour was dinted and his plume shorn away from his helmet. As he entered the house he was met by his wife, who had run downstairs as she heard his horse stop at the door. A glance at his face was sufficient to tell the news.

"We have lost the day," he said. "Warwick and Monague are both killed. All is lost here for the present. Which will you do, my love, ride with me to the West, where Queen Margaret will speedily land, if indeed she has not landed already, or take sanctuary here with the boy?"

"I will go with you," she said. "I would vastly rather do so."

"I will tell you more on the road," he said. "There is no time to be lost now."

The woman of the house was called, and at once set her son to saddle the other horse and to give a feed to that of the knight. Dame Tresham busied herself with packing the saddle-bags while her husband partook of a hasty meal; and ten minutes after his arrival they set off, Gervaise riding behind his father, while the latter led the horse on which his wife was mounted. A thick mist hung over the country.

"This mist told against us in the battle, wife, for as we advanced our forces fell into confusion, and more than once friend attacked friend, believing that he was an enemy. However, it has proved an advantage to us now, for it has enabled great numbers to escape who might otherwise have been followed and cut down. I was very fortunate. I had

Sir Thomas Tresham brings his wife news of the lost battle.

left my horse at a little farmhouse two miles in the rear of our camp, and in the fog had but small hope of finding it; but soon after leaving the battle-field, I came upon a rustic hurrying in the same direction as myself, and upon questioning him it turned out that he was a hand on the very farm at which I had left the horse. He had, with two or three others, stolen out after midnight to see the battle, and was now making his way home again, having seen indeed but little, but having learned from fugitives that we had been defeated. He guided me to the farmhouse, which otherwise I should assuredly never have reached. His master was favourable to our party, and let the man take one of the cart-horses, on which he rode as my guide until he had placed me upon the high road to St. Albans, and I was then able to gallop on at full speed."

"And Warwick and his brother Montague are both killed?"

"Both. The great Earl will make and unmake no more kings. He has been a curse to England, with his boundless ambition, his vast possessions, and his readiness to change sides and to embroil the country in civil war for purely personal ends. The great nobles are a curse to the country, wife. They are, it is true, a check upon kingly ill-doing and oppression; but were they, with their great arrays of retainers and feudal followers, out of the way, methinks that the citizens and yeomen would be able to hold their own against any king."

"Was the battle a hard-fought one?"

"I know but little of what passed, except near the standard of Warwick himself. There the fighting was fierce indeed, for it was against the Earl that the king finally directed his chief onslaught. Doubtless he was actuated both by a deep personal resentment against the Earl for the part he had played and the humiliation he had inflicted upon him, and also by the knowledge that a defeat of Warwick personally would be the heaviest blow that he could inflict upon the cause of Lancaster."

"Then do you think the cause is lost?"

"I say not that. Pembroke has a strong force in Wales, and if the West rises, and Queen Margaret on landing can join him, we may yet prevail; but I fear that the news of the field of Barnet will deter many from joining us. Men may risk lands and lives for a cause which seems to offer a fair prospect of success, but they can hardly be blamed for holding back when they see that the chances are all against them. Moreover, as a Frenchwoman, it cannot be denied that Margaret has never been popular in England, and her arrival here, aided by French gold and surrounded by Frenchmen, will tell against her with the country people. I went as far as I could on the day before I left Amboise, urging her on no account to come hither until matters were settled. It would have been infinitely better had the young prince come alone, and landed in the West without a single follower. The people would have admired his trust in them, and would, I am sure, have gathered strongly round his banner. However, we must still hope for the best. Fortune was against us to-day: it may be with us next time we give battle. And with parties so equally divided throughout the country a signal victory would bring such vast numbers to our banners that Edward would again find it necessary to cross the seas."

CHAPTER II
THE BATTLE OF TEWKESBURY

RIDING fast, Sir Thomas Tresham crossed the Thames at Reading before any news of the battle of Barnet had arrived there. On the third day after leaving St. Albans he reached Westbury, and there heard that the news had been received of the queen's landing at Plymouth on the very day on which her friends had been defeated at Barnet, and that she had already been joined by the Duke of Somerset, the Earl of Devon, and others, and that Exeter had been named as the point of rendezvous for her friends. As the Lancastrians were in the majority in Wiltshire and Somerset, there was no longer any fear of arrest by partisans of York, and after resting for a day Sir Thomas Tresham rode quietly on to Exeter, where the queen had already arrived.

The battle of Barnet had not, in reality, greatly weakened the Lancastrian cause. The Earl of Warwick was so detested by the adherents of the Red Rose that comparatively few of them had joined him, and the fight was rather between the two sections of Yorkists than between York and Lancaster. The Earl's death had broken up his party, and York and Lancaster were now face to face with each other, without his disturbing influence on either side. Among those who had joined the queen was Tresham's great friend, the Grand Prior of St. John's. Sir Thomas took up his lodgings in the house where he had established himself. The queen was greatly pleased at the arrival of Dame Tresham, and at her earnest request the latter shared her apartments, while Gervaise remained with his father.

THE BATTLE OF TEWKESBURY

"So this is the young Knight of St. John," the prior said, on the evening of the arrival of Sir Thomas. "I would, Tresham, that I were at present at Rhodes, doing battle with the infidels, rather than engaged in this warfare against Englishmen and fellow-Christians."

"I can well understand that," Sir Thomas said.

"I could not hold aloof here, Tresham. The vows of our Order by no means hinder us from taking part in the affairs of our own country. The rule of the Order is indeed against it, but the rule is constantly broken. Were it otherwise there could be no commanderies in this or any other country; we should have, on entering the Order, to abandon our nationality, and to form part of one community in the East. The Order is true to its oaths. We cannot defend the Holy Sepulchre, for that, for the present, is hopelessly lost; but we can and do wage war with the infidel. For this funds are necessary as well as swords, and our commanderies throughout Europe supply the funds by which the struggle is maintained, and, when it is needed, send out contingents to help those fighting in the East. It was from the neglect of this cardinal point that the Templars fell. Their commanderies amassed wealth and wide possessions, but unlike us the knights abstained altogether from fulfilling their vows, and ceased to resist the infidel. Therefore they were suppressed, and, with the general approval of Europe, a portion of their possessions was handed over to the knights of St. John. However, as I understand, it is your wish that as soon as the boy comes of age to wield arms he shall go to Rhodes and become an active member of the Order. This is indeed the rule with all neophytes, but having served a certain time they are then permitted to return and join one of the commanderies in their native countries."

"I do not wish that for Gervaise," his father said; "at least, I wish him to remain at Rhodes until all the civil troubles are absolutely at an end here. My life has been ruined by them. Loving retirement and quiet, and longing for nothing so much as a life among my tenantry, I have almost from a boy been actively engaged in warfare or have been away as an exile. Here every one of gentle blood has been more or less mixed up in these civil broils. To few of us does it personally matter whether a member of the House of York or Lancaster sits on the throne, and yet we have been almost compelled to take sides with one or the other; and now, in my middle age I am on the eve of another battle in which I risk my life and fortune. If we win I gain naught but the satisfaction of seeing young Edward made King of England. If we lose I am going into exile again, or I may leave my wife a widow, and my child penniless."

"It is too true, Tresham; and as I am as likely to fall as you are, the child might be left without a protector as well as fatherless. However, against that I will provide. I will write a letter to Peter D'Aubusson, who is the real governor of Rhodes, for the Grand Master Orsini is so old that his rule is little more than nominal. At his death D'Aubusson is certain to be elected Grand Master. He is a dear friend of mine. We entered the Order the same year, and were comrades in many a fight with the Moslems, and I am quite sure that when I tell him that it is my last request of him, he will, in memory of our long friendship, appoint your son as one of the Grand Master's pages. As you know, no one, however high his rank, is accepted as a novice before the age of sixteen. After a year's probation he is received into the body of the Order as a professed knight, and must go out and serve for a time in Rhodes. After three years of active service he must reside two more at the convent, and can then be made a commander. There is but one exception to the rule—namely, that the pages of the grand master are entitled to the privilege of admission at the age of twelve, so that they become professed knights at thirteen. Your son is now but nine, you say, and we must remember that D'Aubusson is not yet Grand Master, and Orsini may live for some years yet. D'Aubusson, however, can doubtless get him to appoint the boy as one of his pages. But, in any case, there are three years yet to be passed before he can go out. Doubtless these he will spend under his mother's care;

but as it is as well to provide against everything, I will furnish your dame with a letter to the knight who will probably succeed me as Grand Prior of the English *langue*, asking him to see to the care and education of the boy up to the time when he can proceed to Rhodes. We may hope, my dear Tresham, that there will be no occasion to use such documents, and that you and I may both be able personally to watch over his career. Still, it is as well to take every precaution. I shall, of course, give D'Aubusson full particulars about you, your vow, and your wishes."

"I thank you greatly, old friend," Sir Thomas said. "It has taken a load off my mind. I shall leave him here with his mother when we march forward, and bid her, if ill befalls me, cross again to France, and then to keep Gervaise with her until she can bring herself to part with him. She has her jewels and a considerable sum of money which I accepted from the man who has been enjoying my estates for the last five years, in lieu of the monies that he had received during that time. Therefore, she will not lack means for some years to come. Besides, Queen Margaret has a real affection for her, and will, doubtless, be glad to have her with her again in exile."

"When I am old enough," Gervaise said, suddenly looking up from a missal of the Grand Prior's which he had been examining, "I will chop off the head of the Duke of York, and bring mother back to England."

"You will be a valiant champion no doubt, my boy," the prior said, laughing. "But that is just what your father does not want. Chop off the heads of as many infidels as you will, but leave Englishmen alone, be they dukes or commoners. It is a far more glorious career to be aiding to defend Europe against the Moslem than to be engaged in wars with your own countrymen. If the great lords will fight, let them fight it out themselves without our aid; but I hope that long before you become a man even they will be tired of these perpetual broils, and that some agreement may be arrived at, and peace reign in this unhappy land."

A KNIGHT OF THE WHITE CROSS

"Besides, Gervaise," his father added, "you must bear in mind always that my earnest wish and hope is that you will become a champion of the Cross. I took a solemn vow before you were born that if a son were granted to me I would dedicate him to the service of the Cross, and if I am taken from you, you must still try to carry that oath into effect. I trust that, at any rate for some years after you attain manhood, you will expend your whole strength and powers in the defence of Christianity, and as a worthy knight of the Order of St. John. Too many of the knights, after serving for three years against the infidels, return to their native countries and pass the rest of their lives in slothful ease at their commanderies, save perhaps when at any great crisis they go out for a while and join in the struggle. Such is not the life I should wish you to lead. At the death of your mother and myself, you will have no family ties in England—nothing to recall you here. If the House of York succeeds in establishing itself firmly on the throne, my estates will be forfeited. Therefore, regard Rhodes as your permanent home, and devote your life to the Order. Beginning so young, you may hope to distinguish yourself—to gain high rank in it; but remember that though these are my wishes, they are not my orders, and that your career must be in your own hands."

"I will be a brave knight, father," the boy said firmly.

"That is right, my boy. Now go upstairs to your bed; it is already late. I do not regret my vow," he went on, after Gervaise had left the room, "though I regret that he is my only son. It is singular that men should care about what comes after them, but I suppose it is human nature. I should have liked to think that my descendants would sit in the old house, and that men of my race and name would long own the estates. But doubtless it is all for the best; for at least I can view the permanent loss of my estates, in case the Yorkists triumph, without any poignant regret."

"Doubtless it is for the best, Tresham, and you must remember that things may not, even now, turn out as you think. A knight who has done a brave service does not find much difficulty in obtaining from the Pope a dispensation from his vows. Numbers of knights have so left the Order and have married and perpetuated their name. It is almost a necessity that it should be so, for otherwise many princes and barons would object to their sons entering the Order. Its object is to keep back the irruption of the Moslems, and when men have done their share of hard work no regret need be felt if they desire to leave the Order. Our founder had no thought of covering Europe with monasteries, and beyond the fact that it is necessary there should be men to administer our manors and estates, I see no reason why any should not freely leave when they reach the age of thirty or thirty-five, and indeed believe that it would strengthen rather than weaken us were the vows, taken at the age of seventeen, to be for fifteen years only."

"There is something in that," the knight said thoughtfully. "However, that is far in the distance, and concerns me but little; still, I agree with you, for I see no advantage in men, after their time of usefulness to the Order is past, being bound to settle down to a monastic life if by nature and habit unsuited for it. There are some spirits who, after long years of warfare, are well content so to do, but there are assuredly others to whom a life of forced inactivity, after a youth and manhood spent in action, must be well-nigh unendurable. And now tell me frankly what you think of our chances here."

"Everything depends upon time. Promises of aid have come in from all quarters, and if Edward delays we shall soon be at the head of an overwhelming force. But Edward, with all his faults and vices, is an able and energetic leader, and must be well aware that if he is to strike successfully he must strike soon. We must hope that he will not be able to do this. He cannot tell whether we intend to march direct to London, or to join Pembroke in Wales, or to march north, and until he divines our purpose, he will hardly dare to move lest we should, by some rapid movement, interpose between himself and London. If he gives us a month, our success is certain. If he can give battle in a fortnight, no one can say how the matter will end."

Edward, indeed, was losing no time. He stayed but a few days in London after his victory at Barnet, and on the 19th of April left for Windsor, ordering all his forces to join him there. The Lancastrians had endeavoured to puzzle him as to their intended movements by sending parties out in various directions; but as soon as he had gathered a force, numerically small, but composed of veteran soldiers, he hurried west, determined to bring on a battle at the earliest opportunity. The queen's advisers determined to move first to Wells, as from that point they could either go north or march upon London. Edward entered Abingdon on the 27th, and then, finding the Lancastrians still at Wells, marched to the northwest, by which means he hoped to intercept them if they moved north, while he would be able to fall back and bar their road to London if they advanced in that direction. He therefore moved to Cirencester, and waited there for news until he learned that they had visited Bristol and there obtained reinforcements of men and supplies of money and cannon, and had then started on the high road to Gloucester.

He at once sent off messengers to the son of Lord Beauchamp, who held the Castle of Gloucester for him, assuring him that he was following at full speed, and would come to his aid forthwith. The messengers arrived in time, and when the queen, after a long march, arrived before Gloucester, she found the gates shut in her face. The governor had taken steps to prevent her numerous adherents in the town from rising on her behalf, and, manning the walls, refused to surrender. Knowing that Edward was coming up rapidly, it was evident that there was no time to spare in an attempt to take the town, and the queen's army therefore pressed on, without waiting, to Tewkesbury. Once across the river they would speedily be joined by the Earl of Pembroke, and Edward would be forced to fall back at once.

THE BATTLE OF TEWKESBURY

By the time they reached the river, however, they were thoroughly exhausted. They had marched thirty-six miles without rest, along bad roads and through woods, and were unable to go farther. The queen urged that the river should be crossed, but the leaders of the force were of opinion that it was better to halt. Edward would be able to follow them across the river, and were he to attack them when in disorder, and still further wearied by the operation of making the passage, he would certainly crush them. Moreover, a further retreat would discourage the soldiers, and as a battle must now be fought, it was better to fight where they were, especially as they could choose a strong position. The queen gave way, and the army encamped on a large field in front of the town. The position was well calculated for defence, for the country around was so broken and intercepted with lanes and deep hedges and ditches, that it was extremely difficult of approach.

In the evening Edward came up, his men having also marched some six-and-thirty miles, and encamped for the night within three miles of the Lancastrian position. The queen's troops felt confident of victory. In point of numbers they were superior to their antagonists, and had the advantage of a strong position. Sir Thomas Tresham had, as he proposed, left his wife and son at Exeter when the force marched away.

"Do not be despondent, love," he said to his weeping wife, as he bade her good-bye. "Everything is in our favour, and there is a good hope of a happy termination to this long struggle. But, win or lose, be assured it is the last time I will draw my sword. I have proved my fidelity to the House of Lancaster; I have risked life and fortune in their cause; but I feel that I have done my share and more, and whichever way Providence may now decide the issue of the struggle, I will accept it. If we lose, and I come scathless through the fight, I will ride hither, and we will embark at Plymouth for France, and there live quietly until the time comes when Edward may feel himself seated with sufficient firmness on the throne to forgive past offences and to grant an amnesty to all who have fought against him. In any other case, dear, you know my wishes, and I bid you carry them out within twenty-four hours of your receiving news of a defeat, without waiting longer for my appearance."

As soon as it was light, Edward advanced to the attack. The Duke of Gloucester was in command of the vanguard. He himself led the centre, while the rear was commanded by the Marquis of Dorset and Lord Hastings. The most advanced division of Lancastrians was commanded by the Duke of Somerset and his brother. The Grand Prior of the Order of St. John and Lord Wenlock were stationed in the centre, the Earl of Devon with the reserve. Refreshed by their rest, the queen's troops were in good spirits. While awaiting the attack, she and the prince rode among the ranks, encouraging the men with fiery speeches, and promising large rewards to all in case of victory.

Gloucester made his advance with great difficulty. The obstacles to his progress were so many and serious that his division was brought to a halt before it came into contact with the defenders. He therefore brought up his artillery and opened a heavy cannonade upon Somerset's position, supporting his guns with flights of arrows, and inflicting such heavy loss upon him that the duke felt compelled to take the offensive.

Having foreseen that he might be obliged to do so, he had, early in the morning, carefully examined the ground in front of him, and had found some lanes by which he could make a flank attack on the enemy. Moving his force down these lanes, where the trees and hedges completely hid his advance from the Yorkists, he fell suddenly upon Edward's centre, which, taken by surprise at the unexpected attack, was driven in confusion up the hill behind it. Somerset was quick to take advantage of his success, and wheeling his men round fell upon the Duke of Gloucester's division, and was equally successful in his attack upon it. Had the centre, under Lord Wenlock, moved forward at once to his support, the victory would have been assured; but Wenlock lay inactive, and Somerset was now engaged in conflict with the whole of Edward's force. But even under these circumstances he still gained ground, when suddenly the whole aspect of the battle was changed.

Before it began Edward had sent two hundred spearmen to watch a wood near the defenders' lines, as he thought that the Lancastrians might place a force there to take him in flank as he attacked their front. He ordered them, if they found the wood unoccupied, to join in the fight as opportunity might offer. The wood was unoccupied, and the spearmen, seeing the two divisions of their army driven backwards, and being thereby cut off from their friends, issued from the wood and, charging down in a body, fell suddenly upon Somerset's rear.

Astounded and confused by an attack from such a quarter, and believing that it was an act of treachery by one of their own commanders, Somerset's men, who had hitherto been fighting with the greatest bravery, fell into confusion. Edward's quick eye soon grasped the opportunity, and rallying his troops he charged impetuously down upon the Lancastrians, seconded hotly by Gloucester and his division.

The disorder in Somerset's lines speedily grew into a panic, and the division broke up and fled through the lanes to the right and left. Somerset, after in vain trying to stop the panic, rode furiously back into the camp, followed by his principal officers, and riding up to Lord Wenlock he cleft his head in two with a battle-axe. His resentment, although justified by the inactivity of this nobleman at such a crisis, was yet disastrous, as it left the centre without a leader, and threw it into a state of disorganization, as many must have supposed that Somerset had turned traitor and gone over to the enemy. Before any disposition could be made, Edward and Gloucester poured their forces into the camp, and the Lancastrians at once broke and fled. Many of their leaders took refuge in the church, an asylum which they deemed inviolable, and which the Lancastrians had honourably respected in their hour of triumph.

Among them were the Duke of Somerset, the Grand Prior of the Order of St. John, Sir Humphrey Audely, Sir Gervis of Clifton, Sir William Gainsby, Sir William Cary, Sir Henry Rose, Sir Thomas Tresham, and seven esquires. Margaret of Anjou fell into the hands of the victors. As to the fate of the young prince, accounts differ. Some authorities say that he was overtaken and slain on the field, but the majority related that he was captured and taken before Edward, who asked him, "What brought you to England?" On his replying boldly, "My father's crown and mine own inheritance," Edward struck him in the mouth with his gauntlet, and his attendants, or some say his brothers, at once despatched the youth with their swords.

The king, with Gloucester and Clarence, then went to the church at Tewkesbury, where the knights had taken refuge, burst open the doors, and entered it. A priest, bearing the holy vessels, threw himself before the king, and would not move until he promised to pardon all who had taken sanctuary there. The king then retired, and trusting in the royal word, the gentlemen made no attempt to escape, although it is said that they could easily have done so. Two days later a party of soldiers by the king's orders broke into the church, dragged them from the foot of the altar, and beheaded them outside.

The news of the issue of the fatal battle of Tewkesbury, the capture of the queen, and the death of the prince, was borne to Exeter by fugitives on the following day. Beyond the fact that the Earl of Devon and other nobles were known to have been killed, and Somerset with a party of knights had taken sanctuary, they could give no details as to the fate of individuals. In the deepest distress at the utter ruin of the cause, and in ignorance of the fate of her husband, who she could only hope was one of those who had gained sanctuary, Dame Tresham prepared for flight. This accomplished, she had only to wait, and sit in tearless anguish at the window, listening intently whenever a horseman rode past. All night her watch continued. Gervaise, who had cried himself to sleep, lay on a couch beside her. Morning dawned, and she they knew that her husband would not come, for had he escaped from the field he would long ere this have been with her. The messenger with the news had arrived at eight the previous morning, and, faithful to her husband's wishes, at that hour she ordered the horses to be brought round, and, joining a party of gentlemen who were also making for the coast, rode with them to Plymouth. Arrangements were at once made with the captain of a small ship in the port, and two days later they landed at Honfleur, where Sir Thomas had enjoined his wife to wait until she heard from him or obtained sure news of his fate.

A week after her arrival the news was brought by other fugitives of the violation of the sanctuary by the king, and the murder of Somerset and the gentlemen with him, of whom Sir Thomas Tresham was known to have been one.

The blow proved fatal to Dame Tresham. She had gone through many trials and misfortunes, and had ever borne them bravely, but the loss of her husband completely broke her down. Save to see his wishes concerning their son carried out, she had no longer any interest in life or any wish to live. But until the future of Gervaise was assured, her mission was unfulfilled. His education was her sole care; his mornings were spent at a monastery, where the monks instructed the sons of such of the nobles and gentry of the neighbourhood as cared that they should be able to read and write. In the afternoon he had the best masters in the town in military exercises. His evenings he spent with his mother, who strove to instil in him the virtues of patience, mercy to the vanquished, and valour, by stories of the great characters of history. She herself spent her days in pious exercises, in attending the services of the Church, and in acts of charity and kindness to her poorer neighbours. But her strength failed rapidly, and she was but a shadow of her former self when, two years and a half after her arrival at Honfleur, she felt that if she was herself to hand Gervaise over to the Order of St. John, she must no longer delay. Accordingly she took ship to London, and landing there made her way with him to the dwelling of the Order at Clerkenwell. It was in process of rebuilding, for in 1381 it had been first plundered and then burned by the insurgents under Wat Tyler. During the ninety years that had elapsed since that event the work of re-building had proceeded steadily, each grand prior making additions to the pile which, although not yet fully completed, was already one of the grandest and stateliest abodes in England.

On inquiring for the grand prior, and stating that she had a letter of importance for him, Dame Tresham and her son were shown up to his apartment, and on entering were kindly and courteously received by him when informed that she was the widow of the late Sir Thomas Tresham.

"I am the bearer of a letter for you, given into my hand by my husband's dear friend your predecessor," she said, "a few days before his murder at Tewkesbury. It relates to my son here."

The grand prior opened the letter and read it.

"Assuredly, madam, I will carry out the wishes here expressed," he said. "They are, that I should forward at once the letter he has given you to Sir Peter D'Aubusson, and that until an answer is received from him, I should take care of the boy here, and see that he is instructed in all that is needful for a future knight of our Order. I grieve to see that you yourself are looking so ill."

"My course is well-nigh run," she said. "I have, methinks, but a few days to live. I am thankful that it has been permitted to me to carry out my husband's wishes, and to place my boy in your hands. That done, my work on earth is finished, and glad indeed am I that the time is at hand when I can rejoin my dear husband."

"We have a building here where we can lodge ladies in distress or need, Dame Tresham, and trust you will take up your abode there."

"I shall indeed be thankful to do so," she replied. "I know no one in London, and few would care to lodge a dying woman."

THE BATTLE OF TEWKESBURY

"We are Hospitallers," the grand prior said. "That was our sole mission when we were first founded, and before we became a military order, and it is still a part of our sworn duty to aid the distressed."

A few minutes later Dame Tresham was conducted to a comfortable apartment, and was given into the charge of a female attendant. The next day she had another interview with the grand prior, to whom she handed over her jewels and remaining money. This she prayed him to devote to the furnishing of the necessary outfit for Gervaise. She spent the rest of the day in the church of the hospital, had a long talk with her son in the evening, giving him her last charges as to his future life and conduct, and that night, as if she had now fulfilled her last duty on earth, she passed away, and was found by her attendant lying with a look of joy and peacefulness on her dead face.

Gervaise's grief was for a time excessive. He was nearly twelve years old, and had never until now been separated from her even for a day. She had often spoken to him of her end being near, but until the blow came he had never quite understood that it could be so. She had, on the night before her death, told him that he must not grieve overmuch for her, for that in any case they must have soon been sundered, and that it was far better that he should think of her as at rest, and happy, than as leading a lonely and sorrowful life. The grand prior, however, wisely gave him but little time to dwell upon his loss, but as soon as her funeral had taken place, handed him over to the knights who had the charge of the novices on probation, and instructed them in their military exercises, and of the chaplain who taught them such learning as was considered requisite for a knight of the Order.

The knights were surprised at the proficiency the lad had already attained in the use of his weapons.

"By St. Agatha," one of them exclaimed, after the conclusion of his first lesson, "you have had good teachers, lad, and have availed yourself rarely of them. If you go on like this you will become a distinguished knight of our Order.

With a few more years to strengthen your arms I warrant me you will bear your part well in your first tussle with the Moslem corsairs."

It fortunately happened that a party of knights were starting for Rhodes a few days after the admission of Gervaise to the Hospital, and the letter to Sir Peter D'Aubusson was committed to their charge. They were to proceed to Bordeaux by ship, then to journey by land to Marseilles, and thence, being joined by some French knights, to sail direct to Rhodes. Two months later an answer was received. D'Aubusson wrote to the grand prior saying that he would gladly carry out the last wishes of his dead friend, and that he had already obtained from the grand master the appointment of Gervaise Tresham as one of his pages, and begged that he might be sent out with the next party of knights leaving England. It was three months before such an opportunity occurred. During that time Gervaise remained at the house of St. John's studying diligently, and continuing his military exercises. These were severe; for the scions of noble houses, who hoped some day to distinguish themselves as knights, were put through many gymnastic exercises—were taught to spring on to a horse when clad in full armour, to wield heavy battle-axes, to run and climb, and to prepare themselves for all the possibilities of the mode of fighting of the day.

Gervaise gained the encomiums, not only of his special preceptor, but of the various knights in the house, and of the grand prior himself, both for his strength and activity, and for the earnestness with which he worked. When the time approached for his leaving England, the grand prior ordered for him the outfit which would be necessary in his position as a page of the grand master. The dresses were numerous and rich, for although the knights of St. John wore over their armour the simple mantle of their order, which was a sleeveless garment of black relieved only by a white cross on the chest, they indulged in the finest and most costly armour, and in rich garments beneath their black mantles when not in armour.

THE BATTLE OF TEWKESBURY

"I am well pleased with you, Gervaise," the grand prior said, on the evening before he was to leave, "and I see in you the making of a valiant knight of the Order. Maintain the same spirit you have shown here; be obedient and reverent to your superiors; give your whole mind to your duties; strive earnestly during the three or four years that your pagedom will last, to perfect yourself in military exercises, that when the time comes for you to buckle on armour you will be able to bear yourself worthily. Remember that you will have to win your knighthood, for the Order does not bestow this honour, and you must remain a professed knight until you receive it at the hands of some distinguished warrior. Ever bear in mind that you are a soldier of the Cross. Avoid luxury, live simply and modestly; be not led away by others, upon whom their vows may sit but lightly; keep ever in your mind that you have joined the Order neither to gain fame nor personal advantage, but simply that you may devote the strength and the intelligence that God has given you to protect Christendom from the advance of the infidel. I shall hear of you from time to time from D'Aubusson, and feel sure that the expectations I have formed of you will be fulfilled."

CHAPTER III
THE GRAND MASTER'S PAGE

THE grand prior had, in accordance with Dame Tresham's request, sent the steward of the house to one of the principal jewellers of the city who, as the Order were excellent customers, paid a good price for her jewels. After the payment for the numerous dresses required for the service as a page to the grand master, the grand prior handed the balance of the money Dame Tresham had brought with her, and that obtained by the sale of her jewels, to one of the knights under whose charge Gervaise was to travel, to be given by him to D'Aubusson for the necessities of Gervaise as a page. During their term of service the pages received no remuneration, all their expenses being paid by their families. Nevertheless, the post was considered so honourable, and of such great advantage to those entering the Order, that the appointments were eagerly sought after.

The head of the party was Sir Guy Redcar, who had been a commander in England, but who was now relinquishing that post in order to take a high office in the convent at the Island. With him were four lads between seventeen and twenty who were going out as professed knights, having served their year of probation as novices at the grand priory. With these Gervaise was already acquainted, as they had lived, studied, and performed their military exercises together. The three eldest of these Gervaise liked much, but the youngest of the party, Robert Rivers, a relation of the queen, had always shown a very different spirit from the others. He was jealous that a member of one of the defeated and disinherited Lancastrian families should obtain a post of such honour and advantage as that of page to the grand master, and that thus, although five years younger, Gervaise should enter the Order on an equality with him.

In point of strength and stature he was, of course, greatly superior to Gervaise; but he had been spoilt from his childhood, was averse to exercise, and dull at learning, and while Gervaise was frequently commended by his instructors, he himself was constantly reproved, and it had been more than once a question whether he should be received as a professed knight at the termination of his year of novitiate. Thus, while the other lads treated Gervaise kindly, and indeed made rather a pet of him, Robert Rivers ignored him as much as possible, and if obliged to speak to him did so with a pointed rudeness that more than once brought upon him a sharp reproof from his companions. Gervaise himself was but little affected by Robert's manner. He was of an exceptionally good-tempered nature, and, indeed, was so occupied with his work and so anxious to satisfy his teachers, that Robert's ill-humour passed almost unnoticed.

The journey was performed without incident. During their passage across the south of France, Gervaise's perfect knowledge of the language gained for him a great advantage over his companions, and enabled him to be of much use to Sir Guy. They had fine weather during their passage up the Mediterranean, and on the day their leader gave them their first lessons in the management and discipline of a ship.

"You will be nearly as much at sea as you are on land for the five years you must stay at the convent," he said; "and it is essential to the education of a knight of our Order to know all things connected with the management of a ship, even to its building. We construct our own galleys at Rhodes, using, of course, the labour of slaves, but under our own superintendence; and it is even more essential to us to know how to fight on sea than on land. There is, too, you see, a rivalry among ourselves, for each *langue* has its duties, and each strives to perform more gallant deeds and to bring in more rich prizes than the others. We of England are among the smallest of the *langue*s, and yet methinks we do a fair portion of the work, and gain fully our share of honour. There is no fear of your having much time on your hands, for it is quite certain that there will soon be open war between Mahomet and the Order. In spite of the nominal truce, constant skirmishes are taking place, so that, in addition to our fights with pirates, we have sometimes encounters with the sultan's galleys.

"Seven years ago, a number of our Order took part in the defence of Lesbos, and lost their lives at its capture, and we have sure information that Mahomet is preparing for an attack on the Island. No doubt he thinks it will be an easy conquest, for in '57 he succeeded in landing eighteen thousand men on the Island, and in ravaging a large district, carrying off much booty. Since then, however, the defences of Rhodes have been greatly strengthened. Zacosta, our last grand master, laboured diligently to increase the fortifications, and, specially, built on one side of the entrance to the harbour a strong tower, called Fort St. Nicholas. Orsini has carried on the works, which have been directed by D'Aubusson, who is captain-general of the forces of the Island, and who has deepened the ditches and built a wall on the sea front of the town six hundred feet in length and twenty feet in height, money being found by the grand master from his private purse.

"At present we are not sure whether the great armament that Mahomet is preparing is intended for the capture of Negropont, which belongs to Venice, or of Rhodes. Unfortunately Venice and Rhodes are not good friends. In the course of our war with Egypt in '58 we captured from some Venetian vessels, in which they were travelling, several Egyptian merchants with a great store of goods. The Venetians protested that as the ships were theirs we had no right to interfere with our enemies who were travelling in them, and, without giving time for the question to be discussed, at once attacked our galleys, and sent a fleet against Rhodes. They landed on the Island, and not only

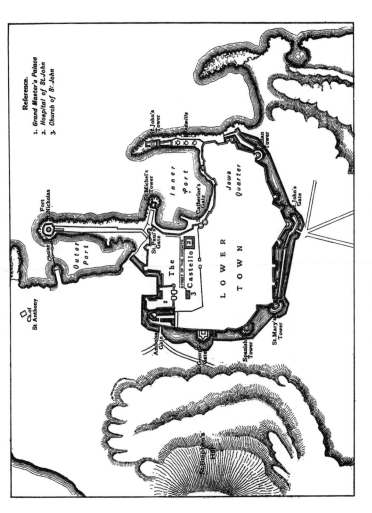

Plan of the Fortress of Rhodes.

pillaged the district of Halki, but, a number of natives having sought shelter in a cave, the Venetians blocked up the entrance with brushwood, set it on fire, and suffocated them all.

"Shortly afterwards, another and larger fleet appeared off Rhodes, and demanded the restitution of the Egyptians and their merchandise. There was a great division of opinion in the council; but, seeing the great danger that threatened us both from the Turks at Constantinople and the Venetians, and that it was madness at such a time to engage in war with a Christian power, the grand master persuaded the council to accede to their request. There has never been any friendly feeling between Venice and ourselves since that time. Still, I trust that our common danger will re-unite us, and that whether Negropont or Rhodes is attacked by the Moslems, we shall render loyal aid to each other."

There was great excitement among Gervaise and his companions when it was announced that Rhodes was in sight, and as they approached the town they gazed with admiration at the castle with its stately buildings, the palace of the grand master and the Hospital of St. John, rising above the lower town, the massive walls strengthened by projecting bastions, and the fortifications of the ports. Of these there were two, with separate entrances, divided from each other by a narrow tongue of land. At its extremity stood Fort St. Nicholas, which was connected by a strong wall running along the promontory to the town. The inner port, as it was called, was of greater importance, as it adjoined the town itself. It was defended in the first place by Fort St. Nicholas, and at the inner entrance stood the towers of St. John and St. Michael, one on either side. Into this the vessel was steered. There were many craft lying there, among them eight or ten of the galleys of the Order.

"We will go first to the house of our *langue*," Sir Guy said, "and tell them to send down slaves to fetch up our baggage; then I will take you, Gervaise, to Sir Peter D'Aubusson, and hand you over to his care."

THE GRAND MASTER'S PAGE

On landing, Gervaise was surprised at the number of slaves who were labouring at the public works, and who formed no small proportion of the population in the streets. Their condition was pitiable. They were, of course, enemies of Christianity, and numbers of them had been pirates; but he could not help pitying their condition as they worked in the full heat of the sun under the vigilant eyes of numbers of overseers, who carried heavy whips, in addition to their arms. Their progress to the upper city was slow, for on their way they met many knights, of whom several were acquainted with Sir Guy; and each, after greeting him, demanded the latest news from England, and in return gave him particulars of the state of things at Rhodes.

At last they arrived at the house of the English *langue*. The Order was divided into *langue*s or nationalities. Of these there were eight—Provence, Auvergne, France, Italy, Germany, England, Aragon, and Castile and Portugal. The French element was by far the strongest. The Order had been founded in that country, and as it possessed no less than three *langue*s, and held the greater part of the high official positions in the Order, it was only kept in check by the other *langue*s acting together to demand their fair share of dignities. The grand master's authority was considerable, but it was checked by the council, which was composed of the bailiffs and knights of the highest order, known as Grand Crosses. Each *langue* had its bailiff elected by itself; these resided constantly at Rhodes. Each of these bailiffs held a high office; thus the Bailiff of Provence was always the grand commander of the Order. He controlled the expenditure, superintended the stores, and was governor of the arsenal. The Bailiff of Auvergne was the commander-in-chief of all the forces, army and navy. The Bailiff of France was the grand hospitaller, with the supreme direction of the hospitals and infirmaries of the Order, a hospital in those days signifying a guest-house. The Bailiff of Italy was the grand admiral, and the Bailiff of England was chief of the light cavalry. Thus the difficulties and jealousies that would have arisen at every vacancy were avoided.

41

A KNIGHT OF THE WHITE CROSS

In the early days of the Order, when Jerusalem was in the hands of the Christians, the care of the hospitals was its chief and most important function. Innumerable pilgrims visited Jerusalem, and these were entertained at the immense guest-house of the Order. But with the loss of Jerusalem and the expulsion of the Christians from Palestine, that function had become of very secondary importance although there was still a guest-house and infirmary at Rhodes, where strangers and the sick were carefully attended by the knights. No longer did these ride out to battle on their war-horses. It was on the sea that the foe was to be met, and the knights were now sailors rather than soldiers. They dwelt at the houses of their respective *langue*s; here they ate at a common table, which was supplied by the bailiff, who drew rations for each knight, and received, in addition, a yearly sum for the supply of such luxuries as were not included in the rations. The average number of knights residing in each of these *langue*s averaged from a hundred to a hundred and fifty.

It was not until some hours after his arrival that Sir Guy could find time to take Gervaise across to the house of the *langue* of Auvergne, to which D'Aubusson belonged. It was a larger and more stately pile than that of the English *langue*, but the arrangements were similar in all these buildings. In the English house Gervaise had not felt strange, as he had the companionship of his fellow-voyagers; but as he followed Sir Guy through the spacious halls of the *langue* of Auvergne, where no familiar face met his, he felt more lonely than he had done since he entered the house at Clerkenwell.

On sending in his name Sir Guy was at once conducted to the chamber occupied by D'Aubusson. The knight was seated at his table, examining some plans. The room was furnished with monastic simplicity, save that the walls were hung with rich silks and curtains captured from Turkish galleys.

THE GRAND MASTER'S PAGE

"Welcome back to us, Sir Guy," D'Aubusson said, rising, and warmly shaking his visitor's hand. "I have been looking for your coming, for we need men with clear heads. Of strong arms and valiant spirits we have no lack; but men of judgment and discretion, who can be trusted to look at matters calmly and not to be carried away by passion, are welcome indeed to us. I was expecting you about this time, and when I heard that a ship had arrived from Marseilles I made inquiries, and was glad to find that you were on board."

"I am heartily glad to be back, D'Aubusson; I am sick of the dull life of a commandery, and rejoice at the prospect of stirring times again. This lad is young Tresham, who has come out in my charge, and for whom you have been good enough to obtain the post of page to the grand master."

"And no slight business was it to do so," D'Aubusson said with a smile. "It happened there was a vacancy when the letter concerning him arrived, and had it been one of the highest offices in the Order there could not have been a keener contention for it. Every bailiff had his candidate ready; but I seldom ask for anything for members of my *langue*, and when I told the other bailiffs that it was to me a matter of honour to carry out the last request of my dead friend, they all gave way. You see, I am placed in a position of some little difficulty. The grand master is so enfeebled and crippled that he leaves matters almost entirely in my hands, and it would be an abuse of my position, and would excite no little jealousy, were I to use the power I possess to nominate friends of my own to appointments. It is only by the most rigid impartiality, and by dividing as fairly as possible all offices between the eight *langues*, that all continue to give me their support. As you know, we have had great difficulties and heartburnings here; but happily they have to a great extent been set at rest by forming a new *langue* of Castile and Portugal out of that of Aragon. This has given one more vote to the smaller *langues*, and has so balanced the power that of late the jealousies between us have greatly subsided, and all are working well together in face of the common danger. Well, young sir, and how like you the prospect of your pageship?"

"I like it greatly, sir, but shall like still more the time when I can buckle on armour and take a share of the fighting with the infidels. I would fain, sir, offer to you my deep and humble thanks for the great kindness you have shown me in procuring me the appointment of page to the grand master."

The knight smiled kindly. "There are the less thanks due, lad, inasmuch as I did it not for you, but for the dear friend who wrote to me on your behalf. However, I trust that you will do credit to my nomination by your conduct here."

"There is a letter from our grand prior which I have brought to you," Sir Guy said. "He commended the lad to me warmly, and seems to be greatly pleased with his conduct."

D'Aubusson cut the silken string that bound the missive together, and read the letter.

"He does indeed speak warmly," he said, as he laid it down on the table.

"He tells me that the lad, young as he was, had been well trained when he came, and that he worked with great diligence during the five months he was in the House, and displayed such skill and strength for his age, as to surprise his preceptors, who prophesied that he would turn out a stout swordsman, and would be a credit to the Order."

"He is well furnished with garments both for ordinary and state occasions," Sir Guy said; "and in this packet are some sixty gold crowns, which are the last remains of his patrimony, and which I was to hand to you in order to pay the necessary expenses during his pageship."

"He could have done without that," D'Aubusson said. "Recommended to me as he is, I would have seen that he lacked nothing, but was provided with all necessaries for his position. I will in the future take care that in all things he is on a par with his companions." He touched a bell on the table, and a servitor entered.

"Tell Richard de Deauville to come here," he said.

A minute later the hangings at the door were pushed aside, and a lad about a year older than Gervaise appeared, and, bowing deeply to the knight, stood in a respectful attitude, awaiting his orders.

"Deauville, take this youth, Gervaise Tresham to your room. He is appointed one of the pages of the grand master. He is English, but he speaks French as well as you do, having lived in France for some years. Take him to your apartment and treat him kindly and well, seeing that he is a stranger and new to all here. To-morrow he will go to the palace."

Gervaise bowed deeply to the two knights, and then followed the page.

"I suppose you arrived in that ship which came in to-day," the latter said, as soon as they had left the room. "You are in luck indeed to have obtained a pageship at the grand master's. You begin to count your time at once, while we do not begin to count ours until we are seventeen. Still, good luck may befall us yet, for if the grand master dies, Sir Peter is sure to be chosen to succeed him. Then, you see, we too shall be pages of the grand master."

"How many are there of you?"

"Only De Lille and myself. Of course D'Aubusson will take on the grand master's present pages; but as there are five vacancies on an average every year, he will be able to find room for us among the number."

"Why, how many pages has the grand master?" Gervaise asked, in surprise.

"Sixteen of them, so you may guess the duties are easy enough, as only two are generally employed, except, of course on solemn occasions."

"Are there any other English besides myself?"

The boy shook his head. "There are eight belonging to the French *langue*s; the others are Spaniards, Italians, or Germans. There, this is our room and this is De Lille. De Lille, this is the grand master's new page, Master Gervaise Tresham, and our lord says we are to treat him kindly and entertain him well until to-morrow, when he will go to the palace. He speaks our language, and has been some years in France."

"How came you to be there?" De Lille asked Gervaise.

"My father was a Lancastrian, and my mother a great friend of our Queen Margaret of Anjou, and they were with her all the time she was in exile."

"How quarrelsome you English are!" De Lille said. "You seem to be always fighting among yourselves."

"I don't think," Gervaise said, with a smile, "there is any love lost between Louis of France and the Duke of Burgundy, to say nothing of other great lords."

"No; you are right there. But though we talk a great deal about fighting, it is only occasionally that we engage in it."

The pages' room was a small one. It contained two pallets, which served as seats by day, and two wooden chests, in which they kept their clothes.

Their conversation was interrupted by the ringing of a bell.

"That is supper," De Lille said, jumping up. "We will leave you here while we go down to stand behind our lord's chair. When the meal is over we will bring a pasty or something else good, and a measure of wine, and have our supper together up here; and we will tell the servitors to bring up another pallet for you. Of course, you can go down with us if you like."

"Thank you, I would much rather stay here. Every one would be strange to me, and having nothing to do I should feel in the way."

The boys nodded, and taking their caps ran off, while Gervaise, tired by the excitement of the day, lay down on the bed which a servant brought up a few minutes after they had left him, and slept soundly until their return.

"I think I have been asleep," he said, starting up when they entered the room again.

"You look as if you had, anyhow," De Lille laughed. "It was the best thing you could do. We have brought up supper. We generally sit down and eat after the knights have done, but this is much better, as you are here." They sat down on the beds, carved the pasty with their daggers, and after they had finished Gervaise gladly accepted the proposal of the others to take a walk round the walls.

They started from the corner of the castle looking down upon the spit of land dividing the two ports.

"You see," De Lille said, "there is a row of small islands across the mouth of the outer port, and the guns of St. Nicholas, and those on this wall, would prevent any hostile fleet from entering."

"I hardly see what use that port is, for it lies altogether outside the town, and vessels could not unload there."

"No. Still, it forms a useful place of refuge. In case a great fleet came to attack us, our galleys would lay up in the inner port, which would be cleared of all the merchant craft, as these would hamper the defence; they would, therefore, be sent round into the outer port, where they would be safe from any attack by sea, although they would doubtless be burnt did an army besiege the town."

Passing along the walls of the grand master's palace, which was a strongly fortified building, and formed a citadel that could be defended after the lower town and the rest of the castle had been taken, they came to the western angle of the fortifications.

"You must know that each *langue* has charge of a separate part of the wall. From the foot of the mole of St. Nicholas to the grand master's palace it is in charge of France. On the line where we now are, between the palace and the gate of St. George, it is held by Germany. From that gate to the Spanish tower Auvergne is posted. England takes the wall between the Spanish tower and that of St. Mary. You defend only the lower storey of that tower, the upper part being held by Aragon, whose charge extends up to the gate of St. John. Thence to the tower of Italy,—behind which lies the Jews' quarter,—Provence is in charge, while the sea-front, thence to the mole of St. Nicholas, is held by Italy and Castile, each taking half. Not only have the *langue*s the charge of defending each its portion of the wall, but of keeping it in order at all times; and I may say that nowhere is the wall better kept or more fairly decorated with carvings than where England holds."

"You have not told me who defends the palace itself."

"That is in charge of a force composed of equal numbers of picked knights from each *langue*."

Gervaise leant on the battlement and looked with admiration at the scene beyond. The land side was surrounded by hills, the ground rising very gradually from the foot of the walls. Every yard of ground was cultivated, and was covered with brilliant vegetation. Groves and orchards occurred thickly, while the slopes were dotted with chapels, summerhouses—in which the natives of the city spent most of their time in the hot season—and other rustic buildings.

"What a rich and beautiful country!" he said.

"It is very pleasant to look at," De Lille agreed. "But all this would be a sore disadvantage to us if the Turks were besieging us, for the groves and orchards would conceal their approaches, the walls and buildings would give them shelter, and our cannon would be of little use until they reached the farther side of the ditch. If the Turks come, I hear it is decided to level all the buildings and walls, and to chop down every tree."

"If they were to plant their cannon on the hills they would do us much harm," Gervaise remarked.

"The Turks are clumsy gunners they say," Deauville replied, "and they would but waste their powder and ball at that distance, without making a breach in our walls."

THE GRAND MASTER'S PAGE

"Even if they did, they could surely scarce pass that deep fosse," Gervaise said, looking down into the tremendous cutting in the solid rock that ran round the whole circuit of the walls; it was from forty to sixty feet deep, and from ninety to a hundred and forty feet wide. It was from this great cutting that the stones for the construction of the walls, towers, and buildings of the town had been taken, the work having been going on ever since the knights established themselves at Rhodes, and being performed by a host of captives taken in war, together with labour hired from neighboring islands. Upon this immense work the Order had expended no small proportion of their revenue since their capture of the island in 1310, and the result was a fortress that, under the conditions of warfare of that age, seemed almost impregnable; and this without any natural advantage of position.

In addition to the five great towers or bastions, the wall was strengthened by square towers at short intervals. On looking down from the wall upon which the three pages were standing, on to the lower town, the view was a singular one. The houses were all built of stone, with flat roofs, after the manner of most Eastern cities. The streets were very narrow, and were crossed at frequent intervals by broad stone arches. These had the effect, not only of giving shelter from an enemy's fire, but of affording means by which troops could march rapidly across the town upon the roofs of the houses to reinforce the defenders of the wall, wherever pressed by the enemy. Thus the town from above presented the appearance of a great pavement, broken only by dark and frequently interrupted lines.

"How different to the towns at home!" Gervaise exclaimed, as, after gazing long upon the beautiful country outside the walls, he turned and looked inward. "One would hardly know that it was a town at all."

"Yes, it is rather different to the view from the top of the tower of Notre Dame, which I ascended while I was staying in Paris. But this sort of building is best here; the thickness of the stone roofs keeps out the heat of the sun,

49

and it is only when it is almost overhead that it shines down into the narrow streets. As you can see by the number of the people on the roofs, they use them as a resort in the evening. Then carpets are spread, and they receive visitors, and can talk to their neighbours over the low walls that separate the roofs. You can trace the divisions. Some of the house roofs are larger than others, but all are upon the same level; this being the regulation, in order that there might be free passage everywhere for the troops."

By the time they had made the circuit of the walls darkness had fallen, and concealed the martial features of the scene. Lights twinkled everywhere upon the stone terraces; the sound of lutes and other musical instruments came up softly on the still air, with the hum of talk and laughter. The sea lay as smooth as a mirror, and reflected the light of the stars, and the black hulls of the galleys and ships in the harbour lay still and motionless.

Greatly pleased with his first experience of the city that was to be his future home, Gervaise returned, with his companions, to the *auberge* of Auvergne.

The next morning the bailiff D'Aubusson bade Gervaise accompany him to the palace of the grand master. Here he introduced him to Orsini, an old and feeble man, who, after a few kind words, handed him over to the chamberlain, who, in turn, led him to the official who was in charge of the pages. That officer took him down to the courtyard, where four young knights were engaged in superintending the military exercises of the pages. The scene was exactly the same as that to which Gervaise had been accustomed at the House in London. Some of the lads were fighting with blunted swords, others were swinging heavy bars of iron, climbing ropes, or vaulting on to the back of a wooden horse. All paused as the official entered with his charge.

"This is your new comrade, boys," he said—"Master Gervaise Tresham, a member of the English *langue*. Be good comrades to him. By the reports I hear I am sure that you will find him a worthy companion."

THE GRAND MASTER'S PAGE

The pages had been prepared to like the new-comer, for it was well known that he owed his appointment to the bailiff of Auvergne, who was the most popular of the officials of the Order, and who was already regarded as the grand master. His appearance confirmed their anticipation. His fair complexion and nut-brown hair tinged with gold, cut somewhat short, but with a natural wave, contrasted with their darker locks and faces bronzed by the sun. There was an honest and frank look in his grey eyes, and an expression of good-temper on his face, though the square chin and firm lips spoke of earnestness and resolution of purpose. The official took him round the circle and presented him first to the knights and then to each of his comrades.

"You may as well join them in their exercises. In that way you will sooner become at home with them."

Gervaise at once laid down his mantle, removed his doublet, and then joined the others. There was but one half-hour remaining before they broke off to go to dinner, which was at half-past ten, but the time sufficed to show the young pages that this English lad was the equal of all,—except two or three of the oldest,—both in strength and in knowledge of arms. He could climb the rope with any of them, could vault on to the wooden horse with a heavy cuirass and backpiece on him, and held his own in a bout with swords against Conrad von Berghoff, who was considered the best sword-player among them. As soon as the exercises were over all proceeded to the bath, and then to dinner. The meal was a simple one, but Gervaise enjoyed it thoroughly, for the table was loaded with an abundance of fruits of kinds altogether novel to him, and which he found delicious.

The official in charge of them sat at the head of the table, and the meal was eaten in silence. After it was over and they had retired to their own rooms discipline was at an end, and they were free to amuse themselves as they liked. There were many questions to be asked and answered, but his display of strength and skill in the courtyard saved Gervaise from a good deal of the teasing to which a new-comer among a party of boys is always exposed.

He, on his part, learnt that the duties of the pages were very light. Two only were on duty each day, being in constant attendance on the grand master, and accompanying him wherever he went. When he dined in public four of them waited on him at table, and one of them performed the duties of taster. If he returned to the palace after dark, six others lined the staircase with torches. On occasions of state ceremony, and at the numerous religious festivals, all were in attendance. By this time Gervaise's trunks had been brought over from the English *auberge*, where they had been conveyed from the ship, and his garments were taken out and inspected by his comrades, who all admitted that they were, in point of beauty of colour and material, and in fashion, equal to their own.

"You will have to get one more suit, Gervaise," one of the lads said. "At one or two of the grand ceremonies every year we are all dressed alike; that is the rule. On other occasions we wear what we choose, so that our garments are handsome, and I think it looks a good deal better than when we are dressed alike; though no doubt in religious processions that is more appropriate. De Ribaumont, our governor, will give orders for the supply of your state costume. He is a good fellow. Of course, he has to be rather strict with us; but so long as there is nothing done that he considers discreditable to our position, he lets us do pretty nearly as we like.

"We have four hours a day at our military exercises, and two hours with the sub-chaplain, who teaches us our books and religious duties. The rest of our time we can use as we like, except that every day eight of us ride for two hours and practise with the lance; for although it is at sea we fight the Moslems, we are expected to become finished knights in all matters. These eight horses are kept for our service, and such as choose may at other times ride them. On Saturdays we are free from all our exercises; then some of us generally go on horseback for long excursions on the island, while others take boats and go out on the sea; one afternoon in the week we all make a trip in a galley, to learn our duties on board."

CHAPTER IV
A PROFESSED KNIGHT

GERVAISE was soon quite at home in the palace of the grand master, and his companions were, like other boys, of varying characters; but as all were of noble families, were strongly impressed with the importance of the Order and the honour of their own position, and were constantly in contact with stately knights and grave officials, their manners conformed to those of their elders; and even among themselves there was no rough fun, or loud disputes, but a certain courtesy of manner that was in accordance with their surroundings. This came naturally to Gervaise, brought up as he had been by his father and mother, and having at frequent intervals stayed with them for months at the various royal castles in which Margaret of Anjou and her son had been assigned apartments during their exile. Even at St. John's house the novices with whom he lived were all a good deal older than himself, and the discipline of the house was much more strict than that at Rhodes.

He enjoyed both his exercises with the knights and the time spent with the sub-chaplain, no small proportion of the hours of study being occupied in listening to stories of chivalry; it being considered one of the most important parts of a knight's education that he should have a thorough acquaintance, not only with the laws of chivalry, but with the brave deeds both of former and of living knights, with the relations of the noble houses of Europe to each other, especially of the many great families whose members were connected with the Order of St. John.

A PROFESSED KNIGHT

These matters formed, indeed, the main subject of their studies. All were taught to read and write, but this was considered sufficient in the way of actual instruction. The rules of the Order had to be committed to memory. Beyond this their reading consisted largely of the lives of saints, especially of those who distinguished themselves by their charity or their devotion to their vows of poverty, to both of which the members of the Order were pledged. Gervaise, however, could see around him no signs whatever of poverty on their part. It was true that they all lived and fed together in the *auberges* of their respective *langues*, and that they possessed no houses or establishments of their own; but the magnificence of their armour and attire, and the lavish expenditure of some upon their pleasures, contrasted strangely with the poverty to which they had vowed themselves. It was true that in many cases the means to support the expenditure was derived from the shares the knights received of the plunder acquired in their captures of Moslem ships; but undoubtedly many must have possessed large private means; the bailiffs, for example, although only required by the rules to place before the knights at their *auberges* the rations they received for them, with such luxuries as could be purchased by their yearly allowance for that purpose, expended annually very large sums in addition, and supplied their tables with every dainty, in order to gain popularity and goodwill among the members of the *langue*.

Not only did the post of bailiff confer upon its owner a very high position at Rhodes, but it was a stepping-stone to the most lucrative offices in their *langue*s. The bailiffs at Rhodes had the right of claiming any of the grand priories or bailiwicks at home that might fall vacant, and the grand master was frequently chosen from among their number, as, by being present at Rhodes, they had many advantages in the way of making themselves popular among the electors. The emoluments of some of these provincial bailiwicks were large; and as the bailiffs at Rhodes were generally elected by seniority—although younger knights who had greatly distinguished themselves were sometimes chosen—they were usually glad to resign the heavy work and responsibility of their position at Rhodes, and to retire to the far easier position of a provincial bailiff. In the majority of cases, doubtless, the fortunes of the high officials were obtained from the money amassed when in possession of rich commanderies at home; but even this was assuredly incompatible with their vows of poverty.

His hours of leisure Gervaise spent either on the water or in the saddle, and his love of exercise of all sorts excited the wonder and even the amusement of his companions, who for the most part preferred spending the time at their disposal in sleep, in idly looking out from a shaded room at what was going on outside, or in visits to friends and relations at the *auberge*s of the *langue*s to which they belonged. The natural consequence was, that by the time he reached the end of his three years' pageship, Gervaise was indisputably superior in strength, activity, and skill in military exercises, to any of his companions. The majority of these, after completing their time, returned to the headquarters of their *langue* at home, to pass their time there, until of an age to be eligible for the charge of a commandery obtained for them by family influence, which had no small share in the granting of these appointments.

As it was known, however, that Gervaise intended to remain permanently in the Island, his progress was watched with particular attention by his instructors; and, seeing his own earnestness in the matter, they took special pains with his training. The bailiff of Auvergne continued to take much interest in him, inquiring often from the officers in charge of the pages, and from his instructors, of his conduct and progress, and occasionally sending for him to his *auberge* and talking with him as to his life and progress. Just before his pageship terminated, he said to him,—

"I was rather puzzled at first, Gervaise, as to what we should do with you when your term of office concluded, but I am so no longer, for, although you are some two years younger than the professed knights who come out here, you are better fitted than the majority to take your place in the naval expeditions, and to fight the Moslem pirates. I will see that you have your share of these adventures. All young knights are, as you know, obliged to make three voyages, but beyond that many of them do not care to share in the rough life at sea, and prefer the bustle, and, I grieve to say, the gaiety and pleasures of this city. For one, then, really eager to distinguish himself, the opportunities are frequent. When danger threatens, or heavy engagements are expected, every knight is desirous of bearing his part in the fray; but this is not the case when the work to be done consists of scouring the sea for weeks, without perchance coming across a single pirate. Of course, as soon as your pageship is over you will go to the English *auberge*, but I shall still keep my eye upon you, and shall do my best to help you to achieve distinction; and I shall take upon myself the providing of your arms and armour as a knight."

Accordingly, on the day on which his duties as a page terminated, two servitors of the *auberge* of Auvergne brought across to the palace a suit of fine armour and a sword, a battle-axe, a lance, and a dagger; also three complete suits of clothes, two of them for ordinary wear, and one for state occasions. The next day Gervaise took the oaths of the Order in the Church of St. John. The aged master himself received the vows, and formally inducted him as a professed knight of the Order, Peter D'Aubusson and the bailiff of the English *langue* acting as his sponsors, vouching that he was of noble blood and in all ways fitted to become a knight of Justice, this being the official title of the professed knights of the Order. Ten newly arrived novices were inducted at the same time, and the ceremony was a stately one, attended by a number of the knights from each *langue*, all in full armour.

The ceremony over, Gervaise bore the title of Sir Gervaise Tresham; but this was an honorary rather than a real title, as the Order did not profess to bestow the honour of knighthood, and it was usual for its members to receive the accolade at the hands of secular knights. At the conclusion of the ceremony, he returned with the bailiff of the English *langue* to the *auberge*, and took up his quarters there. By his frequent visits he was well known to all the members, and in a day or two felt as much at home as he had done in the pages' room in the palace. A week was given to him before he was assigned to any special duty, and he was glad when he was told off as one of the knights who were to take their turn in superintending the work of the slaves employed in strengthening the fortifications, although he would rather that any other employment should have been assigned to him, because he felt deep pity for the unfortunate men who were engaged in the work.

He knew well enough that if he himself were ever made prisoner by the Turks, his lot would be as hard and as hopeless as that of the Moslem captives; but this, although he often repeated it to himself in order to abate his feeling of commiseration, was but a poor satisfaction. He saw one side of the picture, and the other was hidden from him; and although he told himself that after slaving in a Turkish galley he would feel a satisfaction at seeing those who had been his tyrants suffering the same fate, he was well aware that this would not be the case, and that his own sufferings would only make him sympathise more deeply with those of others. He had found, soon after his arrival on the Island, that it was best to keep his feelings on this subject to himself. While the knights were bound, in accordance with their vows, to relieve sufferings of any kind among Christians, they seemed to regard their captives rather in the light of brute beasts than human beings. The slaves were struck on the smallest provocation, and even the killing of a slave was considered a very venial offence, and punished only because the slave was of value to the Order.

It was true that edicts were from time to time published by the council, enjoining fair treatment of slaves, and it was specially ordered that those employed as servants in the *auberges* were not to be struck. The lot of these servants was, indeed, very much easier than that of those engaged on the public works, and such occupation was therefore considered a privilege, the servants being for the most part selected from among the captives of superior rank.

For the next six months Gervaise worked at various duties in the town. He was employed for a fortnight in the infirmary, then for a while he was transferred to the galleys; but for the most part he was with the slaves working on the fortifications. At the end of that time he was, to his great delight, informed by the bailiff that he was one of the six knights of the *langue* told off to join a galley that was on the point of sailing. Among those going in her was Sir Ralph Harcourt, one of his companions on the journey from England.

"So you are to go with us, Gervaise," the young knight said, "to try your luck for the first time against the infidels. This is my third voyage, and I hope that it will be more fortunate than its predecessors, for, beyond picking up two or three small craft, which did not venture upon resistance, we gained neither honour nor booty. I regard you as having specially good fortune, and besides being glad that we shall be together, I expect that you will bring good luck to us, and that we shall meet with foes worth contending with. The corsairs have been very active of late, and have captured many prizes, while, on the other hand, our galleys have been unfortunate, and have but seldom come upon the miscreants."

"How many knights will there be on board?"

"Forty. Aragon, like us, furnishes five, Germany ten, Portugal five, Auvergne ten, and Provence five. We shall be commanded by Sir Louis Ricord, a knight of Auvergne, and we could wish no better, for he has proved himself a good seaman and a brave captain. Two other galleys are to start with us. We are to cruise separately unless one gets news of a force so superior that he will need aid to attack it, when he will meet the others at a rendezvous agreed upon, and we shall work together."

"Who are the other three Englishmen?"

"John Boswell, Marmaduke Lumley, and Adam Tedbond—all, as you know, brave knights and good companions."

That evening Gervaise received a message from D'Aubusson, requesting him to call at his *auberge*.

"So you are going to sea, Sir Gervaise? I hear from your bailiff that you have been working to his satisfaction in the town."

"Yes, sir. I shall indeed be glad to change it for a life at sea. In truth, it is grievous to me to witness the sufferings of the slaves, and I would rather do any other work."

"They are far better off than the Christians who fall into the hands of the Turks," the bailiff said; "and, moreover, it is because their countrymen are preparing to attack us that we are forced to use their labour in strengthening our fortifications. They have naught to complain of in the way of food. Still, I would myself gladly see their lot alleviated; but we could not afford to keep so great a number of captives in idleness; they must work for their living. Had it not been for their labour we could never have built and fortified the city. After all, they are little worse off than our serfs at home; they build our castles and till our land."

"It may be so, sir; but with us in England men are free, and it was, when I first came, strange to me to see them working under the fear of the whip. It is necessary, I know, that such work should be done, but I own that I shall be glad to be away from the sight of the poor wretches, pirates and enemies of the faith though they be."

"I can understand your feelings, and I too felt somewhat the same when I first came here. Nevertheless, there is work that must be done if the Order is not to be crushed by the infidels. Here are captives, for the most part malefactors, who have to be fed; and there is no injustice in their having, like all men, to give work for food. I have learnt to see this and recognise the necessity, though I would that the work could be obtained without the use of harshness and severity. We ourselves are prepared at any moment to sacrifice our lives for the good of the Order and for the great cause, and it would be wrong, nay, sinful, not to use the means that have been placed ready to our hand. Now, Sir Gervaise, I wish you a pleasant voyage. You will find the life somewhat hard, after your three years' residence at the palace, but this I know you will not mind. I have specially commended you to Ricord as one in whom I am personally interested, and from whom I hope great things in the future. Be brave; be resolute. From what you have said I need not say—be merciful. Fulfil all orders promptly and without question; bear yourself courteously to all; above all things, remember that you are a soldier, not only of the Order, but of the Cross."

The next day Gervaise embarked with his companions on board the galley. It was a long, low boat, similar to those in use by the Venetians and Genoese. It was rowed by fifty slaves, who slept at night on or beneath the benches they sat on by day. The knights occupied the great cabins in the poop. There were two tiers of these; the upper one contained the little cabin of the commander, while the rest of the space on this deck, and that below it, was used by the knights in common. In the upper cabin they took their meals, and a third of their number slept there, the remainder in the cabin below. A fourth of their number were, however, always on guard, lest any attempt at a rising or escape should be made by the galley-slaves.

On leaving the harbour the galley, with its two consorts, rowed north, and Gervaise learnt that they were to cruise between the mainland and the islands. Some of these were in the hands of the Turks, while others were still occupied by Greeks.

Except when there was a formal and actual state of war, the Moslem and Christian islands remained in a state of neutrality, trading with each other and avoiding all unfriendly proceedings that would lead to struggles which would be fatal to the prosperity of both. The Archipelago, and indeed the whole of the eastern portion of the Mediterranean, was infested by pirates, fitted out, for the most part, on the mainland. These, when in force, openly kept the sea, attacking the Christian merchant ships, but when cruising alone they hid in unfrequented bays, or behind uninhabited islets, until they could pounce upon a passing ship whose size promised an easy capture. The Order of St. John furnished a maritime police, earning thereby the deep gratitude of Spain, France, and Italy. They were aided occasionally by the Venetians, but these, being frequently engaged in quarrels with their neighbours, did but a small share of this work, only sending their fleets to sea when danger threatened some of their possessions in the Levant.

"This is delightful, Ralph," Gervaise said, as they stood together on the poop, looking back at the receding city.

"What a pleasant change it is from standing in the broiling sun watching those poor wretches toiling at the fortifications! There is only one drawback to my pleasure. I wish that we carried sails, and were moved along by the breeze, instead of by the exertions of the slaves."

"Much chance we should have of catching a pirate under such circumstances!" Ralph said, laughing. "You might as well set a tortoise to catch a hare."

"I don't say that we should not be obliged to carry rowers, Ralph; but all the prizes that have been brought in since I have been at Rhodes carry masts and sails, as well as oars, and, as I understand, for the most part cruise about under sail, and only use the oars when chasing or fleeing."

"That is so; because, you see, in most cases the crew themselves have to row, and I have no doubt if we had no slaves to do the work we should soon take to masts and sails also; but for speed the rowing galleys are the best, for unless a brisk wind were blowing, the mast and sails would but check her progress when the oars were out, and at any rate constrain her to travel only before the wind. I know your weakness about the slaves, Gervaise; but as we could neither build our fortifications nor row our galleys without them, I cannot go as far as you do in the matter, though I own that I am sometimes sorry for them. But you must remember that it is the fault of their people, and not of ours, that they are here."

"All that is true enough, Ralph, and I cannot gainsay you. Still I would rather that we were gliding along with sails instead of being rowed by slaves."

"At any rate, Gervaise, you will not see them ill-treated, for I myself heard Ricord, just before we were starting, tell the slave-overseers that so long as the rowers did fair work they were not to use their whips, and that only if we were in chase of a pirate were they to be urged to their utmost exertions."

"I am right glad to hear it, Ralph, and shall be able to enjoy the voyage all the more, now you have told me that such orders have been issued."

For a fortnight they cruised about among the islands. Several times boats rowed out from the shore to the galley with complaints of outrages by pirates under a notorious corsair named Hassan Ali, who had landed, burnt villages, killed many of the inhabitants, and carried off the rest as slaves; but no one could give any clue to aid them in their search for the corsairs. The time passed very pleasantly. There was no occasion for speed; often they lay all day in some bay, where they could approach near enough to the shore to lie in the shade of trees, while two or three of the knights ascended a hill and kept watch there for the appearance of any vessels of a suspicious character.

One morning, after passing the night at anchor, Harcourt and Gervaise were despatched just before sunrise to take a look round before the galley got under way. From the top of the hill they had an uninterrupted view of the sea, studded with islands on all sides of them. Beyond a few fishing-boats, looking like black specks on the glassy surface, no craft were in sight. They were about to return to the galley when, taking a last look round, Gervaise suddenly exclaimed,—

"Look, Ralph! There is smoke ascending from that island to the south-west. There was none just now."

"You mean from that bay, Gervaise? Yes, I see it; it is not more than a light mist."

"It is growing thicker," Gervaise said, "and spreading. Maybe it is but a hut that has accidentally caught fire, but it seems to me that the smoke is rising from several points."

"I think you are right, Gervaise. Let us hurry down with the news. It may be that it is a village which has been attacked by pirates who have landed on the other side of the island during the night, for I can see no ships in the bay."

A few minutes' run and they stood on the shore.

"Quick, men!" Ralph said to the rowers of the boat that had brought them ashore. "Row your hardest."

The slaves bent to their oars, and they were soon alongside the galley, which lay two or three hundred yards from the shore. Those on board had noticed the young knights running down the hill, and, marking the speed at which the boat was rowing, concluded at once that they must have observed one of the pirate's ships.

"Do you see anything of them, Sir Ralph?" the commander shouted, as they came close.

"We have seen no ships, Sir Louis, but there is smoke coming up from a bay in an island four or five miles away to the south-west. It seems to us that it is far too extensive a fire to be the result of an accident, for there was no smoke until within two or three minutes of the time we left, and before we started it was rising from several points, and we both think that it must come from a village that has been attacked by pirates."

The commander rapidly issued his orders, and in two or three minutes the anchor was weighed, the boat hoisted on deck, and the oars in motion.

"Stretch to your oars!" Ricord shouted to the slaves. "Hitherto we have exacted no toil from you, but you have to work now, and woe be to him who does not put out his full strength."

Grateful for the unusual leniency with which they had been treated, the slaves bent to their oars, and the galley sped rapidly through the water. On rounding the end of the island there was an exclamation of satisfaction from the knights as they saw wreaths of white smoke rising from the distant island.

"There can be no doubt that it is a village in flames," Sir Louis said; "and from the suddenness with which it broke out, it is clear that it must have been fired at several points. You say you saw no craft near?" he asked, turning to Harcourt.

"There were none there, or from the top of the hill we should assuredly have made them out, Sir Louis."

"Then the pirates—if this be, as I hope, their work—must have landed at some other point on the island, and if they catch sight of us they may make for their ship and slip away, unobserved by us. Instead of rowing direct, therefore, we will make for that islet to the right, and row round behind it. There are two others almost adjoining it. Once past these, 'tis not more than half a mile to that island stretching away south. Once round that, we shall be beyond the one from which we see the smoke rising, and can come down on its southern side. The course will be double the distance that it would be if we took a straight line, but except when we cross from island to island we shall not be exposed to their view, and may fall upon their ships before the crews have returned from their work of plunder."

The knights fully agreed, and orders were given to the helmsman accordingly.

"We must not over-fatigue the rowers," the commander said. "We may have a long chase if they have started before we get round."

He therefore gave orders to the slaves that, while they were to exert themselves to the utmost when crossing the open sea, they were to relax their efforts and to row within their strength while coasting along behind the islands. On board, everything was made in readiness for a fight: the knights buckled on their armour, the cooks set cauldrons of pitch over the fire, the cannoneers loaded her eight guns. It was an hour and a half after their start before they rounded the end of the last island. It extended a little farther to the south than did that to which they were making, and as they rounded the point, eager looks were cast in search of the pirate ships. No craft were, however, to be seen.

"They must be in some bay or inlet," the commander said; "they can hardly have left, for it would have taken them half an hour at least to cross the island with their booty and captives, and even if they made straight away after having fired the village, their ship could have gone no great distance, for we must have seen her if she put to sea—unless indeed they were anchored on the east of the island, and have sailed in that direction."

"Keep them rowing along steadily," he said to the overseers of the slaves; "but do not press them too hard. We may have a chase yet, and need all their strength, for most of these pirates are fast craft, and if they should get a start of three or four miles, it will be a long row before we catch them."

They made straight for the island, and on nearing it coasted along its southern side. It was some three miles long, the shore being for the most part steep, but here and there falling gradually to the water's edge. Two or three little clusters of houses could be seen as they rowed along; one of these was on fire.

"That is good," Sir Louis exclaimed, as, on turning a point, they saw the flames. "That cannot have been lighted long, and we are pretty certain to come upon the vessels before the marauders have set sail."

Several inlets and small bays were passed, but all were empty. A few fishing boats lay on the shore, but there were no signs of life, as no doubt the people would, long since, have taken alarm and sought shelter in the woods. There was a sharp point just before they reached the south-eastern extremity of the island, and as the galley shot past this, a shout of exultation rose from the knights, for, near the mouth of an inlet that now opened to their view, there lay four long, low vessels, above each of which floated the

Moslem flag. A number of men were gathered on the shore near the ships, and heavily-laden boats were passing to and fro.

A yell of rage and alarm rose from the ships as the galley came into view. There was a stir and movement on the shore, and numbers of men leapt into the boats there, and started for the ships. These were some quarter of a mile away when first seen, and half that distance had been traversed when a puff of smoke shot out from the side of one of them, followed almost immediately by a general discharge of their cannon. One ball tore along the waist of the galley, killing six of the rowers, and several oars on both sides were broken. Two balls passed through the cabins in the poop. But there was no pause in the advance of the galley. The whips of the slave-masters cracked, and the rowers whose oars were intact strained at them. There was no reply from the guns, but the knights raised loud the war cry of the Order, a war cry that was never heard without striking a thrill of apprehension among their Moslem foes.

As they neared the pirate ships, the helm was put down, and the galley brought up alongside the largest of them and a broadside poured into her; then the knights, headed by their commander, leapt on to her deck.

Although a number of the crew had not yet come off from shore, the Moslems still outnumbered their assailants, and, knowing that their consorts would soon come to their aid, they threw themselves in a body on the Christians. But in a hand-to-hand conflict like this, the knights of the Hospital were irresistible. Protected by their armour and long shields from the blows of their enemies' scimitars and daggers, their long, cross-handled swords fell with irresistible force on turbaned head and coat-of-mail, and, maintaining regular order and advancing like a wall of steel along the deck, they drove the Moslems before them, and the combat would soon have terminated had not a shout been raised by one of the overseers of the slaves. One of the other ships had rowed alongside the galley, and the crew were already leaping on board it. At the same moment another ship came up alongside that they had boarded, while the fourth was maneuvering to bring up under her stern.

"Sir John Boswell," Sir Louis shouted, "do you and your countrymen, with the knights of Spain, finish with these miscreants; knights of Germany and Provence keep back the boarders; knights of Auvergne follow me," and he leapt down into the galley.

The English and Spanish knights redoubled their exertions. The Moslems endeavoured to rally, seeing that help was at hand, and that but a small body were now opposed to them, but their numbers availed little. The ten knights kept their line, and, hewing their way forward, pressed them so hotly that the Turks broke and sprang over the bulwarks into the sea. Then the knights looked round. A fierce fight was going on between those of Germany and Provence and the enemy, who strove desperately to board from the ship alongside. The other vessel was now almost touching the stern, and her crew were swarming to her side in readiness to leap on board as soon as the vessels touched.

"We will keep them at bay there," Sir John Boswell shouted. "Do you, Don Pedro, and your comrades, aid Ricord. When his foes are finished with, you can, come back to help us."

Then, with the four English knights, he ran along the deck, and reached the stern just in time to hurl backwards the Moslems, who had already obtained a footing. For a time the five knights kept back the surging mass of their foes. The deck was wide enough for each to have fair play for his sword, and in vain the pirates strove to obtain a footing.

At last Sir Marmaduke Lumley fell, severely wounded by an arrow from a Moslem marksman, and before the others could close the gap a score of pirates leapt on to the deck.

"Fall back, comrades, fall back; but keep together!" Sir John Boswell shouted, as he cleft the skull of one of the pirate officers who sprang at him. "Sir Louis will soon finish his work, and be here to our aid. Ah!" he exclaimed, looking over his shoulder, as he retired a step, "Provence and Germany are overmatched too."

This was indeed the case. Stoutly as they fought the knights were unable to guard the whole of the line of bulwark, and the Moslems had already obtained a footing on the deck. The discipline of the knights stood them in good stead. Drawing closely together as they retreated, they made a stand on the opposite side of the deck, and were here joined by Sir John Boswell and his companions. They now formed a semicircle, each flank resting on the bulwark, and the pirates in vain endeavoured to break their line. Again and again they flung themselves upon the knights, only to be beaten off with heavy loss. At length a loud cheer arose from the galley, and Sir Louis Ricord, with the knights of Auvergne and Spain having cleared the galley of their foes, and carried the pirate that had grappled with her, sprang on to the deck of the ship, and fell upon the throng that were attacking the knights there, oblivious of what was going on elsewhere. At once the English knights and their comrades took the offensive, and fell upon their assailants who, at the sight of the reinforcement, for a moment stood irresolute. For a short time there was a fierce struggle; then the pirates sprang back to their two ships, and endeavoured to cast off the grapnels. But the knights followed hotly upon them, and, panic stricken now, the pirates sprang overboard. Many were drowned, but the greater part managed to swim to shore.

CHAPTER V
SCOURGES OF THE SEA

BREATHLESS and faint from their tremendous exertions, the knights removed their helmets.

"By St. Mary," Sir Louis said, "this has been as hard a fight as I have ever been engaged in, and well may we be content with our victory! Well fought, my brave comrades! Each of these vessels must have carried twice our number at least, and we have captured four of them; but I fear the cost has been heavy."

Seven knights had fallen, struck down by sword, arrow, or thrust of spear. Of the rest but few had escaped unwounded, for, strong as was their armour, the keen Damascus blades of the Moslems had in many cases cut clean through it, and their daggers had found entry at points where the armour joined; and, now that the fight was over, several of the knights sank exhausted on the deck from loss of blood.

But the dressing of wounds formed part of a knight of St. John's training. Those who were unwounded unbuckled the armour and bandaged the wounds. Others fetched wine and water from the galley. The chains of the galley-slaves were removed, and these were set to clear the decks of the Moslem corpses. The anchors were dropped, for what little wind there was drifted them towards the shore. They had learned from a dying pirate that the vessels were part of the fleet of Hassan Ali, a fact that added to the satisfaction felt by the knights at their capture, as this man was one of the most dreaded pirates of the Levant. They learnt that he himself had not been present, the expedition being under the command of one of his lieutenants, who had fallen in the fight.

SCOURGES OF THE SEA

"Now, comrades, let us in the first place take food; we have not broken our fast this morning. Then let us consider what had best be done, for indeed we have got as much in our hands as we can manage; but let us leave that till we eat and drink, for we are faint from want of food and from our exertions. But we shall have to eat what comes to hand, and that without cooking, for our servants all joined the pirates when they boarded us, and are either dead or are ashore there."

A meal was made of bread and fruit, and this with wine sufficed to recruit their energies.

"It seems to me, comrades," Sir Louis said, when all had finished, "that the first thing is to search the holds of these vessels and see what valuables are stored there. These may be all carried on board one ship, and the others must be burnt, for it is clear that, as there are four of them, we cannot take them to Rhodes; and even with one and our galley we should fare but ill, if we fell in with two or three more of Hassan's ships."

"But how about the pirates on shore, Sir Louis?" a knight asked. "There were very many who could not get off to their ships during the fight, and scores must have swum ashore. I should say that there must be full two hundred, and it will be a grievous thing for the islanders if we leave them there."

"It is certain," the commander said, "that we are not strong enough to attack them, for were we to land, a party would have to be left on board, or the pirates might elude our search, seize some fishing-boats, and regain possession. Certainly, we are in no position to divide our forces."

"Methinks," Sir John Boswell said, "that the best plan would be to send a boat, manned with ten galley-slaves, taking two or three of us to the rendezvous, to fetch hither the other two galleys. With their aid we might take all the four ships safe into port, after first clearing the island of these pirates. It is but forty miles away, and eight hours' rowing would take us there."

There was a general murmur of assent, for all wished that the trophies of their bravery should, if possible, be carried to Rhodes.

"That will certainly be the best plan, Sir John, though it may detain us here for two or three days, or even more, for it is quite uncertain when the other two galleys may put in at the rendezvous. Will you yourself undertake the mission?"

"With pleasure."

"How many will you take with you?"

"Two will be sufficient, for we shall have no fighting to do, as we shall have to trust to our speed if we fall in with an enemy. I will take, with your permission, Sir Ralph Harcourt and Sir Gervaise Tresham, both of whom have to-day fought with distinguished bravery. Indeed, I owe my life to them, for more than once, when I was hotly pressed, they freed me from my assailants. Truly none bore themselves better in the fray than they did."

Three or four others joined in hearty commendations of the two young knights.

"Indeed," one said, "I was greatly surprised to see how Tresham bore himself. He is but a lad, with scarce, one would think, strength to hold his own in such a fray. It chanced that he was next to me in the circle, and for a time I kept my eye on him, thinking he might require my aid; but I soon saw that I need not trouble myself on his account, for he wielded his weapon as doughtily as the best knight of the Order could have done, and one of the proofs is that, while most of us bear marks of the conflict, he has escaped without scratch. I trust, Sir Louis, that when you give an account of the fighting you will specially mention that this, the youngest knight of the Order, bore himself as stoutly as any of them. I say this, Sir John, because, not being of your *langue*, I can speak more warmly than you can do of his skill and bravery."

"I thank you, De Boysey," Sir John Boswell said, "and I am proud that my young countryman should have so gained your approbation. And now," he went on, "while the galley-slaves are getting a meal—which they have right well earned to-day—I should like to see what there is under the hatches of these ships, so that I can give our comrades in the other galleys some idea of the value of this booty we have taken."

They rose from the table, and, going on board the prizes, lifted the hatches.

"Beware!" De Boysey exclaimed, looking down into the hold, when the first hatch was taken off. "There are people below."

A chorus of cries followed his exclamation.

"They are the voices of women and children," Sir Louis exclaimed. "They must be captives."

This turned out to be so. In the holds of the four ships were found over a hundred and fifty women and children; these had been brought on board in the first boat-loads by the pirates, and when the Christian galley had been seen coming round the point, had been thrust below, and the hatches thrown over them. They had heard the din of battle above, but knew not how the conflict had terminated, and, being afraid to cry out, had remained silent until, on the hatch being lifted, they had seen the figures of Christian knights standing in the bright sunshine. All had come from the village on the other side of the island. They related how the pirates had suddenly burst upon them, had slaughtered all the men, set fire to the village, and had driven them before them across the island to the ships. The poor creatures were delighted at their escape from slavery, but at the same time were full of grief at the loss of husbands, fathers, and sons.

Some laughed, others cried; while some thanked God for their rescue others heaped imprecations upon the authors of their misfortunes.

The knights explained to them that for a short time they must remain on board, as half the pirates were still on shore, but that aid would soon arrive that would enable them to clear the island.

A KNIGHT OF THE WHITE CROSS

Half an hour later Sir John Boswell, with the two young knights, started in a rowing boat, manned by ten of the galley-slaves. The wind had sprung up since the fight ceased, and as it was nearly astern, they anticipated that they would make a good passage, and be at the little islet, named as the place of rendezvous, before nightfall.

Among the many bales of rich merchandise in the hold of the pirate vessels an abundance of wine had been discovered, and of this a tankard had been given to each of the slaves, by Sir Louis's orders, as a token of satisfaction at their work in the morning.

They had gone some two miles when, from one of the inlets in the island they had left a large fishing-boat was seen to issue out.

"By St. George!" Sir John exclaimed, "that boat must be full of pirates. And if they see us, which they cannot help doing, and take it in their heads to chase us, we shall have a hard time of it."

The fishing-boat for a few minutes kept along the coast, and then suddenly her course was altered, and her head directed towards their boat.

"Now stretch to your oars," Sir John, who spoke some Turkish, said to the slaves. "Keep ahead of that boat, and I promise you, on my honour as a Christian knight, that I will myself purchase your freedom as soon as we get to Rhodes."

With a shout of delight, the galley-slaves bent to their oars, and the boat flew along at a greatly increased speed.

"There is but small chance of our getting away," Sir John said quietly. "At present we must be rowing as fast as they sail; but wind never tires, while there are limits to the powers of muscle and bone. If those fellows follow us—and I doubt not that they will, for they must be thirsting for vengeance—they will overtake us long before we get to the rendezvous; and even did we reach it, the chances are that we should not find either of the galleys there. We must hold on as long as we can, and as a last resource must run ashore. Unfortunately there are no large islands on our way. Nor have we any hope of assistance from our friends behind. The inlet looks east, and they will know nothing of our danger; nor, if they did, could they help us. The galley is short-handed now, and there are the captured ships to look after, and the captives we rescued. We have only ourselves to depend on."

At the end of an hour's rowing the boat astern had gained little; but the exertions of the rowers were telling severely upon them. They were still doing their best, but their breath came in short gasps, the rowing was getting short and unsteady, and there was a sensible decrease in the speed of the boat. Three miles ahead of them was an islet about half a mile in diameter. In some parts it was covered with foliage, but elsewhere it was bare rock.

"That must be our goal," Sir John said. "They will be close to us by the time we get there." Then he said to the rowers, "Stop for a minute to get breath. We will land at that islet ahead, and I shall hold to my promise if we get there in time. Those of you who like can remain in the boat until your countrymen come up; those who choose can leave the boat and hide yourselves as best you may. I leave the choice to yourselves. If we are overtaken and fall, I cannot keep my promise, and it will be best then for you to remain in the boat."

For three or four minutes the slaves bent forward over their oars; but as soon as Sir John gave the word they straightened themselves up and began rowing again. The rest had done them good, and they again fell into a long, steady stroke.

"Shall we buckle on our armour again?" Sir Ralph Harcourt asked; for they had not put it on when they left the ship, as the heat was very great.

"I think we had better don our mail shirts only. In climbing about that rock ahead of us, the less weight we carry the better, and with this heat I would rather fight unprotected than in casque and armour. Besides, there can be little doubt that, if they come upon us, it will be our last, battle. That craft behind is crowded with men, and, armour or no armour, it will come to the same in the end. If it were not that we have a mission to fulfil, and that it is of all things important to send the galleys to aid our friends, I would say let us choose a spot at the foot of the rocks there, where they cannot attack us in the rear, and there fight it out as becomes knights of the Cross; but as it is our duty above all things to carry this message, we must strive to preserve our lives, and must, if we can, conceal ourselves from these paynims."

"What are you going to do?" Sir John asked the slaves, when they were within a quarter of a mile of the islet. "I should think, after we have left the boat, it will be best for you to sit quietly on your benches till our pursuers arrive."

"They would cut our throats at once, Sir Knight; they will be furious at our having given them so long a chase. Hassan Ali's men care little whom they slay, and, irritated by their misfortune, it will be naught to them whether we are Moslem or Christian. I, for one, shall take to the woods, and hide."

There was a chorus of assent among the other rowers.

"I trust that you may escape," the knight said. "It is for us they will be hunting, and if they catch and slay us they will not trouble to search the island further."

"It seems to me, Sir John," Gervaise said, "that with the aid of these good fellows we may yet have a chance of escape."

"What is your plan, Sir Gervaise?"

"I think, Sir John, that if, when we land, we climb straight up that hill, in full sight of the shore, the pirates, when they see us, will follow at once. The slaves should, therefore, be safe for a time if they hide in that wood to the left of the spot we are making for. Will you tell them to keep down by the water's edge among the bushes, and that after crossing that crest, we will try to make a dash round, so as to join them there. 'Tis probable that most of the pirates will start in pursuit of us, and if we and the slaves make a rush for the shore we may seize our boat, push off, and capture their craft, if there are but a few left on board, knock out a plank and scuttle her, and then row away."

"By St. George, your plan is a good one, Tresham!—a right good scheme, and we will try it."

He at once translated what Gervaise had said to the rowers, by whom it was received with short exclamations of approval, for they were too breathless and exhausted for talk. Already they could hear the yells of the pirates, who, as the boat ran up on the beach were but a quarter of a mile behind.

"Now, away for that wood!" Sir John cried, as he leapt ashore. "Now, comrades, for a climb up the hill!"

It was a steep ascent, and more than once one had to be helped up by the others, and then in turn to assist them to get up beside him. Louder and louder rose the shouts of the pirates, but the knights did not glance back until they reached the top of the hill; then they turned and looked round. A swarm of men were climbing after them, and were already halfway up the cliff.

"Heave them down!" Sir John exclaimed, pointing to some loose rocks, and set the example by lifting a great stone and hurling it over the edge. Harcourt and Gervaise at once did the same, and twenty or thirty rocks were speedily sent rolling down the steep ascent, and yells, shouts, and cries were heard below.

"That will check them a bit. Now let us be off," Sir John Boswell said, and they at once started. After crossing a hundred yards of bare rock they stood at the edge of another slope into a deep valley, beyond which rose the central hill of the island. The valley ran right across, and was filled with trees extending to the sea at either end. Running rapidly down, the knights were within the shelter of the wood before the Moslems had reached the brow behind them. A minute later they heard the shouts of their enemies. Once in the wood they turned to the left, and in a few minutes stood on the sea shore. It was a little bay some two hundred yards across, and at either point the cliffs rose abruptly from the water.

"We shall have to swim round the point," Sir John said.

"Take off your mail shirts. We will make our way along the rocks as far as we can, and then drop them into the sea, otherwise they will know that we have taken to the water."

They hurried along the rocks, and were able to make their way to within fifty yards of the point; then, throwing their mail shirts into the sea, they plunged in. All knew the importance of getting round before any of the pirates, who would be searching the valley, came down on the shore, and they swam their hardest until they rounded the corner. The wood rang with the shouts of their pursuers, but no yell had risen from the water's edge. A hundred yards farther, and they were able to land, and were in a short time in the shelter of the trees that fringed the water to the point where they had left the boat. There was no longer any occasion for speed, and they made their way through the thick bushes and undergrowth quietly, until they recovered breath after their exertions. They had gone a few hundreds yards when from the bushes the slaves suddenly rose up.

"All has gone well," Sir John said to them in their own language. "The pirates are searching for us on the other side of the hill. There are not likely to be many of them left here. We shall soon be in possession of our boat again."

Followed by the slaves, they made their way forward until they stood at the edge of the wood. Five or six pirates were standing on the shore.

"I expect they have been left there," Harcourt said, "to prevent the slaves from carrying off the boat. They must have seen them run into the wood. They won't reckon on our being with them."

Drawing their swords, the three knights rushed out, followed by the slaves. They had but a hundred yards to run. The pirates, on seeing them, raised a yell and drew their scimitars; but the sight of the knights rushing upon them, when they had expected but a few unarmed rowers, was too much for their courage, and when their assailants were still fifty yards away they turned and fled. The fishing craft had been run ashore but a few yards from their boat.

"Get her afloat, Harcourt, and bring her to the stern of the fisherman. Now, Tresham, follow me."

Sir John Boswell climbed up on to the fishing boat, which was a craft of some fifteen tons burden. She was entirely deserted, but the sail still hung from the yard, and a fire was burning on a stone hearth, raised on some logs of wood in the centre of the deck.

"Look for something to stave in a plank, Tresham."

Gervaise leapt down into the hold. There were some nets and spare sails lying there, but nothing that would answer the purpose. He examined the planks. The boat was very strongly and roughly built.

"There is nothing here, Sir John, that will do, and nothing short of a heavy sledge hammer would suffice to smash one of these planks."

"There are a lot of them coming down the hill, Tresham. We have not many minutes to spare, but we must disable the craft. They will soon be after us again; they have run her hard and fast here, but when they all come back they will soon get her off. Let us try one of these sweeps."

He lifted one of the heavy oars, and holding it upright he and Gervaise together tried to drive the handle through the bottom. Again and again they raised it and drove it down; but the plank was too strong, and too securely fastened to the timbers.

"We must give it up," the knight said, with a sigh. "Fortune has befriended us so far, Tresham, but she has deserted us at last. Another three minutes, and we shall have thirty or forty of them upon us."

At this moment the lad's eye fell upon the fire.

"We shall manage yet," he exclaimed, and, seizing a blazing brand, he jumped below and set fire to the sails stowed there; they were as dry as tinder, and the flame shot up at once.

"That is good, Tresham," the knight said; "but they will put it out before it has caught the boat."

"Not before it has burnt the sails," Gervaise replied. "Now for this one," and he applied the brand to the lower edge of the great sail. Without a word Sir John seized another brand, and fired the sail on the other side of the deck. The flames flashed up, and a wild yell of rage and alarm broke from the pirates, who were now rushing down towards the beach.

"Now to the boat, Tresham; we have no time to lose if we would avoid being pounded with stones."

They dropped over the stern into the boat. The galley-slaves dipped their oars into the water, and she shot away just as the foremost of the pirates reached the edge of the water. A few stones were thrown; but the pirates were so anxious about the craft, by which alone they could escape from the island, that the majority at once climbed on board.

At a word from the knight, the slaves stopped rowing a hundred yards from the shore. The sail was already consumed, and the yard and the upper part of the mast were in flames. A dense smoke was rising from the hold, and the pirates were throwing buckets of water down into it. In a few minutes the smoke decreased.

"I thought that they would be able to put it out; but, as far as we are concerned, it matters little. They have lost their sails, and as I saw but four sweeps, we can travel five miles to their one. If we find the galleys we will look in here on our way back, and if they have not left we will fire that craft more effectually, and then the pirates will be trapped, and we can leave them till we have fetched off Sir Louis and his prizes, and then have a grand hunt here. We took no prisoners before, and a hundred slaves will be a useful addition to our wall-builders. Now, Tresham, I have to thank you warmly, for Harcourt and I doubly owe our lives to you. It was thanks to your quickness of wit that we regained our boat, for I would not have given a ducat for our chances had you not thought of that scheme. In the second place, we should assuredly have been overtaken again had it not been for your happy thought of crippling them by burning their sails. By St. George, Harcourt, this young countryman of ours is as quick and as ready of wit as he has shown himself a brave and gallant fighter! We have no lack of sturdy fighters; but the wit to devise and to seize upon the right thing in the moment of danger is vastly more rare. As for myself, I have no shame that this lad, who is young enough to be my son, should have thus, twice in a single hour, pointed out the way to safety. With sword and battle-axe I can, I trust, hold my own with any man; but my brain is dull when it comes to hatching schemes. If we live, we shall see Sir Gervaise one of the most distinguished knights of the Order."

"While I feel gratified indeed, as I may well be by your commendation, Sir John, I must, under your favour, say that you have given me a far greater degree of credit than is my due. There was the fire, and there was the sail, and the thought that the one would destroy the other was simply a natural one, which might have occurred to a child. As to the plan about the boat, seeing that there was the hill and the wood, it flashed upon me at once that we might make a circuit and come back to her."

"Just so, lad; but those thoughts did not flash upon my mind, nor upon that of Harcourt. It is just because those sort of ideas do flash upon the minds of some men, and not of others, that the first rise to the rank of distinguished commanders, while the others remain simple knights who would play their part in a charge or in the defence of a breach, but would be of no account as leaders. Now row along steadily, men," he went on, speaking to the slaves. "We are still in good time, for it was not an hour from the moment we touched the island to our departure from it, and much of that time we have gained by the speed with which you rowed before. At any rate, we shall make out the island before sunset, and whether we arrive there a little sooner or later matters little. Harcourt, hand me that wineskin and a goblet. A draught will do us good after our climb and swim, and these good fellows will be none the worse for a cup also."

Inspired with the hope of freedom, the slaves rowed steadily, and the sun had just set when they entered a little inlet in the rocky isle that was their place of rendezvous.

"Thanks be to the saints!" Sir John exclaimed, as they reached the entrance. "There is Santoval's galley."

There was a stir on board the galley as the boat was seen approaching. The knights had put on their armour, which they had found still lying in the boat, the pirates, in their haste to pursue, having left her unexamined, while those who had remained on guard had abstained from touching anything until the return of their captain and comrades.

"Whence come you, Sir John, and what is the news? No misfortune has befallen Ricord's galley, I hope?" the Spanish knight in command shouted, as the boat came near enough for him to recognize the features of its occupants.

"All is well," Sir John shouted back; "but we have taken more prizes than we can manage, though not without hard fighting. Seven knights have fallen, and at least ten others will not be able to buckle their armour on again for some time to come, so I have been sent here to beg your assistance; and it is well that it should be given speedily, for if more pirate vessels come up before you join, Ricord and his companions will be in a sorry plight."

By this time the boat had reached the side of the galley, and as Sir John and his two companions stepped on board, the knights crowded round to hear the details of the news. Exclamations of approval and satisfaction arose when Sir John related the incidents of the fight, and told them that the four vessels that had fallen into their hands formed part of Hassan Ali's fleet.

"That is good news indeed, Boswell," Don Santoval said; "and I would I had been there to take part in so gallant a fight. It is well you found us here, for with four prizes on hand, and with half his strength dead or disabled, Ricord must be in sore need of aid. We will start to-morrow morning at daybreak. As all the ships were taken, there is little fear of any of the other pirates hearing news of what has happened."

"I don't know," Sir John replied. "There were, as I told you, some two hundred pirates left on the island. About half those, we know, seized a fishing boat and escaped, for they chased us, and we have had as narrow an escape from death as has ever fallen to my lot, though I have been in over a score of hard-fought battles. The rest may well have taken another fishing boat and made off also, for we saw several craft along the shores of the island. If so, they may have made for Hassan Ali's rendezvous, wherever that may be, just as I made here, and by this time some of his ships may be on the way there."

"By St. Anthony, this alters the situation gravely!" Don Santoval said. "Fellow knights, we must lose no time in going to Ricord's assistance. The slaves have had a long row to-day, but they must start on another. Let them have a good meal to strengthen them, and a cup of wine each. Whatever their scruples at other times, they never refuse wine when there is heavy work to be done, knowing full well that a draught of it helps them mightily in their labours. Your men must have rowed well, Sir John, to have brought you here so quickly?"

"I have promised them their freedom," Sir John said; "and they shall have it, even if I have to pay their value into the treasury. As I told you, we were hotly pursued, for the craft with her sail went faster than we with our oars; and, knowing the importance of bringing the news here, I encouraged them by promising them their freedom, should we get away. Not only did they row right manfully, but they proved faithful in our extremity, and, when all seemed lost, stuck to us instead of deserting and joining the pirates."

"But how did you get away, Sir John, if their craft outsailed you?"

"I owe my life entirely to the quick wit of my young countryman, Sir Gervaise Tresham here." And Sir John then related the incidents of their adventure on the island, his narrative eliciting warm expressions of approval from the knights.

"Of course, you will go with us, Boswell?" Don Santoval said, when the master of the slaves announced that these had eaten their meal, and were ready.

"I must do so," Sir John replied. "I want you, on your way, to look in at that island where we had so narrow an escape, and if we find their craft still there we can destroy it. The place is directly in our course; we shall, therefore, lose but little time in looking in. Of course, they may have gone as soon as they got their vessel afloat, but it is hardly likely. They would have no idea of my returning with a galley so soon, and will probably set to to make a dozen more oars before they start, for she had but four on board, which will scarce suffice to send her a mile an hour through the water. Therefore, I fancy they will not put off until to-morrow morning. If that is so, and we destroy their craft, they will be trapped in the islet, and on our return we can capture them all. I think of leaving Harcourt and Tresham in the boat, in order that when Piccolomini's galley comes in, they may direct him also to join us."

"He may be in at any moment; we met him three days since. He had captured a pirate, and sent her off under charge of ten of his knights. We agreed to meet him this evening; and as he is not here, he will probably be in the first thing in the morning."

Gervaise and Harcourt took their places in the boat again. The galley got up its anchor and started. Just as she reached the mouth of the inlet another galley rounded the point and nearly ran into her.

"I am going to Ricord's assistance, Piccolomini," Don Santoval shouted.

"Is it urgent?" the commander of the galley shouted back.

"We have had a very long row, and can go no farther, unless his strait is a very sore one."

"No. Come on in the morning. You will hear all the news from a boat lying two hundred yards astern. Two young English knights are waiting in her to give you the news. Ricord has made a fine capture. Row on, men." And the galley proceeded on her way, while the new-comer proceeded up the harbour.

Harcourt and Gervaise at once went on board, and the former gave the Italian commander an account of the battle that had taken place, and the capture of the four pirate vessels. After the exclamations of satisfaction by the knights had ceased, he recounted their own adventures, which were heard with lively interest.

"I hope indeed that Santoval will burn that fishing boat, and that we shall capture the pirates," the commander said. "We have need of more slaves to carry out the works at Rhodes. Now, let us to supper, gentlemen, and then to sleep. In six hours we will be off again, for if some more of these villains have escaped and carried the news to Hassan Ali, our swords may be sorely needed by Ricord and Santoval to-morrow."

CHAPTER VI
KNIGHTED

A T three in the morning all on board the galley were astir. A ration of bread and meat was served out to the slaves, and the boat was soon afterwards under way. The rowers of the English knight's boat had been warmly commended by the commander and placed in charge of the overseer, with instructions that they were to be treated as free men. As soon as the galley-slaves set to work, however, they seated themselves on the benches and double-banked some of the oars, anxious to please the knights. With the exception of those whose turn it was to be on watch, most of the knights slept until daybreak.

"At the rate we are rowing, Gervaise," Harcourt said, as they went up on to the poop together, "it will not take us very long to join our friends. We are going through the water at fully six miles an hour; and as we have already been two hours under way, in another three we shall be there."

An hour and a half later they passed the island where they had landed. The two young knights pointed out to the others the valley into which they had descended, and the point round which they had swum. In a few minutes they caught sight of the landing-place.

"Look, Gervaise, there is something black showing just above the water."

"I see it. I think it is a line of timbers. There were certainly no rocks there when we ran ashore."

"Then Santoval must have found the craft still there and burnt her," one of the knights standing by remarked," and the pirates are caged up. It will take them some time to make a raft that will carry them to the next island, and before they can do that we shall be back again. I shall be sorry if they escape, for they are as ruthless a set of villains as sail the seas."

The galley had traversed half the remaining distance when the sound of a gun was faintly heard. For a moment there was an absolute hush on the poop; then three or four shots in rapid succession were heard.

"Some more pirate ships must have come up," the commander exclaimed. Then he shouted down to the slaves, "Row, men—row for your lives! Overseer, do not spare your lash if any hang back from their work."

The galley had been travelling fast before, but her speed greatly increased as the slaves rowed their hardest. Fast as she was travelling, the impatience of the knights was extreme. They walked up and down the deck, making vows of candles that should be burnt at the shrine of St. John if they arrived in time to take a share in the fight, stopping at times to listen to the sound of artillery, which was now so frequent as to show that a severe engagement was being fought. Many of the younger knights ran down to the waist and double-banked the oars, and in a shorter time than it seemed possible the galley arrived at the mouth of the bay.

A desperate fight was going on. Ricord's ship lay, idle and deserted, at anchor. Five pirate crafts surrounded Santoval's galley. Two of them were alongside of her; the others were raking her fore and aft with their shot. The young knights left the oars, sprang up to the poop and joined in the shout of encouragement raised by the others, and then, resuming their helmets and armour, stood ready to leap on board an enemy as soon as they reached her. Piccolomini directed the helmsman to lay him alongside one of the ships grappling with Santoval. As they came up, their galley's cannon poured their fire into her, and a moment later the knights sprang on board.

In the din of battle their shout had been unheard. The pirates thronging the other side of their ship were intent only on overcoming the resistance of the knights, and even the discharge of cannon had not called their attention to their foe, until the latter, shouting the war-cry of the Order, fell suddenly upon them. A panic at once seized them. Some were cut down almost unresistingly, but the great majority, running to the bow or stern, threw themselves overboard and swam to the other ships. The pirate ship on the other side of Santoval's galley instantly threw off the grapnels and thrust off from her side, and, immediately hauling in the sheets of the big sail, began at once to draw away, while her three consorts made for the mouth of the bay.

"Back to your galley, comrades," Piccolomini shouted, "or with this brisk wind they will escape us."

The knights at once crossed on to their own craft, the oars were got out, and the chase began. A minute or two later Don Santoval followed them, but soon gave up, as so large a number of the oars had been broken when the two pirate ships ran alongside him, that it would have been hopeless to pursue. The wind was blowing freshly, and was rapidly increasing in strength, so that, in spite of the efforts of the galley-slaves, the pirates gradually drew away, running straight before the wind, and aiding the effects of the sails with oars. Seeing the hopelessness of the chase, Piccolomini abandoned it, after rowing for two miles, and returned to the island. The other two galleys were lying beside each other, and Piccolomini had his craft steered alongside them.

"Thanks, Piccolomini, for arriving so opportunely," Santoval, who was seated on the deck leaning against the bulwarks, said, as his fellow commander leapt on board, and came towards him.

"Would that I had arrived sooner, Santoval, for I see that you have been grievously wounded!"

"Ay. One of the paynims' cannonballs has carried off both my legs below the knee. The leech has been searing the wounds with a hot iron, and says that he thinks I shall get over it; but if so I fear that my fighting days are past, unless, indeed, I fight seated on a chair. However, I ought not to grumble. I have lost many brave comrades, and others are wounded more sorely than I am."

KNIGHTED

Sir Louis Ricord now joined them. He embraced Piccolomini warmly.

"I never heard a more welcome shout, Piccolomini, than that which you gave when you fell upon the Moslems, for in truth the issue of the conflict was doubtful. I was delighted when this morning at daybreak Santoval's galley rowed in. We had all kept watch during the night, thinking the pirates might obtain boats and make an attack upon us; and, with but twenty of us fit to wield a sword, our position would have been a bad one, and at any rate they might have re-captured the prizes. We agreed that Santoval and his knights should land at once. This they did. Sir John Boswell had of course told me how his boat had been chased by a fishing craft, manned by a large number of the pirates, and that he feared the rest might similarly have escaped, and might have gone to bring some more of Hassan Ali's ships upon us.

"As soon as Santoval landed, some of the natives came down and told him that there was not a pirate remaining there, the rest having started in another boat a few minutes after the one that had chased Boswell. Santoval left two of his men with orders to ascend to the highest spot on the island, and to keep watch, and then brought the rest off to his galley. Our first step was, of course, to send all the women and children ashore. Then we consulted as to what had best be done if the pirates should come back in force. We hoped, at any rate, that this would not happen until you arrived. We expected that you would be here before noon; but we decided that, should they get here before you, we from our galley would embark on Santoval's, as it was better to fight in one strongly-manned boat than to divide our forces.

"It was scarce half an hour after Santoval came down before the men, left on the look-out, appeared on the beach. On fetching them off, they told us that as soon as they reached the top of the hill they saw five vessels approaching with sails and oars, and that they would be here in half an hour at the outside. We at once abandoned my galley, brought the rowers and the wounded here, and prepared for the fight. As you saw, they ran their two biggest ships alongside us, and for two hours the fight went on. They were crowded with men, who in vain strove to get a footing on our decks. Had we only had these two to deal with, we should have had nothing to fear, heavily-manned though they were; but the other three kept sailing backwards and forwards, discharging their guns into us as they passed, firing not only shot, but bags of bullets.

"Their gunners were skilful, and, as you see, they have completely riddled our poop. Twenty knights have been killed, and eleven others are sorely wounded. Scarce one has escaped unscathed. You may guess, then, how welcome was your aid, which we had not expected for another three hours. We were on the point of abandoning the waist and gathering on the poop, which we could still have defended for a considerable time, when, as if dropped from the skies, you fell upon the pirates, and turned the tables. How is it that you were here so early?"

"We started at three o'clock, instead of waiting for daybreak. It seemed, from the story of the two young knights, that it was possible you might be attacked early, and, crippled as your command was, and with four prizes on your hands, I deemed it best to come on as soon as the rowers had had a few hours' rest."

"It is well that you did so; it would have been a grievous affair had two of our galleys been captured by the pirates. It would have been a blow to the prestige of the Order, and would have brought such strength to Hassan Ali and other pirate leaders that nothing short of sending out a fleet would have recovered our ascendency; and as every ducat we can spare has to be spent on the fortifications, it would have been a misfortune indeed had we been obliged to fit out such an expedition at present."

"Who have fallen, Sir Louis?"

"Five more of the knights of my galley—Pierre des Vignes, Raoul de Montpelier, Ernest Schmidt, Raymond Garcia, and Albert Schenck. Here is the list of the knights of Santoval's galley."

"'Tis a long list, and a sad one," Piccolomini said, after reading the names. "With the seven who fell in your first fight, twenty-seven knights have fallen, all brave comrades. Truly, we can ill spare such a loss. It is true there are five prizes to show for it, and we have struck Hassan Ali a blow that will resound through the Levant; but the cost is heavy."

"It is indeed," Ricord agreed. "The four vessels are well filled with rich spoil that the scoundrels had gathered, and I doubt not the one you captured is equally rich. Still, had they been ten times as valuable, the booty would be dearly purchased at such a price."

There was now a consultation among the leaders, and it was agreed that six knights should be placed in each of the captured ships, with ten of the galley-slaves to work the sails, the others being equally divided between the three galleys. They were, in the first place, to row to the island where the pirates were imprisoned, and to slay or capture the whole of them; afterwards they were to make direct for Rhodes; with so numerous a fleet there was no fear of their being attacked. The arrangements took but a short time to complete. An hour later they left the port, the three galleys rowing ahead, while the five prizes, under easy sail, followed them.

Sir John Boswell had been wounded, but not so seriously as to altogether disable him, and he was in command of one of the prizes, having Sir Adam Tedbond, Harcourt, Gervaise, and a German knight, with him. Sir Marmaduke Lumley, who, after the first fight was over, was found, to the surprise and pleasure of his comrades, to be still living, was, with the rest of the wounded, on board one of the galleys. Two of the pirates had fallen dead across him, and in the ardour of their attack on the knights, he had lain there unnoticed until the return of Sir Louis and his comrades had driven the pirates overboard. The leech was of opinion that he might yet recover from his wound.

On arriving at the island, sixty of the knights disembarked. The woods near the shore were first searched, but were found untenanted. They were about to advance up the hill when a man appeared on the crest above them waving a white flag. He was told to come down, and on his arrival said that he was sent by his companions to offer to surrender, on the promise that their lives should be spared. The knights were well pleased to be saved the trouble of a long search through the woods, and the messenger left at once to acquaint the pirates that their terms were accepted. In a short time some eighty men made their way down the hill. On reaching the beach they were disarmed, divided equally between the galleys, and distributed among the rowers, filling up the places of those who had been killed by the fire of the Moslems, and of the men drafted into the prizes. They begged for food and water before they began work, and, on being questioned, admitted that their surrender was due principally to the fact that they had been unable to find food of any sort on the island, and that after searching all over it no spring of water could be discovered.

"In that case," Sir John Boswell said, "I have no doubt they have all surrendered. I before thought it probable that a good many of them would have remained hidden, trusting to be able to make a raft after we had left, and so get away, believing rightly enough that we should be disinclined to search every foot of the island for them. As it is, I doubt not, all are here."

The little fleet anchored that night at the rendezvous, and after two more days' rowing reached Rhodes, where the appearance of the three galleys, followed by their five prizes, was greeted with great acclamation. The news, however, that twenty-seven knights had fallen, and that thirteen or fourteen others were very gravely wounded, damped the satisfaction that every one had at first felt. D'Aubusson came down as soon as they reached the mole, and was greatly affected when he received Ricord's report.

"It is an unfortunate loss indeed, Sir Louis," he said, "though it may be that the victory is not too dearly purchased. I do not speak of the captured ships, nor of the spoil they contain, nor even of the slaves you have brought us, welcome though all may be, but of the effect that the defeat and capture of these craft of Hassan Ali's will have. It is plain that the preparations the sultan is making, and the belief that Rhodes is doomed, have so encouraged the infidels that they are becoming really formidable at sea. This blow will show them that the Order has yet power to sweep the sea of pirates. Since, however, this adventure has taught us that a single leader like Hassan sails with at least nine ships under his orders, it is clear that in future our galleys must not adventure singly among the islands. It was fortunate indeed that first Santoval, and then Piccolomini, arrived to your assistance. How was it that they happened to come up so opportunely?"

"Sir John Boswell, with Ralph Harcourt and Gervaise Tresham; went in a boat to the rendezvous we had arranged, and reached it after an adventure, which I will leave Sir John to tell himself. I may say that the two young knights named had in our encounter both obtained very high credit amongst us all for the valour with which they fought. No one bore himself more stoutly, and I am glad to take this early opportunity of bringing their conduct before your notice. As you will learn from Sir John, Gervaise Tresham afterwards showed a quickness of wit that was the means of saving the lives of those with him, and I may say also of all with me, for had they failed to reach the rendezvous we should have fallen easy victims to the five ships Hassan Ali brought against us."

Sending for Sir John Boswell, the grand prior heard from him the details of his adventure in the boat.

A KNIGHT OF THE WHITE CROSS

"I am right glad to hear you speak so warmly of Tresham, Sir John, for I regard him as my special *protégé*, and am pleased indeed to find that at this outset of his career he has proved himself not only a brave knight, but full of resource, and quick at invention. I think, Sir John, that these two young knights have shown themselves well worthy of receiving the honour of secular knighthood."

"Assuredly they have," Sir John agreed. "Then, Sir John, will you bestow it upon them? The Order, as an Order, does not bestow the honour, but its members do not forfeit their right as knights to bestow it individually, and none among us are more worthy of admitting them to your rank than yourself."

"I would gladly do it, Sir Peter; but the honour would come far better from yourself, and would not only be more highly prized by them, but would be of greater value in the eyes of others. I am but a simple knight-commander of the Order, and my name would scarce be known beyond its ranks. But to be knighted by one whose name is known and honoured throughout Europe would give them a standing wherever they went, and place them on a level with the best."

"If that is your opinion, Boswell, I will myself undertake it, and will do it at once; it were better done here than at a conclave of the Order—now, when they are fresh from the battle. Let the knights be summoned from the other galleys at once."

In a few minutes the whole of the knights were assembled on the poop of the galley.

"Friends, and brother knights," D'Aubusson said. "First, in the name of the Order, I have to thank you all most heartily for the brave deeds that you have performed, and for the fresh honour you have won for it. Every man has, as I learn from the three commanders, borne himself as a true and valiant knight, ready to give his life in the cause of the Order and of humanity. Two names have been specially brought before me by commander Ricord, and by the good knight Sir John Boswell; they are those of two young companions who, though knights of our Order, have not yet received secular knighthood, and this, in the opinion of these two knights, they have right worthily won. Sir Ralph Harcourt and Sir Gervaise Tresham, step forward."

The two young knights, colouring with pleasure at this unexpected honour, removed their helmets, and stood with bowed heads before the grand prior. D'Aubusson went on, turning to the knights around him, "I am about, comrades, to undertake the office of knighting them. Sir Louis Ricord and Sir John Boswell stand as their sponsors. But before I proceed I would ask you all whether you, too, approve, and hold that Sir Ralph Harcourt and Sir Gervaise Tresham have proved themselves worthy of the honour of secular knighthood at my hands?"

There was a general reply in the affirmative, the answer of the survivors of Ricord's crew being specially emphatic. The grand prior drew his sword, and the two young knights knelt before him, their sponsors standing beside them.

"Sir Ralph Harcourt, you have now been four years a knight of this Order, but hitherto you have had no opportunity of drawing sword against the infidels. Now that the chance has come, you have proved yourself a true and valiant brother of the Order, and well worthy of the secular accolade. It is in that capacity that I now knight you. It is not the grand prior of Auvergne, but Sir Peter D'Aubusson, of the grand cross of St. Louis, who now bestows upon you the honour of secular knighthood." He touched him lightly with the sword. He then turned to Gervaise.

"You, Sir Gervaise Tresham, are young indeed to receive the honour of secular knighthood; but valour is of no age, and in the opinion of your commanders, and in that of your comrades, you have proved yourself worthy of the honour. You have shown too, that, as Sir John Boswell has related to me, you are not only brave in action, but able, in the moment of danger, to plan and to execute. You were, he tells me, the means of saving his life and that of your comrade, and, by thus enabling him to bear to the

Gervaise and Ralph are knighted by the Grand Prior.

place of rendezvous the news of Sir Louis's danger, were also the means of saving the lives of Sir Louis and his companions, and of bringing home in safety the prizes he had taken. With such a beginning it is easy to foresee that you will win fame yourself some day a distinguished position in the ranks of the Order, and are most worthy of the honour I now bestowed upon you." And he touched him with his sword.

The two young knights rose to their feet, bowed deeply to D'Aubusson, and then retired, with their sponsors. They were at once surrounded by the knights, who shook them by the hand, and warmly congratulated them upon the honour that had befallen them, receiving equally warm congratulations on their arrival at the *auberge* of the *langue*.

The five prizes turned out, when their cargoes were landed to be much more valuable than the cursory examination made by the knights had warranted them in expecting. They contained, indeed, an accumulation of the most valuable contents of the prizes taken by the pirates for a long time previously; and as these desperadoes preyed upon Turkish commerce as well as Christian, the goods consisted largely of Eastern manufactures of all kinds. Costly robes, delicate embroidery, superb carpets, shawls, goldsmiths' work, and no small amount of jewels, were among the spoil collected, and the bulk of the merchandise captured was, two days later, despatched in galleys to Genoa and Marseilles, to be sold for the benefit of the Order.

D'Aubusson without hesitation carried out Sir John Boswell's promise to the slaves who had rowed his boat. They were not only set at liberty, but were each presented with a sum of money, and were placed on board a galley, and landed on the mainland.

The English knights were all proud of the honour that had been won by their young countrymen, the only exception being Robert Rivers, who was devoured with jealousy at their advancement. He did not openly display his feelings, for the reports not only of Sir John Boswell, but of the other two English knights, were so strong that he dared not express his discontent. He himself had twice been engaged with pirates, but had gained no particular credit, and indeed had, in the opinion of his comrades, been somewhat slack in the fray. He was no favourite in the *auberge*, though he spared no pains to ingratiate himself with the senior knights, and had a short time before been very severely reprimanded by the bailiff for striking one of the servants.

"I have more than once had to reprove you for your manners to the servants," the bailiff said. "You will now be punished by the septaine; you will fast for seven days, on Wednesday and Friday you will receive bread and water only, and will be confined to the *auberge* for that period. The next time that I have reason to complain of you, I shall bring the matter before the grand master, and represent to him that it were best to send you home, since you cannot comport yourself to the servants of the *auberge* as befits a knight of the Order. We have always borne the reputation of being specially kind to our servants, and it is intolerable that one, who has been but a short time only a professed knight, should behave with a hauteur and insolence that not even the oldest among us would permit himself. There is not one of the servants here who was not in his own country of a rank and station equal, if not superior, to your own; and though misfortune has fallen upon them, they are to be pitied rather than condemned for it. In future, you are to give no order whatever to the servants, nor to address them, save when at meals you require anything. If you have any complaints to make of their conduct to you, you will make them to me, and I will inquire into the matter; and if I find they have failed in their duty they will be punished. I shall keep my eye upon you in the future. There are other faults that I have observed in you. More than once I have heard you address Sir Gervaise Tresham in a manner which, were not duelling forbidden by our rules, might bring about bloodshed; and from what I have seen when I have been watching the exercises, he is as much your superior in arms as he is in manner and disposition."

This reproof had greatly subdued Robert Rivers; and as he felt that any display of his jealousy of Gervaise would be resented by the other knights, and might result in serious consequences to himself, he abstained from any exhibition of it when they returned to the *auberge*, although he could not bring himself to join in the congratulations offered to them. The next day, however, when he was talking to Ralph Harcourt, he remarked,—

"From what I hear, Harcourt, D'Aubusson praised young Tresham very highly. It seems to me that there was nothing at all out of the way in what he did, and it was very unfair that he should be selected for higher praise than yourself."

"It was not unfair at all," Ralph said warmly, for he was of a generous nature, and incapable of the base feeling of envy. "Tresham did a great deal more than I did. When we saw the pirate boat gaining so fast upon us, it seemed to Sir John Boswell, as well as to myself, that there was scarce a chance of escape, and that all we could do was to choose a spot on which to make a stand, and then to sell our lives as dearly as we could. I could see that Sir John was scanning the hill for a spot where we could best defend ourselves. As to hiding on so small an island, with a hundred men eager for our blood searching for us, it was well-nigh impossible. It was Tresham's suggestion alone that saved our lives and enabled us to fetch succour to Sir Louis. Sir John, who is an old and tried soldier, said that for quickness and merit of conception, the oldest knight in the Order could not have done better; and he is not one to praise unduly. I am four years older than Gervaise Tresham, but I tell you that were he named to-morrow commander of a galley, I would willingly serve under him."

"Well, well, you need not be angry, Harcourt, I have nothing to say against Tresham. No doubt he had a happy thought, which turned out well; but I cannot see that there was anything wonderful in it, and it seemed to me unfair that one who is a mere boy should receive higher praise than yourself, who, as I heard Sir John and Sir Adam Tedbond say last night at the refectory, bore yourself right gallantly."

"I did my best," Ralph said shortly; "but there was small credit in that when we were fighting for our lives. The most cowardly beast will fight under such circumstances. When you see a Moslem rushing at you, scimitar in hand, and know that if you do not cut him down he will cut you down, you naturally strike as hard and as quickly as you can. You have never liked Gervaise, Rivers. I am sure I don't know why, but you always speak in a contemptuous sort of tone about him. True, it does him no harm, but it certainly does you no good. For what reason should you feel a contempt for him? Although so much younger, he is a better swordsman and a better rider than you are. He is liked by every one in the *auberge*, which is more than can be said of yourself; he is always good-tempered, and is quiet and unassuming. What on earth do you always set yourself against him for?"

"I do not know that I do set myself against him," Rivers said sullenly. "I own to having no great liking for him, which is natural enough, seeing that his father was a Lancastrian, while we are Yorkists; but it is not pleasant to see so much made of a boy, merely because D'Aubusson has favoured him."

"I am certain," Harcourt said hotly, "that such an idea has never occurred to any one but yourself. Sir Peter is a great man and will soon be our grand master, but at present he is but grand prior of the *langue* of Auvergne, and whether he favours Tresham or not is a matter that concerns none of us. Gervaise is liked by us for his own good qualities. He bears himself, as a young knight should do, respectfully towards his seniors, and is ever ready to do a service to any one. No one has ever seen him out of temper; he is always kind and considerate to the servants, and when in command of parties of slaves at the public works never says a harsh word to them, but treats them as if they were human beings, and not brute beasts. Besides, though he is more skilful than any of us with his sword, or indeed at any of the military exercises, he is unassuming, and has no particle of pride or arrogance. It is for all these things that he is liked, and the friendship of D'Aubusson has naught whatever to do with it. It is not only D'Aubusson who has prophesied that he will rise to a distinguished rank in the Order. Boswell and Ricord both said the same, and I for one thoroughly believe it. Is there one among us under the age of twenty—and I might go farther—who has already won such credit for himself? One who when but sixteen can make his mark in an Order like ours is certain to rise to high office, and you and I may, before many years are over, be proud to serve under him."

"That I will never do," Rivers said fiercely. "I would rather go and bury myself for life in the smallest commandery in England."

"That may be," Harcourt retorted, his temper also roused, "But possibly you might prefer that to fighting under any other leader."

"That is a reflection on my courage, Sir Ralph Harcourt, I shall lay this matter before the bailiff."

"You can do as you like," Harcourt said disdainfully, "But I don't think you will benefit by your pains."

When his temper cooled down Rivers acknowledged to himself the truth of what Harcourt said. He was not in the favour of the bailiff, while both Harcourt and Tresham stood at the present moment high in his estimation. Any complaint would lead to an inquiry into the matter that had led to the former's words, and even if Harcourt were reprimanded for using them, he himself would assuredly not gain in the estimation of the knights. Harcourt himself thought no more of the matter, though he laughingly told Gervaise that Rivers was by no means gratified at their both attaining the honour of secular knighthood, which virtually placed them over his head.

"He is not a nice fellow," Gervaise said. "But naturally it must be galling to him, and to a good many others who have not yet had the chance of distinguishing themselves.

101

I think it is very good of them that they are all so kind and cordial. Of course it is otherwise with you, who are as old as most of the other professed knights serving here; but with me it is quite different, and as Rivers, somehow, has never been very friendly with me, of course it is doubly galling to him. I hope he will soon get an opportunity of winning his spurs too."

"That is just like you, Tresham. If I were in your place, I should have no good wishes for a fellow who has never lost an opportunity of annoying me, and that without the smallest cause of offence on my part."

"I am sure you would not wish him ill, Harcourt. You would make allowance for him just as I do, and feel that if he had had the same opportunities he would have obtained the same credit and honours."

CHAPTER VII
A FIRST COMMAND

THE first news that the knights heard on their return from their expedition was that the Grand Master Orsini was seriously ill, and that, at his advanced age, the doctors feared there was little hope of his rallying. Gervaise felt a keen regret on hearing that the kind and gentle old man, who had been for three years his master, was at the point of death. Nevertheless, it was generally felt among the knights that, in view of the dangers that threatened Rhodes, it was for the good of the Order that a strong and capable man, whom all respected, and who possessed their entire confidence, should at such a time be invested with absolute power.

D'Aubusson had, indeed, for some years been the real head of the community, but every question had, if only as a matter of form, to be referred to the grand master, in order to obtain his approval and signature. In the state of feebleness to which he had for some months past fallen, much time was frequently lost before he could be made to understand the questions referred to him. Moreover, orders of D'Aubusson could be appealed against, his views thwarted, and his authority questioned; and it was therefore felt that, much as they all respected the old grand master, it would be an advantage to the Order when the supreme authority passed into the hands of D'Aubusson.

Four days after the return of the expedition Orsini died. A few hours later the grand council was convened, and D'Aubusson unanimously elected grand master of the Order. The ceremony of the funeral of his predecessor was an imposing one. Every knight of the Order in Rhodes was present, together with a number of the leading natives of the Island; and although Gervaise had, since his arrival on the Island, seen many stately ceremonies, this far surpassed anything he had previously beheld.

Gervaise had, at one of his first interviews with D'Aubusson after his arrival at the Island, been advised by him to acquire some knowledge of Turkish.

"There are but few knights of the Order who speak the language," he said. "As a rule, while young men are ready to devote any amount of time to acquiring dexterity in all martial exercises, they will bestow no labour in obtaining knowledge that may be fully as useful to them as skill in arms. In our dealings with the Turks, one or other party has to employ an interpreter, and it is often by no means certain that these men convey the full meaning of the speeches they translate. Again, we have large numbers of Turkish slaves, and it is highly to be desired that the knights should be able to give their orders to these men in their own language. Lastly, a knight who has been taken prisoner by the Turks—and even the bravest might meet with such a misfortune—would find it an alleviation of his lot, and might be able to plan and carry out his escape, did he speak Turkish well. I should strongly counsel you to acquire a knowledge of the tongue."

Gervaise had intended to follow the advice of the grand prior, but the duties of his office as page, and the time required for his military exercises and his studies with the chaplain, had rendered it well-nigh impossible, during the first three years, to turn his attention to learning Turkish. As soon as his pageship was at an end, and he found that his duties included supervision of Turkish slaves, he felt the want of a knowledge of the language, and from that time devoted an hour a day to its study, employing one of the servants of the *auberge*, who was a man of rank and education at home, to instruct him.

While he conscientiously spent this amount of time at the work, it was the most disagreeable portion of this day's labour. The events, however, that had taken place during the expedition had impressed him greatly with the utility of a knowledge of Turkish, for had it not been for Sir John Boswell's possessing some acquaintance with the language, it would have been impossible to communicate with the rowers of their boat, or to have arranged the plan by which they had escaped the pirates. He had then and there determined that as soon as he returned to Rhodes he would take the matter up in a very different spirit to that in which he before approached it. He had on the way home spoken to Sir John, who had highly approved of the determination.

"I myself, when I was a young knight of eighteen, was taken captive, twenty-six years ago, at the time when the Egyptian fleet appeared before Rhodes. Our galleys advanced to attack them, but under cover of night they retired, and proceeding to the mainland took shelter under the guns of a Turkish fort. We attacked them there; it was a desperate engagement, but without any decisive advantage on either side. We lost no less than sixty knights, the Egyptians seven hundred men; and their fleet returned to Egypt. I and three others who were left wounded on the deck of one of their ships we had boarded, but failed to capture, were carried to Egypt, and remained there captive for six months, when we were ransomed by the Order.

"During that time I learnt enough of their language, which is akin to Turkish, to be able to make myself understood and to understand what was said to me. I have kept up that much for intercourse with the slaves and servants at Rhodes, and have found it very useful. I consider, then, that you will do well to acquire their tongue; it will be useful not only to yourself, but to others, and when we get back I will, if you like, ask the bailiff to free you from all duty in order that you may devote yourself to it."

The head of the *langue* at once granted Sir John's request.

"I would," he said, "that more of our young knights would give a portion of their time to study; but most of them look to returning home when their term of service here has expired. Many think only of amusement, and all imagine that advancement is best achieved by valour.

Tresham has already distinguished himself very greatly; so much so, that I think it would be well if he did not go on another expedition for a time, but stayed here while others have the opportunity of doing the same. Were we to send him out with the next galleys that start, I should be accused of favouritism, and the lad, who is now deservedly popular with all, would be regarded with envy, and possibly even with dislike.

"At the same time, after what he has done I should have difficulty in refusing, were he to volunteer to sail in the next galley that sets out. The desire, then, on his part to learn Turkish is in all ways opportune. It will, too, in the long run be of great advantage to him in the Order, will give him weight, and bring him into prominence. I do not think there are six in the Order who can fairly translate a Turkish document; there are but two who could write a reply in the same language. Inform him, then, that from the present time he will be excused from all work, except, of course, to join in ceremonials when all are required to be present; and if you, Sir John, will pick out from among the servitors here one who is well instructed and educated, and capable of writing as well as reading his language, I will similarly relieve him of all other work, and place him at the disposal of young Tresham. Tell the lad that I hope he will persevere until he obtains a complete knowledge of the tongue. You can mention to him what I have said as to my opinion of the advantage the knowledge of it will be to him in the Order."

Gervaise accordingly devoted himself to study. His instructor was a Turk of fine presence. He had been a large landowner in Syria, and held a high official position in the province, but had been captured in a galley on his way to Constantinople, whither he was proceeding on an official mission. He was delighted with his new post. Gervaise, both as the youngest member of the community, and from the kind manner in which he always spoke to the servants,— all of whom had acquired some knowledge of English,—was a general favourite among them, and the Turk was glad that he was to be thrown with him. Still more he rejoiced at being appointed his instructor, as it relieved him from all menial work which, although preferable to that to which the bulk of the slaves were condemned, yet galled his spirit infinitely.

Now that he had entered upon the work with the approbation of his superior, and a conviction of its great utility, Gervaise set to work with the same zeal and ardour which he had exhibited in his military exercises. During the heat of the day he sat in the shade reading and writing with his instructor. In the cool of the morning and afternoon he walked with him on the walls, or in the country beyond them. After sunset he sat with him in an unfrequented corner of the roof, all the time conversing with him, either of his own country, or that of his instructor.

At first this was difficult, and he had to eke out the Turkish words he had acquired with English; but it was not long before there was no necessity for this. His intercourse for ten or twelve hours a day with this Turk, and the pains taken by his instructor, caused him to acquire the language with extreme rapidity. Of course, he had to put up with a great deal of banter from the younger knights upon his passion for study. Sometimes they pretended that his mania, as they considered it, arose from the fact that he was determined to become a renegade, and was fitting himself for a high position in the Turkish army. At other times they insisted that his intention was to become a Turkish dervish, or to win a great Turkish heiress and settle in Syria. But as he always bore their banter good-temperedly, and was ready occasionally to join them in the sport when assaults-at-arms were carried on, they soon became tired of making fun of him.

After nine months' constant work, the young knight's studies were abruptly stopped by the receipt of a letter from the Pasha of Syria, offering a considerable sum for the ransom of his instructor. The request was at once acceded to, as it was the policy of the knights to accept ransoms for their prisoners, both because the sums so gained were useful, and because they were themselves compelled sometimes to pay ransom for members of the Order. Suleiman Ali was, it was arranged, to be put on board an Egyptian craft bound for Acre, a safe-conduct having been sent for the vessel and her crew, and for a knight, who was to receive the ransom from the pasha.

"At any rate, Sir Gervaise," the Turk said, when the young knight expressed great regret at his leaving them, "our position as instructor and pupil would have come to an end shortly. For the last three months there has been but little teaching between us; we have talked, and that has been all, save that for a short time each day you read and wrote. But there has been little to teach. You speak the native language now as fluently as I do, and would pass anywhere as a Syrian, especially as there are slight differences of speech in the various provinces. I believe that in Syria you would not be suspected of being anything but a native, and assuredly you would be taken for a Syrian elsewhere. You have learnt enough, and it would be but a waste of time for you, a knight and a soldier, to spend another day in study."

On the following day Gervaise was, to his surprise, sent for by the grand master. Except on the occasion of a few public ceremonies, he had not seen D'Aubusson since he had been elected to his present high dignity, and the summons to attend at the palace therefore came unexpectedly.

"We have become quite strangers, Tresham," the grand master said cordially when he entered. "I have not forgotten you, and have several times questioned your bailiff concerning you. He tells me that you have become quite an anchorite, and that, save at your meals and for an occasional bout-at-arms, you are seldom to be seen. I was glad to hear of your devotion to study, and thought it better to leave you undisturbed at it. Yesterday evening I sent for your instructor. He is a man of influence in Syria, and I wished to learn how he was affected towards us, now that he is about to return there. We talked for some time, and I then asked him what progress you had made, and was surprised and pleased to find that in his opinion you could pass anywhere as a native, and that you were perfectly capable of drawing up and writing any document I might desire to send to the sultan or any of his generals. This is far more than I had expected, and shows how earnestly you must have worked. Your knowledge may prove of much assistance to the Order, and believe me, the time you have spent in acquiring it may prove of much greater advantage to you in your career than if you had occupied it in performing even the most valiant deeds, and that at some future time it will ensure your appointment to a responsible office here. It was partly to assure you of my approbation that I sent for you, partly to inform you that I have appointed you to proceed with Suleiman Ali as the knight in charge of the vessel, and to receive the ransom agreed on, upon your handing him over. The office is an honourable one and one of trust, and it is the first-fruits of the advantages you will gain by your knowledge of Turkish. No, do not thank me. I am selecting you because you are better fitted than any knight I can spare for the mission, and also, I may say, because the choice will be pleasing to Suleiman Ali, whose goodwill I am desirous of gaining. Before now Turkish provinces have thrown off their allegiance to the sultan. They have, I must admit, been usually re-conquered, but such might not be always the case; and if such an event happened in Syria, this man's influence and goodwill might be of great advantage to us, as it might well suit us to ally ourselves with Syria against Constantinople. I am glad to say that I found him at least as well disposed as any man could be who had been some years in slavery. He admitted that, for a slave, he had been kindly and gently treated, and added that any unpleasant memories he might have retained had been obliterated by the nine months of pleasant companionship spent with you."

When Gervaise returned to dinner at the *auberge*, and informed Ralph Harcourt and the other young knights that he had been appointed to take charge of the vessel in which

Suleiman Ali was to be conveyed to Acre, the statement was at first received with incredulity. It seemed incredible that the youngest knight in the *langue* should be chosen for such a mission, involving as it did a separate command. Even the older knights, when the news was passed down the table, were surprised.

"I must say that I am astonished at the grand master's choice. Sir Gervaise Tresham doubtless distinguished himself greatly some months since, but from that time he has not been out with the galleys, or, indeed, done anything that would seem to recommend him for so marked a favour as a separate command."

"I don't know, Wingate," Sir John Boswell said. "It seems to me that when a young knight of seventeen eschews all pleasure, refrains from volunteering for service at sea, and spends his whole time in study, he does distinguish himself, and that very greatly. Of the three or four hundred young knights here I doubt if one other would have so acted. Certainly, none to my knowledge have done so. Yet I do not suppose that D'Aubusson selected him for this duty as a reward for so much self-denial and study, but because by that self-denial and study he is more fitted for it than any of us here, save some three or four knights in the other *langue*s, all of whom are in too high a position to be employed in so unimportant a duty. He can speak Turkish—not a few score of words and sentences such as I can, but, as Suleiman Ali tells me, like a native. Were one of us chosen for this mission, it would be necessary to send an interpreter with him; and every one knows how hard it is to do business in that manner. It seems to me that the grand master has acted wisely in putting aside all question of seniority, and employing the knight who is better suited than any other for it."

"You are right, Boswell," the bailiff said. "I really have been astonished at the manner in which Tresham has given himself up to study. It would have been a natural thing had he, after gaining so much credit, been anxious and eager to gain more. When you spoke to me about his determination to learn Turkish, I thought he would speedily tire of it, and that when the next galley sailed, his name would be among the list of volunteers for the service. I am sure, comrades, that there are few, if any, among us who would not infinitely prefer fighting the Moslems to spending our whole time in learning their language; and I for one consider the fact that he has for nine months laboured so incessantly and assiduously that he has come, as Boswell says, to speak it like a native, is even more to his credit than the deed for which he was knighted."

This conversation took place at the upper end of the table, and was not heard at the lower end where the younger knights were seated.

"I am not chosen from favour," Gervaise said hotly, to one of his companions who had asserted that this was so. "I am simply chosen because I can speak Turkish."

"How much Turkish can you speak?" one of them laughed.

Gervaise turned to the Turkish servant behind them, and said, in his language,—

"Hassan, Sir Giles Trevor wishes to know how well I speak Turkish. You have heard me talking with Suleiman Ali. Will you give him your opinion about it?"

The man turned gravely to Sir Giles Trevor.

"My lord," he said, in English, "Sir Gervaise Tresham, he speaks Turkish same as I do. If he dress up in Turk clothes I suppose him Turk, not know he Christian by his speech."

Exclamations of surprise broke from the young knights.

"Well, you have earned the appointment, Tresham," Ralph Harcourt said heartily. "You always told me when I asked you that you were getting on, but I had not the least idea that you were getting on like this. And can you read and write the Turkish language?"

"Well enough for practical purposes, Ralph. At any rate, I wrote a complimentary letter this morning from the grand master to the governor of Syria, and the bailiff of

Spain, who was, as you know, for ten years a prisoner among the Turks, read it through at D'Aubusson's request, to see that there was no error in it, and was good enough to pass it without alteration."

"I would give a good deal," Sir Giles Trevor said, "if I could follow your example, and shut myself up for nine months with an infidel to study his language; but I could not do it if my life depended on it. I should throw myself off the wall at the end of the first fortnight."

"I don't pretend that I can do what Tresham has done," Ralph Harcourt said. "I always hated our lessons with the chaplain, who gave me the character of having the thickest head of any of his pupils; but I vow"—and he kissed the handle of his dagger—"I will spend half an hour a day in trying to learn something of Turkish. Of course, I know that such time will not be enough to learn a great deal; but if one could get up just enough to be able to give orders to the slaves, to question the captain of a vessel one has captured, and to make them understand a little, if by bad luck one fell into their hands, it would be quite enough for me. I am sure sometimes one is quite at a loss how to pass the hours when the sun is at its hottest, and if one tried one ought to be able to pick up a little without much trouble. Look at the servants; there is not one of them but speaks a little English. And if an infidel can learn enough English to get on with, without any regular study, I can't see why we shouldn't be able to learn enough Turkish in the same way."

Two or three of the other young knights declared that they too would devote a short time during the heat of the day to learning Turkish, and they agreed to begin together forthwith with one of the servants, who spoke English most fluently. Robert Rivers was not present, for he had returned to England six months before, to take up his residence at the House in Clerkenwell, in order that he might bring to bear the interest of his many powerful friends to secure for him an appointment as commander of one of the estates of the Order in England. His departure had caused general satisfaction among the other knights, whom his arrogance and ill-temper had frequently irritated. Gervaise especially was glad at his leaving the Island, for after he received the honour of knighthood, Rivers made a point of always addressing him with an affectation of deference and respect that often tried his temper to the utmost.

"It is well that Rivers has gone," Ralph said, laughing, "for I don't know how he would have supported the chagrin your appointment would have given him. He was devoured with jealousy as it was, but this would have been a trial beyond bearing."

"I am heartily glad he has gone," Gervaise said gravely. "I have put up with a great deal from him, but I don't think I could have stood much more. If our vows had not forbidden our fighting I should have called him to account long ago; but the only thing else to do was for me to lodge a formal complaint before the bailiff, of his continually offensive bearing and manner, which I could not bring myself to do, and indeed there was no special matter that would have seemed to justify me, no single speech that in itself would warrant such grave action on my part. I used to wish over and over again that we could but meet in some quiet spot in England, both unarmed, and could there settle the matter in good English fashion, with our fists, or even with a couple of quarterstaffs."

The others laughed.

"That would be a very unknightly form of contest."

"I care not for that," Gervaise replied. "It would be a very satisfactory one anyhow, and quite serious enough for the occasion. His sneers and petty insults were not sufficient to justify the drawing of blood, and there has been enough of that shed for the last twenty years in England without two brother knights betaking themselves to their swords against each other. But a sound thrashing would have done neither of us harm, and if it had fallen to his lot to get the largest share of it, it might have done him some good."

"He thinks he is sure of an appointment," one of the others said, "but he has been so frequently in trouble here that it is likely that the official report, which is always sent home to the grand prior when the knights return to England, will be so unfavourable that even the most powerful influence will fail to obtain him a post. If so, we may have him back here again, especially if the Turks carry out their threat of assailing us, for an appeal will be made to all the grand priors for knights to aid in the defence."

That evening Gervaise went again to the palace to receive final instructions.

"The craft in which you are to travel is an Egyptian trader. As at present war has not been formally declared between us and the sultan, peaceful traders, as you know, carry on their avocations unmolested either by the war-ships of the Turks or by ours; they do not enter our ports without a special permit, and the crews are never allowed to land, in order that no detailed account of our fortifications may be taken to the sultan. Moreover, brawls might arise between them and the native population, or they might aid slaves to escape. However, you will be altogether safe from interference from Turkish war-vessels, and if overhauled by one of them the safe-conduct will be sufficient to prevent interference with you. But it is not so with pirates. They will plunder their own countrymen as readily as they will Christians, and the safe guard of the governor of Syria will be of no use whatever to you. In this consists the danger of your mission. I cannot send one of our war-galleys on such an errand, and if there are not enough knights on board to beat off any pirate, the fewer there are the better. I hear that the craft is a fast sailer, and as the crew will be as anxious to avoid pirates as you, they will do their best to escape. I leave it to you to take any route. You can either sail hence direct for Acre, or you can coast along the shores of Anatolia and Syria, lying up at night in bays.

"Should you be overtaken I do not think it would be of any use for you to disguise yourself, for some of the crew would be sure to denounce you. Should the worst happen, and you are captured by pirates, you will of course in the first place show them your safe-conduct, and if I find that you do not return I shall send at once to the governor

114

of Syria, complaining of your capture when furnished with his safeguard, and requesting him to order a search for you to be made at every port on the coast, with instructions that you are to be at once released, and either sent to him for return hither, or placed on board a craft bound for any Christian port; while you, on your part, will endeavour to acquaint the Turkish authorities with the fact that you have been seized while travelling with a safe-conduct from the governor of Syria.

"But, more than from any efforts on your part or mine, I rely upon Suleiman Ali, who will, I am sure, as soon as he is set on shore, lose no time in acquainting the pasha of your capture, and in calling upon him to interfere in your favour. In that case, the worst that could befall you would be a temporary detention, unless, indeed, the pirates should take you to Egypt. As that country is friendly with us at present, since Egypt dreads the ever-increasing power of the Turks, it will be but a question of ransom, for I have secret agents there who will inform me without delay of the arrival of a Christian captive."

"I understand, sir, and will do my best in the matter. If I am captured I trust that an opportunity of escape will soon present itself, for I should, if taken, conceal from my captors the fact that I understand their language, and should thus, if I could evade my guard, have every chance of escaping, as in a native dress I could meet and converse with those hunting for me, without their having a suspicion of my being the white slave for whom they were in search."

"Once at Acre you will be safe. But do not land unless it is absolutely necessary, for you might fall a victim to the fanaticism of its inhabitants, and no knight has ever set foot on shore there since the ill-fated day when the Moslems wrested it from us, bathed the ruined walls with the best blood of our Order and the Templars', and destroyed the last hope of our ever recovering the Holy Sepulchre."

The next morning at daybreak Gervaise and Suleiman Ali went on board the Egyptian trader, and sailed for Acre. The current of opinion had changed at the *auberge* when the knights came to think over the mission on which Gervaise was about to start, and the slight feeling of jealousy with which the younger knights had received the news was entirely dissipated. While it did not seem to them that there was any chance of his distinguishing himself, they perceived, as they thought it over, the considerable danger there was of capture by pirates, and Ralph and some of his companions came down to the mole to see him off, with feelings in which envy bore no part whatever.

"I see now, Gervaise, that it is truly no holiday excursion on which you are starting. I should envy you greatly were you going in command of an armed galley, prepared to beat off any craft that might try to overhaul you; but, going alone as you are, it is a very different thing. Should pirates meet you, you could offer no resistance, and your position would be a perilous one indeed. However, I think you are born to good luck, and am confident that your patron saint will look after you, and therefore expect to see you back here in a fortnight's time at the outside."

"I hope so with all my heart, Ralph. It will be no fault of mine if I tarry."

"Will you keep the open sea, or skirt the land, Tresham?" one of the others asked.

"I shall keep the open sea. The grand master left me to choose my course; but I think there is more danger by the coast—where pirates may be hiding in unfrequented bays, in readiness to pounce upon a passing craft—than in the open sea, where we should have at least the advantage that we could not be taken by surprise, and might make a race of it. But the sun will be up in a few minutes, and my orders were to set out at sunrise, so I must say good-bye at once."

As soon as the vessel was under way, Gervaise took a seat on the poop by the side of Suleiman Ali, and related to him the conversation he had had with the grand master.

"The risk that you will run has not escaped me," the Turk said, "and indeed, I now regret that you were chosen as my escort. I almost wish that my son had not purchased my freedom at the present time, since it involves the risk of you losing yours. There is no doubt that the sea swarms with pirates; the sultan is too busy with his own struggles for Empire to bestow any attention upon so small a matter. The pashas and the officers of the ports have not the power, even had they the will, to put down piracy in their districts, and indeed are, as often as not, participators in the spoils. Your Order, which, years back, scoured the seas so hotly that piracy well-nigh ceased, have now for forty years been obliged to turn their attention chiefly to their own defence. They possess a comparatively small fleet of galleys, and their wealth is expended on their fortress.

"What with Egypt and the sultan their hands are too full for them to act as the police of the sea, and the consequence is that from every port, bay, and inlet, pirate craft set out—some mere row-boats, some, like those under the command of Hassan Ali, veritable fleets. Thus the humblest coasters and the largest merchant craft go alike in fear of them, and I would that the sultan and Egypt and your Order would for two or three years put aside their differences, and confine their efforts to sweeping the seas of these pests, to storming their strongholds, and to inflicting such punishment upon them as that, for a very long time to come, peaceful merchants might carry on their trade without fear.

"I heard you tell the captain that he was to steer straight for Acre, and I think you are right in avoiding the coast, where the most harmless-looking fishing boat may carry a crowd of pirates hidden in her hold. At the same time, if you will take my advice you will head much more to the south, so as to be out of the regular track of ships making from Constantinople or the islands to Acre. You may meet pirates anywhere, but they are assuredly thicker along the more frequented routes. The safest plan of all would probably be to bear south, and strike the Egyptian coast well to the east of the mouth of the Nile. Thence, till you get to Palestine, the country is utterly barren and uninhabited, while, running up the coast to Palestine, there are, save at Jaffa, no ports to speak of until you arrive at

Acre; and besides, the inhabitants there, even if pirates, would not venture to disregard the pasha's safe-conduct. I do not by any means say that such a course would be absolutely safe. You may meet with vessels on your way south, and doubtless some of them cruise off the barren coast I speak of, to intercept traders to and from Egypt and Acre, and other Syrian ports; for the trade carried on is considerable, and, although of the same religion, the Turks are disposed to view the Egyptians as enemies rather than as friends, and would have even less hesitation in plundering them than in robbing their own countrymen."

"I think that your suggestion is a good one, and will follow it, at any rate. The course is a good deal longer, but that is comparatively of little moment. The great thing is to carry you safely to Acre."

"And to get back with equal safety," Suleiman said, with a smile.

"That is quite as important in my eyes; in fact, of the two, I would far rather that we were captured on our voyage thither, for in that case I might be able to arrange for the ransom of both of us."

CHAPTER VIII
AN EVENING AT RHODES

SULEIMAN ALI'S advice was carried out. It added considerably to the length of the voyage; but they saw only one doubtful craft. She was lying close inshore under the shadow of the sand-hills, and they did not see her until she hoisted her sails and shot out from the land. They were, however, three miles distant from the land at the time, and the wind was blowing from the north; consequently the pirate was dead to leeward. Every sail was set at once on board the trader, and, being a fast sailer, she maintained her position until nightfall. The wind then dropped, and just as the light faded they could see that the vessel behind them had put out her sweeps. The trader kept up her sails until certain that she could be no longer seen; then the canvas was lowered, and the crew took to the boats and towed her due north.

The night was fortunately a dark one, and those watching anxiously from the deck of the trader were unable to discern her pursuer as she passed behind them. As soon as they were well assured that she must have gone on, the boats were got in, the sails hoisted again, and, taking advantage of every light flaw of wind, they proceeded on their course. In the morning the sails of the galley could be seen on the horizon, but the distance was too great for her to take up the pursuit again with any chance of success, and the trader continued her course to Acre without seeing more of her.

As soon as the trader entered the port, the Egyptian captain went on shore, taking with him a copy of the safe-conduct and the letter from the grand master to the pasha. Going to the residence of the governor, he handed these to him, saying that he had on board Aga Suleiman Ali, and a knight who was charged to deliver him up on payment of the ransom.

"I have been expecting you," the governor said. "I have received a letter from the pasha, stating that he had written to the grand master respecting the ransom of the aga, and sending me the amount which Suleiman's son had offered. The young man was not of age when his father was captured, but he is so now, and was therefore able to raise the sum required. I will go down to the port with you myself, hand over the ransom, and welcome Suleiman, whom I knew well, back from his captivity."

The transfer was speedily made; a heavy purse was handed to Gervaise, and Suleiman was a free man.

"Send me word, if you can, when you return to Rhodes," the latter said, as he bade farewell to the young knight. "I shall be anxious until I hear. Fortune was with us as we sailed hither, but it may desert you on your return. Should aught befall you, tell your captors that if they bring you to me I will pay any ransom that they could, in fairness, require. Should they refuse to do this, send, if possible, a messenger to me, and on receipt of your message I will send a trusty man to purchase your freedom. You have treated me as a friend and an equal, and a friend I shall always remain."

The vessel was to remain four days in port, to discharge her cargo and take in another, and Suleiman had talked of remaining at Acre until she sailed, but Gervaise protested strongly against this.

"You have your family, from whom you have been so long separated, awaiting your return with anxiety, and I pray you to make no stay on my account. I am well content to remain on board here, and to look at the city which has so often been the theatre of great deeds—which Richard the Lion-heart captured, and which so many of the Hospitallers died to defend. I was charged by the grand master not to land, and indeed I feel myself that it would be an act of folly to do so. There are doubtless many on shore who have relatives and friends now working as slaves among us, and some of these might well seek to avenge them by slaying one of the Order. I feel your kindness, but it would be a pain to me to know that you were lingering here on my account, when you must be longing to embrace your children."

The four days passed rapidly. Gervaise had, at the suggestion of the governor, laid aside the mantle and insignia of the Order.

"If you do not do so," he said, "I must place a strong guard of soldiers on board, in order to ensure that the pasha's safeguard is not violated. Sailors are a turbulent race, and were you recognised here they might make a tumult, and slay you before a word of what was going on reached me. In any case I shall place two soldiers on board until you leave the port."

On the morning of the fifth day the sails were got up, and the vessel sailed out from the port. Fortune again favoured them, and they reached Rhodes without any adventure. Gervaise went at once to the palace, and handed over the purse of gold to the treasurer. He then sent up his name to the grand master, and was immediately conducted to his room.

"I am glad to see you back, Tresham. I have been uneasy about you. Have you fulfilled your mission without adventure?"

"Without any adventure, sir, save that we were once chased by a pirate on our way east, but escaped in the darkness. Save for that, the voyage has been wholly uneventful. I have received the ransom, and handed the purse to your treasurer."

"I am glad that your first command has turned out so well. I will see that you do not lack employment; and the fact that you are able to act as interpreter will ensure you a welcome on any galley. At present, however, it is not my intention to send out many cruisers. Every life now is precious, and no amount of spoil that can be brought in will counter-balance the loss of those who fall. However, I may find some mission on which you can be employed. I know that you love an active life; and as, for nine months, you have put a rein on your inclinations, and have devoted yourself wholly to study, so that you might be of greater use to the Order, you have a good right to any employment in which your knowledge can be utilised."

On his arrival at the *auberge*, Gervaise was very heartily greeted by the younger knights.

"I told you you were born lucky, Gervaise," Ralph Harcourt said. "There has been more than one wager made that you would be captured; but I, for my part, was confident that your good fortune would not desert you. Still, though not surprised, we are delighted to see you again. Now tell us about your voyage."

Gervaise gave a brief account of the adventure with the pirate, and then described the visit of the governor to the ship.

"Did he say anything to you?"

"He was courteous and solemn; just the sort of man you would fancy a Turkish governor should be. He looked a little surprised when I accosted him in Turkish, but asked no questions at the time, though I daresay he inquired afterwards of Suleiman how I came to speak the language. The only time he actually said anything was when he requested that I would not wear the mantle of the Order while in port, as sailors were a turbulent race, and it might lead to an attack upon me; and as he was responsible to the pasha that his safe-conduct should be respected, it would be necessary, if I declined to follow his advice, to keep a strong body of soldiers on board. As this would have been a horrible nuisance, especially as I wanted to enjoy in quiet the view of the city, with its castle and walls, I acceded at once to his request, which seemed to me a reasonable one. He did send two soldiers on board, but they remained down in the waist, and did not interfere with my pleasure in any way."

AN EVENING AT RHODES

"Next to Jerusalem, how I should like to see Acre!" Ralph Harcourt exclaimed. "It is, of all other cities, the most closely connected with our Order. We helped to win it, and we were the last to defend it. We have heard so much about the fortress, and it has been so often described to me, that I know the situation of every bastion—at least, as it was when we left it, though I know not what changes the Turks may since have made."

"That I know not, Ralph. Of course, I only saw the seafront, and it was upon the land side that the attack was made. We know that the breaches were all repaired long ago, and it is said that the place is stronger than ever. From the port all was solid and massive. It is indeed a grand and stately fortress. Here we have done all that was possible to make Rhodes impregnable, but nature did nothing for us; there nature has done everything, and the castle looks as if it could defy the assaults of an army, however large. And indeed, it was not wrested from us by force. The knights, when the city walls were stormed and the town filled with their foes fought their way down to the water's edge and embarked there, for they were reduced to a mere handful; and however strong a castle may be, it needs hands to defend it. Still, it well-nigh moved me to tears to see the Turkish banner waving over it, and to think how many tens of thousands of Christian soldiers had died in the effort to retain the holy places, and had died in vain."

"I wonder whether the Turks will ever be forced to relinquish their hold of the holy places?"

"Who can tell, Sir Giles?" the bailiff, who had come up to the group unobserved, said quietly. "Certainly not in our time—not until the Moslem power, which threatens not only us, but all Europe, has crumbled to dust. So long as Acre remains in their power there is no hope. I say not but that by a mighty effort of all Christendom, Palestine might be wrested from the infidels, as it was wrested before; but the past shows us that while men or nations can be stirred to enthusiasm for a time, the fire does not last long, and once again the faithful few would be overwhelmed by the odds that would be brought against them, while Europe looked on impassive, if not indifferent. No, knights; the utmost that can be hoped for, is that the tide of Moslem invasion westward may be stayed. At present we are the bulwark, and as long as the standard of our Order waves over Rhodes so long is Europe safe by sea. But I foresee that this cannot last: the strongest defences, the stoutest hearts, and the bravest of hearts, cannot in the long run prevail against overpowering numbers. As at Acre, we may repel assault after assault, we may cause army after army to betake themselves again to their ships; but, as a rock is overwhelmed by the rising tide, so must Rhodes succumb at last, if left by Europe to bear alone the brunt of Moslem invasion. All that men can do we shall do. As long as it is possible to resist, we shall resist. When further resistance becomes impossible, we shall, I trust, act as we did before.

"We were driven from Palestine, only to fortify ourselves at Rhodes. If we are driven from Rhodes, we shall, I feel assured, find a home elsewhere, and again commence our labours. The nearer we are to Europe the more hope there is that Christendom will aid us, for they will more generally understand that our defeat would mean the laying open of the shores of the Mediterranean, from Turkey to Gibraltar, to the invasion of the Moslems. However, comrades, this is all in the future. Our share is but in the present, and I trust the flag of the Order will float over Rhodes as long, at least, as the lifetime of the youngest of us, and that we may bequeath the duty of upholding the Cross untarnished to those who come after us; and we can then leave the issue in God's hands."

All listened respectfully to the words of their leader, although his opinion fell like cold water upon the fiery zeal and high hopes of his hearers. The possibility of their losing Rhodes had never once entered into the minds of the majority of them. It was likely that ere long they might be called upon to stand a siege, but, acquainted as they were with the strength of the place—its deep and seemingly impassable moat, its massive walls, and protecting towers and bastions—it had seemed to them that Rhodes was capable of withstanding all assaults, however numerous the foe, however oft-repeated the invasion. The bailiff was, as all knew, a man of dauntless courage, of wide experience and great judgment, and that he should believe that Rhodes would, although not in their time, inevitably fall, brought home to them for the first time the fact that their fortress was but an outpost of Europe, and one placed so distant from it that Christendom, in the hour of peril, might be unable to furnish them with aid.

As the bailiff walked away, there was silence for a short time, and then Sir Giles Trevor said cheerfully,—

"Well, if it lasts our time we need not trouble our heads as to what will take place afterwards. As the bailiff says, our duty is with the present, and as we all mean to drive the Turks back when they come, I do not see that there is any occasion for us to take it to heart, even if it be fated that the Moslems shall one day walk over our tombs. If Christendom chooses to be supine, let Christendom suffer, say I. At any rate, I am not going to weep for what may take place after I am turned into dust."

"That sounds all very well, Sir Giles," Ralph Harcourt said, "and I have no argument to advance against it, though I am sure there is much to be said; but if the bailiff, or the chaplain, or indeed any of the elders, had heard you say so, I have no doubt you would have had a fitting reply."

Sir Giles tossed his head mockingly. "I shall fight neither better nor worse, friend Harcourt, because it may be that someday the Moslems are, as the bailiff seems to think, destined to lord it here. I have only promised and vowed to do my best against the Moslems, and that vow only holds good as long as I am in the flesh; beyond that I have no concern. But what are we staying here for, wasting our time? It is the hour for those of us who are going, to be starting for the ball given by Signor Succhi; as he is one of the richest merchants in the town, it will be a gay one, and there is no lack of fair faces in Rhodes. It is a grievous pity that our elders all set their will against even the younger members of the community joining in a dance. It was not one of the things I swore to give up. However, here in Rhodes there is no flying in the face of rules."

Three or four of the other young knights were also going.

"What are you thinking of doing, Gervaise?" Harcourt asked.

"I have nothing particular to do, Ralph, except that, first of all, I must write a letter to Suleiman Ali and hand it to the bailiff, praying him to send it off by the first vessel that may put in here on her way to Acre. If I do not do it now it may be neglected, and I promised to write directly I got here. I will not be half an hour, and after that I shall be ready to do anything you like."

In less than that time, indeed, he rejoined Ralph. "Now what shall we do with ourselves? What do you say to a stroll through the streets? I am never tired of that."

"I like better to go by way of the roofs, Gervaise. The streets are badly lit, and although they are busy enough in some quarters, they are so narrow that one gets jostled and pushed. On the terraces everything is quiet. You have plenty of light and music, and it is pleasant to see families sitting together and enjoying themselves; and if one is disposed for a cup of wine or of cool sherbet, they are delighted to give it, for they all are pleased when one of us joins a group. I have quite a number of acquaintances I have made in this way while you have been working away at your Turkish."

"Very well," Gervaise said. "If such is your fancy, Ralph, let us take one of the paths across the roofs. I might walk there twenty years by myself without making an acquaintance, and I do not pledge myself to join in these intimacies of yours. However, I shall be quite content to amuse myself by looking on at the scene in general, while you are paying your visits and drinking your sherbet."

"There are plenty of fair girls among the Rhodians," Ralph said, with a smile; "and though we are pledged to celibacy we are in no way bound to abstain from admiration."

Gervaise laughed.

"Admire as much as you like, Ralph, but do not expect me to do so. I have scarcely as much as spoken to a woman since I entered the House in London, and I should have no idea what to say to a young girl."

"But it is part of the education of a true knight to be courteous to women. It is one of the great duties of chivalry. And you must remember that we are secular knights, as well knights of the Order."

"The work of the Order is quite sufficient for me at present, Ralph. In time I may come to like the society of women, to admire their beauty, and possibly even to wear the colour of some one, for that seems to be the fashion; though why we, who are bound to celibacy, should admire one woman more than another I cannot understand."

They had by this time descended from the castle, and were taking their way along one of the broad paths that led over the flat roofs of the houses by means of the bridges thrown across the streets.

"These are some acquaintances of mine," Ralph said, stopping at one of the walls, some three feet high, that bordered the path.

Beyond was an enclosure of some fifty feet square. Clumps of shrubs and flowers, surrounded by stonework some eight or ten inches high enclosing the earth in which they grew, were scattered here and there. Lamps were hung to cords stretched above it, while others were arranged among the flowers. In the centre a large carpet was spread, and on this some eight or ten persons were seated on cushions. A girl was playing a lute, and another singing to her accompaniment. She stopped abruptly when her eye fell upon the figures of the two young knights.

"There is Sir Ralph Harcourt, father!" she exclaimed in Italian, which was the language most used on the Island, and spoken with more or less fluency by all the knights, among whom it served as a general medium of

A girl was playing a lute, and another singing to her accompaniment.

communication. "Are you waiting to be invited in, Sir Knight?" she went on saucily. "I thought that by this time you would know you were welcome."

"Your tongue runs too fast, child," her father said, as he rose and walked across to Ralph. "You are welcome, Sir Ralph, very welcome. I pray you enter and join us."

"I will do so with pleasure, Signor Vrados, if you will also extend your hospitality to my friend Sir Gervaise Tresham."

"Most gladly," the merchant said. "I pray him to enter."

The two knights passed through the gate in the wall. All rose to their feet as they went up to the carpet, and greeted Ralph with a warmth which showed that he was a favourite. He introduced Gervaise to them.

"I wonder that I do not know your face, Sir Knight," the merchant's wife said. "I thought I knew all the knights of the Order by sight, from seeing them either at the public ceremonies, or observing them pass in the streets."

"For the last nine months Sir Gervaise has been an anchorite. He has been learning Turkish, and has so devoted himself to the study that even I have scarce caught sight of him, save at meals. As for walking in the streets, it is the last thing he would think of doing. I consider myself a good and conscientious young knight, but I am as nothing in that respect to my friend. I used to look upon him as my little brother, for we were at the House of the Order in London together. He is four years younger than I am, and you know four years between boys makes an immense difference. Now the tables are turned, and I quite look up to him."

"You will believe as much as you like, Signora, of what Sir Ralph says," Gervaise laughed. "As you have, he says, known him for some time, you must by this time have learnt that his word is not to be taken literally."

"We learned that quite early in our acquaintance," the girl who had first noticed them said, with an affectation of gravity. "I always tell him that I cannot believe anything he says, and I am grateful to you, Sir Knight, for having thus borne evidence to the quickness of my perception."

By this time the servants had brought some more cushions, and on these Ralph and Gervaise seated themselves. Wine, sherbet, and cakes, were then handed round. The master of the house placed Gervaise on his right hand, as a stranger.

"You have been among our islands, Sir Gervaise? But indeed, I need not ask that, since I know that you and Sir Ralph were knighted together for your valour in that affair with the ships of Hassan Ali. We come from Lesbos. It is now eighty years since my family settled in Rhodes, and we have seen it grow from a small place to a great fortress."

"'Tis a wonderful place," Gervaise said. "I know nothing of the fortresses of Europe, but it seems to me that no other can well be stronger than this—that is, among places with no natural advantages."

"The knights have always had an abundance of slaves," the merchant said; "so many that they have not only had sufficient for their work here, but have been able to sell numbers to European potentates. Yes, Rhodes is wonderfully strong. That great fosse would seem as if it could defy the efforts of an army to cross; and yet the past has shown that even the strongest defences, held with the greatest bravery, can be carried by generals with immense armies, and careless how they sacrifice them so that they do but succeed. Look at Acre, for example."

"I was looking at it five days ago," Gervaise said, "and thinking that it was beyond the might of man to take."

"Do you mean that you were at Acre?" the merchant asked, with surprise.

"Yes. I went there to hand over a captive who had been ransomed. Of course I had a safe-conduct, and I was glad indeed of the opportunity of seeing so famous a fortress."

AN EVENING AT RHODES

"You were fortunate indeed, Sir Knight, and it was, if you will pardon my saying so, singular that so young a knight should have been chosen. Assuredly, even the senior knights of the Order would rejoice at the opportunity of beholding a fortress so intimately connected with the past history of the Order."

"It was due entirely to my being able to speak Turkish," Gervaise said. "As my friend Sir Ralph was mentioning, I have been studying hard, and can now speak the language fluently; and as this was a necessity on such a mission, and the few knights who can so speak it are all in high office, and could hardly be asked to undertake so unimportant a service, I was selected."

"And you really speak Turkish well? It is an accomplishment that few, save Greeks subject to Turkey, possess. Do you intend, may I ask, to make Rhodes your home? I ask because I suppose you would not have taken this labour had you intended shortly to return to England."

"Yes; I hope to remain here permanently. I know that the first step towards promotion here is generally a commandery at home, but I did not enter the Order with any idea of gaining office or dignity. I desire simply to be a knight of the Cross, and to spend my life in doing faithful service to the Order."

"A worthy ambition indeed, and one that, so far as my experience goes, very few knights entertain. I see yearly scores of young knights depart, no small proportion of whom never place foot on Rhodes again, although doubtless many of them will hasten back again as soon as the danger of an assault from the Turks becomes imminent. You see, we who dwell here under the protection of the Order naturally talk over these things among ourselves; and although, in the matter of fortifications, all will admit that enormous efforts have been made to render the town secure, it is clear that in the matter of knights to defend them there is very much left to be desired. It is all very well to say that the knights from all parts of Europe would flock hither to defend it; but the journey would be a long one, and would occupy much time, and they would probably not receive news that the Turks had sailed until the place was already invested. Then it would be difficult, if not altogether impossible, for ships with reinforcements to make their way through the Turkish fleet, and to enter the port. To man the walls properly would need a force five times as numerous as that which is now here. I recognise the valour of your knights; they have accomplished wonders. But even they cannot accomplish impossibilities. For a time they could hold the walls; but as their number became reduced by the fire of the Turkish cannon and the battles at the breaches, they would at last be too weak any longer to repel the onslaughts of foes with an almost unlimited supply of soldiers."

"That is true enough," Gervaise admitted; "and to my mind it is shocking that four-fifths at least of the Order, pledged to oppose the infidels, should be occupied with the inglorious work of looking after the manors and estates of the society throughout Europe, while one-fifth, at most, are here performing the duties to which all are sworn. Of the revenues of the estates themselves, a mere fraction finds its way hither. Still, I trust that the greater part of the knights will hasten here as soon as danger becomes imminent, without waiting for the news that the Turkish armament has actually set forth."

For an hour the two young knights remained on the roof, Gervaise talking quietly with the merchant, while his companion laughed and chatted with the ladies and friends of their host. After they had left, with the promise that it would not be long before they repeated their visit, Ralph bantered Gervaise on preferring the society of the merchant to that of his daughters.

"I found him a pleasant and very well-informed man, Ralph, and enjoyed my talk with him just as you enjoyed talking nonsense to his daughters and listening to their songs. Who was the man sitting next to the eldest daughter?"

AN EVENING AT RHODES

"He doesn't belong to Rhodes, but is a Greek from one of the islands, though I did not catch from which. I don't know whether he is a relative of the family, or a business connection of the merchant's, or a stranger who has brought a letter of introduction to him. Nothing was said on that head; why do you ask?"

"I don't like the man's face; he is a handsome fellow, but has a crafty expression. He did not say much, but it seemed to me that at times, when he appeared to be sitting carelessly sipping his sherbet, he was really trying to listen to what Vrados was saying to me. He could not do so, for we were on the other side of the circle, and were speaking in somewhat low tones, while the rest of you were chatting and laughing."

"What should he want to listen for, most sapient knight?"

"That I can't tell, Ralph; but I am certain that he was trying to listen."

"Well, as you were no doubt both talking more sensibly than most of us," Ralph laughed, "he certainly showed his discernment."

"I daresay I am wrong," Gervaise said quietly; "but you know we have our spies at Constantinople, and probably the sultan has his spies here; and the idea occurred to me that perhaps this man might be one of them."

"Well, I am bound to say, Gervaise," Ralph said, a little irritably, "I have never heard so grave an accusation brought on such insufficient evidence—or rather, as far as I can see, without a shadow of evidence of any kind. We drop in upon a man who is one of our most respected merchants, whose family has been established here many years, whose interests must be the same as those of the Order; and because a guest of his does not care to take any active part in my joking with the girls, and because you imagine that there is a cunning expression on his face, you must straightway take it into your head that he must be a spy."

A KNIGHT OF THE WHITE CROSS

"Excuse me, Ralph, I simply said that the idea occurred to me that he might be a spy, which is a very different thing to my accusing him of being one. I am ready to admit that the chances are infinitely greater that he is an honest trader or a relation of the merchant, and that his presence here is perfectly legitimate and natural, than that he should be a spy. Still, there is a chance, if it be but one out of a thousand, that he may be the latter. I don't think that I am at all of a suspicious nature, but I really should like to learn a little about this man. I do not mean that I am going to try to do so. It would be an unworthy action to pry into another's business, when it is no concern of one's own. Still, I should like to know why he is here."

Ralph shrugged his shoulders.

"This comes of living the life of a hermit, Gervaise. Other people meet and talk, and enjoy what society there is in the city, without troubling their heads for a moment as to where people come from or what their business is here, still less whether they are spies. Such ideas do not so much as occur to them, and I must say that I think the sooner you fall into the ways of other people the better."

"There is no harm done," Gervaise said composedly. "I am not thinking of asking our bailiff to order him to be arrested on suspicion. I only remarked that I did not like the man's face, nor the way in which, while he pretended to be thinking of nothing, he was trying to overhear what we were saying. I am quite willing to admit that I have made a mistake, not in devoting myself to Turkish, but in going to the merchant's with you this evening. I have had no experience whatever of what you call society, and, so far from it giving me pleasure to talk to strangers, especially to women, it seems to me that such talk is annoying to me, at any rate at present. When I get to your age, possibly my ideas may change. I don't for a moment wish to judge you or others; you apparently enjoy it, and it is a distraction from our serious work. I say simply that it is an amusement which I do not understand. You must remember that I entered the Order in consequence of a solemn vow of my dead father, that I regard the profession we make as a very serious one, and that my present intention is to devote my life entirely to the Order and to an active fulfilment of its vows."

"That is all right, Gervaise," Ralph said good-temperedly. "Only I think it would be a pity if you were to turn out a fanatic. Jerusalem and Palestine are lost, and you admit that there is really very little chance of our ever regaining them. Our duties, therefore, are changed, and we are now an army of knights, pledged to war against the infidels, in the same way as knights and nobles at home are ever ready to engage in a war with France. The vow of poverty is long since obsolete. Many of our chief officials are men of great wealth, and indeed, a grand master, or the bailiff of a *langue*, is expected to spend, and does spend, a sum vastly exceeding his allowance from the Order. The great body of knights are equally lax as to some of their other vows, and carry this to a length that, as you know, has caused grave scandal. But I see not that it is in any way incumbent on us to give up all the pleasures of life. We are a military Order, and are all ready to fight in defence of Rhodes, as in bygone days we were ready to fight in defence of the Holy Sepulchre. Kings and great nobles have endowed us with a large number of estates, in order to maintain us as an army against Islam; and as such we do our duty. But to affect asceticism is out of date and ridiculous."

"I have certainly no wish to be an ascetic, Ralph. I should have no objection to hold estates, if I had them to hold. But I think that at present, with the great danger hanging over us, it would be better if, in the first place, we were all to spend less time in idleness or amusement, and to devote all our energies to the cause. I mean not only by fighting when the time comes for fighting, but by endeavouring in every way to ward off danger."

"When I see danger, I will do my best to ward it off, Gervaise; but I cannot go about with my nose in the air, snuffing danger like a hunting dog in pursuit of game. At any rate, I will not bother you to accompany me on my visits in future."

CHAPTER IX
WITH THE GALLEY-SLAVES

ERVAISE, on consideration, was obliged to own to himself that Ralph was right in saying that he had no ground whatever for suspicion against the Greek he had met at Signor Vrados's; and he could see no means of following the matter up. It would not, he felt, be honourable to go again to the merchant's house, and to avail himself of his hospitality, while watching his guest. He determined to dismiss the matter from his mind, and had, indeed, altogether done so when, a week later, it suddenly recurred to his memory.

A party of slaves, under the escort of overseers and in charge of a knight who had been with them at their work on the fortifications, were passing along the street on their way back to barracks. It was already dusk, and as Gervaise was going the same way as they were, he stood aside in a doorway to let them pass. He was on the point of stepping out to follow them, when he saw a man, who had been standing in the shadow of the wall, fall in with their ranks, and, as he walked engaged in an earnest conversation with one of the slaves. He kept beside him for a hundred yards or so, then passed something into the slave's hand, and turned abruptly down a side opening. There were but few people about, and in the growing darkness the action of the man passed unobserved by the overseers. Gervaise, thinking the occurrence a strange one, turned down the same lane as the man.

He slackened his pace until the latter was fifty yards ahead, so that he would not, had he looked round, have been able to perceive that it was a knight who was behind him. After passing through several streets, the man turned into a refreshment house. The door stood open, and as the place was brightly lit up, Gervaise, pausing outside, was able to see what was going on inside. The man he had followed was on the point of seating himself at one of the tables, and as he did so Gervaise recognised him as the Greek he had met at the merchant's house. He at once walked on a short distance, and then paused to think.

The vague suspicions he had before entertained as to the man now recurred with double force; he was certainly in communication with one or more of the slaves, and such communication, so secretly effected, could be for no good purpose. So far, however, there was nothing he could tax the man with. He would probably deny altogether that he had spoken to any of the slaves, and Gervaise could not point out the one he had conversed with. At any rate, nothing could be done now, and he required time to think what steps he could take to follow up the matter. He resolved, however, to wait and follow the Greek when he came out. After a few minutes he again re-passed the door, and saw that the man was engaged in earnest conversation with another. After considering for a time, Gervaise thought that it would be best for him to follow this other man when he left, and ascertain who he was, rather than to keep a watch on the movements of the Greek, who, as likely as not, would now return to the merchant's.

He walked several times up and down the street, until at last he saw the two men issue out together. They stopped for a moment outside, and then, after exchanging a few words, separated, the Greek going in the direction of the quarter in which lay the house of Vrados, while the other walked towards Gervaise. The latter passed him carelessly, but when the man had gone nearly to the end of the street, he turned and followed him. He could see at once that he was a lay brother of the Order. This class consisted of men of an inferior social position to the knights; they filled many of the minor offices, but were not eligible for promotion. Following for ten minutes, Gervaise saw him approach one of the barracks, or prisons, occupied by the slaves. He knocked at the door, and, upon its being opened, at once entered.

The matter had now assumed a much more serious aspect. This young Greek, a stranger to Rhodes, was in communication not only with some of the slaves, but with a prison official, and the matter appeared so grave to Gervaise that, after some deliberation, he thought it was too important for him to endeavour to follow out alone, and that it was necessary to lay it before the bailiff. Accordingly, after the evening meal he went up to Sir John Kendall, and asked if he could confer with him alone on a matter over which he was somewhat troubled. The bailiff assented at once, and Gervaise followed him to his private apartment.

"Now, what is this matter, Sir Gervaise?" he asked pleasantly.

"Nothing serious, I trust?"

"I don't know, Sir John. That is a matter for your consideration; but it seems to me of such importance that it ought to be brought to your knowledge."

The face of the bailiff grew more grave, and, seating himself in a chair, he motioned to Gervaise to do the same.

"Now, let me hear what it is," he said.

Gervaise told his story simply. A slight smile passed across the bailiff's face as he mentioned that he had met the Greek on the roof of the house of Signor Vrados, and had not liked the expression of his face.

"Vrados has some fair daughters, has he not?" he asked.

"Yes, sir; but I know little of them. That is the only visit that I ever paid there, or, indeed, to the house of any one in the town."

Sir John's face grew grave again as Gervaise recounted how he had seen the man enter into communication with a slave; and he frowned heavily when he heard of his meeting afterwards with one of the prison officers.

"In truth, Sir Gervaise," he said, after a pause, "this seems to be a right serious matter, and you have done wisely in informing me of what you have seen. Assuredly there is mischief of some sort in the wind. The question is how to get to the bottom of it. Of course, the grand master might order the arrest of this Greek and of the prison officer, but you may be sure that neither would commit himself unless torture were applied; and I, for one, have no belief in what any man says under such circumstances. The most honest man may own himself a traitor when racked with torture, and may denounce innocent men. It is at best a clumsy device. What think you of the matter?"

"I have hardly thought it over yet, Sir John; and certainly no plan has yet occurred to me."

"Well, think it over, Sir Gervaise. It is not likely that a few days will make any difference. But I will take measures to see that this Greek does not sail away from the Island at present, and will speak to the port-master about it. I will myself give the matter consideration, but as you have shown yourself so quick-witted in following up the matter so far, I rely upon you more than myself to carry it farther. There may possibly be some simple explanation of the matter. He may come from an island where the Turks are masters, and has, perhaps, brought a message from some relatives of a slave; as to the talk with the prison officer, it may be wholly innocent. If we should find that it is so we will keep this matter to ourselves, if possible, or we shall get finely laughed at by our comrades for having run upon a false scent. If, on the other hand, the matter should turn out to be serious, you will assuredly get great credit for having discovered it. Therefore, turn it over in your mind to-night, and see if you can arrive at some scheme for seeing further into it before we take any steps."

In the morning Gervaise again called upon Sir John Kendall.

WITH THE GALLEY-SLAVES

"Well, Sir Gervaise, I hope that you have hit upon some scheme for getting to the bottom of this matter. I confess that I myself, though I have had a sleepless night over it, have not been able to see any method of getting to the root of the affair, save by the application of torture."

"I do not know whether the plan I have thought of will commend itself to your opinion, sir, but I have worked out a scheme which will, I think, enable us to get to the bottom of the matter. I believe that a galley is expected back from a cruise to-day or to-morrow. Now, sir, my idea is that I should go on board a small craft, under the command of a knight upon whose discretion and silence you can rely, such as, for example, Sir John Boswell, and that we should intercept the galley. Before we board her I should disguise myself as a Turkish slave, and as such Sir John should hand me over to the officer in command of the galley, giving him a letter of private instructions from you as to my disposal. If they have other slaves on board I would ask that I should be kept apart from them, as well as from the rowers of the galley. On being landed I should be sent to the prison where I saw the officer enter last night, and the slaves and rowers should be distributed among the other prisons. Thus, then, the slaves I should be placed with would only know that I had arrived in the galley with other slaves captured by it. I have no doubt I should be able to maintain my assumed character, and should in a short time be taken into the confidence of the others, and should learn what is going on. It would be well, of course, that none of the officials of the prison should be informed as to my true character, for others, besides the one I saw, may have been bribed to participate in whatever plot is going on."

"And do you mean to say, Sir Gervaise, that you, a knight of the Order, are willing to submit to the indignity of being treated as a slave? To keep up the disguise long enough to be taken into the confidence of the plotters, you might have to stay there for some time; and if the prison officials believe you to be but an ordinary slave, you will be put to work either on the walls or in one of the galleys."

"I am ready to do anything for the benefit of the Order, and the safety of Rhodes, that will meet with your approval," Gervaise replied. "It will no doubt be unpleasant, but we did not enter the Order to do pleasant things, but to perform certain duties, and those duties necessarily involve a certain amount of sacrifice."

"Do you think you would be able to maintain the character? Because you must remember that if detected you might be torn in pieces by the slaves, before the officers could interfere to protect you."

"I feel sure that I can do so, Sir John."

"What story would you tell them?"

"I would say that I had come from Syria, and sailed from Acre in a trader, which is perfectly true, and also that I was taken off the ship I was on by a galley—which would not be altogether false, as I crossed one as I landed. I think there would be very little questioning, for I should pretend to be in a state of sullen despair, and give such short answers to questions that I should soon be left alone."

"The scheme is a good one, Sir Gervaise, though full of danger and difficulty. If you are ready to render this great service to the Order, I willingly accept the sacrifice you offer to make. I will send one of my slaves down into the town to buy garments suitable for you, and also stains for your skin. It will, of course, be necessary for you to shave a portion of your head in Turkish fashion. I will also see Sir John Boswell, and ask him to arrange for a craft to be ready to start at noon. The galley is not expected in until evening, but of course she may arrive at any moment now. Come here again in an hour's time, and I will have the clothes ready for you."

"May I suggest, sir, that they should be those appropriate to a small merchant? This might seem to account for my not being placed with the other slaves who may be on board the galley, as it would be supposed that I was set apart in order that I should be sent to one of the *auberges* as a servant; and my afterwards being herded with the others would be explained by its being found that there was no opening for me in such a capacity. I should think there would be no difficulty in obtaining such a suit, as garments of all kinds are brought here in prizes, and are bought up by some of the Greek merchants, who afterwards find opportunities of despatching them by craft trading among the islands."

Just before noon Gervaise walked down to the port with Sir John Boswell, a servant following with a bundle.

"It seems to me a hair-brained scheme, lad," Sir John, who had just joined him, said, as they issued from the *auberge*; "though I own, from what the bailiff tells me, that there must be some treacherous plot on hand, and when that is the case it is necessary that it should be probed to the bottom. But for a knight to go in the disguise of an infidel slave seems to me to be beyond all bounds."

"If one is ready to give one's life for the Order, Sir John, surely one need not mind a few weeks' inconvenience. I shall, at any rate, be no worse off than you were when serving as a Turkish slave."

"Well, no, I don't know that you will," Sir John replied doubtfully. "But that was from necessity, and not from choice; and it is, moreover, an accident we are all exposed to."

"It is surely better to do a thing of one's own free will than because one is forced to do it, Sir John?"

The knight was silent. He was a stout fighting man, but unused to argument.

"Well," he said, after a long pause, "I can only hope that it will turn out all right, and promise that if you are strangled in prison, I will see that every slave who had a hand in it shall be strung up. I have told Kendall frankly that if I were in his place I would not permit you to try such a venture. However, as I could think of no other plan by which there would be a chance of getting to the bottom of this matter, my words had no effect with him. I should not have so much cared if the officers of the gaol knew who you were; but I can see that if there is treachery at work this would defeat your object altogether. What do you suppose this rascal Greek can be intending?"

"That I cannot say, Sir John. He may be trying to get an exact plan of the fortifications, or he may be arranging some plan of communication by which, in case of siege, news of our condition and of the state of our defences may be conveyed to the Turkish commander."

By this time they had reached the port, and embarked at once on a trading vessel belonging to one of the merchants, from whom Sir John had readily obtained her use for a day or two. Her sails were hoisted at once, and she rowed out from the port. Having proceeded some three or four miles, they lowered her sails, and lay to in the course a galley making for the port would take. A sailor was sent up to the masthead to keep a look-out. Late in the afternoon he called down that he could make out a black speck some twelve miles away. She carried no sails, and he judged her to be a galley.

"It will be dark before she comes along," Sir John Boswell said. "You can hoist your sails, captain, and return to within half a mile of the port, or she may pass us beyond hailing distance."

Gervaise at once retired to the cabin that had been set aside for their use, and proceeded to disguise himself. An hour later Sir John came down. He looked at Gervaise critically.

"You are all right as far as appearances go. I should take you anywhere for a young Turk. Your clothes are not too new, and are in accordance with the tale you are going to tell, which is that you are the son of a Syrian trader. If, as Suleiman says, you speak Turkish well enough to pose as a native, I think you ought to be able to pass muster. How long will that dye last? Because if it begins to fade they will soon suspect you."

"It will last a fortnight; at least, so Sir John Kendall says. But he has arranged that if at the end of ten days I have not succeeded in finding out anything, he will send down to the prison, and under the pretence that he wants to ask me some questions about what ransom my father would be likely to pay for me, he will have me up to the *auberge*, and there I can dye myself afresh."

"How are you to communicate with him in case of need?"

"His servant Ahmet, who got the things for me, is to come down every morning, and to be near the door of the prison at the hour when the slaves are taken out to work. If I have aught to communicate I am to nod twice, and Sir John Kendall will send down that evening to fetch me, instead of waiting until it is time for me to renew my dye."

"What is going to be said to Harcourt and the others to account for your absence?"

"The bailiff will merely say that he has suddenly sent me away by ship, on a private mission. They may wonder, perhaps, but none of them will venture to ask him its nature."

"Well, I must say that you seem to have made all your arrangements carefully, Tresham, and I hope it will turn out well. I was against the scheme at first, but I own that I do not see now why it should not succeed; and if there is any plot really on hand, you may be able to get to the bottom of it."

It was an hour after darkness had completely fallen when the regular beat of oars was heard. The ship's boat was already in the water, and Gervaise, wrapped up in his mantle, followed Sir John out of his cabin and descended with him into the boat, which was at once rowed towards the approaching galley. Sir John hailed it as it came along.

"Who is it calls?" a voice said.

"It is I—Sir John Boswell. Pray take me on board, Sir Almeric. It is a somewhat special matter."

The order was given, the galley-slaves ceased rowing, and the boat ran alongside. Gervaise unclasped his mantle and gave it to Sir John, and then followed him on board.

"I congratulate you on your return, and on your good fortune in having, as your letter stated, made a prosperous voyage," Sir John said, as he shook hands with the commander of the galley.

"I would speak a word with you aside," he added in a low voice.

Sir Almeric moved with him a few paces from the other knights.

"I am sent here by our bailiff, Sir Almeric. I have a Turkish prisoner here with me who is to be landed with those you have taken. There are special reasons for this, which I need not now enter into. Will you let him sit down here by the helm? My instructions are that he is not to mingle with the other slaves; and as there are reasons why it is wished that his coming on board in this manner shall not be known to them, I myself am to take him up to one of the prisons, or at least to hand him over to the officer sent down from that prison to take up the captives allotted to it. The matter is of more importance than it seems to be, or, as you may imagine, I should not be charged to intercept you on such an errand."

"Of course, I don't understand anything about it, Sir John, but will do as you ask me."

He went to where Gervaise had crouched down by the bulwark, beckoned him to follow, and, walking aft, motioned to him to sit down there. Then he returned to Sir John, and joined the other knights, who were all too anxious to learn the latest news—who had left the island, and who had come to it since they sailed—to interest themselves in any way with the figure who had gone aft, supposing him, indeed, to be Sir John's servant, the lantern suspended over the poop giving too feeble a light for his costume to be noted.

A quarter of an hour later they anchored in the harbour. Some of the knights at once went ashore to their respective *auberges*, but Sir Almeric and a few others remained on board until relieved of their charge in the morning, an account being sent on shore of the number of captives that had been brought in. No thought was given to Gervaise, who slept curled up on the poop. Sir John Boswell passed the night on board. In the morning an officer came off with a list of the prisons to which the slaves were to be sent. Sir John Kendall had seen the officer charged with the distribution, who had, at his request, not included the prison of St. Pelagius in the list.

A message, however, had been sent to that prison, as well as to the others, for an officer to attend at the landing-stage. In the morning Sir John went ashore in one of the boats conveying the slaves, of whom some forty had been captured. Gervaise followed him into the boat, and took his seat by the others, who were too dispirited at the fate which had befallen them to pay any attention to him.

When he landed, Sir John asked which was the officer from St. Pelagius. One stepped forward.

"This is the only slave for you," he said, pointing to Gervaise. "He is of a better class than the rest, and in the future may be he will do for a servitor at one of the *auberge*s, but none have at present occasion for one, and so he is to go to you. He says that his father is a merchant, and will be ready to pay a ransom for him; but they all say that, and we must not heed it overmuch. As he seems a smart young fellow, it may be that he will be sent to one of the *auberge*s later on; but at present, at any rate, you can put him with the rest, and send him out with the gangs."

"He is a well-built young fellow, Sir John," the officer remarked, "and should make a good rower in a galley. I will put him in the crew of the St. Elmo. Follow me," he said, in Turkish, to Gervaise, and then led the way up to the prison. On entering he crossed a courtyard to a door which was standing open. Within was a vaulted room, some forty feet long by twenty wide; along each side there were rushes strewn thickly.

"The others have just started to their work," he said, "so that for to-day you can sleep."

After he had left, Gervaise looked with some disgust at the rushes, that had evidently been for weeks unchanged.

"I would rather have the bare stones, if they were clean," he muttered to himself. "However, it can't be helped."

He presently strolled out into the courtyard, where some other slaves, disabled by illness or injuries, were seated in the sun. Gervaise walked across to them, and they looked listlessly up at him as he approached.

"You are a new-comer," one said, as he came up. "I saw you brought in, but it didn't need that. By the time you have been here a week or two, your clothes will be like ours," and he pointed to his ragged garments. "When did you arrive? Are there no others coming up here?"

"The galley came in last night," Gervaise said, "but they did not land us until this morning. I wish they had killed me rather than that I should have been brought here to work as a slave."

"One always thinks so at first," the man said. "But somehow one clings to life. We shall die when Allah wills it, and not before."

"What is the matter with your foot?" Gervaise asked.

"I was with the gang quarrying stones, and a mass of rock fell upon it. I have been in the infirmary for weeks, and I own that the Christian dogs treated me well. A slave has his value, you see. I am nearly cured now, but I shall never walk well again. I expect they will put me in one of their accursed galleys."

"How long have you been here?"

"Seven years; it seems a lifetime. However, there is hope yet. They don't tell us much, but we hear things sometimes, and they say that the sultan is going to sweep them out of Rhodes as they were swept out of Acre. When will it be?"

"I know not. I am from Syria, but even there they are making preparations. The sultan has had troubles in the East, and that has delayed him, but he will be here before long, and then we shall see. It will be our turn then."

"It will, indeed!" one of the others exclaimed. "Oh, to see these dogs brought down, and suffering as we have suffered, toiling at oars in one of our galleys, or at the fortifications of one of our castles! It will make amends for all our suffering. Had you a hard fight with them?"

"No. We were but a small craft, and it was vain to attempt resistance. I would gladly have fought, but the sailors said it would only throw away their lives. There was but little on board, and they allowed the vessel to go free with those of the sailors who were too old to be made useful for hard work."

No further questions were asked. The men seemed to have no interest save in their own misery, and Gervaise soon left them, and, sitting down in a shady corner, presently dropped off to sleep.

In the evening all came in from their various work. The officer man who had brought Gervaise in went up to the overseer of the galley-slaves and informed him that he had told off the new slave—pointing to Gervaise—to his gang.

"He was brought in by the galley that arrived last night," he said; "he was the only slave sent up here. I hear that he had been set aside to be appointed a servitor, but there are no vacancies, so they sent him here till one should occur; and I was ordered to make him useful in other ways in the meantime."

"I am two or three hands short," the overseer said. "I wish now I had sent in an application yesterday, for if I had done so, no doubt they would have sent me some more men. However, this fellow will make up an even number, and he is strong and active, though at present he looks sulky enough under his bad fortune."

A few of the slaves spoke to Gervaise as they were waiting for food to be brought them, but the majority dropped upon the rushes, too exhausted with toil and heat to feel an interest in anything. The food consisted of rye bread, with thin broth, brought in a great iron vessel. Each slave had a horn, which was used for soup or water, and which, when done with, he had, by the rule enforced among

Sir Gervaise in prison answers the questions of the galley-slaves.

themselves, to take out to the fountain in the courtyard and wash, before it was added to the pile in the corner of the room.

The cool of the evening aided the meal in restoring the energies of the slaves. Several gathered round Gervaise, and asked questions as to what he knew of the prospects of an early invasion of Rhodes; but as soon as the officer left the room, closing and locking the door after him, the slaves became for the most part silent. A few men sat in groups together, talking in undertones, but the greater number threw themselves down on the rushes, either to sleep or to think alone. Gervaise was struck by the manner in which most of them lay, without making the slightest movement, so long as there was light to enable him to make out their figures. He himself addressed two or three of them, as they lay with their eyes wide open, asking questions with reference to the work; but in no case did he receive any reply. The men seemed altogether unconscious of being addressed, being absorbed in the thought of their far-distant homes and families which they might never see again.

Gervaise walked a few times up and down the room, and as he approached a silence fell each time upon the groups of men talking together. More than once a figure rose soon afterwards from the ground, and, as he came along again, asked him a few questions about himself. As soon as it was dark, he lay down in a vacant space on the rushes. Shortly afterwards talking ceased altogether, and there was quiet in the vaulted room. With the first gleam of daylight they were astir, and, when the doors were opened, poured out into the courtyard, where all had a wash at the fountain. Half an hour later, a meal, precisely similar to that of the previous evening, was served out; then the overseers called over the muster roll, the gangs were made up, and each, under its officer, started for its work.

Gervaise, with the men of his room, proceeded down to the port, and at once took their seats on the benches of the galley, one foot being chained to a ring in the deck, the other to that of a companion at the oar. The slaves were more cheerful now. As there was no work to do at present, they were allowed to talk, and an occasional laugh was heard, for the sun and brightness of the day cheered them. Many, after years of captivity, had grown altogether reckless, and it was among these that there was most talking; the younger men seemed, for the most part, silent and moody.

"You will get accustomed to it," the man next to Gervaise said cheeringly. "When I first came here, it seemed to me that I could not support the life for a month—that the fate was too dreadful to be borne, and that death would be most welcome; but, like the rest, I became accustomed to it in time. After all, the work is no harder than one would do at home. There is no stint of food, and it is no worse than one would have, were one labouring in the fields. Were it not for the loss of those we love, it would be nothing; and in time one gets over even that. I have long ago told myself that if they are not dead, at least they are dead to me. They have their livings to get, and cannot be always mourning, and I have tried to forget them, as they must have forgotten me."

"Do you work hard?" Gervaise asked.

"No. We who are in the galleys are regarded by the others with envy. Sometimes— often, indeed we have naught to do all day. We bask in the sun, we talk, we sleep, we forget that we are slaves. But, generally, we go out for an hour or two's exercise; that is well enough, and keeps us strong and in health. Only when we are away on voyages is the work hard. Sometimes we row from morning to night; but it is only when they are in chase of another craft that we have really to exert ourselves greatly. Then it is terrible. We may be doing our best, our very best, and yet to the impatient knights it seems that we might do more. Then they shout to the overseer, and he lays his whip on our backs without mercy. Then we row until sometimes we drop, senseless, off the benches. But this, you understand, is not very often; and though the work on a cruise is long, it is not beyond our strength. Besides, when we are away in the galley there is always hope. The galley may meet with four or five of our ships, and be captured, or a storm may arise and dash her upon the shore; and though many would lose their lives, some might escape, and each man, in thinking of it, believes that he will be one of the fortunate ones.

"Take my advice: always look cheerful if you can; always put your hand on the oar when the order is given, and row as if you were glad to be at work again; and always make a show, as if you were working your hardest. Never complain when you are struck unjustly, and always speak respectfully to the overseer. In that way you will find your life much easier than you would think. You will be chosen for small boat service; and that is a great thing, as we are not chained in the small boats. Some men are foolish and obstinate, but, so far from doing any good, this only brings trouble on themselves; they come in for punishment daily, they are closely watched, and their lives made hells for them. Even as a help to escape it pays best to be cheerful and alert. We all think of escape, you know, though it is seldom indeed that a chance ever comes to any of us. It is the one thing except death to look forward to, and there is not a man among us who does not think of it scores of times a day; but, small as the chance is, it is greatest for those who behave best. For instance, it is they only who man small boats; and when a small boat rows ashore, it is always possible that the guard may be careless—that he will keep the boat at the landing-place, instead of pushing off at once into deep water, as he ought to do—and that in this way a chance will, sooner or later, come for springing ashore and making a dash for liberty."

CHAPTER X.
A PLOT DISCOVERED.

THE conversation between Gervaise and his fellow-slave was interrupted by the arrival at the side of the quay of a party of knights. Silence instantly fell upon the slaves; all straightened themselves up to the oars, and prepared for a start. Among the knights who took their places on the poop Gervaise saw with amusement his friend Ralph. He had no fear of a recognition, for the darkly-stained skin and the black hair had so completely altered him that when he had looked at himself in a mirror, after the application of the dye, he was surprised to find that he would not have known it to be his own face. Ralph was in command of the party, which consisted of young knights who had but recently arrived at Rhodes; and as it was the first time he had been appointed as instructor, Gervaise saw that he was greatly pleased at what he rightly regarded as promotion.

The galley at once pushed off from the wharf, and rowed out of the port. The work was hard; but as the slaves were not pressed to any extraordinary exertions, Gervaise did not find it excessive. He congratulated himself, however, that the stain was, as he had been assured, indelible, save by time, for after a few minutes' exercise he was bathed in perspiration. As the galley had been taken out only that instruction might be given to the young knights, the work was frequently broken.

Sometimes they went ahead at full speed for a few hundred yards, as if to chase an adversary; then they would swerve aside, the slaves on one side rowing, while those on the other backed, so as to make a rapid turn. Then she lay for a minute or two immovable, and then backed water, or turned to avoid the attack of an imaginary foe. Then for an hour she lay quiet, while the knights, divesting themselves of their mantles and armour, worked one of the guns on the poop, aiming at a floating barrel moored for the purpose a mile out at sea. At eleven o'clock they returned to the port. Bread and water were served out to the slaves, and they were then permitted to lie down and sleep, the galley being moored under the shadow of the wall.

At four o'clock another party of knights came down, and the work was similar to that which had been performed in the morning. At seven o'clock the slaves were taken back to their barracks.

"Well, what do you think of your work?" one of the slaves asked Gervaise, as they ate their evening meal. "It would not be so bad if it was all like that."

"No. But I can tell you that when you have to row from sunrise to sunset, with perhaps but one or two pauses for a few minutes, it is a different thing altogether, especially if the galley is carrying despatches, and speed is necessary. Then you get so worn out and exhausted, that you can scarce move an oar through the water, until you are wakened up by a smart as if a red-hot iron had been laid across your shoulders. It is terrible work then. The whip cracks every minute across some one's back; you are blinded by exhaustion and rage, and you feel that you would give the world if you could but burst your chain, rush on your taskmasters, and strike, if only one blow, before you are killed."

"It must be terrible," Gervaise said. "And do you never get loose, and fall upon them?"

The man shook his head.

"The chains are too strong, and the watch too vigilant," he said. "Since I came here I have heard tales of crews having freed themselves in the night, and fallen upon the Christians, but for my part I do not believe in them. I have thought, as I suppose every one of us has thought, how such a thing could be done; but as far as I know no one has hit on a plan yet. Now and then men have managed to become possessed of a file, and have, by long and patient work, sawn through a chain, and have, when a galley has been lying near our own shore, sprung overboard and escaped; but for every attempt that succeeds there must be twenty failures, for the chains are frequently examined, and woe be to the man who is found to have been tampering with his. But as to a whole gang getting free at once, it is altogether impossible, unless the key of the pad locks could be stolen from an overseer, or the man bribed into aiding us."

"And that, I suppose, is impossible?" Gervaise said.

"Certainly, impossible for us who have no money to bribe them with, but easy enough if any one outside, with ample means, were to set about it. These overseers are, many of them, sons of Turkish mothers, and have no sympathy, save that caused by interest, with one parent more than another. Of course, they are brought up Christians, and taught to hold Moslems in abhorrence, but I think many of them, if they had their free choice, would cross to the mainland. Here they have no chance of ever being aught but what they are—overseers of slaves, or small prison officials. They are despised by these haughty knights, and hated by us, while were they to reach the mainland and adopt their mothers' religion, everything would be open to them. All followers of the Prophet have an equal chance, and one may be a soldier to-day, a bey to-morrow, and a pasha a year hence, if he be brave, or astute, or capable in any way beyond his fellows. Men like these warders would be sure to make their way.

"They cannot have gathered much during their service, therefore the offer of a large sum of money would find plenty among them eager to earn it. But, you see, they are but the inferiors. On our voyages on board the galley, the knights inspect our fetters twice a day, and the keys are kept in the commander's cabin. For an hour or two, when we are not on a long passage, the padlocks are unfastened, in order that we may jump over and bathe, and exercise our limbs; but at this time the knights are always on guard, and as we are without arms we are altogether powerless. It is the same thing here. The senior warders, who all belong to the Order, although of an inferior grade, come round, as you have seen, to examine our fetters, and themselves lock and bar the doors. If one or two of these could be corrupted, escape would be easy enough."

"But is it impossible to do this?" Gervaise asked eagerly. "My father has money, and would I know be ready, if I could communicate with him, to pay a handsome sum, if sure that it would result in my obtaining my freedom."

The man nodded significantly.

"There may be other means of doing it," he said. "Perhaps it will not be long before you hear of it. You seem a stout fellow, and full of spirit, but, as yet, anything that may be going on is known but to a few, and will go no further until the time comes that all may be told. I think not so badly of men of our faith as to believe that any one would betray the secret for the sake of obtaining his own freedom and a big reward; but secrets, when known by many, are apt to leak out. A muttered word or two in sleep, or the ravings of one down with fever, might afford ground for suspicion, and torture would soon do the rest. I myself know nothing of the secret, but I do know that there is something going on which, if successful, will give us our freedom. I am content to know no more until the time comes; but there are few, save those engaged in the matter, that know as much as this, and you can see that it is better it should be so. Look at that man opposite; he has been here fifteen years; he seldom speaks; he does his work, but it is as a brute beast—despair has well-nigh turned him into one. Think you that if such a man as that were to know that there is hope, he would not be so changed that even the dullest would observe it. I see you are a brisk young fellow, and I say to you, keep up your courage. The time is nearer than you think when you will be free from these accursed shackles."

A KNIGHT OF THE WHITE CROSS

Each morning, as he went out to work with his gang, Gervaise saw the servant from the *auberge* standing near; but he made no sign. He was satisfied that his suspicions had been justified, and that he was not leading this life in vain, but he thought it better to wait until the week passed, and he was taken away to have his colour renewed, than to make a sign that might possibly rouse the suspicions of his comrades. On the eighth morning, when the door of the room was unlocked, the overseer said—

"Number 36, you will remain here. You are wanted for other work."

After the gang had left the prison, the overseer returned.

"I am to take you up to the English *auberge*. The knight who handed you over to me when you landed, told me that you might be wanted as a servitor; and as it is he who has sent down, it may be that a vacancy has occurred. If so, you are in luck, for the servitors have a vastly better time of it than the galley-slaves, and the English *auberge* has the best reputation in that respect. Come along with me."

The English *auberge* was one of the most handsome of the buildings standing in the great street of the Knights. Its architecture was Gothic in its character, and, although the *langue* was one of the smallest of those represented at Rhodes, it vied with any of them in the splendour of its appointments. Sir John Boswell was standing in the interior courtyard."

"Wait here for a few minutes," he said to the overseer. "The bailiff will himself question the slave as to his accomplishments; but I fancy he will not be considered of sufficient age for the post that is vacant. However, if this should not be so, I shall no doubt find a post to fit him ere long, for he seems a smart young fellow, and, what is better, a willing one, and bears himself well under his misfortunes." Then he motioned to Gervaise to follow him to the bailiff's apartments.

A PLOT DISCOVERED

"Well, Sir Gervaise," Sir John Kendall exclaimed, as the door closed behind him, "have you found aught to justify this cruel penance you have undertaken?"

"As to the penance, Sir John, it has been nothing unsupportable. The exercise is hard enough, but none too hard for one in good health and strength, and, save for the filth of the chamber in which we are shut up at night, and the foul state of the rushes on which we lie, I should have naught to complain of. No, I have as yet heard nothing of a surety—and yet enough to show me that my suspicions were justified, and that there is a plot of some sort on foot," and he related to the two knights the conversation he had had with the galley-slave.

"By St. George!" the bailiff said, "you have indeed been justified in your surmises, and I am glad that I attached sufficient importance to your suspicions to let you undertake this strange enterprise. What think you, Sir John Boswell?"

"I think with you, that Sir Gervaise has fully justified his insistence in this matter, which I own I considered to be hare-brained folly. What is to be done next, Sir Gervaise?"

"That is what I have been turning over in my mind. You see, I may have little warning of what is going to take place. I may not hear of it until we are locked up for the night and the affair is on the point of taking place, and it will, of course, be most needful that I shall be able to communicate with you speedily."

"That, of course, is of vital importance," the bailiff said. "But how is it to be managed?"

"That is what I cannot exactly see, Sir John. An armed guard remains in our room all night. But, in the first place, he might be himself in the plot, and if not, the slaves would almost certainly overpower him and kill him, as a preliminary to the work of knocking off their chains."

"Is there a window to the room? At least,— of course there is a window, but is it within your reach?"

"There are six small loop-holes—one on each side of the door, and two in each of the side walls; they are but four inches across and three feet in length, and there are two cross-bars to each; they are four feet from the floor."

"At any rate, they are large enough for your arm to pass through, Sir Gervaise, and you might drop a strip of cloth out."

"Certainly I could, Sir John. I could easily hide a piece of white cotton a yard or so long in my clothes, scanty as these are, and could certainly manage, unobserved, to drop it outside the window."

"Then the rest is for us to contrive, Boswell. We must have some one posted in the yard of the prison, with instructions to go every ten minutes throughout the night to see if a strip of white cotton has been dropped out. When he finds it he must go at once to William Neave, the governor. He is a sturdy Englishman, and there is no fear of his having been bribed to turn traitor; but it were well to take no one into our confidence. I think we cannot do better than employ Ahmet on this business, as he already knows that Sir Gervaise is masquerading there. We will have William Neave up here presently. Tell him that for certain reasons we wish Ahmet to pass the night for the present in the prison, and arrange with him on what excuse we can best bestow him there without exciting suspicion. At any rate, Sir Gervaise, that is our affair."

He went to a closet and took out a white mantle, tore a strip off the bottom, and gave it to Gervaise.

"It would be best not to keep you here any longer," he said, "so renew your stain while I speak. As soon as you learn the details of the plot, you will drop this out from the loop-hole on the right-hand side of the door; that is to say, the one on your right, standing inside. If the affair is not to come off at once, it were best for you to proceed as before. Ahmet will be outside when you go out with your gang, and on your nodding to him we will make some excuse to take you away on your return. I say this because if you see that the affair, whatever it is, is not imminent, you might think it better to remain with them longer, so as to learn their plans more fully, instead of having the thing put a stop to at once."

"I understand, Sir John; but, as I have said, I do not think we should all be told until the blow is ready to be struck, as they would be afraid that some one might inform against them, if time and opportunity were granted them."

"I think so too, Sir Gervaise. This afternoon we will call upon the grand master, for we have no means of knowing how serious or how extended this plot may be; it may include only the crew of a single galley, and, on the other hand, the whole of the slaves may be implicated in it. It is evident, therefore, that the matter is too serious to be kept any longer from his knowledge."

Three more days passed. On the third evening, after the allowance of broth and bread had been consumed, and the door was closed and locked upon them for the night, three or four of the galley-slaves, after talking eagerly together, beckoned to the others to gather round them at the end of the room farthest from the door. Two of them took up arms-full of the bedding, and stuffed it into the side windows. Gervaise saw, in the dim light, a look of intense excitement on the faces of the slaves. It had been vaguely known among them that a plot was in hand, although but few had been admitted into the confidence of the leaders. Hitherto all had feared that it concerned only a small number, but the preparations now made to insure that they should not be overheard, showed that, whatever the plan might be, all were to share in it.

"Thanks be to Allah, the All-powerful," one of the men began, "my lips are unsealed, and I can tell you the great news that our hour for escape from bondage is at hand! We need not fear the warder there," he went on, as several eyes were turned apprehensively towards the guard, who, with his spear beside him, was leaning carelessly against the wall at the farther end, looking through the window into the court-yard; "he is with us. You must know that for the last two months an agent from Constantinople has been on the Island, and has been engaged in arranging this affair. Two of our taskmasters belonging to the Order have been bribed by large sums of money, and several of the overseers, who are half of our blood, have eagerly embraced the prospect of returning to their mothers' country, and of avowing openly their belief in our religion. These, again, have bought over many of the guards, ours included, and to-night all will be ready for action. Those not of our party will be killed without ceremony. Duplicate keys have been made of all the padlocks of the fetters; the guards who are with us have each one of them, the others will have been slipped into the hands of one man in each gang as they returned to-night from work. The overseers who are in the plot will, at midnight, go quietly round and unlock the doors, and remove the bars from the outside. We have, therefore, only to overcome the eight or ten men who patrol the prison; and as we shall have the arms of the guards, some thirty in number, we shall make quick work of them.

"The two guards at the outside gates must, of course, be killed. Duplicates of the keys have been made, and will be hidden in a spot known to some of our party, close to the gate. Thus we have but to issue out and rush down, in a body, to the port. I and another are to take the arms of our guard, and two others are told off in each room to do the same. That will give us sixty armed men. We shall make very short work of the guards at the gate leading into the port. Then twenty of us are to run along the mole to Fort St. Nicholas, twenty to the Tower of St. Michael, and twenty to that of St. John. There will be, at the most, but three or four men keeping watch at each fort, and thus we shall have in our possession the three forts commanding the entrance to the harbour. There are, as you know, six galleys manned by crews from our prison there. The crew of each galley will embark upon it, and man the oars; the rest will divide themselves among the galleys. Before starting, we shall seize and set fire to all other galleys and ships in the port. The gangs in four of the rooms have been told off specially for this duty. Before firing them, they are to take out such provisions as they may find, and transport them to the galleys. We who take the forts are provided with hammers and long nails, to drive down the vent-holes of the cannon; when we have done this, we are to wait until one of the galleys fetches us off. Ten minutes should be ample time for all there is to be done, and even if the alarm is given at once, we shall be away long before the knights can be aroused from sleep, buckle on their armour, and get down to the port."

Exclamations of delight and approbation burst from his hearers.

"Then it is only we of this prison who are in the plot?" one said.

"Yes. In the first place, it would have been too dangerous to attempt to free all. In the second, the galleys would not carry them; we shall be closely packed as it is, for there are over a thousand here. I hear that there was a talk of freeing all, and that we, instead of embarking at first, should make for the other prisons, burst open the doors, and rescue the others; but by the time we could do so the knights would be all in arms, and our enterprise would fail altogether, for as but a small proportion of us can obtain weapons, we could not hope to overcome them. Were it not for the strong wall that separates their quarter from the town, we might make straight for their houses and slay them before the alarm could be given. As it is, that would be impossible, and therefore the plan will be carried out as I have told you. The loss of all their galleys and of over one thousand slaves will be a heavy blow for them. Great pains have been taken to prevent confusion when we reach the port. The men in each room have been instructed as to the galleys on which they are to embark. As for you, you know precisely what is to be done; you will simply take your places, and then wait until all are on board. No galley is to push out from the wharf until the last man of those employed in burning the ships has returned, with the provisions found in them. Then the order will be given by the man who has arranged all this, and the six galleys will put out together.

One is to row to each of the forts to carry off the party that will have been engaged in silencing its cannon. Our galley is to row to St. Nicholas, and take off the twenty men I shall lead there. There is no possibility of failure. Everything has, you see, been arranged. One of the overseers who is in the plot walked by my side as we returned from the port, and gave me the instructions, and all the others will have been told in the same way, or else by the guards in charge of them."

The gang now broke up into little groups, talking excitedly over the unlooked-for news, and exulting over the speedy advent of liberty. Gervaise strolled carelessly to the window, and dropped out the white strip of stuff. It was now quite dark, and there was no fear of any one observing the movement. Then he joined the others. After an hour and a half had passed he heard footsteps approaching the door. There was a pause; then the outside bars were taken down, and a key turned in the lock. A deep silence fell on the slaves. Then a voice called,—

"Number 36!"

"What is it?" replied Gervaise, without raising himself from his seat on the bedding. "I have done my share of work to-day, and earned my night's sleep."

"It is a knight from the English *auberge*; he has come to fetch you. It seems that you are to go there as a servitor."

"What a cursed fortune," Gervaise muttered, in Turkish, "just when a road to freedom is open! I have a good mind to say I am ill, and cannot go till the morning."

"No, no!" one of the others exclaimed. "They would only drag you out, and when they saw that there was naught the matter with you, would suspect that there must be some reason why you did not want to go, when, as every one knows, the position of the servitors is in every way preferable to ours."

"Now then, why are you delaying?" a voice said sharply, and a warder entered with a lighted torch. "Get up, you lazy hound! It will be worse for you if I have to speak again."

"I am coming," Gervaise grumbled. "I was just asleep."

A PLOT DISCOVERED

He rose, as if reluctantly, and went forward. The warder gave him an angry push, followed him out, and locked and barred the door after him.

"I suppose this is the right man?" Sir John Boswell said.

"This is Number 36, Sir Knight, the same who was taken over to your *auberge* the other day," and he held the light close to Gervaise's face.

"Yes, that is the man. Follow me," he added, in Turkish. The gate of the courtyard was unbarred, and they passed out unquestioned. Sir John strolled on ahead. Gervaise followed him a pace or two behind. Not until they had passed through the gate of the castle did Sir John turn.

"I have not spoken to you," he said, "as we may have been watched. Keep your news until we reach the *auberge*."

Upon entering it they went up at once to Sir John Kendall's apartments.

"Well, Sir Gervaise, the strip of cotton was brought to us safely. What is your news?"

"It is very serious, Sir John, and I have been in terrible anxiety since I dropped it out, lest it should not come to hand in time. As it is, you have till midnight to make your preparations. He then repeated the statement made by the galley-slave.

"By my faith," Sir John Kendall exclaimed, "this is a pretty plot indeed! And had it succeeded, as it certainly would have done but for your vigilance, it would have been a heavy blow to us. The burning of all our galleys would have crippled us sorely, and the loss of over a thousand slaves would have been a serious one indeed, when we so urgently require them for completing our defences. Get rid of those clothes at once, Sir Gervaise, and don your own. We must go straight to the grand master. You will find your clothes and armour in the next room. I had them taken there as soon as your token was brought me."

In a few minutes Gervaise returned in his usual attire, and with his armour buckled on. The two knights were already in their coats-of-mail, and leaving the *auberge* they went to the grand master's palace. A servitor had already been sent to D'Aubusson to inform him that they were coming, and he advanced to meet them as they entered.

"Welcome, Sir Gervaise!" he said. "Whether your news be good or bad, whether you have found that it is a general rising of the slaves that is intended, or a plot by which a handful of slaves may seize a boat and escape, the gratitude of the Order is no less due to you for the hardships and humiliations you have undergone on its behalf."

"It concerns but one prison: that of St. Pelagius."

"The largest of them," the grand master put in. "The whole of the slaves there are to be liberated at twelve o'clock to-night, are to seize the three water towers and to spike the guns, to burn all the shipping in the harbour, to make off with six galleys, and destroy the rest."

"By St. John!" D'Aubusson exclaimed, "this is indeed a serious matter. But tell me all about it. There must be treachery indeed at work for such a scheme to be carried out."

Gervaise now told him all the details he had learned.

"So two of the Order, though but of the inferior grade, are in the plot?" the grand master said; "and several of the overseers? One of the villains is, of course, the man you saw this Greek talking with. We must get hold of the other if we can. As to the slaves, now that we have warning, there is an end of the matter, though without such warning they would surely have succeeded, for the plans are well laid, and they would have been at sea before we could have gathered in any force at the port. If it were not that it would cost the lives of many of the warders and of the prison guards, I should say we ought to take post outside the gate, for we should then catch the traitors who are to accompany them. As it is, we must be beforehand with them. A hundred men will be more than ample for our purpose. Do you take fifty of your knights, Sir John Kendall, and I will draw fifty of those of Auvergne. At eleven o'clock we will meet at the gate leading down into the town, and will march to the private entrance of the governor's house. I will go in first with a few of you, tell him what we have discovered, and post guards to prevent any one from leaving his house. Then, having admitted the others, we will go quietly out and place a party at each door of the overseers' house, with orders to seize any who may come out. The rest, in small parties, will then go round the prison, and, entering each room, show the slaves that their plot has been discovered. This we must do to save the lives of the guards who may be faithful to their trust. As to the higher officials engaged in the affair, we must obtain their names from the overseers or slaves. It is not likely that the two traitors will quit their houses, as they will leave the matter in the hands of the overseers, who, as you say, intend to first open the doors, and then to accompany the slaves in their escape. Do not warn the knights until it is nearly time to start, Sir John. The less stir made the better, for no one can say whether they may not have suborned some of the servitors to send instant news of any unusual movements in any of the *auberge*s."

At half-past ten Sir John Kendall went round among the knights and bade fifty of them arm themselves quietly, and proceed, one by one, down to the gate, and there await orders. Up to this time Gervaise had remained in the bailiff's room, so as to avoid the questioning that would take place, and he went down to the gate with the bailiff and Sir John Boswell.

The knights assembled rapidly. None were aware of the reason for which they had been called out at such an hour, and there was a buzz of talk and conjecture until Sir John Kendall arrived. He was followed by four of the servants, who at once lighted the torches they carried, when he proceeded to go through the roll, and found that the muster was complete. Many of the knights had gazed in some surprise at Gervaise, whose dark complexion altogether concealed his identity, and it was supposed that he must be some newly arrived knight, though none had heard that any ship had entered the harbour that day.

A KNIGHT OF THE WHITE CROSS

Two or three minutes later fifty knights of the *langue* of Auvergne came down, headed by the grand master himself, whose appearance greatly heightened the surprise of the English knights. The torches were now extinguished, the gate thrown open, and the party descended into the town. Gervaise had purposely fallen in by the side of Harcourt.

"You are but newly arrived, Sir Knight?" the latter said, as they moved off.

"Not so very newly, Ralph," Gervaise replied.

"What! is it you, Gervaise?" Harcourt exclaimed, with a start of surprise. "Why, I did not know you, though I looked hard at you in the torch-light. What have you done with yourself? Where have you been? Do you know what all this is about?"

"I cannot tell you now, Ralph. You must be content to know that I have been in prison, and working in the galleys."

"The saints defend us! Why, what on earth had you done to entail such punishment as that. It is an outrage. The grand master and the council have the right to expel a knight from the Order after due trial and investigation, but not to condemn him to such penalties as the galleys. It is a outrage upon the whole Order, and I would say so to the grand master himself."

"There was no outrage in it, Ralph. Wait until you hear the whole story. That I have not disgraced you, you may judge from the fact that I am in the armour and mantle of the Order, and that, as you saw, I came down with Sir John Kendall himself."

There were no people about in the streets, though the lights still burned on a few of the roofs. For a short distance the knights marched down towards the port, and then turned down a street to the right. After a few minutes' marching they halted under a high wall which all knew to be that of the prison of St. Pelagius. Six knights were posted at the main entrance, with orders that none should be allowed to leave the prison, and that any persons who came up to the gate were to be at once seized and made prisoners.

A PLOT DISCOVERED

The rest marched on to a small door leading into the governor's house. Here they were halted, and told to wait till called in; six knights of England, and as many of Auvergne, being told off to accompany the grand master and Sir John Kendall. A note had been sent to the governor, informing him that the grand master intended to visit the prison at eleven o'clock, but that the matter was to be kept an absolute secret; and that the governor himself was to be down at the gate to admit him.

CHAPTER XI
IN COMMAND OF A GALLEY.

WILLIAM NEAVE, the governor of the prison, looked astonished indeed when, upon his opening the door, the grand master and the bailiff of the English *langue*, with the twelve knights behind them, entered. He had been puzzled when, four days before, he had received an order from the grand master that Ahmet, a servitor in the *auberge* of the English *langue*, should be permitted to pass the night in his house, with authority to move freely and without question, at any hour, in the courtyard of the gaol, and to depart at any hour, secretly and without observation, by the private gate. Still more had he been surprised when he received the message that the grand master would pay him a secret visit at eleven o'clock at night.

"Let no word be spoken until we are in your apartments," D'Aubusson said in a low voice, as he entered. "But first lead four of these knights and post them so that none can enter the gaol from the house. If there are more than four doors or windows on that side, you must post a larger number. It is imperative that there shall be no communication whatever between your servants and the gaol."

As soon as this was done, the rest of the party were taken to the governor's rooms.

"I can now explain to you all," the grand master said, "the reason of our presence here. I have learned that at twelve to-night there will be a general rising of the slaves in this prison, and that, aided by treachery, they will free themselves from their fetters, overpower and slay such of the guards in their rooms as have not been bribed, throw open the gates, make their way down to the port, burn all the shipping there, and make off in the six galleys manned by them, having first overpowered the sentries in the three forts commanding the entrance, and spiked the guns."

Exclamations of astonishment burst from the knights, who now, for the first time, learnt the reason of their being called out. The governor listened with an expression of stupefaction.

"With all deference to your Highness," he said hesitatingly, "it seems to me that some one must have been deceiving you with this tale. It is altogether incredible that such a plot should have been hatched without a whisper of the matter coming to my ears. It could only be possible were there, not one but many, traitors among the officials; if this is so, then indeed am I a dull ass, and unfit for my duty here, of which I shall pray you to relieve me, and to order such punishment as the council may deem just to be allotted to me for having so signally been hoodwinked."

"My news is sure," the grand master said; " but I deem not that you are in any way to blame in the matter. The plot has been matured, not as a consequence of any laxity of discipline in the prison, but from deliberate treachery, against which no mortal being can guard. The traitors are two of the officials who, being members of the Order, none would suspect of connivance in such a deed. With them are several—I know not how many—under-officials, warders, and guards; all these have been bribed by an emissary from Constantinople, now in the town, and who is doubtless furnished with large means. It is well, indeed, for the Order, that this terrible act of treachery has been discovered in time to prevent the plot from coming to a head, for the loss of all our galleys, to say nothing of the disgrace of having been thus bearded by slaves, would be a very heavy blow to it.

"Now that the house is safely guarded, William Neave, you can admit the rest of the knights, who are waiting outside. Then you will, in the first place, conduct a party, and post them so that they may arrest, as they come out to perform their share of the work, all officials, warders, and guards, of whatever rank. When you have posted knights to carry out this—and I need not say that the operation must be performed as silently as possible, for it is above all things necessary that the men concerned shall have no suspicion that their plot has been discovered—you will conduct other parties to the various rooms occupied by the slaves. The guards on duty inside will be made prisoners. The doors will then be locked and barred as before. The appearance of the knights and the arrest of the guards will be sufficient to show the slaves that their plot has been discovered, and there will be no fear of their making any attempt to carry it into execution. I will myself post the main body of the knights in the courtyard. The arrest of the guards is to be carried out at once, as all those not concerned in the plot would be killed when the hour comes for the rising. Therefore this part of the business must be carried out immediately. I should not, however, lead the guards away to a cell, for the less tramping of feet the better. Therefore I shall place two knights in each room, and beg them to remain inside in charge until the traitors outside are secured."

The knights outside were now marched up. The grand master ordered half those of Auvergne to go round to the main gate, which would be opened for them by the governor; they were to enter quietly, and remain in a body close to it until they received further orders. Sir John Kendall told off the rest of the knights to the various duties of watching the houses occupied by the officials and warders, and of entering the prison rooms and remaining in them on guard. The governor, with his private servants, bearing a supply of torches, was to lead them to the various cells, and unlock the doors. The knights were enjoined to move as noiselessly as possible, and to avoid all clashing of arms against armour.

IN COMMAND OF A GALLEY

The governor produced a number of cloths intended to be served out to the slaves. Strips of these were cut off and wrapped round the feet of the English knights, so as to deaden the sound of their boots on the stone pavement. Then, accompanied by the grand master and Sir John Kendall, he went the round of the cells.

In some of these the slaves were found standing up in an attitude of eager expectation, which, as the door opened, and the light of the torches showed a party of knights, changed into one of terror and consternation. Scarce a word was spoken. The guard was ordered to lay down his arms, and to take one of the torches. Two knights placed themselves, one on each side of him, with drawn swords. The door was again locked and barred, and the party proceeded to the next cell. In less than a quarter of an hour this part of the work was finished, and D'Aubusson, Sir John Kendall, and the governor, then took up their station with a party of knights who, concealed behind a buttress, were watching the doors of the officials' houses.

Ten minutes later one of these doors was heard to open, and five dark figures came noiselessly out. They were allowed to go a short distance, in order to see if any others followed; but as no others came out, the governor stepped forward.

"Whither are you going, at this time of night?" he asked. There was a momentary pause, a few hasty words were exchanged, then the five men rushed towards him with bared swords or knives; but before they reached him the knights poured out from their hiding place.

"We are betrayed," one of the men shouted in Turkish. "Fight to the last. Better be killed than tortured and executed." With a yell of fury and despair, they rushed upon the knights. So desperate was their attack that the latter were forced to use their swords, which indeed, burning with rage at the treachery of these men, they were not backward in doing, and in less than a minute the five traitors lay, with cloven heads, dead on the pavement.

"It is as well so," D'Aubusson said, looking sternly down upon them; "perhaps better so, since it has saved us the scandal of their trial. We might have learned more from them, but we have learnt enough, since, doubtless, they have no accomplices among the warders, or they would have been with them. Now we will deal with the arch-traitors. There is no need for further concealment; the noise of this fray will assuredly have been heard by them, for they will be listening for the sounds that would tell them the slaves had been liberated."

Followed by the knights, he went to the door of the house occupied by the overseers, all of whom were members of the lower branch of the Order. It was indeed evident that an alarm had been given there, for lights appeared at the windows. As they opened the door and entered the hall, several half-dressed men rushed down the stairs with drawn swords, two of them carrying torches in their left hands. As the light fell upon the figures of the grand master and the knights, they paused in astonishment.

"There is treachery at work in the prison," D'Aubusson said quietly. "I pray you to collect your comrades and to assemble here at once."

In a minute or two some twenty officials were gathered in the hall.

"Are all here?" D'Aubusson asked the governor.

The latter counted the men.

"There are two short," he said—"Pietro Romano and Karl Schumann. They occupy the same room. Go and fetch them down, four of you."

The four men nearest to the stairs at once went up with two torches. They returned in a minute.

"The door is fastened on the inside, and we can obtain no response."

"Fetch an axe and break it in," the grand master ordered. "Sir John Boswell, do you, with some other knights, take post without; they may attempt to escape by the window, though, as we hold the gates, it would avail them little. Sir Gervaise Tresham, do you follow us."

Gervaise, who had been placed with the party watching the house, followed the grand master and governor upstairs. A few blows with an axe splintered the door; its fastenings gave way, and they entered the room. The window was open, and two figures lay prostrate on the ground near it.

"I half expected this," the grand master said. "They were listening there. The conflict in the yard told them that the plot had been discovered, and as they saw us approaching the house, they dared not meet the punishment of their crimes, and have fallen by their own daggers. Put a torch close to their faces. Sir Gervaise, do you recognise in either of these men the official you saw in conversation with the Greek?"

Gervaise stepped forward and examined the men's faces.

"This is the man," he said, pointing to one of them. "I marked him so closely that I cannot be mistaken."

"That is Pietro Romano," the governor said; "he was an able officer, but discontented with his position and given to quarrelling with his comrades."

"Have a hole dug and bury them in the prison," D'Aubusson said; "they have been false to their vows, and false to their religion. They have chosen their own mode of death; let them be buried like dogs, as they are. But let a careful search be made of their garments and of this room. It may be that they have some documents concealed which may be of use to us."

The grand master then descended to the hall.

"Members of the Order," he said to the overseers, "your guilty companions have met death by their own hands, as the others concerned in this plot have met theirs by the swords of the knights. It were well that this matter were not spoken of outside the prison. The attempt has been detected, and has failed; but were it talked of, it might incite others to repeat the attempt, and possibly with better success. Now," he went on, turning to the governor, "our work is done here. Call up the other warders. Let them take the men now prisoners in the rooms, and place them in a dungeon. Let fresh men be placed on guard, and let all the knights gather in the courtyard."

When this was done, and all the knights again assembled, D'Aubusson said,—

"Our work is nearly done, brothers. The traitors are all dead, and the revolt is at an end. It remains but to capture the author of this attempt; but I believe he is already in our hands. I have given an accurate description of him to Da Veschi, who has taken four knights with him, and they probably will catch him down at the port; if not, he will be arrested the first thing in the morning. As to the slaves, they will be so utterly cowed by the discovery, that there will be no fear of their repeating the attempt. I have ordered the officials of the prison to say naught in the town of what has taken place. There can, however, be no concealment among ourselves. I shall, of course, lay the whole matter before the council. The fact that a strong body of knights has, at so late an hour, started on some unknown mission is, of course, already known in the *auberge*s of Auvergne and England. No concealment of the facts is therefore possible. It is the most serious attempt at a revolt of the slaves that has ever taken place, and will be a warning to us that more vigilance must be exercised. As it is, we have only been saved from the loss of our galleys and slaves by the acuteness of one of the youngest of our knights, who, in the first place, noted a suspicious occurrence which would have been passed by without attracting a moment's thought by ninety-nine out of a hundred men. He laid the matter before his bailiff, Sir John Kendall, who accepted his offer to disguise himself as a slave, to enter the prison under circumstances that would excite no suspicions among the others, and to live and work among them in order to ascertain whether there was any plot on hand. This task—a painful one, as you may imagine—he carried out, and for two weeks he rowed as a galley-slave. His lot was as hard as that of the others, for, as he had reason to believe that some of the officials were concerned in the plot, it was necessary that all should be kept in ignorance that he was other than he seemed to be. Thanks to his perfect knowledge of Turkish, he was able to carry his mission through with complete success, and to obtain full particulars of the plot we have to-night crushed. The knight who has performed this inestimable service is Sir Gervaise Tresham, of the English *langue*. The action he has performed will be noted in the annals of the Order as an example of intelligence and of the extreme of self-sacrifice, as well as of courage; for his life would have been assuredly forfeited had the slaves entertained the slightest suspicion of his real character."

There was a murmur of acclamation among the knights. Not one of them but would have freely risked his life in the service of the Order, but there were few who would not have shrunk from the idea of living as a slave among the slaves, sharing their tasks, and subject to the orders of men of inferior rank and often brutal manners.

The knights now returned to their *auberge*s. It was past midnight, but at the English house the lamps and flambeaux were lighted in the great hall. The servitors were called up, wine placed on the table, and the knights discussed the incidents of the evening.

When the meal had concluded, Sir John Kendall said, "Brother knights,—When the grand master bestowed the honour of secular knighthood upon this young comrade of ours, he predicted that he would rise to high distinction in the Order. I think you will all agree with me that the prediction is already in a fair way of being fulfilled, and that the services he has rendered to the Order justify us, his comrades of the English *langue*, in feeling proud of him. I drink, brothers, to his health."

A loud shout rose from the assembled knights, for upon the return of the party who had been away, the rest of those at the *auberge* had hastily robed themselves and descended to the hall to gather the news. When the shout had died away, and the wine-cups were emptied, Gervaise, who was sitting on Sir John Kendall's right hand, would gladly have retained his seat, but the bailiff told him that he must say a few words, and after standing in embarrassed silence for a minute he said,—

"Sir John Kendall, and brother knights,—I can only say that I am very sensible of the kindness with which you have been pleased to regard what seems to me after all to have been a very ordinary affair. I saw a man, whom I knew to be a stranger in the Island, speaking surreptitiously to a slave, and afterwards saw him conversing with a prison officer. That naturally struck me as curious, and I followed the officer, to see to which prison he belonged. Any one would have thought, as I did, that such a thing was strange, if not suspicious, and the only way to find out whether there was anything in it was to mix with the slaves; as I spoke Turkish well enough to do so I asked Sir John Kendall's permission to disguise myself. He gave me every assistance, and I shared their lot for a fortnight. There was no very great hardship in that—certainly nothing to merit the praise that Sir John Kendall has been kind enough to bestow on me. Nevertheless, I am very glad to have gained your good opinion and very grateful to him and to you for drinking to my health."

Then he sat down abruptly.

Sir John Kendall now rose, and the knights, following his example, betook themselves to their dormitories.

The next morning notices were sent by the grand master to the bailiffs of the *auberges*, and the knights of the grand cross who happened to be in the Island, to assemble in council. Messages were also sent to Gervaise, requesting him to repair at the same hour to the palace, as the council would probably require his attendance.

"Oh dear! I wish this was all over," he said to Ralph, as the latter assisted him to buckle on his armour.

"I don't see anything to sigh about," Ralph said. "I think that you are the most fortunate fellow in the world. I do not say that you have not well deserved it, because it is the tremendous way you worked at Turkish and gave up everything else that has enabled you to do this. Still, there was luck in your noticing that villain talking to the galley-slaves, and then to one of the officers of the prison. Of course, as the grand master said last night, it isn't one in a thousand who would have thought anything more about it, and I am sure I shouldn't; so that, and all the rest, is entirely your own doing. Still, it was a piece of luck that you noticed him talking with a slave. Don't think I envy you, Gervaise; I don't a bit, and I feel as much as any one that you have well deserved the honour you have obtained. Still, you know, it is a sort of consolation to me that luck had a little just a little—to do with it."

"In my opinion luck had everything to do with it," Gervaise said heartily, "and I feel downright ashamed at there being such a fuss made over it. It was bad enough before, merely because I had hit on a plan for our escape from those pirates, but this is worse, and I feel horribly nervous at the thought of having to appear before the grand master and the council."

"Well, that brown dye will hide your blushes, Gervaise. I can only say I wish that I was in your place. By-the-bye, have you heard that they caught that rascal Greek last night?"

"No, I have not heard anything about it."

"Yes. The knights hid themselves behind a pile of goods on the wharf. There was no one about, so far as they could see, but soon after twelve they saw a figure come up on to the deck of a fishing-boat moored by the quay. It was the Greek; he stood there for a minute or two listening, and then went down again; he did this five or six times, and at one o'clock they saw him throw up his arms, as if in despair; he stepped ashore, and was about to make his way up into the town when they rushed out and seized him. There is no doubt as to what his fate will be. I am sorry to say that I hear my friend Vrados has been arrested; but there can be no doubt about his loyalty, and he will assuredly be able to explain to the satisfaction of the council how this man became a resident at his house."

"I am sorry I met him there, Ralph. It is a very unpleasant thing to have gone to a house, to have been received kindly, and then to be the means of bringing trouble upon it."

"Yes. I feel that a little myself, because I took you there; and yet I cannot regret it, for if you had not seen him and taken an objection to him, you might not have noticed him particularly when he spoke to one of the galley-slaves. It is certainly curious that you should have doubted the man, for I have met him there several times, and even after your visit with me I could see nothing in him to justify your dislike."

Gervaise went up to the palace, and while waiting in the great hall until summoned before the council he was warmly accosted by several knights,—some of whom were quite strangers to him,—who all joined in congratulating him on the immense service he had done to the Order. It was upwards of an hour before he was called in.

"The council have received, Sir Gervaise Tresham," the grand master said, "full details from Sir John Kendall of the manner in which you first discovered, and have since followed up the daring plot by which the slaves at St. Pelagius were to have risen, slain the guards who were faithful, spiked the cannon in the three water forts, burnt the merchant shipping, carried off six galleys and burnt the rest, and in their name I thank you for having saved the Order from a great calamity. The members of the council agree with me that you have shown an amount of discernment of the highest kind, and that you are worthy of exceptional favour and reward for your conduct. I therefore in my own name appoint you to the commandery of our manor of Maltby in Lincolnshire, which, having fallen vacant, is in my gift; and I release it from the usual payment of the first year's revenue. Knowing that you desire to establish yourself here, the council have, at my request, decided to make an exception to the general rule that a knight, on promotion to a commandery, must return and take charge of it in two years from the time the grant is made to him. The commandery will therefore be administered by the senior of the knights attached to it.

"The council, on their part, have requested the bailiff of Auvergne, as grand master of the Fleet, to appoint you to the command of the galley now building, and approaching completion. This he has consented to do, feeling, as we all feel, that although such an appointment is unprecedented for a young knight, yet in the present case such an exception may well be made. I may add that the Admiral has—in order that no knight greatly your senior should be placed under your command—determined that he will appoint to it only young knights, who will, we are assured, gladly serve under one who has so distinguished himself, feeling certain that, under his command, they will have ample opportunities against the infidels to prove themselves worthy of the Order. I may add, also, that the bailiffs of all the *langue*s promise that they will select from among the young knights such as may seem best fitted for such service, by their skill in warlike exercises, by their ready obedience to orders, and good conduct. And I foresee that the spirit of emulation, and the desire to show that, though still but professed knights, they are capable of performing as valiant deeds as their elders, will make the galley under your command one of the most successful in the Order.

"As you are aware, it is a stringent rule, which even in so exceptional a case we should not be justified in breaking, that a knight must reside in the Island for five years previous to being promoted to a commandery. It is now two months more than that time since you were received as page to the late grand master, and in promoting you to a commandery I have not, therefore, broken the rule. You may retire, Sir Gervaise."

Gervaise, overwhelmed by the unlooked-for honours thus bestowed upon him, bowed deeply to the grand master and the members of the council, and then retired from the chamber. He passed out of the palace by a side door, so as to avoid being accosted by the knights in the great hall, and took his way out on to the ramparts, where he walked up and down for a considerable time before returning to the *auberge*. He felt no hilarity at his promotion. He had never entertained any ambition for rising to high office in the Order, but had hoped only to perform his duty as a true knight, to fight against the infidels, and some day, if need be, to die for the Order. The commandery was, he knew, a rich one, and as its chief he would draw a considerable revenue from the estate. This afforded him no pleasure whatever, except inasmuch as it would enable him, in his new command of the galley, to keep a handsome table, and to entertain well the knights who served under him.

It seemed to him, however, that the reward and honours were so far beyond his deserts that he felt almost humiliated by their bestowal. The responsibility, too, was great. Would these young knights, the youngest of whom could be but a year his junior, serve willingly under his orders? And, above all, would they be able to emulate the deeds of experienced warriors, and would the galley worthily maintain the fame of the Order?

At the end of two hours he was joined by Ralph Harcourt.

"I have been looking for you everywhere, Gervaise. You seemed to have disappeared mysteriously. None had marked you leave the council chamber, or knew where you had gone; and after searching everywhere I remembered your fondness for walks upon the walls, so I climbed to the top of St. John's tower and thence espied you. Well, I congratulate you most heartily on the honours that have fallen to your share, especially that of the command of a new galley."

"It is too much altogether, Ralph. I feel ashamed at being thus thrust into a post that ought to be given to a knight of age and experience. How can I expect a number of young knights, of whom well-nigh all must be my seniors in age, to obey me as they would an older man?"

IN COMMAND OF A GALLEY

"What has age to do with it?" Ralph said. "You have shown that you have a head to think, and, as you before proved, you have an arm to strike. Why, every young knight in the Order must feel proud that one of their own age has gained such honour. It raises them all in their own esteem, and you will see that you will get the pick among all the professed knights, and of a good many who have finished their profession, and are serving here in the hope of some day getting promotion to a commandery. Not such an one as you have got; that, in the ordinary course of things, does not fall to a knight until he is well on in years, and has served in many commanderies of smaller value. I can tell you, directly Sir John Kendall came back and told us that you had been appointed commander of the new galley, and that it was to be manned wholly by young knights, there was not one of those serving their profession in the *auberge* who did not beg Sir John to put down his name for it; and ten or twelve others, myself among them, who have obtained full knighthood also."

"You don't mean to say that you have put down your name to serve under me, Ralph? It would be monstrous."

"I see nothing monstrous in it, Gervaise. As I said just now, years have nothing to do with it, and, putting aside our friendship, I would rather serve under you than under many knights old enough to be your father. I don't know whether I shall have the luck to be one of the chosen, as Sir John said that there were to be only seven from each *langue*, which will make forty-nine—with yourself fifty. If I am chosen—and, knowing our friendship, I hope that the bailiff will let me go with you—it is likely enough I may be named your lieutenant, as I shall be the only one beside yourself who is a secular knight, and am, therefore, superior in rank to the rest."

"That would be pleasant indeed, Ralph, though I would rather that you had been made commander and I lieutenant; but at any rate, with you to support me, I shall feel less oppressed by the thought of my responsibility."

A KNIGHT OF THE WHITE CROSS

As Ralph had declared would be the case, the young knights in the other *auberges* were as anxious as those of England to be enrolled among the crew of the new galley, and the bailiffs had some trouble in choosing among the aspirants. Very few were selected outside the rank of professed knights, and as great pains were taken to comply with the grand master's wishes that only young knights of good conduct and disposition, and distinguished by their proficiency in warlike exercises, should be chosen, the crew was in every way a picked one. Most of them had made one or two of the three months' voyages in the galleys, though comparatively few had had the good fortune to be absolutely engaged with the Moslem pirates.

To the great satisfaction of himself and Gervaise, Ralph Harcourt was nominated lieutenant of the galley. The fact that so many had volunteered impressed all those who were chosen with the sense that it was at once an honour and a piece of good fortune to be selected, and all were determined that the boy-galley, as the elder knights laughingly termed it, should do honour to the Order.

It was a fortnight before she was launched. Gervaise had heard, with great satisfaction, that it had been decided by the council that no punishment should be inflicted upon the slaves for their share in the intended rising at St. Pelagius. All were guilty, and there was no means of saying who had taken prominent parts in the plot. The council felt that it was but natural that they should grasp at the prospect of freedom, for they themselves would have done the same had they been captives of the infidels. Even the warders and guards were allowed to go unpunished, although their offence was a much more serious one. Those who could have named the men who had accepted bribes were dead, and the lesson had been so severe a one that there was no probability of any again turning traitors. The author of the rising had been publicly executed. Seeing the hopelessness of denial, he had boldly avowed his share in the matter, and

184

had acknowledged that he was acting as agent for the sultan, and had been supplied with ample funds before leaving Constantinople.

He declared that he was absolutely unable to give any names whatever of those concerned in the plot, save those of the two overseers, as these had undertaken the work of suborning the warders and guards, though he admitted that he had on several occasions spoken to slaves as the gangs were on their way back to the prison, and had told them to be prepared to take part in a plan that was on foot for their rescue from slavery. The torture had not been, as was then the usual custom, applied to extort information; partly because his story was probable, still more because the grand master and council did not wish that more publicity should be given to the affair, and were glad that it should be allowed to drop without any further trial of the delinquents. In the city generally it was only known that a plot had been discovered for the liberation and escape of some of the slaves; and, outside the members of the Order, none were aware of its extent and dangerous character. To the satisfaction of Gervaise and Ralph, Vrados was able to produce letters and documents that satisfied the council that he had been deceived as to the character of the Greek, and was wholly innocent in the matter.

CHAPTER XII
THE BOY-GALLEY.

AMONG those most pleased at the appointment of Gervaise to the command of the galley was Sir John Boswell. Ever since the adventure with the pirates, the knight had exhibited an almost fatherly interest in him; had encouraged him in his studies, ridden with him on such occasions as he had permitted himself a short holiday, and had, whenever they were together, related to him stories of war, sieges, battles, and escapes, from which he thought the young knight might gain lessons for his future guidance.

"I doubt, Gervaise," he said one day, as they were riding quietly along the road, "whether our plan of life is altogether the best. We were founded, you know, simply as a body of monks, bound to devote ourselves solely to the care of the sick, and to give hospitality to pilgrims in Palestine. Now this was monkish work, and men who devoted themselves solely to such a life of charity as that in our Hospital at Jerusalem, might well renounce all human pleasures; but when the great change was made by Master Raymond du Puy, and from a nursing body we became a brotherhood-in-arms, it seems to me that the vows of celibacy were no longer needful or desirable. The crusaders were, many of them, married men, but they fought no worse for that. It would have been far better, methinks, had we been converted into an Order pledged to resist the infidel, but without the vows of poverty and of celibacy, which have never been seriously regarded.

"The garrison here might be composed, as indeed it is now, principally of young knights, of those who have not cared to marry, and of the officers of the Order whose wives

186

and families might dwell here with them. This would have many advantages. Among others, the presence of so many ladies of rank would have the excellent effect of discountenancing and repressing extravagances and dissolute habits, which are but too common, and are a shame to the Order. Knights possessing commanderies throughout Europe would be no worse stewards for being married men, and scandals, such as contributed largely to the downfall of the Templars, would be avoided.

"The sole vow necessary, so far as I can see, would be that knights should remain unmarried and disposable at all times for service until ten years after making their profession, and that afterwards they should ever be ready to obey the summons to arms, on occasions when the safety of Rhodes, or the invasion of any Christian country by the Moslems, rendered their services needful, when they would come out just as the knights of Richard the Lion-heart went out as crusaders. I have spent half my life since I joined the Order in commanderies at home, and a dull life it was, and I was glad enough to resign my last command and come out here. Had I been able to marry, I might now have had a son of your age, whose career I could watch and feel a pride in. My life would have been far happier in England, and in all respects I should be a better man than I am now. Methinks it would strengthen rather than weaken the Order. As a fighting body we should be in no way inferior to what we are now, and we should be more liked and more respected throughout Europe, for naturally the sight of so many men leading a luxurious life in commanderies causes a feeling against them."

"But I suppose, Sir John, that there is no great difficulty in obtaining a dispensation from our vows?"

"In this, as in all other matters, everything depends upon interest or money. Of course, dispensations are not common; but doubtless any knight when he had served his term of active service could, especially if his request were backed by the grand master, obtain from the Pope a dispensation of his vows. If he had a commandery it would make a vacancy, and give the grand prior, or the grand master, or the council, in whosoever's gift it might be, an opportunity of rewarding services or of gratifying some powerful family."

"I agree with you that it would have been much better, Sir John. I can understand that monks, ever living a quiet life apart from the world, should be content so to continue; but among a body of warlike knights there must be many who, in time, must come to regret the vows they took when boys. The cadet of a noble family might, by the death of elder brothers, come to be the head of a great family, the ruler over wide domains. Surely it would be desirable that such a man should be able to marry and have heirs."

"Doubtless it could be managed in such cases, Gervaise, but it is a pity that it should have to be managed. I can see no reason in the world why a knight, after doing ten years of service here, should not be free to marry, providing he takes a vow to render full service to the Order whenever called upon to do so. Already the vow of poverty is everywhere broken. Already, in defiance of their oaths, too many knights lead idle and dissolute lives. Already, knights, when in their own countries, disregard the rule that they shall draw sword in no cause save that of the Holy Sepulchre, and, like other knights and nobles, take part in civil strife or foreign wars. All this is a scandal, and it were better by far to do away with all oaths, save that of obedience and willingness to war with the infidel, than to make vows that all men know are constantly and shamelessly broken.

"I am fond of you, Gervaise. I am proud of you, as one who has brought honour to our *langue*, and who, in time, will bring more honour. I am glad that, so far as there can be between a young knight and one of middle age, there is a friendship between us. But see what greater pleasure it would give to my life were you my son, for whom I could lay by such funds as I could well spare, instead of spending all my appointments on myself, and having neither kith nor kin to give a sigh of regret when the news comes that I have fallen in some engagement with the infidels. I often think of all these things, and sometimes talk them over with comrades, and there are few who do not hold, with me, that it would be far better that we should become a purely military Order, like some of the military Orders in the courts of the European sovereigns, than remain as we are, half monk, half soldier—a mixture that, so far as I can see, accords but badly with either morality or public repute.

"However, I see no chance of such a change coming, and we must be content to observe our vows as well as may be, so long as we are willing to remain monks and try to obtain dispensation from our vows should we desire to alter our mode of life. We ought either to have remained monks pure and simple, spending our lives in deeds of charity, a life which suits many men, and against which I should be the last to say anything, or else soldiers pure and simple, as were the crusaders, who wrested the Holy Sepulchre from the hands of the infidels. At present, Gervaise, your vocation lies wholly in the way of fighting, but it may be that the time will come when you may have other aims and ambitions, and when the vows of the Order will gall you."

"I hope not, Sir John," Gervaise said earnestly.

"You are young yet," the knight replied, with an indulgent smile.

"Some day you may think differently. Now," he went on, changing the subject abruptly, "when will your galley be ready?"

"This is my last ride, Sir John. The shipwrights will have finished to-morrow, and the next day we shall take possession of her, and begin to practise, so that each man shall know his duties, and the galley-slaves learn to row well, before we have orders to sail. I wish you were going with us, Sir John."

"I should like it, lad, in many respects. It does one good to see the enthusiasm of young men, and doubtless you will be a merry party. But, on the other hand, unless I mistake, you will be undertaking wild adventures, and my time for these is well-nigh passed. When the Turk comes here, if he ever comes—and of that I have little doubt—I shall be ready to take my full share of the fighting; but I shall seek adventures no longer, and shall go no more to sea. Next only to the bailiff, I am the senior of our *auberge*, and—but this is between ourselves, lad—am like to succeed to the grand priory of England when it becomes vacant, and if not I shall, as the grand master has told me, have the offer of the next high office vacant in the palace."

Two days later Gervaise and his company of young knights went down to the port to take part in the launch of the new galley. This was the occasion of a solemn ceremony, the grand master and a large number of knights being present. A religious service first took place on her poop, and she was named by the grand master the *Santa Barbara*. When the ceremony was over, Gervaise was solemnly invested with the command of the galley by the grand marshal of the navy; then the shores were struck away, and the galley glided into the water, amid the firing of guns, the blowing of trumpets, and the cheers of the spectators who had gathered at the port to witness the ceremony.

The next morning a gang of galley-slaves were marched down. A third of these had been drawn from the crews of other galleys, their places being supplied by new hands. The remainder were taken from the men employed on the fortifications. Three weeks were occupied in teaching the rowers their work, and getting them well together. They were a fine crew, for the governor of St. Pelagius, grateful to Gervaise for the discovery of the plot, had ordered the overseers to pick out from the various gangs men specially suited by age and strength for the work.

The dye by this time had entirely worn off his face, and although his hair was still several shades darker than of old, it differed even more widely from the ebon hue that it had been when he was in prison. Thus, although he recognised three or four men upon the benches who had been fellow-occupants of his cell, he had no fear whatever of their detecting in the commander of the galley their late companion in misfortune.

THE BOY-GALLEY

Only a portion of the knights had been out each day while the crew were learning to row, as there was but little for them to learn. The galley carried no sails, and the knights were soldiers rather than sailors, and fought on the deck of their ship, as if defending a breach, or storming one held by the enemy. Moreover, as all of them had already made one or more voyages, they were accustomed to such duties as they would have to discharge on board.

All were glad when an order was published for the galley to sail. On the eve of departure Gervaise was sent for by the grand master. The general of the galleys was with him when Gervaise entered the room. The bailiff of Auvergne always held the position of grand marshal, and the bailiff of Italy that of second in command, with the title of grand admiral. These officials, however, as heads of their respective *langue*s, had many other duties to perform, and it was only on great occasions that they took any practical share in the work of which they were nominally heads. The real control in all naval questions rested with the general of the galleys, who was elected by the council, but on the nomination of the grand master.

His power when at sea with the fleet was absolute. He could suspend any officer from duty, and had unquestioned power of life and death over the crews. He had been frequently on board the galley since she had been launched, and had been pleased with the attention paid by Gervaise to his duties, and with the ready manner in which the young knights carried out his orders.

"Sir Gervaise Tresham," he said, "it is usual, as you know, to appoint each galley to a certain cruising ground, to which it is confined during its three months' absence. At present there is a galley on each of these stations, and as the last relief took place but a month since, it is better that they should remain at the stations allotted to them. I have therefore, after consultation with his Highness the grand master, decided to give you a free hand. You are as likely to meet with pirates in one quarter as in another, and you will pick up from vessels you may overhaul news of their doings, which will enable you to direct your course to the point where you will be most useful."

"In the first place, however, you will proceed to the coast of Tunis. Visconti's galley is already there, but the coast swarms with corsairs, and we have had many complaints as to their depredations. The Court of Spain has twice represented to us lately that the pirates have grown so bold that vessels have been carried off, even when coasting from one Spanish port to another. Visconti is specially watching the coast near Tunis, and you will therefore perhaps do better to proceed farther west, for every village from Tunis to Tangier is little better than a nest of pirates. I should imagine that you will find ample employment there during your three months' cruise. When I say that you are free to choose your own cruising ground, I do not mean that you should go up the Levant, or to the east of the Mediterranean, but that you are not bound to keep close along the African coast, but may, should you obtain any information to warrant your doing so, seek the pirates along the shores of Spain, Sardinia, Corsica, or Sicily.

"I need not warn you to act with prudence as well as courage, for you have proved that you possess both qualities. Do not allow yourself to be carried away by the impetuosity of your knights; it is more often the duty of a commander to restrain than to encourage his crew, and with such young blood as you have under your command the necessity will be greater than usual. Be kind to your slaves, but be ever watchful; yet this I need not tell you. Maintain a strict but not over-severe discipline. You are all knights and comrades of the Order, and equals when on shore, but on board you are the captain and they are your soldiers. I have this afternoon had a meeting of your knights, and have urged upon them very strongly that, having volunteered to serve under you, they must obey your orders as promptly and willingly as if you were the senior knight of the Order, and that it behoves them specially upon the present occasion, when the crew is composed entirely

of young knights, to show themselves worthy of the honour
that has been done to them by entrusting a galley of the
Order to their charge. I told them I should regard your
report of their individual conduct with the same attention
and respect with which I should that of any other
commander, and that they might greatly make or mar their
future prospects in the Order by their conduct during the
cruise. I am convinced, from what I know of you, that you
will exercise no undue harshness, but will act with tact and
discretion, as well as firmness."

"I will try to do so, your Excellency. I feel that it is a
heavy responsibility and will spare no pains to justify the
unmerited honour that has been bestowed upon me."

"You have seen that the taking in of stores is complete,
and that nothing is wanting for the voyage?"

"Yes, sir. I stood by while the overseer of stores checked
off every sack and barrel as it came on board. The water is
to be brought off this evening, and as I was unable to be
present, Sir Ralph Harcourt is there to count the barrels
and see that all are full."

"Good-bye, Sir Gervaise," the grand master said, as the
interview terminated.

"Hitherto you have given me, from the time you
reached the Island, naught but reason for satisfaction at
my nomination of you as page, and I have no fear that you
will fail this time. Remember that valour, however great,
cannot prevail against overpowering odds. You had a
lesson of that when you served under Ricord, though finally
the affair turned out well. I do not say, don't attempt
desperate undertakings, but don't attempt impossible ones.
Be careful of the lives of your knights. Remember that ere
long every sword may be of the utmost consequence in the
defence of Rhodes, and that even the capture of pirates
may be too dearly purchased; but that, at the same time,
the honour of the flag of the Order must be upheld at all
hazards. Ah!" he broke off, seeing a slight smile on the
young knight's face, "you think my orders contradictory?
It may be so; but you know what I mean, and I fear not that

you will blunder in carrying them out. Be prudent, and yet not over-prudent. I mean, be not rash, unless there are such benefits to be obtained as would justify great risk in obtaining them."

On returning to the *auberge*, Gervaise had a long chat with Ralph.

"I think the admiral's talk with us this afternoon had an excellent effect, Gervaise. I do not say that every one was not before disposed to obey you in all things, willingly and cheerfully; but he put it so strongly to them that they had volunteered specially for service in this galley, knowing well who was to be its commander, and the circumstance that the crew was to consist solely of young knights, and had therefore specially pledged their honour so to act that the enterprise should be in all respects a successful one. To render it so, obedience was even a greater necessity than valour. This was the most important of all the vows taken by the knights of the Order, and it was only by the strictest and most unquestioning obedience on the part of all to the orders of their superiors, that the work of a vast community could be carried on. Passing over the fact that you were their superior in rank, both as being a secular knight and a knight commander of the Order, you had been specially appointed by the grand master and council, as well as by himself, and that they bestowed upon you while at sea, and in the absence of any officers of superior rank, their full powers and authority. You were, in fact, their representative and agent, and therefore to be regarded with the same deference and respect that would be due to the oldest knight similarly placed. 'Lastly,' he said, in a less serious tone, 'you must remember that this is an experiment, and, as some think, a somewhat rash one. Never before did a galley, manned entirely from among the youngest of our knights, put to sea; and you may be sure that, unless successful, the experiment is not likely to be ever repeated. You have been selected from among many other candidates, and you have not only to justify the choice, but to uphold the reputation and honour of the young knights of your Order, by all of whom your doings will be regarded with special interest, as reflecting credit not only upon yourselves individually, but as representatives and champions of them all.'

"I could see that his words had a great effect. He had placed me beside him, and I marked their faces as he spoke. Each face lit up at his appeal, and I do not think there was one but silently registered a vow to do all in his power to prove himself worthy of the confidence placed in him and his companions by the grand master and admiral. I had before no shadow of fear that everything would not go well. I knew almost all of them personally, and if I myself had had the selection from among the whole body of knights in the convent, I could not have made a choice that would have suited me better. It seems to me that in each *auberge* the bailiff has endeavoured to pick out the seven young knights whom he considered would most worthily support the honour of the *langue*. Still, confident as I was before, I feel more so now, after the admiral's address to us."

"I had no fear either, Ralph, though doubtless the admiral's words will carry great weight with them. It was thoughtlessness rather than anything else that I dreaded; but now that the admiral himself has spoken to them, there is no fear that anything will occur to give us trouble. I have particularly noticed that when we have been on board, and have been laughing and chatting together before we got under way, their manner changed directly the first order was given, and that all the commands were carried out with as much goodwill and alacrity as if they were under Ricord himself."

On the following morning the knights all went on board the *Santa Barbara*. Their baggage was carried down by slaves, and by the personal servants from each *auberge* who were to go as their attendants during the voyage. The grand master had advanced Gervaise a sum equal to half a year's income of his commandery, and with this he had purchased a stock of the best wines, and various other luxuries, to supplement the rations supplied from the funds of the Order to knights when at sea. Gervaise had to go round early to the admiral to sign the receipt for stores and to receive his final orders in writing. All were, therefore, on board before him and, when he arrived, were drawn up in military order to receive him.

Every knight was in full armour, and as, at a word from Ralph, they drew their swords and saluted the young commander, Gervaise felt with a thrill of pleasure and of confidence that with such a following he need not fear any encounter with a pirate force, unless in overwhelming numbers.

The young knights were all, with the exception only of Ralph Harcourt, between the ages of seventeen and nineteen, and their young faces, free in most cases even from the suspicion of a moustache, looked almost those of boys. But there was no mistaking the ardour and enthusiasm in their faces, and the lack of breadth and weight, that years alone would give to them, was compensated by skill in their weapons, acquired by long and severe training, and by the activity and tireless energy of youth.

"Knights and comrades," Gervaise said as, after walking through the double line to the end of the poop he turned and faced them, " I am proud indeed to command so gallant a body of knights. The success of our expedition depends upon you rather than upon me, and as I feel assured of your warm co-operation I have no fear as to what the result will be, if Dame Fortune will but favour us by throwing in our way some of those scourges of the sea in search of whom we are about to set out. Many of us have already encountered them, and, fighting side by side with older knights, have borne our share of the work, while those who have not done so will, I am sure, do equally well when the opportunity arrives. We shall not this voyage have the encouragement and confidence inspired by the presence of those who have long and valiantly borne the standard of the Order; but, on the other hand, we have to show that we are worthy of the confidence reposed in us, and that the young knights of the Order can be trusted to emulate the deeds of those who have rendered the name of the Hospitallers a terror to the infidel."

A shout of approbation greeted the close of his address. Gervaise then walked forward to the end of the poop, and looked down upon the slaves, who, with their oars out, were awaiting the order to row.

"Men," he said in Turkish, "it is my desire that, while it is necessary that you should do your work, your lot shall be no heavier than can be avoided. You will not be taxed beyond your powers, save when the enemy is in sight, or there is supreme need for haste, but then you must be called upon for your utmost exertions. I wish your work to be willing. I abhor the use of the lash, and so long as each man does his fair quota of work, I have given the strictest orders that it shall never be used. I have, at my own cost, made provision that your daily rations shall be improved while under my command. Meat will be served out to you daily, when it can be obtained, and for those of you who hold that the strict tenets of your religion may be relaxed while engaged in such severe labour, a ration of wine will also be served out; and such other indulgences as are compatible with the discipline and safety of the ship, will also be granted to you."

There was a murmur of gratitude among the slaves. Gervaise then gave the order to row, and the galley started on her voyage. The knights had now fallen out from their ranks, and were soon laughing and talking gaily. Being all of noble families and knightly rank, there was, except when on actual duty, a tone of perfect equality and good fellowship prevailing among them. French was the common language, for as the Order was of French foundation, and three of the seven *langue*s belonged to that country, most of the high dignitaries being chosen from their ranks, it was natural that the French language should be the general medium of communication between them.

A KNIGHT OF THE WHITE CROSS

Until noon the slaves rowed steadily and well. Work was then stopped, for there was scarce a breath of wind stirring the water. Even under the awning that had, as the sun gained power, been erected over the poop, the heat was oppressive. The knights had all divested themselves of their armour, and most of them retired below for a siesta. As soon as the slaves stopped rowing, an awning, which Gervaise had purchased, and which was rolled up under the break of the poop, was, to their astonishment, drawn over them.

"Don't you think you are spoiling your slaves, Sir Gervaise?" one of the Spanish knights asked doubtfully.

"On the contrary, Sir Pedro, I hope that I am improving them. You have not worked as a galley-slave, but I have, and I can assure you that I used to feel the hours when we were lying broiling in the sun, doing nothing, much more trying than those during which I was at work. I used to be quite giddy and sick with the heat, and on getting out the oars again had scarce strength to work them. But this is not the most important point. In port the slaves always sleep in the prison, but at sea they must rest on their benches; and to do so with clothes soaked with the heavy dew must be a severe trial, and most prejudicial to the health. The awning cost but a few ducats, and I reckon that, putting aside the comfort to the slaves, it will be very speedily repaid by their better health and capacity for labour. When away in the galley with Sir Louis Ricord, I used to feel the greatest pity for the unfortunate wretches when at daybreak, in their drenched clothes, and shivering with cold and wet, they rose to commence their work. I then took a vow that if ever I should come to command a galley I would provide an awning for the slaves."

Two or three of the knights standing by expressed their warm approval of what Gervaise said. There was, in those days, but little of that sentiment of humanity that is now prevalent, and slaves were everywhere regarded as mere beasts of burden rather than as human beings. When, however, they had the question put to them, as Gervaise had done, they were ready to give a hearty agreement, although it was the utilitarian rather than the humanitarian side of the question that recommended it to them. After three hours' rest the journey was renewed, and just at nightfall the galley anchored off an islet lying to the north of Carpathos.

While the servants were laying the tables along the poop for the evening meal, Gervaise went down to see that his orders were carried out regarding the food for the slaves. They were already eating their bread and meat with an air of satisfaction that showed how warmly they appreciated the unusual indulgence, while there were few indeed who did not hold up their drinking horns as a servant passed along between the benches with a skin of wine. Gervaise spoke to many of them.

"Ah, my lord," one of them said, "if we were always treated like this, slavery would be endurable. For ten years have I rowed in Christian galleys, but never before has an awning been spread to keep off the sun or the dew. We shall not forget your kindness, my lord, and will row our hardest right cheerfully when you call upon us for an effort."

There was a murmur of assent from the galley-slaves around.

"May Allah be merciful to you, as you are merciful to us!" another slave exclaimed. "The blessing of those whom you regard as infidels can at least do you no harm."

"On the contrary, it can do me good," Gervaise said. "The God you Moslems and we Christians worship is, I believe, the same, though under another name."

Gervaise had, indeed, during his long conversations with Suleiman Ali, often discussed with him the matter of his faith, and had come, in consequence, to regard it in a very different light to that in which it was viewed by his companions. There was faith in one God at the bottom of both Mohammedanism and Christianity. The Mohammedans held in reverence the lawgivers and prophets of the Old Testament, and even regarded Christ Himself as being a prophet. They had been grievously led away by

Mahomet, whom Gervaise regarded as a false teacher; but as he had seen innumerable instances of the fidelity of the Moslems to their creed, and the punctuality and devotion with which the slaves said their daily prayers, exposed though they were to the scorn and even the anger of their taskmasters, he had quite lost, during his nine months of constant association with Suleiman Ali, the bigoted hatred of Mohammedanism so universal at the time. He regarded Moslems as foes to be opposed to the death; but he felt that it was unfair to hate them for being hostile to Christianity, of which they knew nothing.

CHAPTER XIII
THE FIRST PRIZES

AFTER leaving the slaves, Gervaise joined his companions on the poop. They were engaged in an animated discussion as to whether it was advisable to grant indulgences to slaves. The majority approved of the steps Gervaise had taken, but some asserted that these concessions would only lead them to look for more, and would create discontent among the crews of other galleys not so favoured.

"Well, comrades," said Gervaise, "I think that so far I am better qualified than any of you to give an opinion; but it may be that it will fall to the lot of some of you to be a slave in Turkish hands. In that case, I can affirm with certainty, that you will keenly appreciate any alleviation, however small, of your lot. You must remember that the one feeling of the slave is dull despair. Death is the only relief he has to look forward to. Do you think that a man so feeling can do his best, either at an oar or at any other kind of work? I am sure it would not be so in my case. But if you brighten his life a little, and show him that he is not regarded as merely a brute beast, and that you take some interest in him, he will work in a different spirit. Even viewed from a merely monetary point of view it must pay well to render him as content as possible with his lot. You know how great is the mortality among the slaves—how they pine away and die from no material malady that can be detected, but simply from hopelessness and weariness of life, aided, undoubtedly, in the case of the galley-slaves, by sleeping in the damp night air after an exposure all day to the full heat of the sun. This brings an answer to your second objection. Undoubtedly it might cause discontent among the slaves of other galleys when they hear that others are treated better than themselves. But I hope that if, on our return, we bring back all our slaves in good condition and health, the contrast between their appearance and that of the slaves in most other galleys will be so marked that the admiral may consider it would be well to order awnings to be fixed to all the vessels of the Order, and even to grant to all slaves, when away on voyages, the little indulgences I have given them here. The expense would be very trifling, and it would certainly add a great deal to the average life of a slave, and would render him capable of better work. There is another advantage. If the Turks learn that their countrymen in our hands are treated with a certain amount of kindness and consideration, it might lead them to act similarly to those of our Order who may be unfortunate enough to fall into their hands."

"There is a great deal in what you say, Sir Gervaise," one of the knights, who had before taken the opposite point of view, said. "There is no reason why our galley should not be a model one, and though, like enough, the seniors will laugh at our making innovations, D'Aubusson is a reformer, and will certainly support anything that he sees to be beneficial, from whatever quarter it comes."

Supper was now served, and the young knights were well pleased with the entertainment provided for them. It was the principal meal of the day. Their fast was broken by a glass of wine, a manchet of bread, and fruit soon after rising. At eleven o'clock they sat down to a more substantial meal; but in that climate the heat was at that hour considerable, and as there were duties to be performed, there was no sitting long at table. At supper the day's work was over, their appetite was sharpened by the cool evening breeze, and the meal was hearty and prolonged. After it was concluded, several of the knights brought up from below viols and other instruments of music; for the ability to accompany the voice with such an instrument was considered an essential part of the education of a knight.

For some hours the songs and romances, so popular at the time, were sung in the various languages represented on board; then the knights, one by one, went down to their sleeping places, until only the seven knights of the *langue* of Auvergne, who were to watch the first night, remained on deck. Five of these wrapped themselves in their mantles and lay down on the benches. One of the others descended to the waist, walked along the plank between the lines of sleeping slaves, and took up his place in the bow, while the other paced up and down the poop, the fall of his footsteps being the only sound to break the silence that reigned throughout the ship.

In the morning, as soon as the knights had all taken a plunge in the sea, the oars were got out, and the galley proceeded on her way. Passing through the islands and skirting the southern shore of Greece, she continued her course west. Malta was sighted, but they did not put in there. Pantellaria was passed, and in a fortnight after leaving Rhodes, Cape Bon, at the entrance to the bay of Tunis, was sighted. Until Greece was left behind them, the nights had generally been spent in small ports, where supplies of fresh meat, fish, and fruit, were obtainable. So far no incident had marked the voyage. The weather had continued fine, and they had heard nothing, from ships they had fallen in with, of any Moslem pirates having been seen. A few hours, however, after sighting the coast of Africa, a dark object was seen ahead.

"It is a ship of some sort," Ralph said; "but her masts have gone. It may be that she is a merchantman that has been captured and sacked by the Moorish pirates."

Orders were given to the rowers to quicken their pace, and in little over an hour they were alongside the hull. As soon as the vessels were close enough for those on the poop of the galley to look down on to the deck of the other craft, it was seen that Ralph's suppositions were correct. Two bodies lay stretched upon it. One was crushed under the fallen mast; the other lay huddled up in a heap, a cannon-ball having almost torn him asunder. The knights leapt on to the deck as soon as the galley ran alongside. Gervaise made first for the man lying beneath the mast; as he came up to him, the sailor opened his eyes and murmured, "Water!" Gervaise called out to one of the servants to bring water from the galley, and, as soon as it came, poured some between the man's lips, and the knights by their united efforts lifted the mast from across his body. It was evident, however, that he had but a short time to live, and the dew of death was on his face. After a few minutes he rallied a little, and looked gratefully at his rescuers.

"You have been attacked by pirates," Gervaise said. "Was there one galley, or two?"

"Three galleys," the man replied in a faint whisper.

"Do you know where they were from?"

"Tripoli."

"How long ago?"

"It was about three hours after sunrise when we saw them coming up," the man said, his voice gaining in strength, as some wine they gave him took effect. "It was useless to fight, and I hauled down our flag, but in spite of that one of the pirates fired a broadside, and one of the shot hit the mast and brought it down, and I was crushed under it. They boarded us, took off all the crew as captives, and emptied the hold; I knew that I was done for, and begged them to kill me; but they paid no attention. I know a little of their language, and as I lay there I caught something of what they were saying; they are bound for the Island of Sardinia, where they have a rendezvous, and are to join a great gathering of their consorts. I don't know the name of the place, but it is on the east coast. More water!"

Gervaise knelt to pour some water between his lips, when he gave a sudden cry, a shudder ran through his frame, and he was dead.

"Let us return on board, gentlemen," Gervaise said, rising to his feet. "We can do nothing here."

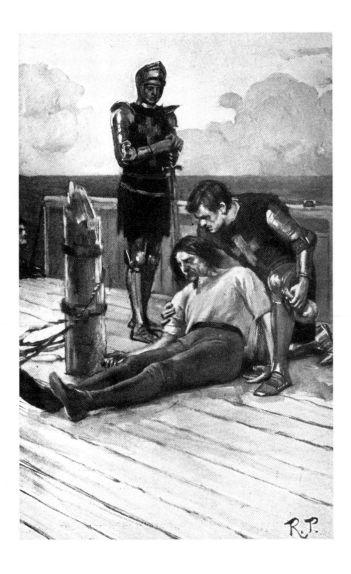

"You have been attacked by pirates," Gervaise said.

As soon as he regained the deck of the galley, he signed to Ralph to follow him below.

"Now, Ralph," he said, "this is one of those cases in which we have to decide whether we ought or ought not to be prudent. From what that poor fellow said, the pirates have about five hours' start of us, and as they can have no idea that they are pursued, we can doubtless overtake them before they reach Sardinia. The question is, ought we to pursue them at once, or ought we to coast along until we find Visconti's galley? Three of these Tripoli pirates, crowded as they always are with men, would prove serious opponents, yet we might engage them with a fair hope of victory. But we may be seriously disabled in the fight, and should be, perhaps, unable to carry the news to Genoa that there are many pirate ships gathering on the coast of Sardinia to prey upon their commerce."

"We might be days, or even weeks, before we light upon Visconti's galley, Gervaise, and even when we found it, he might not consider himself justified in leaving the coast where he is stationed. Besides, while we are spending our time looking for him, the pirates will be committing terrible depredations. It must be a big expedition, under some notorious pirate, or they would never venture so far north."

"Then you think that I should be justified in pursuing them alone. It is a fearful responsibility to have to decide."

"I think so, Gervaise. There is no saying what misfortunes might happen if we did not venture to do so."

"Very well then, so be it. But before deciding finally on so grave a matter, I will lay it before the company."

"There is no doubt as to what their decision will be," Ralph said, with a smile.

"Perhaps not, Ralph; but as they will be called upon to risk their lives in a dangerous enterprise, it is as well that they should have a say in the matter."

When they returned on to the poop, there was an expression of eagerness and excitement on the faces of the young knights which showed how anxiously they had been awaiting the result of the conference below. Gervaise stepped on to a bench, and motioned to them to close up round him.

"Comrades," he said, "although the responsibility of whatever course may be taken must rest upon my shoulders, yet I think it but right that, as a general before a battle often calls a council of war to assist him with its advice, so I should lay before you the two courses open to us, and ask your opinion upon them. Sir Ralph Harcourt and I are of one mind in the matter, but as the decision is a grave one we should be loth to act upon it without your concurrence." He then repeated the alternatives as he had laid them before Ralph. "Now," he went on, "as you see, there is grave danger, and much risk in the one course; but if successful its advantages are obvious. On the other hand, the second plan is more sure, more prudent, and more in accordance with the instructions I have received. I ask you to let me know frankly your opinion on the subject. If your view agrees with ours, although it will not relieve me from the responsibility of deciding, it will at least, in the event of things turning out badly, be a satisfaction to know that the course had your approval, and that it was your desire, as well as ours, that we should undertake it. First, then, let all who are in favour of following the pirates go to the starboard side of the deck, while those who are in favour of joining Visconti, and laying this serious matter we have discovered before him, move to the larboard side."

There was a rush of the knights to the right, and not one moved to the other side.

"Your decision is the same as ours," Gervaise said. "To the north, then! If there is great peril in the adventure, there is also great honour to be gained."

The knights gave a shout of satisfaction at finding that their choice was also that of the officers.

"Lay her head to the north," Gervaise said to the pilot. Then he went to the end of the poop, and ordered the slaves to row on. "Row a long, steady stroke, such as you can maintain for many hours. We have a long journey before us, and there is need for haste. Now is the time for willing work."

The oars dipped into the water, and the galley was soon moving along at a much faster pace than that at which they had performed the journey from Rhodes. The slaves had not, from their benches, been able to see what had passed on board the dismantled vessel, but from the order and the change of course, they had no doubt that the knights had obtained some clue to the direction taken by the corsairs who had captured and sacked the ship.

"There is but little wind," Gervaise said to Ralph, "and their sails will be of slight use to them; therefore we shall go fully three feet to their two. It is quite possible that we may not catch sight of them, for we cannot tell exactly the course they will take. We shall steer for Cape Carbonara, which is some hundred and thirty miles distant. If we do not see them by the time we get there, we shall be sure that we have passed them on the way, unless, indeed, a strong wind should spring up from the south. However, I hope that we shall catch sight of them before that, for we shall be able from our look-out to discover their masts and sails some eight or ten miles away, while they will not be able to see us until we are within half that distance. They cannot be more than twenty miles away now, for the light breeze will aid them but little, and as they will see no occasion for haste, they will not be rowing at their full power, with so long a passage before them."

Already, indeed, one of the knights had perched himself on the seat at the top of a low mast some fifteen feet above the poop, that served as a look-out.

"You can see nothing yet, I suppose, Cairoli?"

"No; the line of sea is clear all round."

It was indeed some four hours before the knight on the look-out cried that he could make out three dark specks on the horizon. Gervaise at once ascended to the look-out, by the ladder that was fixed against the post.

THE FIRST PRIZES

"They are making to the left of the course we are taking. Turn her head rather more to the west. That will do. They are directly ahead now." He then came down to the deck again. "I would that we had seven or eight more hours of daylight, Ralph, instead of but three at the outside. However, as we know the course they are taking, we are not likely to miss them, for as we shall not be near enough for them to make us out before the sun sets, there will be no chance of their changing it. Do you think they will row all night?"

"I should not think so. If the land were nearer they might keep on until they make it, but as they have had no wind since daylight, they will lie on their oars until morning. You see, at sunset they will still be some eighty miles from Cape Carbonara, and the slaves could not possibly row that distance without rest; so that if we keep on we may take them by surprise."

"That is what I have been thinking, Ralph, but it would be well not to attack them until nearly daybreak. We should capture one galley easily enough; but the others, being ignorant of our force, might make off in different directions, and we might lose both of them. If, on the other hand, we could fall upon them a short time before daylight, we should be able to keep them in sight, and, even if they separated, they would soon come together and continue their course, or, as I hope, when they see that we are alone, bear up and fight us. I think that our best plan will be to row on until it is dark, then give the slaves six hours' rest, and after that go on quietly. If we can make them out, which we may do if they have lights on board, we will stop, and wait until it is the hour to attack them. If we miss them, we will row on to Sardinia and lie up, as we proposed, until they come along."

"I think that will be a very good plan, Gervaise."

Before sunset the three pirate ships could be clearly made out from the deck, but the pilot judged them to be fully ten miles away. Half an hour later the slaves were told to cease rowing. Gervaise had ordered the cooks to prepare them a good meal, and this was at once served, together with a full ration of wine. As soon as they had consumed it, they were told to lie down and sleep, as at one o'clock the galley would be again under way.

The knights' supper was served below, as lights on the poop might be made out, should a look-out be placed by the corsairs in their tops.

"We had better follow the example of the galley-slaves," Gervaise said, rising as soon as the meal was finished, "and, with the exception of Spain, who is on watch, turn in to sleep till we are off again. All of you will, of course, don your armour on rising."

At the appointed hour the galley was again under way. There was not a breath of air, and before starting, pieces of cloth were wrapped round the oars at the rowlocks to deaden the sound, which might otherwise have been heard at a considerable distance on so still a night. After an hour and a half's rowing, the knight on the look-out said that he could see a light some distance ahead. The pilot, an experienced old sailor, joined him, and speedily descended to the poop again.

"It is a ship's light," he said. "I should say that it was a lantern on board the ship of the captain of the expedition, and is shown to enable the other two to keep near him. I cannot say how far it is away, for I do not know at what height it hangs above the water; but I should imagine, from the feebleness of the light, that it must be some two miles distant."

As soon as the light had been noticed, the slaves had been ordered to cease rowing, and they were now told that they would not be required again for fully two hours. When the first gleam of dawn appeared in the east they were called to their work again. The lantern was still burning, and, in a quarter of an hour, the knights on the poop were able, in the broadening light, to make out three shadowy forms some two miles ahead of them. They decreased this distance by more than half before they could discern any signs of life or motion on board. Then a sudden stir was apparent; they could hear shouts from one vessel to another, oars were thrust out, and an effort made to get the heads of the ships in the same direction, so as to catch the light breeze that had just sprung up.

The moment he saw that the galley was discovered, Gervaise shouted down to the slaves to row their hardest, and told the pilot to steer for the ship farthest to the east. She was some four or five hundred yards from her nearest consort, and the same distance separated that vessel from the third craft.

"We shall have time to carry her, Ralph, before the others come to her assistance, and they will only arrive one at a time. If we were to lie alongside the middle craft, which is probably that of the chief, as it is she that has the light burning, we might have the other two upon us before we had done with her, for she is evidently the largest, and most likely the strongest handed, of them."

The leader of the pirates evidently saw that there was no chance of evading the fight. A flag was run up to the masthead of his ship, and the three vessels began to endeavour to turn, so as to meet the galley. The operation, however, took some time. In the confusion, orders were misunderstood, and instead of all the slaves on one side rowing whilst those on the other side backed, all order was lost, and long before the craft for which the galley was making had got round, the latter was upon her.

"Shall I ram her, Sir Gervaise?" the pilot asked.

"No; we might damage ourselves; besides, I do not want to sink her. Sheer away the oars on one side!"

The galley carried eight guns—three on each side of the poop, and two forward; and these had been loaded with small pieces of iron. A few shots had been fired by the pirates, but, owing to the confusion that prevailed on board, the guns were discharged so hurriedly that the shot either flew overhead or passed wide of the galley. Excited as the young knights were, and eager for the fray, a general laugh broke out as the galley swept along by the pirate-ship, breaking many of her oars, and hurling all the slaves who manned them backwards off their benches. A moment later the guns poured their iron contents among the pirates who clustered thickly on the forecastle and poop, and as the vessels grated together the knights sprang on board the corsair.

The members of the English *langue* had each been provided with short pieces of rope, and before joining their companions in the fray they lashed the vessels together, side by side. The fight was a very short one. France and Auvergne, led by Ralph Harcourt, boarded at the bow, the other five *langue*s at the poop; and so impetuous was their onset that the pirates, who had still scarce recovered from their surprise at being hastily aroused from sleep to repel the attack of the foe who had so suddenly sprung out from the darkness upon them, offered but a feeble resistance. Many threw themselves overboard, and swam to the ship nearest to them; others were cut down; and the rest flung away their arms, and cried for quarter.

All who did so were, without the loss of a minute's time, thrown down into the hold of their ship, and the hatches secured over them. It had before been arranged that Ralph should take the command of the corsair, having with him France, Auvergne, and Germany. As soon, therefore, as the captives were fastened below, Gervaise called the knights of the other four *langue*s back to the deck of the galley. The lashings were cast off, she was pushed from the side of the prize, and the oars were got out. There was no time to be lost, for the largest of the three pirate-ships, which had, directly it was seen that her consort was captured, poured two heavy broadsides into the prize, was now approaching—rowing but slowly, however, for the third vessel to come up.

She was but a hundred yards away when the galley swept round the bow of the prize and advanced to meet her. As she did so, Ralph discharged the eight guns of the prize, which he had at once re-loaded, into the bow of the corsair, the shot raking the crowded deck from end to end. When but a few yards distant, the two bow guns of the galley poured in a shower of missiles, and a moment later she ran alongside the pirate, the poop guns, as before, preparing the way for the boarders. But no sooner had they leapt on deck than they were met by the pirates, headed by their captain.

Gervaise had specially charged the knights not to allow themselves to be carried away by their ardour. "We are sure to be greatly outnumbered, and, when we first spring on board, we must cut our way across the deck, and then form ourselves in a double or treble line across it, and, so fighting, gradually force them before us."

This, in spite of the efforts of the pirates, was accomplished, and, once formed, the corsairs strove in vain to break through the wall of steel. For a time, however, no forward movement could be made, so furious were the attacks upon them, led by the pirate chief. Several times breaches were made in the front rank, but the knights behind each time bore back the assault, and restored the line. The knights had won their way half along the poop when a yell of exultation rose from the corsairs as the third of their vessels rowed up on the other side of the galley, and her crew sprang on board it. Gervaise called the knights of the second line from their places, and ranged them along the bulwark, to prevent the Moors from boarding from the poop of the galley.

Then for a moment he looked round. The prize was creeping up, and was a length or two away, coming up alongside. Its approach was also noticed by the pirates, who, with wild shouts, flung themselves upon their opponents. Gervaise sprang forward to take the place of a young Italian knight, who staggered back, with his helmet cleft by a heavy blow from the keen yataghan of the pirate captain. The corsair, shouting his war-cry of "Allah!" sprang with the bound of a wild cat upon Gervaise; his weapon descended on his uplifted guard, and shore right through the stout blade. With a shout of triumph, the corsair raised his arm to repeat the blow; but Gervaise in turn sprang forward, and struck with all his force with the pummel of his sword on the forehead of his opponent. The latter fell as if shot, his weapon dropping from his hand beside him.

Dismayed at the fall of their leader, his followers recoiled for a moment. Another tall pirate sprang forward to take his place, and, shouting to them to follow, was about to throw himself upon Gervaise, when a gun crashed out close alongside. A storm of iron swept away the front line of Moors, and the shout of "St. John!" "St. John!" rose above the din. It was one of the bow guns of the prize, and as she swept along gun after gun poured its contents among the pirates.

"Do you clear the galley, Ralph. We can manage here now," Gervaise said, as Ralph leapt on board. The latter, followed by his party of knights, rushed across the poop, and sprang on to the galley among the pirates, who had been striving in vain to break through the line of defenders. Gervaise called to his party to follow him, and, taking the offensive, fell upon the remnant of the corsairs who still held the forward end of the poop.

The discharge of the cannon at such close quarters had wrought terrible havoc among them, and the pirates, with but slight resistance, turned, and either ran down the ladder or leapt into the water. The knights followed them forward among the benches of the rowers, who cheered loudly in many tongues as they passed them. At the forecastle the Moors made another stand, but the knights forced their way up, and in two minutes all was over.

"Now to the aid of our comrades!" Gervaise shouted, as the last of the corsairs was struck down.

Ralph's party had indeed cleared the poop of the galley, but they in vain endeavoured to climb up on to that of the third pirate-ship, whose superior height gave a great advantage to its defenders. Gervaise leapt down on to the bow of the galley, followed by the knights, and then ran aft until he could climb into the waist of the pirate. So intent were the corsairs upon defending the poop that they did not see what was going on elsewhere, and Gervaise had obtained a fair footing before he was noticed. Then a number of men ran down and attacked his party. But it was too late, for the whole of the knights had, by this time, leaped on board. Their assailants were forced back, and, pressing close upon them, the knights gained the poop before the main body of the pirates were aware of their coming.

Warned by the shouts and shrieks of their comrades that they had been taken in the rear, the Moslems who were defending the side of the poop wavered for a moment. Ralph took advantage of their hesitation, and sprang on board, his companions pouring in after him. There was a stern and desperate fight. The Moslems fought with the fury of despair, disdaining to ask or accept quarter. A few leapt overboard, preferring death by drowning to that by the swords of the Christians; but the great majority died fighting to the last. A shout of triumph rose from the knights as the last of the Moslems fell.

The first impulse of all of them was to take off their helmets in order to breathe the fresh air, and for a while they all stood panting from their exertions.

"Nobly and gallantly done, comrades!" Gervaise exclaimed. "This is indeed a victory of which we have all a right to be proud. Now, the first thing is to free the slaves of their shackles; there are many white faces among them. Let our *langue* look after the wounded, while the released captives clear the decks of the bodies of the fallen pirates."

It took an hour's hard work to knock off the chains of the slaves. The greater portion of them were Christians— Greeks, Italians, Spaniards, and French, who had been captured in various raids by the corsairs; and among them were the crew of the ship that had been overhauled by the galley on the previous day. Besides these, there were a few Moslems who had been sentenced to labour in the galleys for various crimes.

Among the Christians, the joy at their liberation was intense. Some laughed, some cried, others were too overcome to speak coherently. Among the rest were found, to the intense pleasure of their rescuers, three knights of the Order who had for years been missing. They had been taken prisoners on an island at which the galley to which they belonged had touched. Many of the knights had landed, and three of them, all belonging to the *langue* of Italy, had wandered away from the rest, and had not returned. A search had been made for them, and it was discovered that a struggle had taken place. As there were no marks of blood, it was supposed that they were suddenly pounced upon by a party of hidden marauders, who had been watching them from some hiding-place, and had thrown themselves upon the knights before they had had time to draw their swords. Following the trail by bushes broken down, and plants crushed under foot, it was found to lead to a creek on the other side of the island. Here there were signs that a craft had been anchored, as there were the ashes of fires, fragments of food, and other matters, scattered about on the shore. Hours had passed before the knights had been missed, and therefore the craft in which they had been carried off was long out of sight. Letters were written by the grand master to the Pasha of Syria, to the Emperor of Egypt, and to the Bey of Tunis, offering to ransom the knights, but all replied that they were unaware of any such captives having been landed.

An attempt had then been made to ascertain whether they had been carried to Tripoli; but the bey had little authority over the various tribesmen along the coast, and only replied that no such captives had been sold in the city. Thus all hope of ransoming them had died away, and their names were inscribed in the list of those who had fallen into the hands of the infidels, but of whose subsequent fate no clue could be obtained.

All were greatly emaciated, and their faces showed signs of the sufferings they had undergone. The young knights were all familiar with their names, but personally none had known them, for they had been carried off two or three months before Gervaise and Ralph Harcourt had arrived at Rhodes.

THE FIRST PRIZES

All three had struggled desperately to break their chains while the fight was going on, and had, as soon as the contest was decided, risen to their feet and shouted the battle-cry of the Order; then, overcome by their emotions, they sank down upon their benches, and remained as if in a stupor until the knights, who had hurried first to them, struck off their fetters. Then the three men grasped each other's hands, while tears streamed down their cheeks.

"It is no dream, comrades," one of them said, in a hoarse voice. "We are free again. Let us first return thanks to God for our release, and then we can thank these our brothers."

The three knights knelt at the benches where they had toiled and suffered, and hid their faces in their hands. No sounds came from their lips, but their stifled sobs and the heaving of their naked shoulders, seamed and scarred by the strokes of their taskmasters' whips, told the young knights, who stood unhelmeted and silent around, how deep was their emotion. Then they rose.

"I am Fabricius Caretto," one said; "this is Giacomo Da Vinci; this Pietro Forzi: all knight commanders of the Order, and now for six years prisoners in the hands of these corsairs. Assuredly no one would know us, so changed are we." He looked round inquiringly for a familiar face. "Your commander must surely be a comrade of ours?"

"We know all your names," Gervaise said, coming forward, "though none of us reached the convent until after your capture. I have the honour to command this galley. My name is Gervaise Tresham, and I have for my lieutenant Sir Ralph Harcourt. All of us, glad as we are at the capture we have effected of these three corsairs, are still more pleased that we should have been the means of rescuing three noble knights of our Order from captivity. Now, I pray you first of all to accompany me on board the galley, where we will do all we can to make you forget the sufferings you have gone through. After you have bathed, and re-clad yourselves, I will present to you the knights my

The three knights of the Cross give thanks for their release.

comrades, amongst whom are seven of your own *langue*. Three of these I will tell off to see to your comfort, for, as you will understand, I have my hands full indeed at present."

"First, before all things, Sir Knight, let me express to you all our deep gratitude and our admiration of the gallant deed that you have accomplished in thus, single-handed, capturing three vessels belonging to the fiercest and most dreaded of the corsairs of Tripoli. God bless you all, sirs"— and his voice broke again—"for the deed you have done, and for bringing us out of this living hell!"

Gervaise called to three of the Italian knights, and, followed by them and the released captives, led the way to the galley. Here he left them in charge of their countrymen. "Give them each a draught of old Cyprus, and something to eat," he said aside to one of the knights; "they sorely need refreshment before aught else, for, as you see, they are well-nigh dazed with this unlooked-for change. I will put out clothes enough for one of them; the others you must supply for the present from your stores. Now I must be off."

There was indeed much to be done. Four of the knights were told off to attend upon the most urgent cases among their own wounded. Only two of their number had been killed outright, but there were four serious cases among the wounded, while eight or ten others had received wounds that required bandaging and attending to. As fast as the slaves' fetters were struck off, food and wine were given to them, together with such garments as could be found at the moment. Then the bodies of the fallen pirates were thrown overboard, while the wounded were attended to, and the released Christians were divided equally between the three prizes. To each of these the knights of one of the *langue*s were told off, the seniors being appointed to the command. There were in all some ninety Christian captives on board the three ships. Thus each vessel had a complement of seven knights and thirty Christians, and to these were added ten of the thirty Moslems found at the oars, and fifteen of the pirates to whom quarter had been given.

It was past noon before all these arrangements had been made, and during the time so occupied, the ships lay idly side by side, drifting slowly before the wind, the sails having been lowered as soon as the struggle was over. Up to this time, the knights had been too busily engaged to think of food, but they were right glad when they were summoned to a meal on board the galley.

Gervaise found the three knights in the cabin, dressed in the usual attire of the Order. They presented a very different appearance, indeed, to that which they wore when he had first seen them. They had bathed, and combed their matted hair, which was alone sufficient to transform them, but the feeling that they were once more free men, and knights of an honoured Order, had done even more to effect the change; and although they looked thin and worn, the martial bearing had come back naturally as they donned their knightly robes and buckled on swords.

"I am glad to see that you are better," Gervaise said, as he went up to greet them. "Twenty years seem to have dropped off your shoulders since this morning."

"We are not the same men, Sir Gervaise. We were slaves, and are now free. We were Christian dogs; now we are Christian knights. We were subject to scoffs and blows; now, thank God, we have swords to strike with, and though as yet our arms may not have regained their full strength, we could at least bear a share in a fray. Our comrades have been telling us somewhat of how this wonderful thing has come about, and have been explaining what at first filled us with surprise, that a galley should be manned solely by young knights, of whom their commander is one of the youngest. We can testify, at least, that had the grand master been himself in command, and his crew composed of veteran knights, he could have done no better."

THE FIRST PRIZES

"We were fortunate in taking them so much by surprise that the first of their ships fell into our hands before her consorts could come to her assistance; and her guns did us good service in our struggle with the others."

"The matter was well arranged, as well as gallantly fought," one of the other knights said. "Had you first fallen foul of the chief's galley, it would have gone hard with you, for his crew were so strong that you could scarce have overcome them before the other two vessels came up to his assistance."

"Now let us to our meal," Gervaise said.

The three knights were placed at the head of the table by him, and it was pleasant to see how they enjoyed their food.

"I can scarce persuade myself that I am not dreaming," Caretto said. "Sometimes, when lying at night, wet through with the damp air, I have wondered to myself whether I could ever have lived thus, and whether I should ever exchange my hard bread-and-water for what seemed to me fabulous luxuries, though at the time one had taken them as a matter of course. You cannot tell how strange it feels to me to come back to the old life again."

"You will soon be accustomed to it," Gervaise said, with a smile, "and then you will look upon your captivity as a dream, just as you then regarded your past life."

"I suppose, Sir Gervaise," Pietro Forzi said, "that you will sail direct for Rhodes with your prizes?"

"No indeed," Gervaise replied. "At the same time that we learned, from a dying man left on board the ship the pirates captured yesterday, of the course they had taken, and were so enabled to follow them, we also learned that they were on their way to join a corsair fleet that was collecting at some point on the eastern side of Sardinia, with the intention of sweeping the coast of Italy. It was this, rather than the capture of these three vessels, that induced us to disobey the general instructions we had been given to cruise along the northern coast of Africa, and determined us to push north to give warning along the coast from

Naples to Genoa of the danger that threatened, and, if possible, to enable Genoa to fit out her galleys to encounter the corsairs. That duty has still to be fulfilled, though I fear that Genoa will be able to do little, for of late she has been engaged in a long civil struggle between her great families, and has taken but a small part in maritime affairs. However, we can at least warn her, as well as Naples, Pisa, and other towns, and may possibly find some opportunity for ourselves striking another blow against the pirates."

"If so, certainly we shall be glad to accompany you, if you will allow us to serve under you; for nothing would please us so much as the opportunity of paying off a small share of the vengeance we owe them. But of course, if you would rather, we will sail for Rhodes in the prizes."

"I am not thinking of sending them to Rhodes at present," Gervaise said. "It seems to me that we may be able, in some way, to utilise them to advantage. They have their sails, and rowers for the oars. There will be, in each, besides seven knights of the Order, thirty men who, like yourselves, must feel willing to strike a blow at their late oppressors. I need hardly say that I shall be glad indeed to have the company and aid of three such well-known knights of the Order, and would, could I do so, gladly resign my command into your experienced hands. But this I cannot do, and, anticipating that you would be willing to join us in this expedition, I have been thinking how I could best utilise your aid. I have thought that, if you would accept the positions, I would appoint one of you to each of the prizes, to act, not as its commander, but as the leader of the band of released captives. Most of them are sailors, of course, and with them you could work the guns and give effective aid to the little party of knights in any actual fight."

The three knights all exclaimed that they would gladly accept the posts he offered them.

THE FIRST PRIZES

"The idea is a capital one, Sir Gervaise; and, as long as it does not come to close fighting, the three ships should be able to render efficient aid to your galley in any encounter. They will be, at any rate, a match for their own number of pirate ships," Caretto said.

As soon as the meal concluded, the Moslem captives were questioned one by one as to the rendezvous at which the pirate fleet was to assemble; all, however, protested that the place was known only to the three commanders, all of whom had fallen in the fight.

CHAPTER XIV
THE CORSAIR FLEET

AN hour later all was ready for a start. The knights of the *langue*s of France, Germany, and Spain went on board their respective ships, as did the three parties of released captives, with the knights who were to command them, while the rowers took their seats on the benches, shackled with the chains that had recently held the Christians. The wind was from the south, and with sails and oars the prizes were able to keep fairly abreast of the galley. With a few short intervals of rest, the slaves continued their work all night, until, shortly before daybreak, land was seen ahead, and the pilot at once pronounced it to be Cape Carbonara.

"A good landfall, Gervaise," Ralph said. "The pilot has done right well. I suppose you mean to anchor when you get there?"

"Certainly, Ralph. The slaves will have rowed nearly eighteen hours, with only two hours' rest. They must have some hours, at least, of sleep before we go on. As you and I have been up all night, we will turn in also. We will send a boat ashore to try and find out from the natives they may come across whether any vessels, bearing the appearance of Moorish corsairs, have been seen passing up the coast, and also to find out what bays and inlets there are where they would be likely to anchor. Some of the Italian knights had best go with the boat, for though I believe these people speak a different dialect to those of the mainland, they would have more chance of understanding them than any of the others."

THE CORSAIR FLEET

The sun had risen when the little fleet came to an anchor close to the cape. A boat was at once prepared to go ashore, and Gervaise begged Fabricius Caretto, the senior of the rescued Italian knights, to endeavour to find out whether a swift-sailing craft of some kind could be hired. If so, he was to secure her on any terms, and come off in her at once to the galley.

Gervaise had already talked the matter over with Ralph, and they agreed that a strongly-manned craft of this kind would go faster than any of those they had taken, and that, moreover, it would be a pity to weaken their force by sending one of the prizes away. Having seen them off, Gervaise retired to the cabin and threw himself down for a short sleep, leaving the knights who had been off watch during the night, to see that all went well. In two hours he was roused. A native craft had come alongside with Sir Fabricius Caretto.

"I think she is just the craft for us," the knight said, as Gervaise came on deck. "She belongs to a large fishing village just round the point to the left. There were several boats there, but the villagers all said that this was the speediest vessel anywhere along the coast. She belongs to two brothers, who, with four men, constitute her regular crew; but I have arranged for twelve others to go in her, in order that they may row her along at a good pace if the wind falls light."

"Are your companions come off yet?"

"No; but we can hoist a flag for their recall."

"Do so. I shall be greatly obliged if you will undertake this mission to the seaports. It needs one of name and rank to speak with the nobles and officials authoritatively."

"I will gladly do so, Sir Gervaise. Give me your instructions, and you can rely upon my carrying them out."

"I thank you greatly, Sir Fabricius, and shall be glad if you will take with you any two of the knights you may select. I have to write letters for you to deliver to the authorities at Naples, Pisa, and Genoa. I shall write but briefly, and leave you to explain matters more fully. I shall merely say that I have intelligence of the arrival here of a fleet of Moorish corsairs, of whose strength I am ignorant, but that assuredly their intention is to make a raid on the commerce of the coast, and perhaps to land at unprotected places. At Ostia, after warning the authorities to send orders along the coast for the inhabitants to be on their guard, pray them to carry word at once to Rome, and request his Holiness the Pope to order some armed galleys to put to sea as soon as possible. Beg them at Naples and Pisa to do the same thing. But of course it is from Genoa that we must hope for the most assistance.

"In each place you will, if possible, see the syndic himself, and such of his council as can be got quickly together. The moment you have done all you can at Genoa sail for the Island of Madalena, which lies off the north-eastern point of the island. There you will either find us, or a boat with a message where to direct your course. I think perhaps it will be best to omit Naples—it will save you fully a day, if not two, to do so. Pray them at Ostia to send off news down the coast, or to request the papal authorities to despatch mounted messengers. 'Tis likely that, at first, at any rate, the corsairs will try the narrower waters to the north. From here to Ostia is nigh two hundred miles, and if the wind is brisk you may arrive there to-morrow afternoon, and start again at night, arriving at Pisa before noon on the following day; while, allowing for four or five hours to ascend the river there, you may be at Genoa next morning.

"Three hours should suffice to gather from the authorities what force they can despatch, and as soon as you have learned this, embark again and sail south. You may reach Madalena in two days. Thus, at the earliest, it must be from six to seven days before you can bring us the news there; if you meet with calms or foul winds you may be well-nigh double that time. If at Ostia you can get a faster craft than this, hire it, or take a relay of fresh rowers. I will furnish you with means when I give you the letters."

THE CORSAIR FLEET

In less than half an hour Gervaise was on deck again. The boat had returned with the other Italian knights. An ample store of provisions had been placed on board the *Speronára*, both for the crew and for the three knights, and, without a minute's delay, these took their places on board, the great sails were hoisted, and the craft glided rapidly away.

"The villagers spoke truly as to her speed," Ralph said, as they looked after her. "Even with this light wind, she is running fully six miles an hour, and as, by the look of the sky, there will be more of it soon, she will make the run to Ostia well within the time we calculated."

Gervaise now questioned the other Italian knights as to what information they had gained.

They said the peasants had told them that several strange craft, using both oars and sails, had been noticed passing northwards, and that so strong was the opinion that these were either Algerines or Tunisians that, for the last three or four days, none of the fishing craft had ventured to put to sea. They were able to tell but little as to the bays along the coastline, which they described as very rugged and precipitous. Five or six little streams ran, they knew, down from the mountains. They thought the most likely places for corsairs to rendezvous would be in a deep indentation north of Cape Bellavista, or behind Cape Comino. If not at these places, they might meet in the great bay at whose entrance stands Tavolara Island, and that beyond, there were several deep inlets on the north-eastern coast of the Island. Gervaise had a consultation with Ralph.

"The first thing is to find out where these corsairs have their meeting-place, Ralph; and this must be done without their catching sight of the galley or of the prizes, which some of them would be sure to recognise."

Ralph nodded.

"It is a difficult question, Gervaise. Of course, if we had a boat speedy enough to row away from the corsairs it would be easy enough; but with wind and oars they go so fast that no boat could escape them."

A KNIGHT OF THE WHITE CROSS

"That is quite certain, Ralph; and therefore, if it is done by a boat, it must be by one so small and insignificant that they would pay but little attention to it if they caught sight of it. My idea is that we should take our own little boat, which is a fast one, paint it black, to give it the appearance of a fisherman's boat, and hire a couple of good rowers from the village. This, with one knight dressed as a fisherman, should go ahead of us, and explore every inlet where ships could be sheltered. We would follow ten miles behind. When we get near the places where the natives think the fleet is likely to be, the boat must go on at night, while we anchor. In that way they ought to be able to discover the corsairs, while themselves unseen, and to gain some idea of their numbers and the position in which they are anchored, and bring us back news."

"Shall I go myself, Gervaise?"

"I could not spare you, Ralph. The risk of capture does not seem to me to be great, but there certainly is a risk, and I dare not part with you. It had better be an Italian, because there will doubtless be an opportunity of landing at villages and questioning the inhabitants, therefore we will send Fosco. If there are some eight or ten corsairs gathered in any of these bays the news is sure to travel along the shore, and we may get some tidings in that way. The first thing is to send off to the village again to fetch two young fishermen; they must be active fellows, strong, and possessed of some courage. I will ask da Vinci to go himself and select them. While he is away we will paint our boat black, and make ready for her to start at once; the sooner she is off the better."

The Italian knight at once undertook the mission, and started for the shore. Fosco, who had been chosen principally because he was light of frame, as well as very shrewd and intelligent, was then called up, and his mission explained to him. He was delighted at having been selected. Gervaise took him down to the cabin, and they consulted the maps with which the galley was furnished.

THE CORSAIR FLEET

"You will row on to Muravera; it is some twenty miles from here. You see, the village lies at the mouth of a river. As soon as you arrive there, you will land and find out whether there is any report of Moorish pirates having been seen along the coast. We shall be there this evening, and you will come on board and report. Next day you will get to Lunasei, which is about five miles on this side of Cape Bellavista, and they will certainly know there if the pirates are lying behind the cape. If they are so, you will row back to meet us; if they are not, you will remain there until we come up in the evening. Remember that, should you on either day be seen and chased, and you find they are overtaking you, you will make for the shore, land, and conceal yourselves. We shall keep along near the coast, and as we pass you can come down to the water's edge and signal to us to take you off. Now you had better disguise yourself, so as to be in readiness to start as soon as da Vinci comes off with the men. You will only need to take a small stock of provisions, as each night you can replenish them here."

An hour later da Vinci came off with two stalwart young fishermen. The little boat had already been painted, and it was lowered at once; Fosco stepped into it, and started.

Two hours later the prizes got up sail, and, accompanied by the galley, coasted quietly along the shore, arriving, late in the afternoon, at Muravera. Fosco at once came on board.

"There is no news here beyond that which we gained this morning, Sir Gervaise," he said. "Strange ships have certainly been seen sailing north, but they did not approach the coast."

A similar report was given at Lunasei; there were certainly no corsairs lying behind Cape Bellavista, or news would assuredly have reached the village. At Orosei, next day, the report was the same; there were no strange ships at Cape Comino. They had been warned overnight that the coast beyond the cape was so precipitous, that there would be no villages at which to make inquiries, and arranged with

Fosco that the ships should anchor north of the cape, and that he should go on at once to inspect the next bay. If he found ships there, he was to return at once; if not, he was, at daybreak, to land at one of the villages in the bay, and to make inquiries.

No news was brought in by him during the night.

"It is evident the pirates are not in the bay, Gervaise," Ralph said, as they came on deck at daybreak.

"Yes; and I am glad of it. It is a large bay, and if the Genoese send half-a-dozen galleys, some of the pirates might still escape, while the next bays are deeper and narrower, and it would be more easy to entrap them all. I have all along thought it most probable that they would rendezvous there. The maps show no villages for many miles round, and they might lie there for weeks without so much as a shepherd getting sight of them from the cliffs. Moreover, it is the nearest point for cutting off ships coming down between Corsica and the mainland, and they can, besides, snap up those proceeding from the south to Marseilles, as these, for the most part, pass between Sardinia and Corsica."

At eight o'clock the boat was seen coming round the point.

"Any news, Fosco?" Gervaise asked, as it approached the galley.

"None, Sir Gervaise. They have heard nothing of pirates, nor seen anything of them."

Exclamations of disappointment broke from the knights.

"That makes it all the more likely," Gervaise said, " that they are lying in one of the inlets to the north. You see, lower down they kept comparatively close to the shore, being careless who might notice them; but as they approached their rendezvous, they would be more careful, and might either pass along at night, or keep far out. If they had not been anxious to conceal their near presence, they would have been likely to put into this bay in search of plunder and captives; for Tempe, one of the largest of the Sardinian towns, lies but a short distance away, and there must be a considerable amount of traffic."

"There are four or five small craft lying there," Fosco, who had by this time stepped on board, put in, "and a considerable number of fishing boats. When I came upon the ships in the dark, I thought at first that I had lighted on the pirates, but on letting the boat drift closely by them I soon saw they were not corsair galleys."

"Shall we get up anchor and go into the bay?" Ralph asked.

"It were safer not to do so, Ralph. Possibly one of the craft lying there might be presently captured by them, and they might learn from her crew of the presence of a galley of the Order there. Therefore I think it best to remain where we are till nightfall, and then to proceed and anchor on the north side of the Island of Madalena, if we can find a sheltered cove where we could not be seen either from the land or by passing ships."

During the day there was a good deal of discussion among the knights as to whether the corsairs might not already have sailed away. It was evident that if all their ships had arrived, there would be no motive for delay. Three ships they knew would never join them, and others might have been detained, from some cause or another. There could be no doubt that the pirates had already ample force for capturing as many merchant vessels as they might come across. But it might be intended to carry out some more daring project—to sack and burn towns along the coast, carry off the leading people for ransom, and fill the vessels with slaves—the attack being made simultaneously on several unprotected towns. A vast amount of plunder could thus be reaped, together with captives of even greater money value. Were this their plan, they would doubtless delay until all those who had promised to join in the expedition had arrived. The balance of opinion, then, was that the corsairs were still in hiding.

By daybreak next morning they were moored in a sheltered little bay to the north of Madalena, the galley lying inside the prizes, so as to be concealed as much as possible from view of any craft that might happen to pass the mouth of the bay. Fosco started as soon as darkness fell in the evening, and returned early in the morning.

"They are there," he shouted, as he neared the galley, "hidden in a deep inlet that runs into one of the narrow bays."

"How many are there of them?"

"Seventeen or eighteen, I could not say which. They are all moored side by side."

By this time Fosco's boat had reached the galley.

"You have done well indeed," Gervaise said, as the young knight ascended to the poop. "Now give us a full account of what you have seen."

"As you know, Sir Gervaise, the bay opposite this island splits up into two, running a long way inland, like the fangs of a great tooth. I had, of course, no difficulty in finding the entrance to the bay itself, as it is but a short distance across the strait. I steered first for the left-hand shore, and kept close along under the shadow of the cliffs, which, in many cases, rise almost straight out from the water. We rowed very quietly, fearing to run against a rock; for although it was light enough to see across the water, and to make out any craft that might be anchored there, it was very dark along the foot of the cliffs. There was no need for haste, as I knew I had plenty of time to explore both arms of the bay, and to be back here before day began to break.

"We rowed up to the end of the inlet, and then, having assured ourselves that it was empty, came down the other side, and turned up the western arm. We had got some distance along when I fancied I heard voices, and so let the boat drift along, only dipping the oars in the water occasionally. I could make out no signs whatever of the corsairs, when suddenly we came upon a break in the cliffs. It was only some fifty yards across, and here a creek came in at right angles to the shore. I could have given a shout of pleasure as I looked up it, for there a score of lights were burning above a dark mass, and we could hear the sound of talking and laughter. It was but a glimpse I caught, for the men at once backed water, and we were soon round the corner again.

"Up till then the fishermen had been ready enough to go where I wanted, but the sight of that clump of galleys regularly scared them, and they wanted to row straight away; but of course I pointed out to them that they had taken pay to do this thing, and that they had to do it. They said that if caught they would be either killed or made slaves of, and I could not contradict them, but said that, in the first place, as I was ready to run the risk, there was no reason why they shouldn't do so, and in the second, there was no chance whatever of their being taken, as, if discovered, we should get so long a start that we could either escape them altogether or run the boat ashore at some point where the trees came down to the water's edge, carry the boat up and hide it, and then move up into the hills until the corsairs had gone.

"We waited there three or four hours, looking round the point occasionally. At the end of that time all was quiet. Two or three of the lanterns still burned, but there was no sign of life or movement on their decks. After waiting another half-hour to ensure the crews being asleep, we rowed quietly up the creek, keeping within an oar's length of the rocks. There was not much to see; the galleys lay two abreast, and as there was no space between them, I supposed the whole were lashed together. There were eight of them on the side we went along, but I think there were only seven on the other side. As I thought it did not much matter whether there were fifteen or sixteen, and as the men were in a state of horrible fright, we turned and went back again, and I own I felt very glad myself when we got round the point without an alarm being given. We came quietly out, and it was fortunate we did so, for we had not gone a quarter of a mile when we heard the sound of oars, and, lying silently under the cliff, we saw two large galleys row past us."

"It is a strong force, Gervaise," Ralph said, as they paced up and down the poop together. "Probably in each of those galleys are eighty or a hundred men, in addition to the rowers. It is evident that unless Genoa sends us help we shall not be able to interfere with their plans."

"I don't know, Ralph. I think we may injure them sorely, though we might not be able to defeat them altogether. I want you to-night to take one of the prizes, and row round to the bay we passed, and there to buy three coasting vessels and six or eight fishing-boats. Get as much pitch, oil, and other combustibles, as you can purchase in the villages on the shore. If you can engage a score of fishermen to man them, all the better. My idea is that if Caretto returns with news that the Genoese have no galleys ready for sea, we must do what we can to injure these corsairs. If we smear these craft you are going to fetch with pitch and oil, and fill the holds with combustibles, and so turn them into fire-ships, we may at least do the pirates a tremendous lot of harm. When we get to the mouth of this inlet, we could have the fire-ships rowed in by three or four men in each, they having a boat behind in which to escape as soon as the boats are lighted. The sight of a dozen craft coming down on them in flames would cause a terrific panic, for, moored closely together, as they are, if one took fire there would be little chance of the others escaping. Of course, we should add to the confusion by opening a fire with all our guns, and could hope to capture some at least of them as they tried to make their way out."

"It is a grand idea, Gervaise; a splendid idea! It would be a terrific blow to the Moors, and would make the sea safe from them for a long time."

"When you buy the other things, Ralph, get a quantity of black cloth—it matters not how coarse, or of what material; and also some white. As soon as you come back with it, all hands shall set to work to make the stuff up into mantles of the Order, with the white cross. We will put these on to the Christians in the prizes, and the Moors will suppose that they are attacked by four of the galleys of the Order. If you can get some more arms and some iron headpieces, all the better."

"I will do what I can, Gervaise; the arms will certainly be wanted, for those we found on the decks were sufficient only to arm half the Christians. As to the steel caps, that will not matter so much, as in the darkness and confusion the sight of the mantles will be quite enough to convince the corsairs that we are all knights of the Order. By the way, Gervaise, we have not yet looked into the holds of the prizes."

"That is so, Ralph; we knew, of course, that as the ships had but just started we should find nothing in them save the cargo of that unfortunate craft they captured."

On searching they found, as they had expected, that the cargo of the captured ship had been of no great value. It consisted of wine, olive oil, and grain. These were all useful, for the number of mouths to be fed was considerable, and heavy inroads had already been made on the stores of the galley. The rowers of the four vessels were at once set to work to crush the grain between flat stones brought from the shore, and an ample supply of coarse flour for their use for at least a fortnight was obtained before sunset.

As soon as darkness fell, Ralph and two of the French knights started in one of the prizes. Late on the following afternoon a sail was seen coming from the north, and before the sun set they were able to make her out to be the craft in which Caretto had sailed. The anchor of the galley was at once got up, and she rowed out to meet the boat and conduct her into the little bay. It was almost dark when they came within hailing distance.

"What news do you bring, Sir Fabricius?"

"Bad news, I regret to say. I do not think that Genoa will be able to send out any galleys for at least a fortnight. There have been civil dissensions, and fighting between rival factions, and in consequence her ships are all dismantled and laid up. Crews will have to be collected for them, repairs executed, and officers chosen; a fortnight will be the earliest time in which they can be here. Pisa has no war-galleys, and unless the Pope sends some out directly he gets the news, the corsairs will have it their own way. Have you discovered them?"

"Yes; they lie but a few miles from here. There were fifteen or sixteen of them two days ago, and two others joined them that night. You have lost no time indeed. We had scarce begun to expect you, Sir Fabricius," he added, as the knight and his two comrades stepped on board.

"I have done my best," the knight said angrily. "But I am in a rage with my ill success. All I have accomplished is that no merchant vessels will put to sea at present. At Ostia they would only send off a message to Rome, to ask for orders. At Pisa the authorities at first treated my story as a fiction, and, I believe, took me for an impostor; but on the news spreading, some knights came forward and recognised me. Then we had a meeting of the council. All talked, wrangled, and protested. They said that it was absurd to suppose that they could, at a moment's notice, fit out ships to cope with a fleet of corsairs; and their sole idea was to man the forts, and to repel an attack. However, mounted messengers were sent off at once, up and down the coast, to give warning to the inhabitants of the towns to put themselves into a posture of defence, and to the villagers to fly with their wives and families into the interior as soon as they saw galleys of doubtful appearance approaching. I was there but four hours, and then started for Genoa."

"There was almost a panic there too, as the members of the council were mostly merchants, and were filled with dismay for the safety of their ships and goods at sea. Of course, there was no thought that the corsairs, however strong, would venture an attack upon Genoa itself. I told them that you had captured three of the corsairs with a single galley, and that if they could send you ten others you would probably be able to make head against the pirates;

but, as I have told you, Genoa is at peace with all the world; her war-galleys are laid up, and most of them would need repair and recaulking before they would be fit to send to sea. Although they maintained that no more than a week should elapse before they would be ready to sail I am right sure that it will be double that time before they are fitted out.

"Of course, in Genoa I was well known, though my family estates lie near Mantua, and my acquaintances flocked round me and urged me to stay until the galleys were ready for sea. This I would not hear of, and, six hours after my arrival, started again. We made the voyage to Corsica at a good speed, but since then we have had the oars constantly out to help the sails. The men have well earned their pay, I can assure you. It is enough to make one mad with rage to think that these pirates will be able to harry the coast of Italy at their pleasure; for there can be little chance that they will abide quiet much longer at this rendezvous."

"It is annoying, indeed," Gervaise agreed; and a murmur of disappointment ran round the assembled knights. "However, we have the consolation that we have done all we could, and I am sure that we shall do so in the future."

Gervaise had charged Ralph to say nothing about the object of his mission, and the general supposition was that he had sailed to endeavour to purchase some bullocks, as the supply of meat was nearly exhausted. Ralph himself had let drop a few words to this effect, and had indeed been charged by Gervaise to bring off a few oxen if they could be obtained without loss of time.

Gervaise was on deck at midnight, and soon afterwards the beat of oars was heard. It was a still night, and one of the knights on watch remarked to him,—

"It seems to me, Sir Gervaise, that the sound is a confused one, and that there must be several vessels rowing. Shall I call up our companions? It may be that it is the pirate fleet coming out."

"You need not do that," Gervaise replied. "I am expecting Sir Ralph to bring back with him some fishing-boats, for which I think I can find a use. We should have heard before this if the corsairs had been putting out. Fosco is in his boat watching the mouth of the inlet, and would have started with the news had there been any stir on board their galleys."

It was a quarter of an hour before a number of dark objects entered the little bay. As soon as they did so, they ceased rowing, and the splashes of the anchors as they fell into the water were heard. Then came the sound of a boat's oars, and Ralph was soon alongside.

"I see that you have succeeded, Ralph."

"There is no fear of failing when one is ready to pay the full value of what one wants to get. I have bought three coasters and eight fishing-boats, and have a sufficient store of pitch and oil, with plenty of straw and faggots. There was no difficulty in getting men to come with me. As soon as they heard that a fleet of eighteen Moorish galleys was in the next bay, they were ready enough to aid in any plan for their destruction, for they knew well enough that some of them would be sure to make raids all along the coast, sacking and burning, and carrying off men, women, and children, as slaves. I said I only wanted two men for each craft, but so many were willing to come that I have some thirty more than the number I asked for, and we can divide these among us. They are strong, active-looking fellows."

"We will keep them here then, Ralph. You see, there are one-and-twenty of our knights in the three prizes, and as we lost two in the capture, and four others are not fit to put on armour, we have but six-and-twenty, and the addition will be very welcome. What are they armed with?"

"They have bows and arrows, and long pikes and axes."

"Good. Have you managed to collect any more arms?"

"Yes. The people are all charcoal burners and woodmen in winter, and I was therefore able to get together some thirty or forty axes and hatchets, which will be ample, with the arms we took from the Moors, to equip the ninety Christians."

"I think we can depend upon these for fighting, Ralph."

"I don't think there is any doubt about that. A few of them are pretty well worn out with labour and suffering, but all have gained strength and spirits greatly in the past week, and you may be sure that they will fight to the death rather than run the risk of another turn in the galleys."

"And have you got the stuff to make the mantles?"

"Yes. There was plenty of the coarse black cloth which they wear in summer—in winter, of course, they are clad in sheepskins; and I have sufficient white cotton cloth to make the crosses."

"We have only one thing to wish for now, Ralph, and that is, that the corsairs may not take it into their heads to sail to-morrow. Fosco will bring me news at daybreak, and we will at once send another boat off to watch the mouth of the bay when he leaves it. If they sail, we cannot venture to attack them as long as they keep together, the odds are far too heavy, and our only plan will be to follow them at a distance, when we can just keep their upper sails in sight, and then to attack any detachment that may separate from the main body."

"I hope it will not come to that, Gervaise. It would be hard indeed, when you have devised such a splendid plan, and we have got everything ready to carry it out, if they were to give us the slip. Do the others know anything about it yet?"

"No. I thought it better to keep silence till to-morrow. No doubt some of the galley-slaves understand enough of one or other of our languages to gather what is on foot. Besides, their late captives might, in their satisfaction at the thought of revenge, say enough to them to let them know that an attack on their fleet was intended, and one of them might, in some way, free himself from his irons and swim ashore. We know there is a small fishing village across the island, and there would be no difficulty in stealing a boat and making off with the news. I do not say that the risk is great; still, it were better not to throw away even a chance. The knights have all turned in in a very gloomy mood, for Caretto has returned with news that there is no hope of assistance from Genoa for a fortnight, and it seemed, therefore, that all our pains had been thrown away. And now we may as well turn in until daylight."

CHAPTER XV
A SPLENDID EXPLOIT

GERVAISE was up again at dawn. He was amused at the wonder of the knights, as they came up one by one, at the sight of the little fleet anchored outside them. As soon as it was fairly daylight, he sent off to the three prizes to request all the knights to come on board the galley. When all were assembled there he said, "You are all aware, comrades, that Sir Fabricius Caretto has brought news that the galleys at Genoa are all laid up, and that it will be a fortnight before they can put to sea. Long before that, the corsairs will assuredly be ravaging all the villages and small towns along the coast of Italy, unless we can prevent their doing so. It would be simple madness to try to attack them at sea; of that I feel sure you are all conscious. It would be only throwing away our lives and our galley."

There was a murmur of assent among the knights. They were ready for any encounter in which there was a chance, however faint, of success; but all saw that for a single galley to attack one of the largest corsair fleets that had ever set out, would be nothing short of insanity. Their leader's words, however, seemed to show that he had some plan in his mind by which he hoped to strike a blow at the enemy, and all listened eagerly for what was coming.

"We have heard from our comrade Fosco that their ships lie moored in two lines, side by side in a narrow inlet. He has returned this morning with the news that they are still there. He thinks that three or four more have arrived during the last two days, and it is probable they are waiting for the three we captured to join them. To-night it is my intention to attack them, but not by rowing in and boarding them, for that would hopeless. Yesterday Sir Ralph Harcourt went, as you are aware, to fetch provisions. But this was a part only of the object of his trip. He has, as you see, brought back eleven craft with him; these, I may tell you, are laden with combustibles—pitch, oil, straw, and faggots. They will be rowed and towed to the inlet to-night, set on fire, and launched against the pirates."

An enthusiastic cheer broke from the knights. They saw at once that, lying as the corsairs were, side by side, the destruction of many of them was certain.

"He has also brought fishermen," Gervaise went on, "two or three of whom will go in each fire-ship, having a boat towing behind, in which they will escape as soon as the craft are alongside the galleys. The galley and the three prizes will take their post at the mouth of the inlet. The fire of our guns will add to the confusion among the pirates, and we shall endeavour to fall upon any galleys that may extricate themselves from the mass, and try to make their escape. Sir Ralph has brought back materials for making ninety mantles of the Order, for the Christians on board the three prizes, and thirty fishermen to bring the crew of our galley up to its full strength. The light of the flames will suffice to show the pirates that, as they will believe, four vessels, manned by knights of the Order, are barring the entrance. Many will, we may calculate, jump overboard and swim ashore rather than face us, and we shall be able, at any rate, to capture three or four of their craft, for, as they come out, one by one, we can all close round them; and with nearly fifty knights, ninety released captives, burning for vengeance, and some fifty or sixty fishermen—for those from the fire-ships will, of course, join us—we shall make short work of them, and may even hope to entirely destroy their fleet."

A SPLENDID EXPLOIT

Again a joyous shout rose from the knights. This would indeed be an exploit that all might be proud to share in, and, breaking the ranks in which they had stood while Gervaise addressed them, they crowded round him with exclamations of enthusiasm and devotion.

"Now," he said, as soon as silence was a little restored, "the knights of the *langues* on board the prizes will send at once to the coaster on the left of the other two. Sir Ralph will go there now, and supply each with materials for making the mantles for the Christians; he has brought thread, and fish-bone needles. You will see that the stuff is cut up into suitable lengths, and handed over to your crews, and that each man makes up his mantle. There can be but little sewing required for these sleeveless gowns, nor need it be carefully done. The great thing is that the white crosses shall be conspicuous. As soon as you have set them to work, you will examine the state of the arms, see how many more are needed to complete the list, and then send off to Sir Ralph, who will furnish as many as are required: the fishermen have brought their own weapons. See that the slaves are all well fed to-day, and, before evening, inspect well their fetters, so that you may be free from all anxiety as to an attempt by them to escape during the conflict.

"The rest of you will go on board these native craft, and see that the combustibles are fairly distributed among them, the wood and straw soaked with pitch and oil, as also the sails and ropes, and that the decks are well coated; this is a most important duty. Get some torches made also, so that there shall be two on board each craft; these are to be lighted the last thing before we get to the point, and will be thrown down into the straw and faggots in the hold, by the fishermen when they get close to the corsairs. All this can be prepared before our morning meal, and when you assemble here I hope to receive your reports that everything is in readiness. One of the other coasters has some bullocks on board. Sir Ralph will send one to each of the prizes, and one to us. They had better be killed and cut up at once, in order that the crews may have two good meals to-day of fresh meat. See that the galley-slaves have their share."

No time was lost in carrying out the orders. Ralph, as soon as the cloth, arms, and meat were distributed, went round in a boat to see that the combustibles were properly laid for firing, and everything done to insure that the flames should spread rapidly. The Sards shared in the work, and rations and wine were distributed to them; and when the knights sat down to their meal on board the galley, they were able to report that everything was in perfect readiness, and that the work of sewing the mantles was making good progress.

The day passed slowly to the young knights, all of whom were burning with excitement at the thought of the coming fray. The released Christians were no less exultant at the prospect of taking vengeance for the sufferings they had so long endured, and the scene on board all four ships was most animated.

After talking it over with Ralph, Gervaise told off three more of the knights to each of the prizes, so that there should be ten on board each. This reduced the strength on board the galley to seventeen; but as they would have the assistance of a strong band of Sards they considered this to be ample, under the circumstances. It was arranged that the galley, with one of the prizes, should close with the first corsair that came out, and that the other two prizes should attack the second. After capturing these, they were to assist each other as circumstances might dictate. Gervaise strongly impressed upon the knights in command of each prize that they were not, single-handed, to attack a corsair unless one of their consorts was near, and free to give assistance.

"We must run no risk of a reverse," he said. "We are certain of destroying many of their vessels and of breaking up their fleet, and it is far better that a few should escape than that we should run the risk of losing ten of our number, to say nothing of those we have rescued from captivity. In the excitement of the fight this order must be strictly borne in mind. Our victory must be marred by no misfortune brought on by headstrong rashness. The corsairs are bound to be very strongly manned, and ten knights, even aided by such assistance as they may get from the Christians, might find themselves altogether over-matched against a crowd of desperate men."

As soon as it was dusk the anchors were drawn up, and the fleet got under way. They proceeded but slowly, for the wind was light, and the fishing-boats moved heavily through the water. There was, however, no occasion for speed, for Gervaise did not wish to commence the attack until past midnight. The guns had all been loaded before starting, and a pile of ammunition was placed near each. Presently the wind nearly died out, and the galley and prizes then took the coasters and fishing craft in tow. It was nearly one o'clock when they got within half a mile of the inlet. The tow-ropes were then thrown off, the fishermen got out sweeps, and the galley led the way, the fire-ships followed in a body, and the three prizes brought up the rear. The oars had all been muffled, and slowly they made their way, until Fosco, who was standing next to Gervaise on board the galley, said that the point just ahead marked the entrance to the inlet. They then stopped rowing until the fire-ships were all close up.

These were, as had previously been arranged, in two lines. Five fishing-boats, each manned by four men and having its small boat in tow behind it, formed the first line; the three coasters, each with six men at the oars, and the three other fishing-boats, formed the second. The torches were now lighted. Ralph took his place in the centre boat of the first line; Gervaise went on board one of the coasters, and the order was given to the men to row. What wind there was was favourable, blowing from the north-west, and therefore right into the inlet. Scarcely had the first boats reached the entrance when a shout was heard.

A KNIGHT OF THE WHITE CROSS

"Row, men, your hardest now!" Ralph shouted; the Sards bent to their oars, and the five boats advanced rapidly towards the corsairs. As they did so, a babel of shouts and cries rose from the dark mass of ships, which swelled into a tumult of alarm as on Ralph's order, "Throw your torches into the straw!" a flash of flame leapt up from each boat. Five more strokes, and they were alongside the two outside ships. As they crashed heavily into them, the men leapt from their seats and sprang over into the small boats, threw off the painters, and rowed astern, opening on either hand to allow the second line of fire-ships to pass. These, by Gervaise's directions, divided, and three bore along on either side of the corsairs, and then ran in among them, throwing grapnels to fasten the fire-ships alongside. Then, as the flames sprang up from the holds, the crews betook themselves to their boats, and rowed out of the inlet.

By the time they reached the galley and prizes, the eleven fire-ships were a mass of flame, which was spreading to the corsairs. Lying packed together as these were, the confusion was terrible. Numbers of men endeavoured to push off the fire-ships, but it was too late; others tried to extricate their galleys from the mass, throwing off the hawsers, and striving with hand and oar to push their vessels out of the line. As soon as the boats were alongside the galley, the guns of the four vessels opened fire with grape into the crowded ships, now lit up by the flames as clearly as at noontide, while the battle-cry of the Order sounded high above the din.

"Nothing can save the ships near this end of the line," Ralph said, "but some of those behind may make their way out between the others and the rocks. I can see that some of them there are lowering their yards and sails to prevent their catching fire as they pass."

The knights distributed among the guns worked them incessantly, directing their fire chiefly against the outside ships, so as to hinder the crews in their endeavours to arrest the progress of the flames; but they were soon able to fire impartially into the mass. As the heat of the flames drove

246

the pirates back, scores of men leapt overboard, and made for the shore. Presently, two or three ships were seen making their way along the narrow line of water on either side of the flaming group in front. As the first advanced, the galley and one of the prizes rowed a short distance forward to meet it. Its deck was crowded with men, among whom a discharge of the cannon from both ships created terrible slaughter.

A moment afterwards they closed with it, one on either side, and the knights, the released captives, and the Sards, sprang down on to its deck. The fight lasted but a minute. Appalled by the disaster that had befallen them, by the terrible effect of the broadsides, poured in at a few yards' distance, and by the sight of so many of the dreaded warriors of the Cross, some of the corsairs threw down their arms and flung themselves on the deck or into the hold, crying for quarter; those who resisted fell either under the swords of the knights, the vengeful axes of the late captives, or the pikes of the Sards; but the great bulk, leaping from the bow or stern, swam ashore.

"Back to your ships!" Gervaise shouted, the moment resistance ceased. "Leave her floating here; she will help to block the way."

Six vessels alone managed to make their escape from the blazing mass of ships, and all of these were captured almost as easily as the first had been. As soon as it seemed that all the remainder were involved in the flames, boats were lowered and sent on board the prizes to take possession. Save for the wounded on the decks, they were entirely deserted by their crews, as those who had run below, as soon as they found that their captors had left the vessels, dropped into the water, and made their way, either by swimming or with the assistance of oars, to the shore. There remained only the slaves, chained to their benches. A few of these had been killed by the broadsides; but the guns had been aimed at the poops and forecastles, where the corsairs were clustered together, and consequently the number of galley-slaves who had fallen was comparatively small.

In none of the galleys was the proportion of Christians anything like so large as that in the three prizes first taken, the greater portion being men of inland tribes who had been captured in warfare, or malefactors who, instead of being executed, had been sold to the corsairs. Nevertheless, in the six galleys some seventy Christians were found, and at once freed. It was terrible to think that in the galleys that had been destroyed a large number of Christians must have perished in the flames, and Gervaise expressed bitter regret that he had not considered that his attack by fire-ships must necessarily involve the loss of so many Christian lives.

"It can't be helped," Ralph said, as Gervaise poured out his feelings to him. "To very many of them death must have been welcome, and if we had not attacked them as we did, and they had sailed for Italy, hundreds, if not thousands, of Christians would have been killed, and as many more carried away into captivity; so, you see, the balance is all in favour of the course we adopted."

Gervaise admitted this, but nevertheless his regret at the fate of so many unfortunate captives quite overpowered for the time his satisfaction at the complete success that had been achieved. The victory had been almost a bloodless one on the part of the assailants. A few of the knights had received wounds. Two among the Christian crews had been killed, and four Sards; while two score had received wounds more or less serious, as, unlike the knights, they had no defensive armour. While waiting for daylight to appear, all their wounds were dressed and bandaged by the knights. In the morning the captured galleys were towed out, and anchored a short distance away, and then Gervaise rowed up to the head of the inlet, followed by the other three ships. They found that eleven of the corsairs had been burnt, and to their satisfaction, they discovered four uninjured galleys lying there, deserted, save by the slaves.

A SPLENDID EXPLOIT

Seeing the fate of their comrades who had first issued out, the commanders had, instead of trying to escape, rowed quietly to the head of the inlet, the movement being covered by the flame and smoke, and had there landed, having laden themselves with stores for their support on shore. This was a great satisfaction to the knights, for not only did it swell the list of prizes, but it reduced by over thirty the number of Christian slaves who had perished in the flames. Taking the galleys in tow, they rowed out of the inlet, whose banks were strewn with half-charred timbers, oars, and relics of the fight.

As soon as they had anchored by the side of their first prizes, a council was held on board the *Santa Barbara*. It was clearly impossible to take thirteen prizes to Rhodes, for there would be but three or four knights to each, and were they to fall in with but one Moorish pirate, they might suffer great disaster, while, should they meet with a storm, they would fare badly indeed, as they could not depend upon the rescued Christians for the management of the sails and oars in heavy weather. At the same time, all were most anxious that the prizes should be carried to Rhodes. Never, save as the result of some great battle, had such a fleet of captured galleys been brought in, and the knights were prepared to endure all dangers rather than part with one of them. Finally, after much discussion, it was determined that they should make for Genoa. From thence the rescued captives would be able to find their way to their homes. The great majority were Italians and Spaniards; the former could proceed by land or sea to their respective homes, while the Spaniards would have no long time to wait before a vessel of their own nationality entered the port, even if one were not lying there when they arrived. Moreover, in any case it would be necessary to despatch a vessel to Genoa, in order that it might be known that the danger was averted, and that there was no longer any necessity for getting the galleys ready for sea.

The chief ostensible reason, however, for going to Genoa was that there would be no difficulty in engaging many sailors as might be necessary to take the prizes to Rhodes. Underlying all the arguments was another reason which Ralph laughingly stated.

"It is all very well to bring forward one argument after another, but not one of you has the courage to say what I am sure all of you have at the bottom of your hearts. You know very well that you want to go to Genoa to enjoy a triumph. The Rhodians are all very well, but there are very many more fair faces at Genoa. Fie, Sir Knights! Such a spirit is little in accordance with the vows of the Order. Are we not bound to humility? And here you are all longing for the plaudits of the nobles and ladies of Genoa!"

Some of the young knights laughed, others coloured hotly.

"They need not be ashamed of the feeling," Caretto said. "Is it not the ardent desire of all true knights to do gallant deeds, and do they not value above all things the guerdon of applause from the fair eyes of ladies. Your comrades have performed the gallant deeds, and well deserve the reward. Now, Sir Gervaise, if not for this reason, at any rate for the others that have been brought forward, I suppose we are all agreed that we sail for Genoa. For our part we are heartily glad that such is your decision. We, and the young knights of our *langue*, have many friends there, and in their name I am sure I can promise you a reception as hearty and sincere as that which we shall ourselves receive."

It was settled that the rescued captives should be divided equally among the thirteen prizes, and that three knights should go in each. The Moorish captives were also divided equally among them, to aid with the sails, and to row a few oars, in case of a dead calm setting in. The commands were distributed according to seniority, the three rescued Italian knights remaining on board the *Santa Barbara* with Gervaise.

A SPLENDID EXPLOIT

The Sards were anxious to return to their villages, in order to carry the news that several hundreds of Moorish pirates had landed.

"We shall have great trouble with them," one of the young fishermen, who spoke a little Italian, said to Gervaise. "There are always a great number of swine, and herds of goats, up among the forests on the hills. We must send up and drive in as many of these as possible, and of course we shall send messengers to Tempe; but it will need a very large force to combat these pirates, who will be able to come down and plunder and destroy, and then retire to the hills, whence it will be hard to dislodge them."

"I am sorry indeed that such trouble should have been caused to you," Gervaise replied; "but I am afraid that I can give you no assistance."

"We shall hunt them down in time," the Sard said confidently.

"There are many villages scattered about Tempe, and what with us fishermen, and the woodmen and charcoal-burners, we shall soon get a strong body together. Besides, we know the mountains, and they do not."

"I should say that you had best avoid a pitched battle with them, but keep on harassing them by night and day, cutting off all who separate themselves from the main body, until at last they are completely worn out."

"We shall deal with them, Sir Knight. We are all hunters, for there are wild boars and stags in the forest, and wolves too, and wild sheep on the higher mountains. Every man among us can use his bow skilfully, and wield pike and hatchet. The hunt will not be unprofitable, either, for we can get a good price for all we take alive, to work in the mines."

An hour later one of the galleys started with the Sards for their villages in the bay of Tempe. After landing them, she was to rejoin the rest of the fleet at their former anchorage at Madalena. By nightfall all were gathered there, and the next morning they set out for Genoa. The wind was light; but in their anxiety to return home as soon as possible the released captives all volunteered to take their former places on the benches, and the vessels were kept going at a fair rate of speed. Two days' rowing took them to Bastia, where their approach created unbounded excitement until the banner of the Order was seen floating from the stern of the *Santa Barbara*, while smaller flags, that had been hastily manufactured, flew from the mastheads of the thirteen prizes. Even then the inhabitants feared to put out, believing that the flags were but a ruse, and numbers of them fled at once, with their families and valuables, to the mountains. It was not until a boat was lowered, and Ralph, accompanied by three or four other knights, rowed ashore, that the panic was allayed.

As soon as it was understood that the galley of the knights had not only captured the thirteen corsairs, but had destroyed eleven others, and had thus annihilated a fleet that was intended to prey upon the commerce of Italy, and ravage the western coast, the alarm was succeeded by the wildest enthusiasm. By the time Ralph had obtained the fresh meat and stores he came ashore to purchase, the greater part of the population were gathered on the shore, and a flotilla of boats put out with him, filled with picturesquely-dressed men and women. Some carried flags, others green boughs, while the ladies had bouquets and baskets of fruit. The galley was the first attraction, and, mounting her sides, the ladies presented their offerings of fruit, while the men cheered, and waved their hats; many musicians came out in the boats, and these played on bagpipes and three-reeded flutes a succession of airs peculiar to the island.

Gervaise received his visitors on the poop. These were at first altogether incredulous when told that it was the lad before them who had commanded the galley, had performed such a remarkable feat, and had freed them from a terrible danger. The youth of the knights of the Order no less surprised them, and had not Gervaise assured them that it was altogether contrary to the rules of the Order for a knight to allow himself to be embraced, many of the ladies would have taken this form of showing their enthusiasm and gratitude. The next morning the fleet started for Genoa. The wind was much stronger than it had been on the previous day, and it was therefore unnecessary for the oars to be put out, except, indeed, on board the galley. There, at nightfall, the Christians relieved the slaves for some hours at their benches, and the next morning the circle of hills round Genoa, with the city nestling at their feet on the water's edge, and climbing for some distance up their slopes, was in view. Caretto at once suggested that it would be well to signal to the fleet to lie to.

"If we do not do so," he said, "they will assuredly think that it is the corsair fleet advancing to attack and burn the vessels in port, and you may be saluted as you approach by a shower of cannon-balls. If you will permit me, Sir Gervaise, I will go forward in one of the prizes and explain matters, and will return here in a short time."

"Thank you, Sir Fabricius. As such mischance as you mention might indeed very well occur, we will lower sail and lie here until you return."

While Caretto was away, the knights and crews breakfasted, and the former put on their armour and gayest attire, in readiness for the landing. Gervaise, although with much inward vexation, considered it necessary to do the same.

"I do wish," he said to Ralph, who was smiling at his rueful face, "that you could for to-day take my place, and let me pass as lieutenant."

"I should not mind at all, Gervaise. But you must put up with the disagreeables as well as the advantages of being commander, and must submit to be honoured and fêted here, as well as getting no end of credit at Rhodes. You will have the satisfaction of well deserving it, for I am sure the plan of attacking them with fire-ships would never have occurred to any one else, and if it had not been for that, we should have had the mortification of seeing them sail off without being able to move a finger to interfere with them."

"If one were fighting for fame and honour, all that would be true enough; but members of an Order, whose sole object is to defend Christendom from the Moslems, should strive only to do their duty, and care nothing for such things as honour and glory."

"Human nature is human nature, and I don't see any reason why one should despise honour and glory when they come to one in the course of duty. I fancy you will think so too, Gervaise, in course of time. I am quite sure that among the fifty knights, there is not one who does not feel well content that he has not only done his duty to the Order, but has gained a share in the credit and honour that will certainly be given to all who have taken a part in so crushing a defeat of the corsairs. As for myself, I do not for a moment pretend that I am not sensible of the fact that, as second in command of the galley, my chances of obtaining promotion in the Order are very greatly improved."

It was nearly two hours before Caretto returned.

"It was well indeed that I went in," he said to Gervaise, "for I found the city in an uproar. The alarm bells of the churches were calling all citizens to arms, and troops were being hurried down to the forts and batteries. Rumour had of course exaggerated the strength of the fleet, and half the population believed that the safety of the city itself was menaced by the approach of a mighty squadron. As soon as my news was bruited abroad, and they learned that the fleet consisted solely of prizes captured from the Moors by a galley of the Order, alarm quickly changed into delight, the sharp, angry clang of the bells was succeeded by peals of gladness, and the joy of the citizens at being relieved from the cloud of anxiety that had hung over the city since my last visit, was unbounded. I went at once to the council-chamber, where I found many of the leading citizens already assembled, having been summoned in hot haste as soon as our approach was made out. At first they were almost incredulous when I told them that every ship of the pirate fleet had been either destroyed or captured, and that the fleet in the offing consisted entirely of your galley and the thirteen corsairs she had captured. As soon as they really grasped the fact, they sent off messengers to the churches to order the joy-bells to be rung, and to the dockyard to arrest all work upon the galleys. Then I had to give them a short account of the surprise and destruction of the corsair fleet, and finally they begged me to ask you to delay your entry to the port for a couple of hours, in order that they might have time to prepare a suitable reception for you."

"I suppose there is no help for it," Gervaise said. "Is there anything that we ought to do?"

"I should decorate the galley with all the flags on board: should set every one to work to make great flags with the cross of the Order to hoist to the masthead of the prizes, instead of the little things that are now flying; and under them we will hoist the flags of the corsairs, among which are those of Tripoli, Tunis, and Algiers. I do not know that there is aught else we can do."

CHAPTER XVI
FESTIVITIES

A T last the fleet, headed by the galley, to which all the knights had returned, rowed towards the port. A gun flashed out from the fort at its entrance, and at once those from all the other batteries responded; bells pealed out again, and a confused roar of cheering broke from the crowds occupying every spot from which a view of the harbour could be obtained. The ships in the port were all decked with flags, and the front windows and balconies of every house were hung with tapestries and bright curtains. As soon as the galley entered the port, a state barge, flying the flag of the Republic, advanced to meet her from the wharf. As she approached, Ralph gave orders for the oars to be laid in, and the barge was soon alongside. The knights were already ranged along the poop, and, accompanied by Ralph and Caretto, Gervaise moved to the gangway to receive the visitors. At their head was Battista Fragoso, the doge, in his robe of state, and following him were a body of the highest nobles of Genoa, all brilliant in gala costume.

"This, my lord duke," Caretto said, "is Sir Gervaise Tresham, a knight commander of our Order, and the commander of this, their galley. He has before, as you may well believe from his appointment to so honourable a post, highly distinguished himself, but what he has before accomplished is far surpassed by the brilliant action that he has now achieved. He has won a victory that not only reflects the highest honour upon the Order, but is an inestimable service to Italy, and has freed her from a corsair fleet that would have been a scourge to her, both at sea and to the towns and villages along the coast. Not only has he, with the brave knights under his orders, annihilated the corsair fleet, burning eleven of their galleys, and capturing thirteen others, but he has restored to freedom no less than two hundred Christian captives, among them the cavaliers Giacomo da Vinci, Pietro Forzi, and myself."

"In the name of the Republic, Sir Gervaise Tresham, and I may say in that of all Italy, I thank you most heartily for the splendid service that you have rendered us. It would have seemed to me well-nigh incredible that a single galley, even if commanded and manned by the most famous knights of your great Order, should have accomplished so extraordinary a feat. Still more strange is it that it should have been performed by so young a knight, with a crew composed, as Sir Fabricius Caretto has told us, of knights chosen from among the youngest of the Order."

"You give far more credit to us, your Highness, than we deserve," Gervaise replied. "Three of the ships were indeed captured in fair fight, but we caught the rest asleep and massed together as to be incapable of successful resistance, and they fell easy victims to the fire-ships we launched against them. Any credit that is due to me is shared equally by my sub-commander here, Sir Ralph Harcourt, and indeed by every knight of my company."

"This, doubtless, may be so, Sir Gervaise," the doge said, with a slight smile, "but it is to the head that plans, rather than to the hand that strikes, that such success as you have achieved is due; and the credit of this night attack is, as the cavalier Caretto tells me, wholly yours, for until you issued your final orders it seemed to him, and to the two good knights his companions, that there was naught to do but to remain in port and watch this corsair fleet sail away to carry out its work of destruction."

By this time they had reached the poop of the galley. Gervaise now called forward the knights one by one, and presented them to the doge, who expressed to them all the gratitude felt by himself and the whole of the citizens of

Genoa for the service they had rendered to the Republic. This ceremony being over, the knights broke up their ranks and conversed for a few minutes with those who had come on board with the doge. The latter then took his place in the barge with his companions, inviting Gervaise and Ralph to accompany him. As the barge left the side of the galley, which followed closely behind her, the guns again thundered out their welcome, and a roar of greeting rose from the inhabitants. On landing, the party waited until the knights had joined them, and then proceeded up the street to the ducat palace, amidst enthusiastic cheering from the crowd that lined the road, occupied the windows and balconies, and even scrambled on the house-tops, the ladies waving their handkerchiefs and scarves.

At the palace were assembled all the municipal authorities, and the congratulations given on board were here repeated. After this there was a great banquet, at which Gervaise was placed on the right hand of the doge, who, at the conclusion of the feast, called upon the assembled guests to drink to the health of the knights of St. John, who had saved the commerce and sea-coast of Italy from the greatest danger that had menaced them since the days when the Northern rovers had desolated the shores of the Mediterranean. The toast was drunk with enthusiasm, and Gervaise then replied with a few words of thanks for the honour done to himself and his comrades.

The party then left the banqueting-hall for the great reception-rooms, where the wives and daughters of all the nobles and principal citizens of Genoa were assembled. Most of the young knights, belonging as they did to noble families, and accustomed from childhood to courtly ceremonies and festivities, were quite at home here. Caretto, his two companions, and their six Italian comrades, speedily introduced them, and each was soon surrounded by a group of ladies, anxious to hear from his lips the details of the exploits of the galley.

"But how is it that you are all so young, Sir Ralph?" one of the ladies, to whom Harcourt had been introduced as the second in command, asked him, when he had finished his account of the capture of the galleys. "We heard from those who met you on landing, that all your comrades were young, but we were filled with surprise when you entered the room, for many of them are but lads."

"You may say that all of us are but lads, Countess. I am the oldest of the party, and am but little over twenty-two, but few of the others are over nineteen; they are all professed knights of the Order, who, as you doubtless know, come out to Rhodes when only sixteen. Some, of course, do not join until later, but I think that all here entered at the earliest age permitted, and almost all had served in two or three voyages in the galleys before they were appointed to the *Santa Barbara*. The reason why so young a crew was chosen was that our commander was also young. He had done such exceptional service to the Order that he was appointed to the command of a galley, and he has, as all will allow, well justified the choice. It was because it was deemed inexpedient to place knights many years his senior under his command, and partly, perhaps, to encourage the younger knights, by giving them an exceptional opportunity of distinguishing themselves, that the crew was chosen entirely from their ranks. I was selected as second in command because Gervaise and I had been special friends when we came out from England in the same ship, and had before fought side by side against the Moslems."

"I see that you wear gilded spurs, Sir Ralph," another lady said; "you must therefore be a dubbed knight?"

"Yes; I had the good fortune to be knighted by D'Aubusson himself, at the same time that Sir Gervaise was also so honoured. It was for an affair with the Turkish pirates. It was Gervaise who really won the honour, for I had no share in the affair, save that of doing my best in the fight."

"And who could do more?" the countess queried.

"Gervaise could do more, Countess, as was shown in that attack on the corsairs by means of fire-ships. He has a head to plan, and, in the case I speak of, a happy thought of his not only saved the lives of ourselves and Sir John Boswell, but, indirectly, was the means of preventing two of our galleys being captured by the corsairs."

"Which is Sir Gervaise?" one of the ladies asked.

Ralph smiled.

"Look round the hall, signoras, and see if any of you can pick him out from the rest of us."

The ladies looked round the hall.

"There are only about twenty here; the rest are in the other rooms. Do not set us to work guessing, if he is not in sight, Sir Ralph."

"Oh yes, he is in sight. Now do each of you fix on the one you think most accords with your ideas of what a knight, brave in action and wise and prudent in council, would be like."

The six ladies each fixed on one of the young knights.

"You are all wrong," said Ralph.

"How can we choose?" the countess said laughingly, "when none of them resemble our ideal hero? Most of them are pleasant and courtly-looking youths, but as yet there is scarce a vestige of hair on their faces, and one could not fancy any of them as the destroyer of the fleet of corsairs."

"Do you see the one speaking to the elderly lady in the recess?"

"Yes; she is the wife of Fragoso. You do not mean to say that that lad is the commander of the galley? Why, he looks the youngest of you all."

"He is between seventeen and eighteen, and there are several others who are no older. Yes, that is Sir Gervaise, Knight Commander of the Order of St. John."

"But how can he possibly have served his time as a professed knight?"

"He was one of the grand master's pages, and his time in that service counted just as it would have done had he entered as a professed knight; and at fifteen, therefore, he stood in the same position as those three or four years older than himself. He speaks Turkish as well as our own tongue, and, as I told you, we received the accolade at the hands of the grand master, a year and a half ago. He is now a knight commander, and will assuredly one day occupy one of the highest posts in the Order."

"You do not speak as if you were jealous, Sir Ralph; and yet methinks it cannot be pleasant for you all to have one younger than yourselves placed at your head."

"I do not think there is one of us who so feels," Ralph said earnestly. "In the first place, he has performed excellent service; in the next place, even those who did not know him before, have felt, since we started, that he is a born leader. Then, too, we regard with pride one who has brought credit upon the younger members of the Order. Moreover, we all owe our posts in the galley to the fact that he was chosen for its command. It is a difficult position for him to fill, but he has managed so that, while all obey his orders as cheerfully and willingly as if he were a veteran, when off duty we regard him as one of ourselves."

"You are a staunch friend, Sir Ralph."

"I am a staunch friend of Sir Gervaise, Countess, for the more I know of him the more I care for him. He well deserves the promotion and honour that have fallen to his share."

"Will you bring him across here to us, Sir Ralph? I want to talk to this hero of yours, and I am sure that my daughter is longing to be introduced to him."

Ralph waited until Gervaise was disengaged, and then brought him across, and, after introducing him, moved away at once, leaving Gervaise to be interrogated by the ladies.

"You must be accustomed to festivities, Sir Gervaise, for we have just heard that you were one of the grand master's pages?"

"I am accustomed to them, signora; but that is not at all the same thing as liking them."

The reply was given so earnestly that all the ladies smiled.

"Your taste is quite exceptional. Do you mean to say that you would rather be on board your galley than here?"

"It would not be polite," Gervaise said, with a laugh, "if I were to say that I would infinitely rather be on board; but indeed I have not, like most of my comrades, been brought up in court or castle. Until the day I joined the Order, we led the lives of exiles. My father belonged to the defeated party in England, and, save for a few months when the cause to which he was attached was triumphant, we lived quietly on the estates he had recovered, our life being one of care and anxiety. So, you see, I had no training in gaiety and pleasure. At Rhodes there are state receptions and religious pageants, but a meeting such as this, is, of course, impossible in a convent; and since I was eleven years old I think I have only once spoken to a woman. So you can well understand, signora, that I feel awkward in speech, and I pray you to make allowance for my ignorance of the language of courtesy, such as would naturally be expected in a knight, even though belonging to a religious Order."

"There is naught to make allowance for," the countess said gently. "Women can appreciate simple truth, and are not, as men seem to think, always yearning for compliments. Those who are most proficient in turning phrases are not often among those foremost in battle, or wisest in council, and I can tell you that we women value deeds far higher than words. Sir Fabricius Caretto is a cousin of mine, and has this afternoon been speaking so highly of you to me and my young daughter here, that I am glad indeed to make your acquaintance. How long do you intend to stay in Genoa?"

"No longer than it will take me to engage men to carry the prizes to Rhodes. I am afraid that sounds rude," he broke off, as he noticed a smile on the faces of the ladies.

"Not rude," said the countess; "though most knights would have put it differently, and said that their duty compelled them to leave as soon as the prizes could be manned. But it comes to the same thing. Of course, you will remain the guest of the doge as long as you are here; otherwise, it would have given us the greatest pleasure to have entertained you. My cousin is, of course, staying with us, and you see we all feel a very deep obligation to you. He has been so long a slave among the Moors, that we had almost come to hope death had freed him from his fetters; so you may imagine our pleasure when he arrived here so suddenly ten days ago. We were expecting that he would remain with us for some time, but he says that he must first go back to Rhodes, after which he will ask for leave, and return here. We have a banquet to-morrow evening to celebrate his return, and earnestly hoped that you would be present, but, since you say that you do not care for such gaieties, we shall, if you prefer it, be glad if you will come to join us at our family meal at twelve."

"Thank you, countess, I should very greatly prefer it, and it will give me real pleasure to come."

"Your friend, Sir Ralph Harcourt, has been telling us how you have destroyed the corsair fleet that has been so alarming us. He, too, is an Englishman, though he speaks Italian well."

"Yes, he speaks it a great deal better than I do," Gervaise said. "He is a dear friend of mine, and it is, indeed, chiefly owing to his support and influence that I have been able to manage so pleasantly and well in the command of a body of young knights, most of whom are my seniors."

"He tells us that you speak Turkish?"

"Yes; I thought that it would be very useful, and spent nearly a year in acquiring it, the bailiff of my *langue* being kind enough to relieve me of all other duties. I was fortunate enough to find in one of the servants of the *auberge* a well educated and widely-informed Turk, who was a very pleasant companion, as well as an excellent instructor, and I learnt much from him besides his language. The knowledge of Turkish has already proved to me most useful, and was indeed the means by which I obtained both my commandery and my appointment as captain of the galley."

"Perhaps you will tell us the story to-morrow; that is, if it is too long to tell us now?"

"It is indeed much too long; but if it will interest you I shall be glad to recount it to-morrow."

The next day Gervaise went to the palace of the Countess Da Forli. She was a widow with no children, except Claudia, the young daughter who had accompanied her to the *fête* the evening before. Caretto, and four or five relations of the family, were the only guests beside himself. It was a quiet and sociable meal, and served with less ceremony than usual, as the countess wished to place Gervaise as much as possible at his ease. During the meal but little was said about the affair with the pirates, Caretto telling them some of his experiences as a captive.

"It is well, Claudia," he said, laughing, "that you did not see me at the time I was rescued, for I was such a scarecrow that you would never have been able to regard me with due and proper respect afterwards. I was so thin that my bones almost came through my skin."

"You are thin enough now, cousin," the girl said.

"I have gained so much weight during the last ten days that I begin to fear that I shall, ere long, get too fat to buckle on my armour. But, bad as the thinness was, it was nothing to the dirt. Moreover, I was coming near to losing my voice. There was nothing for us to talk about in our misery, and often days passed without a word being exchanged between Da Vinci, Forzi, and myself. Do you know I felt almost more thankful for the bath and perfumes than I did for my liberty. I was able at once to enjoy the comfort of the one, while it was some time before I could really assure myself that my slavery was over, and that I was a free man again."

"And now, Sir Gervaise," the countess said, when the meal was over, "it is your turn. Claudia is longing to hear your story, and to know how you came to be in command of a galley."

"And I am almost as anxious," Caretto said. "I did not like to ask the question on board the galley, and have been looking forward to learning it when I got to Rhodes. I did, indeed, ask the two knights who accompanied me on my mission here, but they would only tell me that every one knew you had performed some very great service to the Order, and that it concerned some intended rising among the slaves, the details being known to only a few, who had been, they understood, told that it was not to be repeated."

"It was a very simple matter," Gervaise said, "and although the grand master and council were pleased to take a very favourable view of it, it was, in fact, a question of luck, just as was the surprise of the corsairs. There is really no secret about it—at least, except in Rhodes: there it was thought best not to speak of it, because the fact that the attempt among the slaves was almost successful, might, if generally known, encourage others to try to escape, and perhaps with greater success. I told you last night, Countess, that I had only once before in the last six or seven years spoken to a woman, and it was on that occasion that the adventure, so far as I was concerned, had its commencement."

He then, beginning at his visit with Ralph Harcourt to the Greek merchant and his family on the roof of the house, recounted the suspicions he had entertained, the manner in which they were confirmed, and the method by which he had discovered the plot for the rising. He was interrupted several times when he attempted to abbreviate the story, or to omit some of the details, and there were exclamations of surprise at his proposal to personate a Turkish prisoner, and to share the lot of the slaves in their prison, and on the benches of the galley.

"I had no idea, Sir Gervaise," Caretto said, when he had concluded, "that you too had been a galley-slave, and I understand now the care you showed to render the lot of the rowers as easy as possible. It was a splendid scheme, and well carried out. Indeed, I no longer wonder that you were appointed to the command of a galley, and received a rich commandery in England at the hands of the grand master himself. What think you, Countess; did I speak too highly in his favour?"

"Not one jot, cousin. Why, Sir Gervaise, it seems to me that you have been born two centuries too late, and that you should have been a knight errant, instead of being sworn to obey orders, and bound to celibacy. Do you wear no lady's favour in your helm? I know that not a few of your Order do so."

"As I have said, Countess, I know no ladies who would bestow favours upon me; in the second place, I am but eighteen, and it would be ridiculous for me to think of such matters; lastly, it seems to me that, being vowed to the Order, I can desire no other mistress."

Claudia, who had listened with rapt attention to the story, whispered in her mother's ear. The latter smiled.

"It seems to me, Sir Gervaise," she went on, "that after what you have done for Italy there are many fair maidens who would feel it an honour that their colours should be borne by one who has shown himself so valiant a knight. You see, a gage of this kind does not necessarily mean that there is any deep feeling between the knight who bears it and the lady who bestows it; it shows only that she, on her part, feels it an honour that her gage should be worn by a distinguished knight, and, on his part, that he considers it as somewhat more than a compliment, and wears it as a proof of regard on the part of one whose good opinion at least he values. It is true that among secular knights it may mean even more than this, but it ought not to mean more among knights of an Order like yours, pledged to devote their lives to a lofty and holy aim. My daughter Claudia whispers to me that she would deem it an honour indeed if you would wear her token, accepting it in the spirit in which I have spoken. She is fourteen now, and, as you know, a maid of fourteen here is as old as one of sixteen or seventeen in your country."

Gervaise turned to the girl, who was standing by her mother's chair, looking earnestly at him. He had noticed her the evening before; she had asked no questions, but had listened so intently that he had felt almost embarrassed. Claudia's was a very bright face, and yet marked by firmness and strength. He turned his eyes again to the countess.

"I never thought of wearing a woman's favour," he said; "but if your daughter will bestow one upon me, I shall be proud to wear it, and trust that I may carry it unstained. I shall feel honoured indeed that one so fair, and, as I am sure by her face, so deserving of all the devotion that a knight of our Order can give, has thought me worthy of being one of those on whom she could bestow so high a favour, with the confidence that it would be ever borne with credit and honour."

"What shall I give him, mother?" Claudia asked the countess, without a shadow of the embarrassment with which Gervaise had spoken.

"Not a kerchief, Claudia. In the rough work of the knights, it could not be kept without spot or stain. Moreover, if I judge Sir Gervaise rightly, methinks he would prefer some token that he could wear without exciting attention and remark from his comrades. Go, fetch him any of your jewels you may think fit."

"Then I will give him this," the girl said; and unfastening a thin gold chain she wore round her neck, she pulled up a heart-shaped ornament, in pink coral set in gold and pearls.

Her mother uttered a low exclamation of dissent.

"I know, mother; it was your last gift, and I prize it far beyond anything I have; therefore, it is all the more fit to be my token." Then she turned to Gervaise, and went on, without the slightest tremor in her voice, or accession of colour in her cheeks. "Sir Gervaise Tresham, I bestow upon you this my favour, and shall deem it an honour indeed to know that it is borne by one so brave and worthy. You said that you would be glad to be one of those who bore my favours. You will be more than that, for I vow to you that while you live no other knight shall wear a favour of mine."

"Claudia!" her mother said disapprovingly.

Claudia gives Sir Gervaise a chain of gold to wear as her favour.

"I know what I am saying, mother. I have often wondered why maidens should so carelessly bestow their favours upon every knight who begged for them, and have said to myself that when my time came I would grant it but once, and only then to one whom I deemed worthy of it in all ways—one in whose loyalty and honour I could trust implicitly, and who would regard it as something sacred, deeming it an honour to wear it, as being the pledge of my trust and esteem. Kneel, Sir Gervaise, while I fasten this round your neck."

Gervaise took out the small brooch, that fastened the collar of his silken doublet, and then knelt on one knee. The girl fastened the clasp round his neck, and as he rose he hid the heart beneath the doublet, and fastened the collar. "Lady Claudia," he said earnestly, "I accept your favour in the spirit in which you bestow it. So long as I live I shall prize and value it beyond any honour I may gain, and as I feel it next to my heart, it will ever recall to me that you gave it me as a pledge of your esteem and trust, and I will strive to the utmost so to bear myself that I may be worthy of the gift."

None of the others spoke while the little ceremony was being performed. Caretto glanced at the countess with an amused smile, but the latter looked grave, and somewhat vexed. However, she made an effort to dispel the cloud on her face, and, when Gervaise ceased speaking, said,—

"This has been a somewhat more serious business than I intended, Sir Gervaise. But do not think that I regret in any way the course it has taken; 'tis well for a maiden on the threshold of womanhood that she should place before herself a lofty ideal, and that she should entertain a warm feeling of friendship for one worthy of it. So also it is good for a young knight to know that he has the trust and confidence of a pure and innocent maiden; such a knowledge will aid him to be in all ways true to the vows he has taken, and to remember always that he is bound to be not only a valiant knight of his Order, but a sincere soldier of the Cross." Then she went on more lightly. "Have you heard, Sir Gervaise, that there is a question of making you a noble of Genoa?"

"No, indeed," Gervaise replied, in great surprise; "such an idea never entered into my thoughts."

"Nevertheless, I know that it was spoken of last night, and although it has not yet been finally settled, and will not be until the council meet this afternoon, I should not tell you if I did not think that it was as good as agreed upon; and I am pleased to be the first to whisper to you that it is intended to bestow upon you an honour that is jealously guarded and seldom granted, even to crowned heads, unless as a token of gratitude for some signal service done to the Republic."

"I should feel most honoured and most grateful, Countess, for so extraordinary a favour, did I feel that I had done any extraordinary action to merit it. There can be no doubt that the destruction of the corsairs has saved Genoa and all the maritime towns from immense loss by damage to their trade, and by the raids that would have been made at various points on the coast. But I cannot see that the mere fact that we have destroyed their fleet merits any marked honour. They were caught in a trap, and half of them burned, and this might have been done equally as well by the Sardinian fishermen, unarmed, and without our aid. As to the fighting, it was of small account. The first three craft we captured offered a much stouter resistance, and we lost two of our number; but in the other affair no knight was killed, or even seriously wounded, and believe me, Countess, I feel absolutely ashamed at the fuss that is made over it. It seems to me that I am a sort of impostor, obtaining credit under false pretences."

"No man is a fair judge of his own actions, Sir Gervaise," Caretto said. "A man may believe himself a Solon, or a Roland; others may consider him as a fool, or an empty braggart; and it must be taken that the general opinion of the public is the judgment from which there is no appeal. It is not the mob of Genoa only who regard the services that you have rendered as extraordinary, but it is the opinion of the councillors and authorities of the Republic, and of those who, like myself, have borne our share in warfare, that not only is the service great, but that it is due to the singular ability with which you, in command of only a single galley, have wholly destroyed or captured the fleet that threatened our commerce. As our councillors, therefore, all competent judges, are unanimous in their opinion that you have deserved the highest honours that Genoa can bestow upon you, it is useless for you to set up your own opinion to the contrary. Take the good things that fall to you, Sir Gervaise, and be thankful. It is seldom that men obtain more honours than they deserve, while it very often happens that they deserve far more than they obtain. Fortune has doubtless some share in every man's career; but when it is not once, but several times, that a knight gains special credit for deeds he has performed, we may be sure that fortune has less to do with the matter than his personal merits. Three times have you earned special credit; upon the first occasion, the grand master—no mean judge of conduct and character—deemed you worthy of secular knighthood, an honour which has not, in my memory, been bestowed at Rhodes upon any young knight; on the second, you were promoted to the command of a galley, though never before has such a command been given to any, save knights of long experience; and now, for the third time, the councillors of one of the greatest of Italian cities are about to do you honour. It is good to be modest, Sir Gervaise, and it is better to under-estimate than to overrate one's own merits, but it is not well to carry the feeling to an extreme. I am quite sure that in your case your disclaimer is wholly sincere and unaffected; but take my advice, accept the honours the world may pay you as not undeserved, determining only in your mind that if you deem them excessive, you will at least do all in your power to show that they are not ill-bestowed. You will not, I trust, take my counsel amiss."

"On the contrary, Sir Fabricius," Gervaise said warmly. "I am really but a boy yet, though by good fortune pushed strangely forward, and I am glad indeed to receive council from a knight of vastly greater experience than myself; and, in future, however much I may be conscious in my own mind that anything I have done is greatly overrated, I will at least abstain from protest. And now, Countess, I must pray you to excuse me. I know that Sir Ralph Harcourt is, before this, down at the dockyard waiting my coming to engage sailors."

"You will come to-morrow at the same time, I hope, Sir Gervaise. As Claudia's sworn knight we have now a claim upon you, and for the short time that you remain here you must regard this as your home, although you must necessarily remain the guest of the doge."

"He is a fine young fellow, indeed," Caretto said, after Gervaise had left. "There is no affectation about his modesty, and he really considers that this success he has gained is solely a stroke of good fortune. Of course, I have been asking many questions about him of the young knights of his own *langue*, Harcourt among them. They tell me that he is always in earnest in everything he undertakes. He is without a rival among the younger knights of the convent in his skill in arms, and for strength and activity in all exercises; he seems to care nothing for the ordinary amusements in which they join at Rhodes, and for nine months was scarcely ever seen by those in the *auberge*, save when they gathered for meals, so continuously did he work to acquire a perfect command of Turkish. How thoroughly he succeeded is evident from the fact that he was able to live among the galley-slaves without exciting any suspicions in their minds that he was other than he pretended to be, a Syrian captive. That he is brave goes without saying, though perhaps no braver than the majority of his companions. The extraordinary thing about him is that although, as he himself says, little more than a boy, he has the coolness to plan, and the head to carry out, schemes that would do credit to the most experienced captain. He is already a credit to the Order, and, should he live, will assuredly rise to the highest offices in it, and may even die its grand master. In the stormy times that are coming on, there will be ample opportunities for him still further to distinguish himself, and to fulfil the singular promise of his youth. That he possesses great tact, as well as other qualities, is shown by the enthusiasm with which his companions regard him. In no case, among those to whom I have spoken, have I discerned the smallest jealousy of him. The tact that is needed to stand thus among fifty young knights, almost all his seniors in age, will assuredly enable him later on to command the confidence and affection of older men."

When the other guests had left, and Caretto only remained, the countess turned to Claudia. "You went too far, Claudia. I was willing enough, when you asked me, that you should bestow a favour upon him. Most young knights wear such a favour, which may be a sign of devotion, but which far more frequently is a piece of gallantry. In the case of a knight hospitaller it can only be the latter; it is in his case merely a sign that he has so distinguished himself that some maiden feels a pride that her gift should be carried into battle by him, and, on his part, that he too is proud of the gift so bestowed by one whose goodwill he prizes. In that way I was willing that you should grant him your favour. But the manner in which you gave it was far more serious than the occasion warranted, and your promise to grant no similar favour to another as long as he lived, surprised, and, I may almost say, shocked me. You are, according to our custom here, considered almost a woman, and had not Sir Gervaise belonged to a religious Order, and were he of a presuming disposition, he might well have gathered a meaning from your words far beyond what you intended, and have even entertained a presumptuous hope that you were not indifferent to his merits. In the present case, of course, no harm is done; still, methinks that it would be far better had the words been unspoken. Your cousin here will, I am sure, agree with me."

Caretto did not speak, but stood playing with his moustache, waiting for Claudia's reply. The girl had stood with downcast eyes while her mother was speaking.

"I only expressed what I felt, mother," she said, after a pause, "and I do not think that Sir Gervaise Tresham is likely to misunderstand me. It seems to me that never among those whom I have met have I seen one so worthy. No praises can be higher than those with which my cousin has spoken of him. He has rescued him, whom we dearly love, from slavery; he has saved Genoa from great disaster, and many towns and villages from plunder and ruin. I do indeed feel proud that such a knight should wear my gage, and, were there no other reason, I should be unwilling that, so long as he carried it, another should possess a similar one from me. I am sure that Sir Gervaise will have felt that this was the meaning of my words; I wished him to see that it was not a favour lightly given by a girl who might, a few weeks hence, bestow a similar one upon another, but was a gage seriously given of the honour in which I held him."

"Very well said, Claudia," Caretto broke in, before the countess could reply. "I warrant me the young knight will not misunderstand your gift, and that he will prize it highly and carry it nobly. He is not one of those who will boast of a favour and display it all times, and, except perhaps to his friend Sir Ralph Harcourt, I will wager he never tells a soul who was its donor."

When Claudia shortly afterwards left the room, he said to the countess,—

"Excuse me for breaking in, Agatha, but I felt that it was much better to agree with her, and not to make overmuch of the matter; she is just of an age to make some one a hero, and she could hardly have chosen a better subject for her worship. In the first place, he is a knight of St. John; in the second, he is going away in a few days, perhaps to-morrow, and may never cross her path again. The thought of him will prevent her fancy from straying for a time, and keep her heart-whole until you decide on a suitor for her hand."

"Nevertheless, I would rather that it had not been so. Claudia is not given to change, and this may last long enough to cause trouble when I bring forward the suitor you speak of."

"Well, in any case it might be worse," Caretto said philosophically. And then, with a smile in answer to her look of inquiry, "Knights of the Order have, ere now, obtained release from their vows."

"Fabricius!" the countess exclaimed, in a shocked voice.

"Yes, I know, Agatha, that the child is one of the richest heiresses in Italy, but for that very reason it needs not that her husband should have wide possessions. In all other respects you could wish for no better. He will assuredly be a famous knight; he is the sort of man to make her perfectly happy; and, lastly, you know I cannot forget that I owe my liberation from slavery to him. At any rate, Agatha, as I said before, he may never cross her path again, and you may, a year or two hence, find her perfectly amenable to your wishes."

CHAPTER XVII
CAPTURED

UPON the following day the doge requested Gervaise to accompany him to a meeting of the council. Upon entering the grand hall he found not only the members of the council assembled in their robes of office, but a large gathering of the nobles and principal citizens of Genoa, together with the knights of the galley whom, under Ralph Harcourt's orders, Gervaise found, to his surprise, drawn up in order across the Hall. Here, in the name of the Republic, Battista Fragoso announced to him that, by the unanimous decision of the council, he had been elected a noble of Genoa; an honour, he added, on only one or two previous occasions in the history of the Republic bestowed upon any but of princely rank, but which he had nobly earned by the great service he had rendered to the State. His name was then inscribed in the book containing the names and titles of the nobles of Genoa. Next, Battista Fragoso presented him with a superb suit of Milanese armour, as his own personal gift, and then with a casket of very valuable jewels, as the gift of the city of Genoa. Each presentation was accompanied by the plaudits of the assembly, and by the no less warm acclamations of the knights. Ralph was then called forward, and presented with a suit of armour but little inferior to that given to Gervaise, and each knight received a heavy gold chain of the finest workmanship of Genoa.

CAPTURED

Two days later the preparations for departure were complete, and a sufficient number of men were engaged to man the prizes. This charge, also, Genoa took upon itself, and put on board much stronger crews than Gervaise deemed necessary for the navigation of the ships. The weather was fine and the wind favourable, and a quick passage was made to Rhodes. When the harbour was in sight, the ships were ordered to proceed in single file, the galley leading the way with a huge banner of the Order floating from her stern, and smaller flags on staffs at each side. It was not until they passed by the two forts guarding the entrance that the flags fluttering at the mast-heads of the prizes afforded to those on shore an intimation of the event that had taken place, and even then none supposed that this fleet of prizes had been taken by the one galley that headed them.

As the *Santa Barbara* slowly rowed up the harbour, the State barge of the grand master put off to meet it, and D'Aubusson, with a party of knights, soon stepped on board.

"Welcome back, Sir Gervaise ! although I little expected to see you return so soon. What is the meaning of this procession that follows you? By their rig and appearance they are Moors, but how they come to be thus sailing in your wake is a mystery to us all."

"They are Moors, your Excellency; they form part of an expedition fitted out by the corsairs of Algiers, Tripoli, Tunis, and other piratical strongholds, for the purpose of destroying the commerce and ravaging the coasts of Western Italy. Fortunately, we fell in with a ship that had been plundered by three of them on their way north, and learned from the dying captain, who was the only one of her crew left with life on board, the direction they were taking, and something of the nature of the expedition. We pursued the three galleys, came up with them, had the good fortune to capture them, and then had the delight of finding among their rowers the noble knights, Fabricius Caretto, Giacomo Da Vinci, and Pietro Forzi."

277

The grand master, and the knights with him, uttered an exclamation of joy, and, as the three knights named stepped forward, embraced them with the liveliest pleasure.

"My dear Caretto," the grand master exclaimed, "it is almost a resurrection, for we have all long mourned you as dead; and your return to us at the present time is indeed fortunate; for upon whose judgment and aid could I better rely than those of my old comrade in arms?" Then, turning to Gervaise, he went on: "It was a daring and brilliant exploit indeed, Sir Gervaise, and in due time honour shall be paid to you and your brave companions, to whom and to you I now tender the thanks of the Order. But tell me the rest briefly, for I would fain hear from these noble knights and old friends the story of what has befallen them."

"My tale is a very brief one, your Highness. The Cavalier Caretto sailed at once in a swift craft from the south of Sardinia, to carry warnings to the cities on the coast of Italy of the danger that threatened them, and in order that some war-galleys might be despatched by Genoa to meet the corsair fleet. During his absence we discovered the little inlet in which the pirates lay hidden, waiting doubtless the arrival of the three ships we had captured, to commence operations. On the return of the knight with the news that it would be at least a fortnight before Genoa could fit out any galleys, and fearing that the pirates might at any moment put to sea, we procured some small Sardinian craft, and fitted them as fire-ships; with the captives we had rescued, and some Sard fishermen, we manned the three prizes, distributing the knights between them, and at night launched the fire-ships against the corsairs, whose ships were crowded together. Eleven of them were burnt; six we captured as they endeavoured to make their way out, and took possession of four others whose crews had run them ashore and deserted them. None escaped."

Exclamations of astonishment and almost of incredulity broke from the knights.

CAPTURED

"And is it possible, Sir Gervaise, that these thirteen vessels that follow you are all prizes captured by your galley alone?"

"It is, as I have the honour to tell your Highness. But their capture, except in the case of the first three, was due almost solely to good fortune and to the position in which we found them, almost incapable of defence."

"What think you, knights and comrades?" the grand master said to his companions. "There were some of you who deemed it rash to entrust a galley to so young a commander and so youthful a crew. What say you now? Never in the annals of the Order has such a sight been witnessed as that of thirteen prizes being brought in by a single galley, to say naught of eleven others destroyed. Caretto, you and your comrades must have had some share in this marvellous victory."

"By no means," the Italian replied; "beyond having the honour of aiding to carry out the orders of Sir Gervaise Tresham, the commander of the galley. The plan was wholly of his own devising, its execution solely due to his arrangement of the details, and that without the slightest suggestion on the part of myself or my comrades. I will presently narrate to you the whole story; it will come better from my lips than from those of Sir Gervaise, whose disposition is to wholly under-estimate the merit of the action he has performed. But I must also bear testimony, not only to the bravery displayed by Sir Gervaise, Sir Ralph Harcourt, his lieutenant, and every one of the knights his crew, but to the admirable discipline, order, and good fellowship on board the galley, which would have done credit to the most experienced commander and to the most veteran knights of the Order."

The grand master paused a moment, and then said in a loud voice,—

"Sir Gervaise Tresham, Sir Ralph Harcourt, and knights of the seven *langues* of the Order—As yet I can hardly appreciate the full extent of the service that you have rendered. I thanked you but now for the capture of three corsairs; but what can I say when I learn that you have destroyed or taken a whole fleet? I invite you all to a banquet that I shall hold to-night, where the Cavalier Caretto will relate to us all the details of this marvellous exploit."

Within a few minutes after the return of the grand master and his party ashore, the flags of the Order were run up to the flagstaffs of every fort and bastion: the bells of the churches chimed out a triumphant peal, and a salute was fired from the guns of the three water forts, while along the wall facing the port, the townspeople waved numberless gay flags as a welcome to the galley. Most of the knights went ashore at once, but Gervaise, under the excuse that he wished to see that everything was in order before landing, remained on board until it was time to go to the banquet, being sure that by that time the knights would have fully told the story at their respective *auberge*s, and that there would be no more questions to answer. The banquet differed but little from that at Genoa, and Gervaise was heartily glad when it was over.

The next day the grand master sent for him.

"If I judge rightly, Sir Gervaise, the thing that will best please you at present, is an order to put to sea again at once, to conclude the usual period of service of the galley."

"It is indeed," Gervaise replied earnestly. "But I should be glad, sir, if you will allow that the time should begin to count afresh from our present start. We have really had but a short period of service, for we wasted a week at Genoa, and ten days on our journey back here, so that we have had really no more than a month's active service."

"Yes, if you count only by time," D'Aubusson said, with a smile. "Reckoning by results, you have done a good five years' cruise. However, so small a request can certainly be granted. The places of the two knights who were killed, and of four others whose wounds are reported to me as being too severe for them to be fit for service for some time, shall be filled up at once from the *langue*s to which each belonged. You will cruise among the Western islands, whence complaints have reached us of a corsair who has been plundering and burning. Sometimes he is heard of as far north as Negropont, at others he is off the south of the Morea; then, again, we hear of him among the Cyclades. We have been unwilling to despatch another galley, for there is ample employment for every one here. After the blow you have struck on the Moorish corsairs, they are likely to be quiet for a little. You had best, therefore, try for a time if you cannot come across this pirate. You must let me know how much you paid for the vessels you used as fire-ships, and to the Sards; this is an expense chargeable to the general service. I may tell you that to me it is due that no recognition of your exploits, such as that which Genoa bestowed upon you, will be made. At the council this morning it was urged that some signal mark of honour should be granted; but I interposed, saying that you had already received exceptional promotion, and that it would not be for your good, or that of the Order, for so young a knight to be raised to an official position of a character usually held by seniors, and that I was perfectly sure you would prefer remaining in command of your galley to any promotion whatever that would retain you on the Island."

"Indeed I should, your Highness. I wish to gain experience and to do service to the Order, and so far from pleasing me, promotion would trouble and distress me, and, could it have been done, I would most gladly have sent home the prizes, instead of going to Genoa, and would myself have continued the cruise."

"So the Cavalier Caretto told me," the grand master replied. "Very well, then. In three days you shall set out again. The admiral tells me that never before has a galley returned with the slaves in such good health and condition, and that unquestionably your plan of erecting an awning to shelter them from the midday heat and the night dews has had a most beneficial effect on their health; he has recommended its general adoption."

A KNIGHT OF THE WHITE CROSS

Three days later the *Santa Barbara* again left port, and was soon upon her station. For some weeks she cruised backwards and forwards along the coast and among the islands. They often heard of the pirate-ship, but all their efforts to find her were unavailing.

One evening there were signs of a change of weather, and by morning it was blowing a furious gale from the north; in spite of the efforts of the rowers, the galley narrowly escaped being driven ashore; but she at last gained the shelter of an island, and anchored under its lee, the slaves being utterly worn out by continuous exertion. As soon as the gale abated they again put to sea, and, after proceeding for some miles, saw a ship cast up on shore. Some people could be made out on board of her, and a white flag was raised.

"She must have been driven ashore during the gale," Gervaise said. "We will row in to within a quarter of a mile of her and see what we can do for them."

As soon as the anchor was dropped a boat was lowered.

"I will go myself, Ralph, for I shall be glad to set my foot on shore again. There must be people on the island; I wonder none of them have come to the aid of those poor fellows. I suppose the villages are on the other side of the island, and they have not yet heard of the wreck."

Gervaise asked three of the knights to accompany him, and the boat, rowed by galley-slaves, was soon on its way. All were glad at the change afforded to the monotony of their life on board, and at the prospect of a scamper on shore.

There were but five or six men to be seen on the deck of the wreck, and these had, as the boat approached, come down to the rocks as if to meet those who came to their aid; but as the knights leapt out, they threw themselves suddenly upon them with knives and scimitars that had hitherto been concealed beneath their garments, while at the same moment a crowd of men appeared on the deck of the ship, and, leaping down, ran forward with drawn swords. Two of the knights fell dead before they had time to draw

282

their weapons. The third shook off his two assailants, and for a minute kept them both at bay; but others, rushing up, cut him down.

Gervaise had received a slight wound before he realised what was happening. He snatched his dagger from its sheath, and struck down one assailant; but ere he could raise it to strike again, another leapt on to his back, and clung there until the rest rushed up, when he shouted, "Take him alive! take him alive!" and, throwing down their weapons, half a dozen of the pirates flung themselves upon Gervaise, and strove to pull him to the ground, until at last, in spite of his desperate resistance, they succeeded in doing so. His armour was hastily stripped off, his hands and feet bound, and then at the orders of the pirate who had leapt on his back, and who was evidently the captain, half-a-dozen men lifted him on to their shoulders. As they did so four guns from the galley flashed out, and the balls flew overhead. The pirates, who had already begun to quarrel over the armour and arms of the fallen knights, at once took to their heels, followed by the galley-slaves from the boat.

"Make haste," the captain said to the men carrying Gervaise.

"They are lowering their boats; we must be under way before they come up."

In a minute or two Gervaise was set down on his feet, the cords round his legs were cut, and he was made to hurry along with his captors. In a short time an inlet was reached, and here Gervaise saw, to his mortification, the pirate craft for which the *Santa Barbara* had in vain been searching. As soon as the party were all on board, the ropes by which she was moored to two trees were thrown off; the great sails hoisted, and she sailed boldly out. Although the gale had entirely abated, there was still a brisk wind blowing, and it was evident to the captain of the corsair that under such circumstances he could out-sail the galley that had long been searching for him; when, therefore, the *Santa Barbara* came in sight, just as he and his crew had finished stripping the wreck of its contents, the idea had occurred to him to attempt to entice some of the knights to land.

As soon as the vessel was under way he abused his followers hotly for not having obeyed his orders to capture the knights without bloodshed; but they pleaded that it was as much as they had been able to do to capture Gervaise in that way, and that they could never have overcome the four together, before the boats would have had time to come from the ship.

Gervaise had been told to sit down with his back to a mast and in this position he could, when the vessel heeled over to the breeze, obtain a view of the sea. It was with a feeling of bitter mortification and rage that he saw the galley lying but half a mile away, as the corsair issued from the inlet. A moment later he heard a gun fired, and saw the signal hoisted to recall the boats.

"If the wind had been favourable," the captain said to his mate, "we would have borne down upon her, and could have reached and captured her before the boats got back, for you may be sure that they have landed almost all their men. However, we can't get there against the wind, and we will now say good-bye to them."

Gervaise knew well that at the pace they were running through the water the galley would have no chance whatever of overtaking her, and that, ere the knights came on board again, she would be already two or three miles away. A point of land soon concealed the galley from view, and when he caught sight of her, as she rounded the point, she was but a speck in the distance.

They passed several islands in the course of the day, changing their direction to a right angle to that which they had at first pursued, as soon as they were hidden from the sight of the galley by an intervening island. As night came on they anchored in a little bay on the coast of the Morea. The sails being furled, the sailors made a division of the booty they had captured on the island, and of the portable property found on board the wreck. A gourd full of water was placed to Gervaise's lips by one of the men of a kinder disposition than the rest. He drank it thankfully, for he was parched with thirst excited by the pain caused by the tightness with which he had been bound.

He slept where he sat. All night four men remained on guard, although from what he heard they had no fear whatever of being overtaken. In the morning his arms were unbound, and they stripped off his tunic and shirt. They had evidently respect for his strength, for before loosing his arms they tightly fastened his ankles together. The removal of his shirt exposed Claudia's gift to view.

"Take that from him and give it to me," the captain said. As the two men approached, Gervaise seized one in each hand, dashed them against each other, and hurled them on the deck. But the exertion upset his equilibrium, and after making a vain effort to recover it, he fell heavily across them. The captain stooped over him, and, before he could recover himself, snatched the chain from his neck.

"You are a stout fellow," he said, laughing, "and will make a fine slave. What have you got here that you are ready to risk your life for?" He looked at the little chain and its pendant with an air of disappointment. "'Tis worth but little," he said, showing it to his mate. "I would not give five ducats for it in the market. It must be a charm, or a knight would never carry it about with him and prize it so highly. It may be to things like this the Christians owe their luck."

"It has not brought him luck this time," the mate observed with a laugh.

"Even a charm cannot always bring good luck, but at any rate I will try it; "and he put it round his neck just as Gervaise had worn it. The latter was now unbound, and permitted to move about the deck. The strength he had shown in the struggle on shore, and the manner in which he had hurled, bound as he was, two of their comrades to the deck, had won for him the respect of his captors, and he was therefore allowed privileges not granted to the seamen of the vessel that had had the ill fortune to be cast on shore so close to the spot where the corsair was hiding. These had been seized, driven to the ship, and having been stripped of the greater portion of their clothes, shut down in the hold.

Although angry that but one out of the four who landed had been captured, the captain was in a good humour at having tricked his redoubtable foes, and was disposed to treat Gervaise with more consideration than was generally given to captives. The latter had not spoken a word of Turkish from the time he was captured, and had shaken his head when first addressed in that language. No suspicion was therefore entertained that he had any knowledge of it, and the Turks conversed freely before him.

"Where think you we had better sell him?" the mate asked the captain, when Gervaise was leaning against the bulwark watching the land, a short quarter of a mile away. "He ought to fetch a good ransom."

"Ay, but who would get it? You know how it was with one that Ibrahim took two years ago. First there were months of delay, then, when the ransom was settled, the pasha took four-fifths of it for himself, and Ibrahim got far less than he would have done had he sold him as a slave. The pashas here, and the sultans of the Moors, are all alike; if they once meddle in an affair they take all the profit, and think they do well by giving you a tithe of it. There are plenty of wealthy Moors who are ready to pay well for a Christian slave, especially when he is a good-looking young fellow such as this. He will fetch as much as all those eight sailors below. They are only worth their labour, while this youngster will command a fancy price. I know a dozen rich Moors in Tripoli or Tunis who would be glad to have him; and we agreed that we would run down to the African coast for awhile, for that galley has been altogether too busy of late for our comfort, and will be all the more active after this little affair; besides, people in these islands have got so scared that one can't get within ten miles of any of them now without seeing their signal smokes rising on the hills, and finding, when they land, the villages deserted and stripped of everything worth carrying away."

This news was a disappointment to Gervaise. He had calculated that he would be sold at one of the Levant ports, and had thought that with his knowledge of Turkish he should have no great difficulty in escaping from any master into whose hands he might fall, and taking his chance of either seizing a fishing-boat, or of making his way in a trading ship to some district where the population was a mixed one, and where trade was winked at between the merchants there, and those at some of the Greek towns. To escape from Tunis or Tripoli would be far more difficult; there, too, he would be beyond the reach of the good offices of Suleiman Ali, who would, he was sure, have done all in his power to bring about his release. Of one thing he was determined: he would not return to Rhodes without making every possible effort to recover Claudia's gage, as he considered it absolutely incumbent on him as a knight to guard, as something sacred, a gift so bestowed. The fancy of the corsair to retain the jewel as a charm he regarded as a piece of the greatest good fortune. Had it been thrown among the common spoil, he would never have known to which of the crew it had fallen at the division, still less have traced what became of it afterwards; whereas now, for some time, at any rate, it was likely to remain in the captain's possession.

Had it not been for that, he would have attempted to escape at the first opportunity, and such an opportunity could not fail to present itself ere long, for he had but to manage to possess himself of Moslem garments to be able to move about unquestioned in any Turkish town. When it became dark he was shut up in the hold, which was, he found, crowded with captives, as, in addition to the crew of the wreck, between forty and fifty Greeks, for the most part boys and young girls, had been carried off from the villages plundered. It was pitch dark below, although the scuttle had been left open in order to allow a certain amount of air to reach the captives; Gervaise, therefore, felt his way about cautiously, and lay down as soon as he found a clear space. Save an occasional moan or curse, and the panting of those suffering from the heat and closeness of the crowded hold, all was still. The majority of the captives had been some time in their floating prison, and their first poignant grief had settled down into a dull and despairing acceptance of their fate; the sailors, newly captured, had for hours raved and cursed, but, worn out by their struggle with the elements, and their rage and grief, they had now fallen asleep.

It was long before Gervaise dozed off. He was furious with himself for having fallen into the trap; if he had, as he said to himself, lain off the beach in the boat, and questioned the supposed shipwrecked sailors, their inability to reply to him would have at once put him on his guard; as it was, he had walked into the snare as carelessly and confidently as a child might have done. Even more than his own captivity, he regretted the death of his three comrades, which he attributed to his own want of care.

The next morning he was again allowed on deck. The vessel was under way, and her head was pointing south. To his surprise some of the crew gave him a friendly greeting; he was unable to understand a manner so at variance with their hatred to the Christians, until one of them said to him in a mixture of Greek and Italian,—

"We have heard from our countrymen who were in the boat with you, that they received much kindness at your hands, and that of all the Christians they had served under, you were the kindest master. Therefore, it is but right now Allah has decreed that you in turn should be a slave to the true believers, that you should receive the same mercy you gave to Moslems when they were in your power."

The captain came up as the man was speaking. He talked for a time to the sailor, who then turned again to Gervaise. "The captain says that he is told you were the commander of that galley; he has questioned the eight men separately, and they all tell the same story: and yet he cannot understand how so young a man should command a galley manned by warriors famous for their deeds of arms, even among us who are their foes."

"This galley was an exception," Gervaise replied; "the knights on board were all young, as they could be better spared than those more experienced, at a time when your sultan is known to be preparing for an attack on Rhodes."

The captain was silent for a minute when this was interpreted to him; he had at the time noticed and wondered at the youth of the four knights, and the explanation seemed to him a reasonable one.

"I wish I had known it," he said after a pause; "for had I done so, I would have fought and captured her yesterday; I have half a mind to go back and seek her now."

He called up one of the ex-slaves who was a native of Tripoli, and who had now taken his place as a member of the crew, and asked him a number of questions. Gervaise felt uncomfortable while the man was answering. Fortunately, his rowers had agreed to say nothing whatever of the destruction of the corsair fleet, of which no word had as yet reached the pirates, deeming that, in their anger at the news, the pirates might turn upon them for the part that they had, however involuntarily, borne in it.

As soon as he perceived that the captain entertained the idea of returning to engage the galley, the man felt that if he were to avoid a return into captivity he must deter him from taking such a step. He therefore, in answer to his questions as to the strength of the crew of the galley and the fighting powers of the knights, reported the capture of the three vessels. The captain listened almost incredulously to his statement, and, calling up another two of the men, questioned them also as to the occurrence. Having heard them, he turned away and paced the deck, in evident anger; however, he gave no instructions for a change of course, and, to the great satisfaction of the eight rescued slaves, the vessel continued her course southward.

A KNIGHT OF THE WHITE CROSS

As they neared the African coast, Gervaise kept an eager look-out, in hopes that Visconti's galley might appear in sight. The captain's temper had not recovered from the effect of the news of the capture of three Moorish vessels by the galley commanded by Gervaise, and the latter, seeing the mood he was in, kept forward so as to avoid coming in contact with him. He had early taken the opportunity of saying to one of the released galley-slaves, "I pray you, if you have any feeling of kindness towards me for the efforts I made to alleviate your condition, say no word of my knowledge of Turkish, and ask the others also to remain silent on this point."

The man had nodded, and the request was observed by them all.

The captain's irritation showed itself in his treatment of the other captives. These were brought up every day from the hold, and kept on deck until dark, as the price they would fetch in the slave-market in Tripoli would depend greatly upon their health and appearance; but when the captain came near them he several times struck them brutally, if they happened to be in his way. Gervaise had the greatest difficulty in restraining his indignation, and, indeed, only did so because he felt that his interference would but make things worse for them. When at last the ship cast anchor off Tripoli, the captain ordered the boats to be lowered. As he walked towards the gangway, he happened to push against one of the captives, a Greek girl of some ten years of age. With an angry exclamation he struck her to the deck. Gervaise sprang forward.

"You brute!" he exclaimed in English. "I have a good mind to throw you overboard, and will do so the next time you strike one of these children without cause."

Infuriated by Gervaise's interference and threatening attitude, the corsair drew his long knife; but before he could strike, Gervaise caught his wrist; the knife fell from his hand, and Gervaise kicked it through the open gangway into the sea. The captain shouted to his men to seize the Christian, but the young knight's blood was up now. The first man who came at him he seized by the sash round his waist, and threw overboard; the two next he stretched on the deck with blows from his clenched fist. Some of the others now drew their weapons, but the captain shouted to them to sheath them.

"Fools!" he yelled. "Is it not enough that your cowardice has already cost us the lives of three knights, whose capture would have brought us a big sum? Throw him down and bind him. What ! are fifty of you afraid of one unarmed man? No wonder these Christians capture our ships, if this is the mettle of our crews!"

Goaded by his words, the men made a general rush upon Gervaise, and, in spite of his desperate efforts, threw him on to the deck and bound him; then the captain, seizing a heavy stick in his left hand, his right being still powerless, showered blows upon him until Gervaise almost lost consciousness. "Throw some water over the dog," the corsair said, as he threw down the stick, panting with his exertions; and then, without waiting to see if his order was obeyed, he took his place in the boat, and was rowed ashore.

As soon as he had left, three or four of the ex-galley-slaves carried Gervaise into the shade of the sail. The sailors, several of whom bore signs of the late struggle, looked on sullenly, but offered no opposition when the men took off the ropes and raised him into a sitting posture against the mast. He had not entirely lost consciousness, and was now fast recovering himself.

"Is there anything we can do for you?" one of the men asked in Italian.

"No; I shall soon be all right again, although I am bruised all over, and shall be stiff for a day or two. You had best leave me now, or you will incur the enmity of these fellows."

Gervaise was indeed bruised from his neck to his heels. Even in his passion the pirate had avoided striking him on the head, as a disfiguring mark on the face would diminish his value. Sitting there, he congratulated himself that he had been beaten with a stick and not with a whip; a stick is a weapon, and he did not feel the same sense of dishonour that he would have experienced had he been beaten with a whip. That such might be his lot in slavery he recognised. The backs of Caretto and his two companions were seamed with the marks inflicted by the gang-master's whip, and he could scarce hope to escape the same treatment; but at present he hardly felt a slave. There was another reflection that to some extent mitigated the pain of his bruises; the pirate captain held his treasured gage, and it was his fixed determination to recover it. The man had at first in a rough way treated him fairly, and had allowed him more liberty than the other captives, and he would have felt reluctant to take extreme measure against him to recover the gage. Now he was not only free from any sense of obligation, but had a heavy score to settle with him.

After a time he got up and walked stiffly and painfully up and down the deck, knowing that this was the best plan to prevent the limbs from stiffening. The corsair did not return until night set in; he was accompanied by an Arab, whose dress and appearance showed that he was a person of importance. The other slaves had all been sent below, but Gervaise still remained on deck, as the mate had not cared to risk another conflict by giving him orders in the absence of the captain. As the pirate stepped on deck he ordered some torches to be brought.

"This is the Christian I spoke of," he said to the Arab, pointing to Gervaise, who was leaning carelessly against the bulwark.

"He is, as you see, capable of hard work of any kind; his strength is prodigious, for it took ten of my best men to bind him this morning."

"Why did you wish to bind him?" the Arab asked coldly; "you told me that although so strong he was of a quiet disposition, and would make a good household slave."

"I struck a slave girl who stood in my way," the captain said, "and he came at me so suddenly that I had to call upon the men to bind him. He threw one of them

292

overboard, and with his naked hands knocked down two others; and, as I have told you, it took all the efforts of eight or ten more before they could overcome him."

The Arab took a torch from one of the sailors, walked across to Gervaise, who was naked from the waist upwards, his upper garments having been torn into shreds in the struggle, and examined him closely.

"And then you beat him," he said, turning to the captain.

"Certainly I beat him. Do you think that a slave is to mutiny on board my ship, and escape unpunished?"

The Arab, without replying, again inspected Gervaise.

"You ask a large sum for him," he said.

"I should ask twice as much," the captain replied, "if it were not for the regulation that one slave from each cargo brought in belongs to the sultan, and his officers would as a matter of course choose this fellow, for the others are merely such as are sold in the market every day. This man is one of the accursed Order of Rhodes, and would fetch a ransom many times greater than the sum I ask for him, only I have not the time to wait for months until the affair could be arranged."

"And, moreover, Hassan," the Arab said grimly, "it has doubtless not escaped you that as the Sultan of Turkey is fitting out an expedition to destroy the community of Rhodes, the chance of their ransoming their comrade is a very slight one."

"Threatened men live long," the captain said. "The sultan has been talking of attacking them for years, and something has always happened to prevent his carrying out his intention. It may be the same again."

"I will take him," the Arab said shortly. "Here is a purse with the sum you named; count it, and see that it is right."

As he stood apart while the pirate counted out the money, the eight released slaves came up in a body, and one of them, bowing low before the merchant, said,—

A KNIGHT OF THE WHITE CROSS

"My lord, we have long been slaves of the Christian knights at Rhodes, and have worked in their galleys. We were rescued the other day when this knight was taken prisoner. Our life has been a hard one. We have borne toil, and hardship, and blows, the heat of the sun by day, and the damp by night, but we would humbly represent to you that since we were placed in the galley commanded by this knight our lot has been made bearable by his humanity and kindness. He erected an awning to shade us from the sun's rays, and to shelter us from the night dews. He provided good food for us. He saw that we were not worked beyond our strength, and he forbade us being struck, unless for good cause. Therefore, my lord, now that misfortune has fallen upon him, we venture to represent to you the kindness with which he has treated us, in the hope that it may please you to show him such mercy as he showed to us."

"You have done well," the Arab said, "and your words shall not be forgotten. When you land to-morrow, inquire for the house of Isaac Ben Ibyn. You are doubtless penniless, and I may be able to obtain employment for those of you who may stop at Tripoli, and to assist those who desire to take passage to their homes elsewhere. We are commanded to be grateful to those who befriend us, and as you have shown yourselves to be so, it is right that I, an humble servant of the Great One, should in His name reward you."

Motioning to Gervaise to follow him, the Arab stepped into his boat. Gervaise turned to the men, and said in Italian,—

"Thanks, my friends, you have well discharged any debt that you may think you owe me. Will you tell that villain"— and he pointed to the captain threateningly—"I warn him that some day I will kill him like a dog!" Then, turning, he stepped into the bow of the boat, and the two men who rowed it at once pushed off.

CHAPTER XVIII
A KIND MASTER

WHEN the boat reached the shore the Arab handed a long bernouse to Gervaise, signed to him to pull the hood well over his head, and then led the way through the streets until he stopped at a large house, standing in a quiet quarter of the town. He struck on the door with his hand, and it was at once opened by a black slave.

"Call Muley," the Arab said.

The slave hurried away, and returned in a minute with a man somewhat past middle age, and dressed in a style that indicated that he was a trusted servant.

"Muley," his master said, "I have bought this Christian who has been brought in by Hassan the corsair. He is one of the knights who are the terrors of our coasts, but is, from what I hear, of a kind and humane disposition. I am told that he was a commander of one of their galleys, and though I should not have believed it had I only Hassan's word, I have heard from others that it was so. My wife has long desired to have a Christian slave, and as Allah has blessed my efforts it was but right that I should gratify her, though in truth I do not know what work I shall set him to do at present. Let him first have a bath, and see that he is clad decently, then let him have a good meal. I doubt if he has had one since he was captured. He has been sorely beaten by the corsair, and from no fault of his own, but only because he opposed the man's brutality to a child slave. If any of his wounds need ointment, see that he has it. When all is ready, bring him to the door of my apartments, in order that I may show to my wife that I have gratified her whim."

Then he motioned to Gervaise to follow Muley, who was the head of his household. Gervaise resisted the impulse to thank his new master, and followed in silence.

He was first taken to a bath-room, furnished with an abundance of hot and cold water. Muley uttered an exclamation as, on Gervaise throwing off his bernouse, he saw that his flesh was a mass of bruises. After filling the bath with hot water, he motioned to Gervaise to get in, and lie there until he returned. It was some time before he came back, bringing a pot of ointment and some bandages. It was only on the body that the wounds needed dressing, for here the blows had fallen on the naked skin. When he had dressed them, Muley went out and returned with some Turkish garments, consisting of a pair of baggy trousers of yellow cotton, a white shirt of the same material, and a sleeveless jacket of blue cloth embroidered with yellow trimming; a pair of yellow slippers completed the costume. Muley now took him into another room, where he set before him a dish of rice with a meat gravy, a large piece of bread, and a wooden spoon.

Gervaise ate the food with a deep feeling of thankfulness for the fate that had thrown him into such good hands. Then, after taking a long draught of water, he rose to his feet and followed Muley into the entrance hall. The latter stopped at a door on the opposite side, knocked at it, and then motioned to Gervaise to take off his slippers. The door was opened by the Arab himself.

"Enter," he said courteously, and led Gervaise into an apartment where a lady and two girls were sitting on a divan. They were slightly veiled; but, as Gervaise afterwards learnt, Ben Ibyn was not a Moor, but a Berber, a people who do not keep their women in close confinement as do the Moors, but allow them to go abroad freely without being entirely muffled up.

A KIND MASTER

"Khadja," the merchant said, "this is the Christian slave I purchased to-day. You have for a long time desired one, but not until now have I found one who would, I thought, satisfy your expectations. What think you of him?"

"He is a noble-looking youth truly, Isaac, with his fair, wavy hair, his grey eyes, and white skin; truly, all my neighbours will envy me such a possession. I have often seen Christian slaves before, but they have always been broken-down and dejected-looking creatures; this one bears himself like a warrior rather than a slave."

"He is a warrior; he is one of those terrible knights of Rhodes whose very name is a terror to the Turks, and whose galleys are feared even by our boldest corsairs. He must be of approved valour, for he was commander of one of these galleys."

The girls looked with amazement at Gervaise. They had often heard tales of the capture of ships that had sailed from Tripoli, by the galleys of the Christian knights, and had pictured those fierce warriors as of almost supernatural strength and valour. That this youth, whose upper lip was but shaded with a slight moustache, should be one of them, struck them as being almost incredible.

"He does not look ferocious, father," one of them said. "He looks pleasant and good-tempered, as if he could injure no one."

"And yet this morning, daughter, he braved, unarmed, the anger of Hassan the corsair, on the deck of his own ship; and when the pirate called upon his men to seize him he threw one overboard, struck two more on to the deck, and it needed eight men to overpower him."

"I hope he won't get angry with us!" the younger girl exclaimed.

Gervaise could not suppress a laugh, and then, turning to the merchant, said in Turkish,—

"I must ask your pardon for having concealed from you my knowledge of your tongue. I kept the secret from all on board the corsair, and meant to have done the same here, deeming that if none knew that I spoke the language it would greatly aid me should I ever see an opportunity of making my escape; but, Ben Ibyn, you have behaved so kindly to me that I feel it would not be honourable to keep it a secret from you, and to allow you and the ladies to talk freely before me, thinking that I was altogether ignorant of what you were saying."

"You have acted well and honourably," Ben Ibyn said, putting a hand on his shoulder kindly. "We have heard much of the character of the Order, and that though valiant in battle, your knights are courteous and chivalrous, deeming a deceitful action to be unworthy of them, and binding themselves by their vows to succour the distressed and to be pitiful to the weak. We have heard that our wounded are tended by them in your hospitals with as much care as men of their own race and religion, and that in many things the knights were to be admired even by those who were their foes. I see now that these reports were true, and that although, as you say, it might be of advantage to you that none should know you speak Arabic, yet it is from a spirit of honourable courtesy you have now told us that you do so.

"I did not tell you, wife," he went on, turning to her, "that the reason why he bearded Hassan to-day was because the corsair brutally struck a little female captive; thus, you see, he, at the risk of his life, and when himself a captive, carried out his vows to protect the defenceless. And now, wife, there is one thing you must know. For some time, at any rate, you must abandon the idea of exciting the envy of your friends by exhibiting your Christian captive to them. As you are aware, the sultan has the choice of any one slave he may select from each batch brought in, and assuredly he would choose this one, did it come to his ears, or to the ears of one of his officers, that a Christian knight had been landed. For this reason Hassan sold him to me for a less sum than he would otherwise have demanded, and we must for some time keep his presence here a secret. My idea is that he shall remain indoors until we move next week into our country house, where he will be comparatively free from observation."

"Certainly, Isaac. I would not on any account that he should be handed over to the sultan, for he would either be put into the galleys or have to labour in the streets."

"I will tell Muley to order the other slaves to say nothing outside of the fresh arrival, so for the present there is no fear of its being talked about in the town. Hassan will, for his own sake, keep silent on the matter. I have not yet asked your name," he went on, turning to Gervaise.

"My name is Gervaise Tresham; but it will be easier for you to call me by my first name only."

"Then, Gervaise, it were well that you retired to rest at once, for I am sure that you sorely need it." He touched a bell on the table, and told Muley, when he appeared, to conduct Gervaise to the place where he was to sleep, which was, he had already ordered, apart from the quarters of the other slaves.

"The young fellow is a mass of bruises," Ben Ibyn said to his wife, when the door closed behind Gervaise. "Hassan beat him so savagely, after they had overpowered and bound him, that he well-nigh killed him."

An exclamation of indignation burst from the wife and daughters.

"Muley has seen to his wounds," he went on, "and he will doubtless be cured in a few days. And now, wife, that your wish is gratified, and I have purchased a Christian slave for you, may I ask what you are going to do with him?"

"I am sure I do not know," she said in a tone of perplexity. "I had thought of having him to hand round coffee when my friends call, and perhaps to work in the garden, but I did not think that he would be anything like this."

"That is no reason why he should not do so," Ben Ibyn said. "These Christians, I hear, treat their women as if they were superior beings, and feel it no dishonour to wait upon them; I think you cannot do better than carry out your plan. It is certain there is no sort of work that he would prefer to it; therefore, let it be understood that he is to be your own personal attendant, and that when you have no occasion for his services, he will work in the garden. Only do not for the present let any of your friends see him; they would spread the news like wildfire, and in a week every soul in the town would know that you had a good-looking Christian slave, and the sultan's officer would be sending for me to ask how I obtained him. We must put a turban on him. Any one who caught a glimpse of that hair of his, however far distant, would know that he was a Frank."

"We might stain his face and hands with walnut juice," Khadja said, "he would pass as a Nubian. Some of them are tall and strong."

"A very good thought, wife; it would be an excellent disguise. So shall it be." He touched the bell again. "Tell Muley I would speak with him. Muley," he went on, when the steward appeared, "have you said aught to any of the servants touching the Christian?"

"No, my lord; you gave me no instructions about it, and I thought it better to wait until the morning, when I could ask you."

"You did well. We have determined to stain his skin, and at present he will pass as a Nubian. This will avoid all questions and talk."

"But, my lord, they will wonder that he cannot speak their tongue."

"He must pass among them as a mute; but indeed he speaks Arabic as well as we do, Muley."

The man uttered an exclamation of surprise. "He had intended to conceal his knowledge," Ben Ibyn went on, "which would have been politic; but when he found that my intentions were kind, he told us that he knew our tongue, and now revealed his knowledge, as he thought it would be dishonourable to listen to our talk, leaving us under the impression that he could not understand us."

A KIND MASTER

"Truly these Christians are strange men," Muley said. "This youth, who has not yet grown the hair on his face, is nevertheless commander of a war-galley. He is ready to risk his life on behalf of a slave, and can strike down men with his unarmed hand; he is as gentle in his manner as a woman; and now it seems he can talk Arabic, and although it was in his power to keep this secret he tells it rather than overhear words that are not meant for his ear. Truly they are strange people, the Franks. I will prepare some stain in the morning, my lord, and complete his disguise before any of the others see him."

The next morning Muley told Gervaise that his master thought that it would be safer and more convenient for him to pass as a dumb Nubian slave. Gervaise thought the plan an excellent one; and he was soon transformed, Muley shaving that part of the hair that would have shown below the turban, and then staining him a deep brownish-black, from the waist upwards, together with his feet and his legs up to his knee, and darkening his eyebrows, eyelashes, and moustache.

"Save that your lips lack the thickness, and your nose is straighter than those of Nubians, no one would doubt but that you were one of that race; and this is of little consequence, as many of them are of mixed blood, and, though retaining their dark colour, have features that in their outline resemble those of the Arabs. Now I will take you to Ben Ibyn, so that he may judge whether any further change is required before the servants and slaves see you."

"That is excellent," the merchant said, when he had carefully inspected Gervaise, "I should pass you myself without recognizing you. Now you can take him into the servants' quarters, Muley, and tell them that he is a new slave whom I have purchased, and that henceforth it will be his duty to wait upon my wife, to whom I have presented him as her special attendant, and that he will accompany her and my daughters when they go abroad to make their

Sir Gervaise is disguised as a Nubian slave.

purchases or visit their friends. Give some reason, if you can think of one, why you have bestowed him in a chamber separate from the rest."

Gervaise at once took up his new duties, and an hour later, carrying a basket, followed them into the town. It was strange to him thus to be walking among the fanatical Moors, who, had they known the damage that he had inflicted upon their galleys, would have torn him in pieces. None gave him, however, more than a passing look. Nubian slaves were no uncommon sight in the town, and in wealthy Moorish families were commonly employed in places of trust, and especially as attendants in the harems. The ladies were now as closely veiled as the Moorish women, it being only in the house that they followed the Berber customs. Gervaise had learnt from Muley that Ben Ibyn was one of the richest merchants in Tripoli, trading direct with Egypt, Syria, and Constantinople, besides carrying on a large trade with the Berber tribes in the interior. He returned to the house with his basket full of provisions, and having handed these over to the cook, he went to the private apartments, as Khadja had requested him to do. Here she and her daughters asked him innumerable questions as to his country and its customs, and then about Rhodes and the Order to which he belonged. Their surprise was great when they heard that the knights were bound to celibacy.

"But why should they not marry if they like?—why should they not have wives, children, and homes like other people?" Khadja asked.

"It is that they may devote their whole lives to their work. Their home is the convent at Rhodes, or at one of the commanderies scattered over Europe, where they take charge of the estates of the Order."

"But why should they not marry then, Gervaise? At Rhodes there might be danger for women and children, but when they return to Europe to take charge of the estates, surely they would do their duty no worse for having wives?"

Gervaise smiled.

"I did not make the rules of the Order, lady, but I have thought myself that although, so long as they are doing military work at the convent, it is well that they should not marry, yet there is no good reason why, when established in commanderies at home, they should not, like other knights and nobles, marry if it so pleases them."

In the evening the merchant returned from his stores, which were situated down by the port. Soon after he came in he sent for Gervaise. "There is a question I had intended to ask you last night," he said, "but it escaped me. More than two months since there sailed from this port and others many vessels—not the ships of the State, but corsairs. In all, more than twenty ships started, with the intention of making a great raid upon the coast of Italy. No word has since been received of them, and their friends here are becoming very uneasy, the more so as we hear that neither at Tunis nor Algiers has any news been received. Have you heard at Rhodes of a Moorish fleet having been ravaging the coast of Italy?"

"Have you any friends on board the ships that sailed from here, or any interest in the venture, Ben Ibyn?"

The merchant shook his head. "We Berbers," he said, "are not like the Moors, and have but little to do with the sea, save by the way of trade. For myself, I regret that these corsair ships are constantly putting out. Were it not for them and their doings we might trade with the ports of France, of Spain, and Italy, and be on good terms with all. There is no reason why, because our faiths are different, we should be constantly fighting. It is true that the Turks threaten Europe, and are even now preparing to capture Rhodes; but this is no question of religion. The Turks are warlike and ambitious; they have conquered Syria, and war with Egypt and Persia; but the Moorish states are small, they have no thought of conquest, and might live peaceably with Europe were it not for the hatred excited against them by the corsairs."

A KIND MASTER

"In that case I can tell you the truth. Thirteen of those ships were taken into Rhodes as prizes; the other eleven were burnt. Not one of the fleet escaped."

Exclamations of surprise broke from Ben Ibyn, his wife, and daughters.

"I am astonished, indeed," the merchant said. "It was reported here that the Genoese galleys were all laid up, and it was thought that they would be able to sweep the seas without opposition, and to bring home vast spoil and many captives, both from the ships they took and from many of the villages and small towns of the coast. How came such a misfortune to happen to them? It will create consternation here when it is known, for although it was not a state enterprise, the sultan himself and almost all the rich Moors embarked money in the fitting out of the ships, and were to have shares in the spoil taken. How happened it that so strong a fleet was all taken or destroyed, without even one vessel being able to get away to carry home the news of the disaster?"

"Fortune was against them," Gervaise said. "Three ships on their way up were captured by a galley of our Order, and her commander having obtained news of the whereabouts of the spot where the corsairs were to rendezvous, found them all lying together in a small inlet, and launched against them a number of fishing-boats fitted out as fire-ships. The corsairs, packed closely together, were unable to avoid them, and, as I told you, eleven of their ships were burnt, four were run ashore to avoid the flames, while six, trying to make their way out, were captured by the galley, aided by the three prizes that were taken and which the knights had caused to be manned by Sards."

"The ways of Allah the All-seeing are wonderful," the merchant said. "It was indeed a marvellous feat for one galley thus to destroy a great fleet."

"It was the result of good fortune rather than skill and valour," Gervaise said.

"Nay, nay; let praise be given where it is due. It was a marvellous feat; and although there is good or bad fortune in every event, such a deed could not have been performed, and would not even have been thought of, save by a great commander. Who was the knight who thus with one galley alone destroyed a strongly-manned fleet, from which great things had been looked for?"

Gervaise hesitated. "It was a young knight," he said, "of but little standing in the Order, and whose name is entirely unknown outside its ranks."

"By this time it must be well known," Ben Ibyn said; "and it will soon be known throughout Christendom, and will be dreaded by every Moor. What was it?"

Gervaise again hesitated.

"I would not have told you the story at all, Ben Ibyn, had I supposed you would have cared to inquire into the matter. Of course, I will tell you the name if you insist upon it, but I would much rather you did not ask."

"But why?" the merchant asked, in surprise. "If I hear it not from you, I shall assuredly hear it ere long from others, for it will be brought by traders who are in communication with Italy. I cannot understand why you should thus hesitate about telling me the name of this commander. When known it will doubtless be cursed by thousands of Moorish wives and mothers; but we Berbers are another race. None of our friends or kindred were on board the fleet; and we traders have rather reason to rejoice, for, in the first place, so severe a lesson will keep the corsairs in their ports for a long time; and in the second, had the fleet succeeded according to general expectation, so great a store of European goods would have been brought home that the market would have been glutted, and the goods in our storehouses would have lost all their value. What reason, then, can you possibly have in refusing to tell me the name of the commander who has won for himself such credit and glory?"

Gervaise saw that Ben Ibyn was seriously annoyed at what he deemed his unaccountable obstinacy.

A KIND MASTER

"I will tell you, Ben Ibyn, rather than excite your displeasure, though I would much have preferred not to do so, for you speak so much more highly of the affair than it merits. I had myself the honour of being in command of that galley."

The ladies broke into exclamations of surprise, while the merchant regarded him with grave displeasure.

"I had thought you truthful," he said; "but this passes all belief. Dost tell me that a beardless youth could with one galley overcome a great fleet, commanded by the most noted captains on our coast?"

"I thought that you would not believe me," Gervaise said quietly; "and, therefore, would have much preferred to keep silence, knowing that I had no means of supporting my claim. That was not the only reason; the other was, that already a great deal too much has been said about an affair in which, as I have told you, I owed everything to good fortune, and am heartily sick of receiving what I consider altogether undue praise. Ah!" he exclaimed suddenly, "the thought has just occurred to me of a way by which you can obtain confirmation of my story; and, as I value your good opinion and would not be regarded as a boaster and a liar, I entreat you to take it. I heard you tell the eight men who were rowers in my boat when I was captured, to call upon you to-day, that you might do something for them."

"They came this morning to my store," the merchant said. "They told me their wishes. I promised them that I would make inquiry about ships sailing East; and they are to come to me again to-morrow."

"Then, sir, I beseech you to suffer me to go down with you to your stores and meet them there. The galley of which I was in command at the time I was captured is the same as that in which a few weeks before I fought the corsairs, and these eight men were with me at that time. I begged them for my sake to maintain an absolute silence as to that affair, and I have no doubt that they have done so, for in the fury the news would excite, they might fall victims to the first outburst, though, of course, wholly innocent of any share

307

in the misfortune. Did you question them without my being present, they might still keep silent, fearing to injure me. But if, before you begin to do so, I tell them that they can speak the truth with reference to me, they will, I am sure, confirm my story, incredible as it may now appear to you."

"That is a fair offer," the merchant said gravely, "and I accept it, for it may be that I have been too hasty, and I trust it may prove so. I would rather find myself to be in fault than that the esteem with which you have inspired me should prove to be misplaced. We will speak no further on the subject now. I have not yet asked you how it is that you come to speak our language so well."

Gervaise related how he had studied with Suleiman Ali, and had escorted him to Syria and received his ransom.

"I had hoped," he said, "that the corsair would have taken me to Syria, for there I could have communicated with Suleiman, who would, I am sure, have given me such shelter and aid as he was able, in the event of my making my escape from slavery and finding myself unable to leave by sea."

The next day Gervaise went with Ben Ibyn to his stores. The eight men arrived shortly afterwards, and the merchant, in the presence of Gervaise, questioned them as to whether they knew anything of a misfortune that was said to have befallen some ships that had sailed for the coast of Italy. The men, surprised at the question, glanced at Gervaise, who said,—

"Tell Ben Ibyn the truth; it will do neither you nor me any harm, and will be mentioned by him to no one else."

Accordingly the story was told. Ben Ibyn listened gravely.

"It was the will of Allah," he said, when it was concluded. "I have wronged you, Gervaise, but your tale seemed too marvellous to be true. Do not speak of this to others;" he went on to the eight men. "Now as to yourselves. For the four of you who desire to return to Syria I have taken passage in a trader that sails to-morrow and will touch at Joppa and Acre. Here is money to provide yourselves with garments and to carry you to your homes. For you," he said to two who were natives of the town, "I can myself find employment here, and if your conduct is good, you will have no reason to regret taking service with me. The two of you who desire to go to Smyrna I will give passage there in a ship which will sail next week; in the meantime, here is money for your present wants."

Two days later the merchant's family moved to his house two miles outside the town, and here Gervaise remained for six months. His life was not an unpleasant one; he was treated with great kindness by the merchant and his wife, his duties were but slight, and he had no more labour to perform in the garden than he cared to do. Nevertheless, he felt that he would rather have fallen into the hands of a less kind master, for it seemed to him that it would be an act almost of treachery to escape from those who treated him as a friend; moreover, at the country house he was not in a position to frame any plans for escape, had he decided upon attempting it, nor could he have found out when Hassan made one of his occasional visits to the port.

One evening the merchant returned from the town accompanied by one of the sultan's officers and four soldiers. Ben Ibyn was evidently much depressed and disturbed; he told Muley as he entered, to fetch Gervaise. When the latter, in obedience to the order, came in from the garden, the officer said in Italian,—

"It having come to the ears of the sultan my master that the merchant Ben Ibyn has ventured, contrary to the law, to purchase a Christian slave brought secretly into the town, he has declared the slave to be forfeited and I am commanded to take him at once to the slaves' quarter."

"I am at the sultan's orders," Gervaise said, bowing his head. "My master has been a kind one, and I am grateful to him for his treatment of me."

Gervaise, although taken aback by this sudden change in his fortunes, was not so cast down as he might otherwise have been; he would now be free to carry out any plan for escape that he might devise, and by his being addressed in Italian it was evident to him that his knowledge of Turkish was unsuspected. When among the other slaves he had always maintained his character of a mute; and it was only when alone in his master's family that he had spoken at all. He had no doubt that his betrayal was due to one of the gardeners, who had several times shown him signs of ill-will, being doubtless jealous of the immunity he enjoyed from hard labour, and who must, he thought, have crept up and overheard some conversation; but in that case it was singular that the fact of his knowledge of Turkish had not been mentioned. Gervaise afterwards learned that Ben Ibyn had been fined a heavy sum for his breach of the regulations.

He was now placed between the soldiers, and marched down to the town, without being allowed to exchange a word with the merchant. On his arrival there he was taken to the slaves' quarter; here his clothes were stripped from him, and he was given in their place a ragged shirt and trousers, and then turned into a room where some fifty slaves were lying. Of these about half were Europeans, the rest malefactors who had been condemned to labour.

The appearance of all was miserable in the extreme; they were clothed in rags, and the faces of the Europeans had a dull, hopeless look that told alike of their misery and of their despair of any escape from it. They looked up listlessly as he entered, and then an Italian said, "*Cospetto*, comrade; but I know not whether your place is with us, or with the Moslems across there. As far as colour goes I should put you down as a Nubian; but your hair is of a hue that consorts but badly with that of your flesh."

"I am an Englishman," Gervaise replied; "but I have been passing under a disguise which has unfortunately been detected, so you see here I am."

The mystery explained, his questioner had no further interest in the matter, and Gervaise, picking out a vacant place on the stone floor, sat down and looked round him. The room, although large, was roughly built, and had doubtless been erected with a view to its present purpose. There were only a few windows; and these were small, strongly barred, and twelve feet above the floor.

"Not easy to get out of them," Gervaise said to himself; "at least, not easy without aid; and with these Moslems here it is clear that nothing can be done."

They were roused at daybreak next morning, and were taken out to their work under the guard of six armed Moors, two overseers, provided with long whips, accompanied them. The work consisted of cleaning the streets and working on the roads, and at times of carrying stones for the use of the masons employed in building an addition to the palace of the sultan. This was the work to which the gang was set that morning, and it was not long before the vigour with which Gervaise worked, and the strength he displayed in moving the heavy stones, attracted the attention of the overseers and of the head of the masons.

"That is a rare good fellow you have got there, that black with the curious hair," the latter said.

"What is the man? I never saw one like him."

"He is a Christian," one of the overseers said. "He was smuggled into the town and sold to Ben Ibyn the Berber, who, to conceal the matter, dyed him black; but it got to the ears of the sultan, and he had him taken from the Berber, and brought here; I have no doubt the merchant has been squeezed rarely."

"Well, that is a good fellow to work," the other said. "He has just moved a stone, single-handed, that it would have taken half a dozen of the others to lift. I wish you would put him regularly on this job; any one will do to sweep the streets; but a fellow like that will be of real use here, especially when the wall rises a bit higher."

"It makes no difference to me," the overseer said. "I will give orders when I go down that he shall be always sent up with whichever gang comes here."

The head mason, who was the chief official of the work, soon saw that Gervaise not only possessed strength, but knowledge of the manner in which the work should be done.

Accustomed as he had been to direct the slaves at work on the fortifications at Rhodes, he had learned the best methods of moving massive stones, and setting them in the places that they were to occupy. At the end of the day the head mason told one of the slaves who spoke Italian to inquire of Gervaise whether he had ever been employed on such work before. Gervaise replied that he had been engaged in the construction of large buildings.

"I thought so," the officer said to the overseer; "the way he uses his lever shows that he knows what he is doing. Most of the slaves are worth nothing; but I can see that this fellow will prove a treasure to us."

Gervaise returned to the prison well satisfied with his day's work. The labour, hard though it was, was an absolute pleasure to him. There was, moreover, nothing degrading in it, and while the overseers had plied their whips freely on the backs of many of his companions, he had not only escaped, but had, he felt, succeeded in pleasing his masters. The next morning when the gangs were drawn up in the yard before starting for work, he was surprised at being ordered to leave the one to which he belonged and to fall in with another, and was greatly pleased when he found that this took its way to the spot at which they were at work on the previous day.

At the end of the week, when the work of the day was finished, the head mason came down to the prison and spoke to the governor; a few minutes afterwards Gervaise was called out. The governor was standing in the courtyard with an interpreter.

"This officer tells me that you are skilled in masonry," the governor said, "and has desired that you shall be appointed overseer of the gang whose duty it is to move the stones, saying he is sure that with half the slaves now employed you would get as much work done as at present. Have you anything to say?"

"I thank you, my lord, and this officer," Gervaise replied. "I will do my best; but I would submit to you that it would be better if I could have the same slaves always with me, instead of their being changed every day; I could then instruct them in their work. I would also submit that it were well to pick men with some strength for this labour, for many are so weak that they are well-nigh useless in the moving of heavy weights; and lastly, I would humbly submit to you that if men are to do good work they must be fed. This work is as heavy as that in the galleys, and the men there employed receive extra rations to strengthen them; and I could assuredly obtain far better results if the gang employed upon this labour were to receive a somewhat larger supply of food."

"The fellow speaks boldly," the governor said to the head mason, when the reply was translated.

"There is reason in what he says, my lord. Many of the slaves, though fit for the light labour of cleaning the streets, are of very little use to us, and even the whip of the drivers cannot get more than a momentary effort from them. If you can save twenty-five men's labour for other work, it will pay to give more food to the other twenty-five. I should let this man pick out his gang. He has worked in turn with all of them, and must know what each can do; besides, it is necessary that he should have men who can understand his orders."

Gervaise accordingly was allowed to pick out his gang; and he chose those whom he had observed to be the strongest and most handy at the work.

"You will be responsible," the governor said to him, "for the masons being supplied with stone, and if you fail you will be punished and put to other labour."

So far from there being any falling off in the work, the head mason found that, even though the walls began to rise and the labour of transporting the stones into their positions became greater, the masons were never kept standing. The men, finding their position improved, both in the matter of food and in the immunity they enjoyed from blows, worked cheerfully and well. Gervaise did not content himself with giving orders, but worked at the heaviest jobs, and, little by little, introduced many of the appliances used by the skilled masons of Rhodes in transporting and lifting heavy stones. Gradually his own position improved: he was treated as an overseer, and was permitted to sleep under an arcade that ran along one side of the yard, instead of being confined in the close and stifling cell. His dye had long since worn off.

One day as he was going up with his gang under charge of the usual guards to the building, he saw Hassan, who grinned maliciously.

"Ah, ah, Christian dog!" he said; "you threatened me, and I have not forgotten it. The last time I was here I made it known to an officer of the sultan that Ben Ibyn had a Christian slave who had been smuggled in; and here you are. I hope you like the change. Look, I have still got your amulet, and it has brought me better luck than it did you. I have been fortunate ever since, and no money could buy it from me."

He had been walking close to Gervaise as he spoke, and one of the guards pushed him roughly aside.

Time passed on. One day on his return from work a well-dressed Moor met him as the gang broke up in the courtyard.

"I have permission to speak to you," he said to Gervaise, and drew him aside. "Know, O Christian, that I have received a letter from Suleiman Ali, of Syria. He tells me that he has heard from Ben Ibyn, the Berber, that you are a slave, and has asked me to inquire of the sultan the price that he will take for your ransom, expressing his willingness to pay whatever may be demanded, and charging me to defray the sum and to make arrangements by which you may return to Europe. This I am willing to do, knowing Suleiman Ali by report as a wealthy man and an honourable one. I saw the sultan yesterday. He told me that I should have an answer this morning as to the ransom that he would take. When I went to him again to-day, he said that he had learnt from the governor of the prison and from the head mason that you were almost beyond price, that you had been raised to the position of superintendent of the slaves employed in the building of his palace, and that you were a man of such skill that he would not part with you at any price until the work was finished. After that he would sell you; but he named a price threefold that at which the very best white slave in Tripoli would be valued. However, from the way in which Suleiman Ali wrote, I doubt not that he would pay it, great as it is, for he speaks of you in terms of affection, and I would pay the money could you be released at once. As it is, however, I shall write to him, and there will be ample time for an answer to be received from him before the building is finished."

"Truly I am deeply thankful to my good friend, Suleiman Ali; but for reasons of my own I am not desirous of being ransomed at present, especially at such a cost, which I should feel bound in honour to repay to him; therefore, I pray you to write to him, saying that while I thank him from my heart for his kindness, I am not able to avail myself of it. In the first place, I am well treated here, and my position is not an unpleasant one; secondly, the sum required for ransom is altogether preposterous; thirdly, I am not without hopes that I may some day find other means of freeing myself without so great a sacrifice; and lastly, that I have a reason which I cannot mention, why, at present, I would not quit Tripoli, even were I free to-morrow. You can tell him that this is the reason which, most of all, weighs with me. Do not, however, I pray you, let the sultan know that I have refused to be ransomed, for he might think I was meditating an escape, and would order extra precautions to be taken to prevent my doing so. Will you also see Ben Ibyn, and thank him from me for having written to Suleiman Ali on my behalf?"

CHAPTER XIX
ESCAPE

GRADUALLY a greater amount of liberty was given to Gervaise. Escape from Tripoli was deemed impossible, especially as he was supposed to be entirely ignorant of Arabic. He was, indeed, scarcely regarded now as a slave by the head mason, and instead of being clad in rags was dressed like other overseers. He was no longer obliged to walk with the gang to and from the palace, and was at last granted permission to go into the town for an hour or two after his work was over, instead of returning direct to the prison. The first time this permission was given to him he placed himself on the road by which Ben Ibyn would leave the town, choosing a quiet spot where the meeting would not be observed. Gervaise had for some time taken to staining his face, hands, and legs with walnut juice, beginning with a weak solution, and very gradually increasing the strength until he had reached a shade approximating to that of the lighter-coloured portion of the population. The head mason had on one occasion noticed it, and said,—

"The sun is darkening your skin, Gervaise, until you might verily pass as a Moor."

Gervaise detected an expression of doubt in the tone the officer had spoken to the interpreter, and replied at once,—

"It is not altogether the sun. Since I have obtained permission to come to my work alone, I have taken to slightly darkening my skin, in order to go to and fro unmolested, and free from the insults that the boys and beggars hurl at Christians."

The master mason nodded approvingly when the answer was translated to him.

"It is a wise step," he said; "for truly the hatred of Christians is very strong among the lower classes, especially since it became known that the galleys that sailed from here nearly two years ago were, with all the fleet from which so much was expected, utterly destroyed. It is well, then, that you should pass unnoticed, for were there a tumult in the street you might lose your life, and I should lose the best labour-overseer I have ever had."

Thus, then, as Gervaise walked through the streets on the first occasion of obtaining his liberty, he attracted no attention whatever. When he saw Ben Ibyn approaching he stepped out to meet him. The merchant looked in his face, but for a moment failed to recognise him, then he exclaimed suddenly,—

"It is Gervaise! Ah, my son, I am indeed rejoiced to see you. We have spoken of you so often at home, and sorely did my wife and daughters grieve when you were torn from us. I did not dare to send any message to you, for the sultan pretended great anger against me, and used the opportunity to squeeze me hardly; but I have frequently made inquiries about you, and was glad indeed to find that even in prison you received promotion; had it been otherwise—had I found that you were in misery—I would have endeavoured, whatever the risk, to aid you to escape."

"I have indeed nothing to complain of, and was sorry to learn that you had suffered on my account. Have you ever learned how it came about that I was denounced?"

"No, indeed; I would have given much to know, and assuredly the dog, whoever he was, should have been made to suffer."

"It was Hassan. The villain met me when I was with the gang, and boasted that it was he who had sent me there. He had told the news to some official, who had, of course, repeated it to the sultan; doubtless he concealed his own share in the matter, otherwise he too would, next time he returned here, have had to pay for his part in it."

"I will make him pay more heavily than the sultan would," Ben Ibyn said sternly; "I will speak to my friends among the merchants, and henceforth no Berber will buy aught from him; and we have hitherto been his best customers. But let us not waste our time in speaking of this wretch. How comes it that you are walking freely in the streets of Tripoli? I can see that your face is stained, although you are no longer a Nubian."

Gervaise told him how it was that he was free to walk in the city after his work was done.

"I shall now," he went on, "be able to carry out any plan of escape that may occur to me; but before I leave, as I shall certainly do ere long, I mean to settle my score with Hassan, and I pray you to send one of the men who were with me in the galley, and whom you took into your employment, directly you hear that his ship is in harbour. Do not give him either a note or a message: bid him simply place himself in the road between the prison gate and the palace, and look fixedly at me as I pass. I shall know it is a signal that Hassan is in the port."

"Can I aid you in your flight? I will willingly do so."

"All that I shall need is the garb of a peasant," Gervaise said. "I might buy one unnoticed; but, in the first place, I have no money, and in the second, when it is known that I have escaped, the trader might recall the fact that one of the slave overseers had purchased a suit of him."

"The dress of an Arab would be the best," the merchant said. "That I will procure and hold in readiness for you. On the day when I send you word that Hassan is here, I will see that the gate of my garden is unbarred at night, and will place the garments down just behind it. You mean, I suppose, to travel by land?"

"I shall do so for some distance. Were I to steal a boat from the port, it would be missed in the morning, and I be overtaken. I shall therefore go along the coast for some distance and get a boat at one of the villages, choosing my time when there is a brisk wind, and when I may be able to get well beyond any risk of being overtaken. Now, Ben Ibyn, I will leave you; it were better that we should not meet again, lest some suspicion might fall upon you of having aided in my escape. I cannot thank you too much for all your past kindness, and shall ever bear a grateful remembrance of yourself and your family."

"Perhaps it were better so," Ben Ibyn said; "for if the Moors can find any excuse for plundering us, they do so. Have you heard the news that the Sultan of Turkey's expedition for the capture of Rhodes is all but complete, and will assuredly sail before many weeks have passed?"

"I have not heard it," Gervaise replied; "and trust that I may be in time to bear my share in the defence. However, the blow has been so often threatened that it may be some time before it falls."

"May Allah bless you, my son, and take you safely back to your friends! Be assured that you shall have notice as soon as I know that Hassan has returned, and you shall have the bundle with all that is needful, behind my gate."

Another two months passed. Gervaise looked in vain for Ben Ibyn's messenger as he went to and from the palace, and chafed terribly at the delay, when, for aught he knew, the Turkish fleet might already have brought Mahomet's army to Rhodes. At last, as he came back from work, he saw with intense satisfaction one of the men, whose face he recognised, leaning carelessly against the wall. The man gave no sign of recognition, but looked at him earnestly for a minute, and then sauntered off up the street. Gervaise went up into the town as usual, walked about until it became quite dark, and then went to the gate that led into the merchant's garden. He found that it was unfastened, and, opening it, he went in and closed it behind him. As he did so he started, for a voice close by said,—

"Master, it is I, the messenger whom you saw two hours since. Ben Ibyn bade me say that he thought you might require some service, and, knowing that I could be trusted, bade me wait for you here. He thought that you might possibly need a messenger to Hassan."

"The very thing," Gervaise exclaimed. "I have been puzzling myself in vain as to how I could get speech with him in some quiet place; but with your assistance that will be easy; but first let me put on this disguise."

This was easily effected, even in the dark. A loose flowing robe of white cotton, girt in at the waist, a long bernouse with hood to cover the head, a sash with a dagger, and a scimitar, completed the disguise.

"Here is a pouch," the man said, "with money for your journey, and a long sword, which he says you can hang at your back beneath your bernouse."

Gervaise gave an exclamation of pleasure. By its length and weight he was sure that the weapon must have been the property of a Christian knight.

"Shall I carry the message this evening?" the man asked. "It is early still, and it were best that you should not linger in the city, where there is sure to be a strict search for you in the morning."

"But perhaps he may recognise your face?"

"It is blackened, my lord, and I am dressed as you were when with Ben Ibyn."

"Let us settle our plans, then, before we sally out from here; we could not find a safer place for talking. What message, think you, would be the most likely to tempt Hassan to come ashore? You do not know what spoil he has brought?"

"No; besides, if a merchant wanted to buy he would go on board to inspect Hassan's wares. We must have something to sell. It must be something tempting, and something that must be disposed of secretly. I might tell him that my employer—and I would mention some merchant whose name would carry weight with him—has received from the interior a large consignment of slaves, among whom are three or four girls, who would fetch high prices in Egypt, and as he believes they have been captured from a tribe within the limits of the sultan's territory, he is anxious to get rid of them, and will either dispose of them all cheaply in a lot, or will hand them over to him to take to Egypt to sell, giving him a large commission for carrying them there and disposing of them."

"I do not like tempting even an enemy by stories that are untrue," Gervaise said doubtfully.

"I have no scruples that way," the man said, with a laugh; "and it is I who shall tell the story, and not you."

Gervaise shook his head.

"Could you not say that you came from one who owes him a heavy debt and desires to pay him?"

"I do not think that would bring him ashore. Hassan doubtless trades for ready money, and must be well aware that no one here can be greatly in his debt. No, my lord; leave the matter in my hands. I will think of some story before I go on board that will fetch him ashore. But first we must settle where I am to bring him; there are some deserted spots near the wall on the east side of the town."

"I know where you mean," Gervaise agreed; "let us go in that direction at once, for the sooner you are off the better."

In half an hour a spot was fixed on, near some huts that had fallen into ruin. Here Gervaise seated himself on a sand heap, while the man hurried away. The moon had just risen, it being but three days since it was at its full. The night was quiet; sounds of music, laughter, and occasional shouts came faintly from the town. Seated where he was, Gervaise could see the port and the ships lying there. Half an hour later he saw a boat row off to one of them, which he had already singled out, from its size and general appearance, as being that of Hassan; ten minutes later he saw it returning. At that distance separate figures could not be made out, but it seemed to him that it loomed larger than before, and he thought that certainly one, if not more, persons, were returning with his messenger. Presently he heard men approaching; then Hassan's voice came distinctly to his ears.

"How much farther are you going to take me? Remember, I warned you that unless I found that my journey repaid me, it would be bad for you."

"It is but a few yards farther, my lord. There is my master the sheik of the Beni Kalis awaiting you."

Gervaise rose to his feet as Hassan and two of his crew came up.

"Now," the former said roughly, "where have you bestowed these captives you want to sell me?"

"Will you please to follow me into this courtyard?" Gervaise said. He had, while waiting, reconnoitred the neighbourhood, and found an enclosure with the walls still perfect, and had determined to bring Hassan there, in order to prevent him from taking to flight. Hassan entered it unsuspectingly, followed by his two men. Gervaise fell back a little, so as to place himself between them and the entrance. Then he threw back the hood of his bernouse.

"Do you recognise me, Hassan?" he said sternly. "I am the captive whom you beat almost to death. I told you that some day I would kill you; but even now I am willing to forgive you and to allow you to depart in peace, if you will restore the amulet you took from me."

The corsair gave a howl of rage.

"Christian dog!" he exclaimed. "You thought to lead me into a trap, but you have fallen into one yourself. You reckoned that I should come alone; but I suspected there was something hidden behind the story of that black, and so brought two of my crew with me. Upon him, men! Cut him down!" So saying, he drew his scimitar, and sprang furiously upon Gervaise. The latter stepped back into the centre of the gateway, so as to prevent the men, who had also drawn their swords, passing to attack him from behind. He had undone the clasp of his bernouse, and allowed it to fall to the ground as he addressed Hassan, and his long sword flashed in the moonlight as the corsair sprang forward.

Hassan was a good swordsman, and his ferocious bravery, had rendered him one of the most dreaded of the Moorish rovers. Inferior in strength to Gervaise, he was as active as a cat, and he leapt back with the spring of a panther, avoiding the sweeping blow with which Gervaise had hoped to finish the conflict at once; the latter found himself therefore engaged in a desperate fight with his three assailants. So furiously did they attack him that, foot by foot, he was forced to give ground. As he stepped through the gateway one of the pirates sprang past him, but as he did so, a figure leapt out from beyond the wall, and plunged a dagger into his back, while at the same moment, by cutting down another pirate, Gervaise, rid himself of one of his assailants in front; but as he did so, he himself received a severe wound on the left shoulder from Hassan, who, before he could again raise his weapon, sprang upon him, and tried to hurl him to the ground.

Gervaise's superior weight saved him from falling, though he staggered back some paces; then his heel caught against a stone, and he fell, dragging Hassan to the ground with him. Tightly clasped in each other's arms, they rolled over and over. Gervaise succeeded at last in getting the upper hand, but as he did so Hassan twisted his right arm free, snatched the dagger from Gervaise's girdle, and struck furiously at him. Gervaise, who had half risen to his knees, was unable to avoid the blow, but threw himself forward, his weight partly pinning the corsair's shoulders to the ground, and the blow passed behind him, inflicting but a slight wound in the back; then, with his right hand, which was now free, he grasped Hassan by the throat with a grip of iron. The pirate struggled convulsively for a moment, then his left hand released his grasp of his opponent's wrist. A minute later Gervaise rose to his feet: the pirate was dead.

Gervaise grasped Hassan by the throat with a grip of iron.

ESCAPE

Gervaise stooped and raised the fallen man's head from the ground, felt for the chain, pulled up Claudia's gage, and placed it round his own neck; then he turned to his guide.

"I have to thank you for my life," he said, holding out his hand to him.

"It would have gone hard with me if that fellow had attacked me from behind. I had not bargained for three of them."

"I could not help it, my lord. It was not until Hassan had stepped down into the boat that I knew he was going to take any one with him; then he suddenly told two of his men to take their places by him, saying to me, as he did so, 'I know not whether this message is a snare; but mind, if I see any signs of treachery, your life at any rate will pay the forfeit.' I knew not what to do, and indeed could do nothing; but, knowing my lord's valour, I thought that, even against these odds, you might conquer with such poor aid as I could give you."

"It was not poor aid at all," Gervaise said heartily. "Greatly am I indebted to you, and sorry indeed am I, that I am unable to reward you now for the great service that you have rendered me."

"Do not trouble about that, my lord. I am greatly mistaken if I do not find in the sashes of these three villains sufficient to repay me amply for my share in this evening's work. And now, my lord, I pray you to linger not a moment. The gates of the town shut at ten o'clock, and it cannot be long from that hour now. But first, I pray you, let me bind up your shoulder; your garment is soaked with blood."

"Fortunately my bernouse will hide that; but it were certainly best to staunch the blood before I start, for it would be hard for me to get at the wound myself."

The man took one of the sashes of the corsairs, tore it into strips, and bandaged the wound; then with another he made a sling for the arm. As he took off the sashes a leather bag dropped from each, and there was a chink of metal. He placed them in his girdle, saying, "I shall have time to count them when I get back."

Gervaise sheathed his sword, and put on the bernouse, pulling the hood well over his head; then, with a few more words of thanks, started for the gate, leaving the man to search Hassan's girdle.

The gate was a quarter of a mile distant. Gervaise passed through with the usual Arabic salutation to the sentry, and with difficulty repressed a shout of exultation as he left Tripoli behind him.

Following the coast road he walked till daylight; then he left it and lay down among the sand-hills for five or six hours. He calculated that no pursuit would be begun until midday. His absence was not likely to be noticed until the gangs began work in the morning, when an alarm would be given. The sentries at the gates on the previous evening would be questioned, and when it was found that no one answering to his description had passed out before these were closed, there would be a rigid search throughout the city and port. The vessels would all be examined, and the boatmen questioned as to whether any craft was missing. Not until the search proved absolutely fruitless would it be seriously suspected that he had, either by passing through the gates in disguise, or by scaling the walls, made for the interior. None knew that he could speak Arabic, and it would be so hopeless an undertaking for any one unacquainted with the language to traverse the country without being detected, that the Moors would be slow to believe that he had embarked upon such adventure. However, when all search for him in the town and in the vessels in the port proved fruitless, doubtless mounted men would be despatched in all directions; some would take the coast roads, while others would ride into the interior to warn the head men of the villages to be on the look-out for an escaped slave.

ESCAPE

After a sleep of five hours, Gervaise pursued his journey. He had walked for eight hours, and calculated that he must be fully thirty miles from Tripoli, and that not until evening would searchers overtake him. After walking four miles he came to a large village. There he purchased a bag of dates, sat down on a stone bench by the roadside to eat them, and entered into conversation with two or three Moors who sauntered up. To these he represented that he belonged to a party of his tribe who had encamped for the day at a short distance from the village in order to rest their horses before riding into Tripoli, whither they were proceeding to exchange skins of animals taken in the chase, and some young horses, for cotton clothes, knives, and other articles of barter with the tribes beyond them.

After quenching his thirst at a well in front of the mosque, he retraced his steps until beyond the village, then struck out into the country, made a detour, came down into the road again, and continued his journey eastward. He walked until nightfall, and then again lay down.

He was now fully fifty miles from Tripoli, and hoped that he was beyond the point to which horsemen from that town would think of pursuing their search. It was likely that they would not have gone beyond the village at which he had halted on the previous day; for when they learned from the inhabitants that no stranger, save an Arab, had entered it, they would content themselves with warning the head man to be on the watch for any stranger unable to speak their tongue, and would not consider it necessary to push their steps farther.

For four days Gervaise continued his journey. At each village through which he passed he added to his stock of dates, until he had as many as he could carry under his bernouse without attracting observation. He also purchased a large water-bottle, which he slung round his neck.

All this time the sea lay to his left like a sheet of glass, and he knew that until a change of weather occurred, it was useless for him to attempt to escape by boat. On the fifth day there were signs of a change. He saw a dark line far out at sea; it came across the water rapidly, and presently a gentle breeze began to blow from the north-west; it gradually increased in strength, and when, in the afternoon, he stopped at a village, the waves were breaking upon the shore.

After repeating his usual story, he sauntered down to the water's edge. There were several boats hauled up, and a hundred yards out two or three larger craft were lying at anchor. He entered into conversation with some of the fishermen, and his questions as to the boats led them to believe him altogether ignorant of the sea. The craft were, they told him, used sometimes for fishing, but they often made voyages to towns along the coast with dates and other produce. Each boat carried a single short mast, to the top of which was attached a long tapering spar, on which the sail was furled.

Gervaise knew that these small feluccas were generally fast sailers and fair sea boats, and resolved to seize one of them, trusting that when once the sail was shaken out he would be able to manage it single-handed. Accustomed to boats, he picked out that which he thought would be the fastest, and then walked away for half a mile, and lay down to sleep until the village was silent for the night. He had with him some oaten cakes he had bought there, a string of fish he had purchased from the boatmen, and with these and the dates he thought he could manage for four or five days at least. As to water, he could only hope that he should find a supply on board the boat. When he judged it to be about ten o'clock he went down to the shore again, took off his clothes and made them into a bundle; then, wading out into the water to within fifty yards of the felucca, swam off to it, towing the bundle behind him.

He had no difficulty in climbing on board, and after dressing himself in the clothes he had worn at Tripoli, and had kept on underneath the Arab attire, he pulled the head rope until the craft was nearly over the anchor. He then loosened the line that brailed up the sail, got the stone that served as an anchor on board, hauled the sheet aft, and took his place at the tiller. The wind had dropped a good deal with the sun, but there was still sufficient air to send the light craft fast through the water. He steered out for a time, and then, when he thought himself a good mile from the shore, headed east. By the appearance of the water as it glanced past, he thought that he must be making from five to six miles an hour, and when the sun rose at five o'clock, believed that he was nearly forty miles on his way. He now fastened the tiller with a rope and proceeded to overhaul the craft.

It was decked over forward only, and he crept into the cabin, which was little more than three feet high. The first thing his eye lit on was a bulky object hanging against the side, and covered with a thick black blanket of Arab manufacture. Lifting this, he saw, as he expected, that the object beneath it was a large waterskin well filled; the blanket had evidently been placed over it to keep it cool when the sun streamed down on the deck above it. There was also a large bag of dates, and another of flat cakes, and he guessed that these had all been put on board the evening before, in readiness for a start in the morning. This relieved him of his chief anxiety, for he had been unable to think of any plan for replenishing his supply, or to concoct a likely tale that, were he obliged to go on shore, would account for his being alone in a craft of that size.

The wind increased again after sunrise, and being unable to reef the sail single-handed he managed partially to brail it up. All day the craft flew along with the wind on the quarter, making six or seven miles an hour; and he felt that by morning he would be well beyond pursuit. On the run he passed several craft engaged in fishing, but these gave him no uneasiness. He had in the morning, with some old sails he found, constructed three rough imitations of human figures, one with the Arab dress and another with the bernouse, and had placed them against the bulwarks, so that at a short distance it would appear that there were three men on board. Feeling confident that the deception would not be noticed, he kept his course without swerving, and passed some of the fishing boats within hailing distance, waving his hand and shouting the usual Arab salutation to their crews.

During the day he contented himself with eating some dates and an oatmeal cake or two; but at sunset he added to this two or three fish that he had split open and hung up to dry in the sun and wind. There was charcoal on board, and a flat stone served as a hearth in the bottom of the boat, but he had no means of lighting a fire, for this the fishermen would have brought off when they came on board in the morning. After he had finished his meal and taken his place again at the tiller he altered his course. Hitherto he had been steering to the south of east, following the line of coast, but he now saw before him the projecting promontory of Cape Mezurata, which marks the western entrance of the great Gulf of Sydra; and he now directed his course two points north of east, so as to strike the opposite promontory, known as Grenna, more than a hundred miles away. The wind fell much lighter, and he shook out the sail to its full extent. All night he kept at his post, but finding the wind perfectly steady he lashed the tiller so as to keep the boat's head in the direction in which he was steering, and dozed for some hours, waking up occasionally to assure himself that she was keeping her course.

At sunrise he indulged in a wash in sea water, and felt freshened and revived. He now kept a sharp look-out for distant sails, for he was out of the ordinary course a coaster would take, and would have attracted the attention of any corsair coming out from the land; the sea, however, remained clear of ships. All day the felucca made rapid progress, for although the wind freshened, Gervaise did not lessen sail as before, being now accustomed to the boat and confident of her powers. As soon as the wind died away again after sunset, he lay down for a good sleep, feeling this was an absolute necessity, and knowing that before morning he should be obliged to keep a sharp look-out for land. He slept longer than he had intended, for the day was breaking when he opened his eyes. He sprang to his feet, and saw the land stretching ahead of him at a distance, as he thought, of some fifteen miles, and at once put the helm down and bore more to the north.

He judged, from what he had heard on the coast, that he must be nearly off Cape Tejones, behind which lies the town of Bengasi, and was confirmed in the belief on finding half an hour later that the coast, which had run nearly north and south, trended sharply away to the north-east. All day long he kept about the same distance from the land, and at night, instead of keeping on his course, brailed up the sail entirely, and allowed the vessel to drift, as he knew that before morning he should lose the coast if he continued as he was going. He slept without moving until daylight, and then saw, to his satisfaction, by means of landmarks he had noticed the evening before, that the boat had drifted but a few miles during the night. As the day went on, he saw that the coast-line was now east and west, and felt that he must be off the most northerly point of the promontory; he accordingly laid his course to the north-east, which would take him close to Cape Saloman, the most easterly point of Crete, and from two hundred and fifty to three hundred miles distant.

For twenty-four hours he sailed quietly on, the wind dropping lighter and lighter; then it suddenly died out altogether; for some hours there was not a breath to stir the surface of the water, and the heat was stifling. Gervaise slept for some time; when he awoke the same stillness reigned, but there was a change in the appearance of the sky; its brightness was dulled by a faint mist, while, although the sea was of a glassy smoothness, there was an imperceptible swell that caused the felucca to sway uneasily. Gervaise had sufficient experience of the Levant to know that these signs were ominous of a change, and he at once set to work to prepare for it. Although he saw that it would be difficult for him unaided to hoist the long spar back into its place, he decided to lower it. This was not difficult, as its weight brought it down on to the deck as soon as he slackened the halliards; he unhooked it from the block, and then lashed the sail securely to it. When he had done this he looked round. A bank of dark clouds lay across the horizon to the north-west, and in a short time he could see that this was rising rapidly.

Before taking down the spar and sail, he had deliberated as to whether it would be better to run before the coming gale or to lie to, and had decided on the latter alternative, as, were it to continue to blow long, he might be driven on to the Egyptian coast. Moreover, the felucca's bow was much higher out of water than the stern, and he thought that she would ride over the waves with greater safety than she would did they sweep down upon her stern. He had heard that the Greeks, when caught in a sudden gale in small boats, often lashed the oars together, threw them overboard with a rope attached, and rode to them safely through a sea that would otherwise have overwhelmed them. After much consideration as to what had best be done, he took the anchor rope, which was some sixty yards in length, fastened one end to each end of the spar, and then lashed the middle of the rope to the bow of the felucca; then, using an oar as a lever, he with great labour managed to launch the spar over the bow, with the sail still attached to it.

When he had completed this, he looked round at the state of the weather. The clouds had risen so fast that their edge was nearly overhead, spanning the sky like a great arch. Ahead of him it seemed almost as black as night. He had not been out in many of the gales that at times sweep the eastern waters of the Mediterranean with terrible violence, but had seen enough of them to know that it was no ordinary one that he was about to encounter. He looked over the bow; the spar at present was lying in contact with the stem. With an oar he pushed it across so as to be at right angles with the craft, and then, there being nothing else to do, sat down and waited for the storm to burst. In a short time he heard a dull moaning sound, a puff of wind struck the boat, but in a few seconds died out; it was sufficient to give the light craft stern way, and she drifted backwards, the rope tightening, until the spar lay across her bows, and some twenty yards away.

The dull moaning had grown louder; and now ahead of him he saw a white line. It approached with extraordinary rapidity. Knowing the fury with which it would burst upon him, he leapt down, and stood at the entrance to the cabin, with his head just above the deck. With a deafening roar the wind struck the boat, which staggered as if she had on her full course struck on a rock, while a shower of spray flew over her. Half blinded and deafened, Gervaise crawled into the cabin, closed the door, and lay down there; whatever happened, there was nothing he could do. He was soon conscious that the spar and sail were doing their work, for the boat still lay head to wind. The noise overhead and around was deafening; above the howl of the wind could be heard the creaking of the timbers, and the boat seemed to shiver as each fresh gust struck her.

In half an hour he looked out again. There was, as yet, but little sea; the force of the wind seemed to flatten the water, and the instant a wave lifted its head it was cut off as if by a knife, and carried away in spray. The boat herself was moving rapidly through the water, dragging the spar behind her, and Gervaise almost trembled at the thought of the speed at which she would have flown along had it not been for the restraint of the floating anchor. Gradually the sea got up, but the light craft rode easily over it, and Gervaise, after commending his safety to God, lay down, and was soon fast asleep. In spite of the motion of the vessel, he slept soundly for many hours. When he awoke he opened the cabin door and looked out. A tremendous sea was running, but he thought the wind, although so strong that he could scarce lift his head above the shelter of the bulwark, was less violent than it had been when it first broke upon him. He saw to his satisfaction that the felucca breasted the waves lightly, and that although enveloped in spray she took no green water over the bows.

The spar and sail acted not only as a floating anchor, but as a breakwater, and the white-crested waves, which came on as if they would break upon the boat, seemed robbed of half their violence by the obstruction to their course, and passed under the felucca without breaking. For forty-eight hours the gale continued; at the end of that time it ceased almost as suddenly as it had begun. The sun shone brightly out, the clouds cleared entirely away. It was some hours before the sea went down sufficiently for Gervaise to attempt to get the spar on deck again. It was a heavy task, taxing his strength to the utmost, but after a deal of labour it was got on board, and then raised to its position at the mast-head; the sail was shaken out, and the felucca again put on her course.

CHAPTER XX
BELEAGUERED

ONE morning towards the end of May, 1480, Sir John Boswell was standing with some other knights on St. Stephen's Hill, near the city, having hurried up as soon as a column of smoke from a bonfire lighted by the look-out there, gave the news that the Turkish fleet was at last in sight. A similar warning had been given a month previously, but the fleet had sailed past the island, being bound for Phineka, which was the rendezvous where Mahomet's great armament was to assemble. There could be but little doubt that the long-expected storm was this time about to burst. The fleet now seen approaching numbered a hundred and sixty large ships, besides a great number of small craft, conveying a force variously estimated at from seventy to a hundred thousand men.

"'Tis a mighty fleet," Sir John said; "and the worst of it is that we know there are more to follow; still, I doubt not we shall send them back defeated. Our defences are all complete; our recent peace with Egypt has enabled us to fill up our magazines with provisions of all kinds; the inhabitants of the Island have had ample warning to move into the town, carrying with them everything of value; so the Turks will obtain but little plunder, and will be able to gather no means of subsistence on the island, as every animal has been driven within the walls, and even the unripe corn has been reaped and brought in. However long the siege lasts, we need be in no fear of being reduced to sore straits for food. Look over there. There is a small craft under sail, and it comes not from the direction of Phineka. See ! one of the Turkish galleys has separated from the rest and is making off in that direction. It may be that the little craft contains one or two of our comrades who are late in coming to join us."

"It may well be so, Sir John, for they have been straggling in by twos and threes for the last month."

"I will get the grand master's leave to put out in one of the galleys," Sir John said, "for, by the way they are bearing, the Turks will cut the little craft off before she can gain the port."

He hurried to D'Aubusson, who was standing a short distance apart from the others, gazing at the Turkish fleet. A minute later he was running down the hill to the town, accompanied by three or four other knights; they made direct for the outer port, where two galleys were lying in readiness, leapt on board one of them, which already contained its quota of knights, and at once rowed out of the port. Just as they did so the Turkish galley fired a gun.

"I fear we shall be too late," Sir John said; "the Turk is gaining fast on the other craft, whatever she may be. There goes another gun. Row your hardest!" he shouted down to the slaves.

The Turkish ship did not fire again; the wind was light, and they were going two feet through the water to every one sailed by the other craft. The galley from Rhodes was still half a mile away when the Turk was close to the boat that was trying to escape. Sir John and the knights chafed as they saw they would be too late.

"I can't make out why the boat did not use her oars," the former said. "Of course, she could not have kept away from the galley, but if she had rowed it would have made some difference, and we might have been nearly up."

"I can only see one man on board of her, Sir John," one of the younger knights said; and two or three others murmured that they were of the same opinion.

BELEAGUERED

"The others must be lying down; she cannot have less than from fifteen to twenty men. The Turk is close alongside. They still hold on. There! She has gone about and escaped the attempt to run her down. Now she is heading for us again! Brave fellows! brave fellows!" Sir John exclaimed, while a cheer broke from those around him; "but they have done for themselves. They must have seen us coming out, and if they had surrendered might have hoped to have been re-taken. Their chance of getting quarter was truly not great, for expecting—as the Turks do—to carry off both us and all the inhabitants of the Island, a dozen fishermen would have seemed to them scarcely worth keeping. However, by holding on they have thrown away any chance they may have had. The Turks are alongside; they are leaping down into the little craft. Ah! Two more galleys have just left their fleet, and are heading here."

"See, Sir John," one of the knights exclaimed, "there is a single man standing in the bow of that craft: he is facing the Moors alone. See how they crowd there; you can see the weapons flashing in the sun. They have to press past the mast to get at him, and as yet he seems to hold them all at bay."

"He has chosen his post well, D'Urville. The number of his assailants prevents the archers on the Turkish craft using their bows. Fire those bow guns!" he shouted to the knights forward: "Take steady aim at the galley. It will distract their attention."

"Nobly done indeed!" one of the other knights shouted. "I have seen him strike down four of the Turks."

"Row, men, row! 'Tis useless!" Sir John muttered, as he clenched the hilt of his sword. "Useless! A Roland could not long maintain so unequal a fight."

A groan broke from those around him as suddenly the dark mass of the assailants made a forward move, and the single figure was lost to sight. It was but for an instant; a moment later the crowd separated, and a man was seen to spring overboard.

"They will riddle him with their spears when he comes up; we shall have nothing to do but to avenge him. To your stations, comrades! It is our turn now, and we have no time to lose, for the other two Turks will be up in twenty minutes, and I had orders not to fight if it could be avoided: but we must take this fellow."

Five minutes later the galley ran alongside the Turk, to which those who had captured the boat had already hastily returned. The ships discharged their guns into each other, and then, as the galley ran alongside, the knights tried to leap on board of her. They were opposed by a dense mass of Turks, for in addition to her usual crew the Moslem was crowded with troops. For three or four minutes the knights tried, but in vain, to get a footing on board; then Sir John shouted to them to forbear, and gave orders to the rowers at once to push off. A cloud of arrows swept across the poop as they did so; but for the most part these fell harmless from the armour of the knights. For a time the cannon on both sides continued to fire, but as the Christians increased their distance it gradually ceased.

They had gone but a hundred yards from the Turk when a head appeared over the stern railing of the poop, and a figure swung itself on to the deck. The man was attired in Turkish garments, but his head was bare, and the exclamation, "A Christian!" broke from the knights.

The man strode up to Sir John Boswell.

"You used to say you would make matters even with me some day, Sir John, and you have more than kept your word."

Sir John fell back a pace in astonishment, and then with a shout, "By St. George, it is Tresham!" threw his arms round Gervaise's neck, while the knights thronged round with exclamations of satisfaction.

"And it was you whom we saw keep the Turks at bay for three good minutes single-handed," Sir John said, holding Gervaise at arm's length to gaze into his face. "Truly it seemed well-nigh impossible that any one who was like to be on that craft could have performed so doughty a deed. And how did you escape?"

"It was simple enough," Gervaise replied. "As soon as I dived I turned and swam along under the boat and came up by the stern, and then held on by the rudder, sheltered from their sight. I saw that the galley would be up in five minutes, and had no fear of their wasting time to look for me. Directly you came alongside her I dived again, and rose under your stern. I did not think that you would be able to take her, for all their craft are crowded with troops; so I contented myself with holding on until you were out of reach of their arrows, and then I climbed up."

"I am delighted to see you again, Gervaise. I was feeling very sore at the moment, and I know the others felt the same, at being obliged to sheer off without making a capture; but the grand master's orders were strict. We noted your craft pursued by the Turks, and I asked leave to take out a galley to cut her off. He said, 'Take one, Sir John, but do not adventure an attack against the Turk unless she is likely to fall an easy prize to you. Her capture would be of little benefit to us, and would be dearly purchased at the cost of a knight's life. Therefore, as soon as we engaged her, and I found that she was full of troops and could not be captured without heavy loss, and that two of her consorts might arrive before we accomplished it, it was plainly my duty to abandon the attempt, although, you may guess, it went sorely against the grain to give the order, especially as I knew that a host would be looking on from St. Stephen's Hill. However, your rescue more than makes up for our failure; and thankful indeed am I that I made the suggestion that we should put out to save that little craft, though I thought it contained but a few fishermen or some coasting sailors, who had, in ignorance that the Turks were at hand, tried to enter Rhodes. One of those looking on with me did, indeed, suggest that she might have on board a knight or two coming to join us, but I did not give the matter a second thought."

"And how go things, Sir John? And how are old friends?"

"Ralph Harcourt and, I think, all your comrades in the *Santa Barbara*, except the three who fell by your side when you were captured, are well, and at present on the Island, as, for the last two years, none have been allowed to depart. As to other matters, they go not so well as one could wish. The commanderies have not responded to our call for aid as they should have done. For this, however, they are not altogether to blame, for we have been so often threatened with attack, and have so frequently applied for aid in money or men, that they must have begun to doubt whether the danger was really imminent. In other respects we are well prepared. We have obtained large stores of provisions from Egypt, and shall have no ground for uneasiness on that score. The defences have been greatly strengthened, and no one fears that we shall not be able to beat off an attack. We have destroyed the principal buildings outside the walls, though it would have been better could we have gone much further in this direction. And now let us have your adventures and escape."

"'Tis a long story, Sir John, and I must pray you to let me defer it for a time. In the first place, I have two or three wounds that I shall be glad to have bandaged."

"Why did you not say so at once?" Sir John exclaimed. "In those dark clothes, soaked with water as they are, I did not see the blood-stains; but I ought to have looked for them, for surely no one could have gone through that fight—altogether unprotected with armour too—without being wounded. Come below, and we will attend to them."

"Also order me some wine and food, Sir John; I have touched nothing save water for twenty-four hours, and before that fasted somewhat strictly."

By the time Gervaise's wounds, which were not severe, had been bandaged, and he had eaten a hasty meal, the galley was alongside the mole, between the two harbours.

He was provided with some clothes, and went with Sir John straight to the English *auberge*, where the knight insisted that he should at once lie down.

"I will report your return to D'Aubusson, and will tell him it is by my orders that you are resting. Your wounds are not very deep, but you must have lost a good deal of blood, and were you to exert yourself now, and be pestered with questions, it would probably bring on an attack of fever. There is nothing to do at present, for it must be some days before they can land and bring up their guns."

Gervaise obeyed the orders not unwillingly, for he felt that he was really weak, and was greatly worn out by want of sleep. Sir John Kendall, at Boswell's request, issued orders that he was on no account whatever to be disturbed, and that no one was to enter his room unless he sounded the bell placed by the bedside. Gervaise indeed, falling off to sleep a few minutes after he had lain down, did not awake until the following morning. Having no idea that he had slept more than two or three hours, he sounded the bell in order to inquire whether Ralph had returned to the *auberge*. He was surprised to find his friend had just risen, and that he himself had been asleep some eighteen hours!

A few minutes later Ralph hurried into the room.

"Thank God that you are back again, Gervaise!" he said, as he grasped the hand of his friend. "I did not return until late in the evening, having been at work with a large body of slaves at the fortifications; and you may guess what joy I felt at the news. You are changed a good deal."

"I don't suppose you will think so at the end of a day or two, Ralph. I lost a good deal of blood yesterday, and have been on short rations; but I shall very soon pick up again."

"They will bring you some broth and wine directly, Gervaise. Early as it is, the grand master has already sent down to inquire as to your health."

"I will reply in person as soon as I have had a meal and dressed."

"And I suppose we must all wait to hear what you have been doing until you return, Gervaise?"

"I suppose so, Ralph. Of course it is a long story; but I must tell you at once that there is nothing very exciting in it, and that it differed little from that of others who have been prisoners among the Moors, save that I was strangely fortunate, and suffered no hardships whatever. And now I want to ask you about clothes. Have my things been sold, or are they still in the store?"

"No; the question was raised but a short time since. It was mooted, by the way, by that old enemy of yours, Robert Rivers, who returned here some three months ago with a batch of knights from the English commanderies. Sir John Boswell answered him roundly, I can tell you, and said that they should be kept, were it for another fifty years, for that he would wager his life that you would sooner or later make your escape."

"I am sorry that fellow has returned, Ralph. Has he got a commandery yet?"

"No; I believe that Sir John Kendall sent home so bad a report of him, that even the great influence of his family has not sufficed to obtain his appointment, and that he has been merely the assistant at one of the smaller manors. Sir John Boswell told me in confidence that he understood that Rivers did not at first volunteer to come out in response to the appeal of the grand master, but that the grand prior informed him that unless he took this opportunity of retrieving his character, he might give up all hope of ever obtaining advancement. Ah, here is your breakfast."

An hour later Gervaise presented himself at the palace, clothed in the suit of armour that had been given to him by Genoa. Although he was engaged with several members of the council at the time, the grand master ordered him to be at once admitted as soon as he heard that he was in attendance.

"Welcome back, Sir Gervaise Tresham," he said warmly, as he entered. "We all rejoice greatly at your return, and I consider it a happy omen for the success of our defence that so brave and distinguished a knight should at the last moment have arrived to take a share in it."

The others present all shook Gervaise cordially by the hand, and congratulated him on his return.

"You must dine with me this evening," D'Aubusson went on, "and tell us the story of your captivity and escape. At present, as you may suppose, we have too many matters on hand to spare time for aught that is not pressing and important. You will need a few days' rest before you are fit for active service, and by that time we will settle as to what post will best suit you."

Twice that day had Gervaise to recount his adventures, the first time to Sir John Kendall and the knights of his *auberge*, the second to the grand master. Most of the leading members of the Order were assembled at the palace, and, among others, he was introduced to the Viscount de Monteuil, the elder brother of D'Aubusson, one of the most famous leaders of the day. He had brought with him a considerable body of retainers, and, although not a member of the Order, had offered his services in defence of the town. The council had gratefully accepted the offer, and had unanimously named him Commander of the Forces. Many other knights and soldiers had come from different parts of Europe, animated alike by the desire to aid in the defence of Christendom against the advance of the Moslems, and to gain credit and honour by taking part in a siege that was sure to be a desperate one.

"My brother has already spoken of you to me, Sir Gervaise," the viscount said, when the young knight was presented to him; "although indeed there was no occasion for him to do so, since the name of the knight who two years ago saved the commerce of Italy from ruin, and with a single galley destroyed or captured a great fleet of over twenty Barbary pirates, and thus for a time put a stop to the depredations of the infidels, is known throughout

Europe. By the way, I am the bearer of a message to you. I took ship at Genoa on my way hither, and stayed two or three days there while she was being got ready for sea. Knowing that I was bound hither, a certain very beautiful young lady of noble family, to whom I had the honour of being introduced, prayed me that if you should by any chance have escaped from captivity—and she said that she was convinced that you would, when you heard that Rhodes was threatened, assuredly endeavour to escape and to come hither to take a share in the defence—I was to tell you that she trusted you still bore her gage, and that she, on her part, had held fast to the promise she made you."

"I still have her gage, Viscount; for though I was for a long time deprived of it, I succeeded in regaining it when I made my escape," Gervaise said quietly; and De Monteuil at once turned the conversation to another topic.

Gervaise found that no attempt was to be made to take the offensive against the Turks, and that they were to be permitted to advance against the city without interference. Many of the more fiery spirits among the knights chafed at this prohibition. The records of the past showed that armies as large as that of Mahomet had suffered defeat at the hands of bodies of knights no stronger than that gathered for the defence of Rhodes. D'Aubusson, however, knew that between the undisciplined hordes that gathered in countless numbers to oppose the crusaders, and the troops of Mahomet, well-trained in warfare, who had borne his standard victoriously in numerous battles, there was but little comparison. They were commanded, too, by Paleologus, a general of great capacity. Under such circumstances, although victory might be possible, the chances of defeat would be far greater, and while victory could be only won at a great sacrifice of life, defeat would mean annihilation to the garrison, and the loss of the city upon whose fortifications such an enormous amount of money and labour had been expended.

BELEAGUERED

On the other hand, he felt perfectly confident that the city could be successfully defended, and that at a cost of life far less than would be attained by a victory in the open field, while the blow that would be inflicted upon the prestige and power of the enemy, by being ignominiously compelled to retire to their ships, after the failure of all their attacks, would be as great as if their army had been defeated in the field. Therefore the grand master, with the full assent of his leaders, turned a deaf ear to the entreaties of the younger knights, that they might be allowed to make a sortie. He calmly waited behind the formidable defences he had for the past ten years been occupied in perfecting, in anticipation of the assault of the Moslem host. Accordingly, after disembarking at their leisure, the Turkish army moved forward, and took their post upon St. Stephen's Hill. From this eminence they commanded a full view of the town, the hills sloping gently down to the foot of the walls. In later times the first care of a general commanding the defence would have been to construct formidable works upon this commanding position. But the cannon of that period were so cumbrous and slowly worked, and so inaccurate in their aim, that the advantage of occupying a position that would prevent an enemy from firing down into a town was considered to be more than counterbalanced by the weakening of the garrison by the abstraction of the force required to man the detached work, and by the risk of their being surrounded and cut off without the garrison of the town being able to aid them.

That the defence of St. Stephen's Hill was considered unnecessary for the safety of Rhodes is shown by the fact that no attempt had been made to fortify it when, forty years later, the Moslems again besieged the city.

There was no shadow of apprehension felt by the garrison of Rhodes as the great array of their foes was seen moving on to the hill, and preparing to pitch its camp. On the summit was the great tent of the pasha; round this were the marquees of the other commanders, while the encampments of the troops stretched far away along the upper slopes of the hill.

Previous to the despatch of the expedition, the sultan had made preparations for aiding his arms by treachery. The agent he had sent to propose a temporary truce had, during his stay on the Island, made himself thoroughly acquainted with the outline of the works. A very accurate plan of them had also been obtained from an inhabitant of Rhodes, who had abandoned Christianity and taken service with the Turks.

In addition to this he had arranged with a renegade German, known as Maître Georges, a man of very great ability as an artilleryman and engineer, to desert to the city, and there do all in his power to assist the besiegers, both by affording them information and by giving bad advice to the besieged. On the day after Paleologus, who was himself a renegade Greek, had established his camp, he sent in a herald to summon the city to surrender, at the same time making lavish promises that the lives and property of the native population should be respected, and that they should be allowed to continue to reside there, to enjoy the full exercise of their religion and of all other rights they possessed. The pasha had no real hope that the knights would obey the summons, but he thought that he might excite a spirit of disaffection among the townspeople that would, when the crisis came, greatly hamper the efforts of the defenders.

The Rhodians, however, were well satisfied with the rule of the Order. The knights, although belonging to the Catholic Church, had allowed the natives of the Island, who were of the Greek faith, perfect freedom in the exercise of their religion, and their rule, generally, had been fair and just. The wealth and prosperity of the Island had increased enormously since their establishment there, and the population had no inclination whatever to change their rule for that of the Turks. The summons to surrender being refused, the enemy made a reconnaissance towards the walls.

BELEAGUERED

D'Aubusson had no longer any reason for checking the ardour of the knights, and a strong body of horsemen, under the command of De Monteuil, sallied out and drove the Turks back to their camp.

Maître Georges, who was acting as the military adviser of the pasha, saw at once that the weakest point of the defence was Fort St. Nicholas, at the extremity of the mole along the neck of land dividing the outer from the inner port. At a short distance away, on the opposite side of the port, stood the church of St. Anthony, and in the gardens of the church a battery was at once erected. The garden was but three hundred yards from St. Nicholas, and the danger that would arise from the construction of the battery was at once perceived, and an incessant fire opened upon it from the guns on the wall round the grand master's palace. Numbers of the workmen were killed, but the erection of the battery was pushed on night and day, and ere long three of the immense cannon that had been brought from Constantinople,—where sixteen of them had been cast under the direction of Maître Georges—were placed in position. These cannon were eighteen feet in length, and carried stone balls of some twenty-six inches in diameter.

Before these were ready to open fire, Gervaise had entirely regained his health and strength. The grand master, being unwilling to appoint him to a separate command over the heads of knights many years his senior, had attached him to his person in the capacity of what would now be called an *aide-de-camp*.

"I know, Gervaise, that I can rely upon your coolness and discretion. I cannot be everywhere myself, and I want you to act as my eyes in places where I cannot be. I know that the knights, so far as bravery and devotion are concerned, will each and every one do his best, and will die at their posts before yielding a foot; but while fighting like paladins they will think of naught else, and, however hardly pressed, will omit to send to me for reinforcements. Nay, even did they think of it, they probably would not send, deeming that to do so would be derogatory, and might be taken as an act of cowardice. Now, it is this service that I shall specially look for from you. When a post is attacked, I shall, when my presence is required elsewhere, send you to represent me. I do not, of course, wish you to interfere in any way in the conduct of the defence, in which you will take such share as you can; but you are specially to observe how matters go, and if you see that the knights are pressed and in sore need of assistance to enable them to hold the post, you will at once bring the news to me, and I will hurry there with reinforcements."

No post could have been more in accordance with the desire of Gervaise, for the portion of the wall defended by the English *langue* was far removed from the point selected by the Turks for their first attack, the sea front being defended half by the *langue* of Italy, and half by that of Castile. Fort St. Nicholas was under the command of the Cavalier Caretto, and as soon as the Turkish battery was completed, Gervaise went down there with an order from the grand master that he was for the present to consider himself as forming part of the garrison. This was pleasant for both Caretto and himself, for the Italian knight had conceived a strong friendship for the young Englishman, and had rejoiced greatly at his return from captivity, but had been so much occupied with his duty of placing the castle in all respects in a state of defence, that he had had no opportunity for a private conversation with him since his return to Rhodes.

Gervaise, on his part, was no less pleased. Caretto had shown so much tact after his release from the Moors, and had so willingly aided him in any capacity allotted to him, without in the slightest degree interposing his council unasked, that Gervaise had come to like him greatly, even before their arrival at Genoa. Circumstances there had brought them closely together, and their friendship had been cemented during their voyage to Rhodes. Caretto had gone back to Italy, where he had a commandery, a few days after Gervaise had sailed on his last voyage, and had only returned to Rhodes three months before Gervaise escaped from captivity.

"This is turning the tables," Caretto said, with a laugh, when Gervaise presented the grand master's order. "I was under your command last time, and now it seems that you are to be under mine. I suppose you applied to come here, in order to have a fresh opportunity of distinguishing yourself. I heard that you had been placed on D'Aubusson's own staff."

"Yes, and am on it still; and it is by his orders and not by my own solicitation that I am here. I will tell you what my duties are. The grand master knows the commanders of posts have their hands so full that they will have no time for sending complete reports to him, and he considers, moreover, that they might, in some cases, however pressed, hesitate to ask for aid until too late for reinforcements to be brought up. My duty will be to let the grand master know how matters are going, and to send to him at once if it seems to me that help is needed. I should, of course, always send for reinforcements, at the request of a commander; but it is only in the event of his being too busy in the heat of the fray to think of aught but resisting an attack, that I should exercise my own judgment in the matter."

Caretto nodded.

"It is a good thought of D'Aubusson's. When one is in the thick of a fight in a breach, with the Moslems swarming round, it does not occur to one to draw out of the fray to send off messages. For myself, I shall be glad indeed to have that matter off my mind, though it is not every one I should care to trust with such a responsibility. Some might send off for aid when it was not needed, others might delay so long that help might come too late; but with one so cool-headed as yourself I should not fear any contingency. And now, as I am not busy at present, let us have a comfortable talk as to what has happened since we met last. I was at the banquet at the grand master's on the night when you related your adventures. You had certainly much to tell, but it seems to me for some reason or other you cut short certain details, and I could not see why, as there seemed no prospect of escape open to you, you did not accept the offer of Suleiman Ali to ransom you."

"I saw no chance of escape at the moment, but I did not doubt that I could get away from the town whenever I chose, although it was not clear how I should proceed afterwards. It was for this opportunity I was waiting, and I felt sure that, with my knowledge of the language, it would come sooner or later. In the next place, my captors had fixed an exorbitant sum for my ransom, and I did not wish to impose upon the generosity of Suleiman. There was another reason—a private one."

"You don't mean to say that you had fallen in love with a Moorish damsel, Sir Gervaise?" Caretto laughed.

"For shame, Cavalier! As if a Christian knight would care for a Moslem maiden, even were she as fair as the houris of their creed!"

"Christian knights have done so before now," Caretto laughed, greatly amused at the young knight's indignation, "and doubtless will do so again. Well, I suppose I must not ask what the private matter was, though it must have been something grave indeed to lead you, a slave, to reject the offer of freedom. I know that when I was rowing in their galleys, no matter of private business that I can conceive would have stood in my way for a single moment, had a chance of freedom presented itself."

"It was a matter of honour," Gervaise said gravely, "and one of which I should speak to no one else; but as you were present at the time, there can, I think, be no harm in doing so. At the time that I was captured, I was stripped of everything that I had upon me, and, of course, with the rest, of the gage which the Lady Claudia had given me, and which hung round my neck where she had placed it. It was taken possession of by the captain of the pirates, who, seeing that it bore no Christian emblem, looked upon it as a sort of amulet. I understood what he was saying, but, as I was desirous that my knowledge of Turkish should not be suspected, I said nothing. I was very glad that he so regarded it, for had he taken it to be an ordinary trinket, he might have parted with it, and I should never have been able to obtain a clue as to the person to whom he sold it. As it was, he put it round his neck, with the remark that it might bring him better luck than had befallen me. He told me jeeringly months afterwards that it had done so, and that he would never part with it. Given me as it was, I felt that my honour was concerned in its recovery, and that, should I ever meet Lady Claudia again, I should feel disgraced indeed, if, when she asked whether I still bore her gage, I had to confess that it was lost."

"But lost from no fault of your own," Caretto put in.

"The losing was not indeed from any fault of my own, and had the pirate thrown it into the sea I should have held myself free from disgrace; but as it was still in existence, and I knew its possessor, I was bound in honour to recover it. At the time Suleiman Ali's messenger arrived the corsair was away, and there was no saying when his ship would return; therefore, I decided at once not to accept the offer of freedom. Had it not been for that, I own that I should have done so, for I knew that I could repay Suleiman from the revenues of my commandery, which would have accumulated in my absence; but if I had had to wait ten years longer to regain the gage, I felt that I was in honour bound to do so. It was, in fact, some six months before the corsair put into that port again. The moment he did so I carried out the plans I had long before determined upon. I obtained a disguise from Ben Ibyn, and by a ruse succeeded in inducing the pirate to meet me outside the town, believing that I was an Arab chief who wished to dispose of some valuable slave-girls he had brought in. I had with me one of my old galley-slaves, who had been taken into Ben Ibyn's employment; and when the pirate came up with two of his crew, and furiously attacked me as soon as I threw off my disguise, it would have gone hard with me had he not stood by me, and killed one of them who was about to attack me in the rear. I slew the other and Hassan, and the gage is in its place again."

CHAPTER XXI
THE FORT OF ST. NICHOLAS

WELL, you have proved indeed," Caretto said, when Gervaise finished his story, "that you are worthy of the bestowal of a gage by a fair damsel. I do not think that many knights, however true they might be to the donor, would have suffered months of slavery in order to regain a token, lost by no fault or carelessness of their own; and no lady could have blamed or held them in any way dishonoured by the loss."

"I had a message by the Viscount De Monteuil from Lady Claudia the other day, saying that she trusted I had kept her gage. I can assure you that the six months of slavery were cheaply purchased by the pleasure I felt that I still possessed it; and I was glad, too, to learn that I had not been forgotten by her."

"Of that you may well assure yourself, Tresham; my commandery is not far from Genoa, and I was frequently with her, but never without her drawing me aside and asking me if I had heard any news of you, and talking over with me the chances there might be of your escape. I can tell you that there are not a few young nobles of Genoa who would give much to be allowed as you are to carry her gage, or wear her colours. You should see her now; you would scarce know her again, so altered and improved is she; there is no fairer face in all Italy."

"I hope some day to meet her again, " Gervaise replied; "although I own to knowing it were better that I should not do so. Until she gave me her gage I had scarcely noticed her. I have, as you know, no experience of women, and had so much on my mind at the time, what with the fuss they were making about us, and the question of getting the prizes here, that in truth I paid but slight attention to the fair faces of the dames of Genoa. But the gracious and earnest way in which, though scarce more than a child, she gave me her gage, and vowed that no other knight should possess one so long as I lived, struck me so greatly that I own I gave the matter much more thought than was right or becoming in one of our Order. The incident was much more gratifying to me than all the honour paid me by the Republic, and during the long months of my captivity it has recurred to me so frequently that I have in vain endeavoured to chase it from my thoughts, as sinful thus to allow myself constantly to think of any woman. Do not mistake me, Sir Fabricius. I am speaking to you as to a confessor, and just as I have kept her amulet hidden from all, so is the thought of her a secret I would not part with for my life. I do not for a moment deceive myself with the thought that, beyond the fact that her gift has made her feel an interest in me and my fate, she has any sentiment in the matter: probably, indeed, she looks back upon the gift as a foolish act of girlish enthusiasm that led her into making a promise that she now cannot but find unpleasantly binding; for it is but natural that among the young nobles of her own rank and country there must be some whom she would see with pleasure wearing her colours."

Caretto looked at him with some amusement.

"Were you not bound by your vows as a knight of the Order, how would you feel in the matter?"

"I should feel worse," Gervaise said, without hesitation. "I have oftentimes thought that over, and I see that it is good for me I am so bound. It does not decrease my chances, for, as I know, there are no chances; but it renders it more easy for me to know that it is so."

"But why should you say that you have no chances, Tresham?"

"Because it is easy to see that it is so. I am, save for my commandery and prospects in the Order, a penniless young knight, without home or estate, without even a place in my country, and that country not hers. I know that it is not only sinful, but mad, for me to think so frequently of her, but at least I am not mad enough to think that I can either win the heart or aspire to the hand of one who is, you say, so beautiful, and who is, moreover, as I know, the heiress to wide estates."

> " *'There was a squire of low degree*
> *Loved the king's daughter of Hungarie,'* "

Caretto sang, with a laugh. "You are not of low degree, but of noble family, Gervaise. You are not a squire, but a knight, and already a very distinguished one; nor is the young lady, though she be a rich heiress, a king's daughter."

"At any rate, the squire was not vowed to celibacy. No, no, Sir Fabricius, it is a dream, and a pleasant one; but I know perfectly well that it is but a dream, and one that will do me no harm so long as I ever bear in mind that it is so. Many a knight of the Order before me has borne a lady's gage, and carried it valiantly in many a fight, and has been no less true to his vows for doing so."

"Upon the contrary, he has been all the better a knight, Gervaise; it is always good for a knight, whether he belongs to the Order or not, to prize one woman above all others, and to try to make himself worthy of his ideal. As to the vow of celibacy, you know that ere now knights have been absolved from their vows, and methinks that, after the service you have rendered to Italy by ridding the sea of those corsairs, his Holiness would make no difficulty in granting any request that you might make him in that or any other direction. I don't know whether you are aware that, after you sailed from here, letters came from Rome as well as from Pisa, Florence, and Naples, expressive of the gratitude felt for the services that you had rendered, and of their admiration for the splendid exploit that you had performed."

"No; the grand master has had his hands so full of other matters that doubtless an affair so old escaped his memory. Indeed, he may have forgotten that I sailed before the letters arrived."

"Do not forget to jog his memory on the subject, for I can tell you that the letters did not come alone, but were each accompanied by presents worthy of the service you rendered. But as to the vows?"

"As to the vows, I feel as I said just now, that I would not free myself of them if I could, for, being bound by them, I can the more easily and pleasantly enjoy my dream. Besides, what should I do if I left the Order without home, country, or means, and with naught to do but to sell my sword to some warlike monarch? Besides, Caretto, I love the Order, and deem it the highest privilege to fight against the Moslems, and to uphold the banner of the Cross."

"As to that, you could, like De Monteuil and many other knights here, always come out to aid the Order in time of need. As to the vows, I am not foolish enough to suppose that you would ask to be relieved from them, until you had assured yourself that Claudia was also desirous that you should be free."

"It is absurd," Gervaise said, almost impatiently. "Do not let us talk any more about it, Caretto, or it will end by turning my head and making me presumptuous enough to imagine that the Lady Claudia, who only saw me for three or four days, and that while she was still but a girl, has been thinking of me seriously since."

"I do not know Claudia's thoughts," Caretto remarked drily, "but I do know that last year she refused to listen to at least a score of excellent offers for her hand, including one from a son of the doge himself, and that without any reasonable cause assigned by her, to the great wonderment of all, seeing that she does not appear to have any leaning whatever towards a life in a nunnery. At any rate, if at some future time you should pluck up heart of grace to tell her you love her, and she refuses you, you will at least have the consolation of knowing that you are not the only one, by a long way, whose suit has been rejected. And now as to our affairs here. Methinks that to-morrow that battery will open fire upon us. It seems completed."

"Yes, I think they are nearly ready," Gervaise said, turning his mind resolutely from the subject they had been discussing. "From the palace wall I saw, before I came down here, large numbers of men rolling huge stones down towards the church. Our guns were firing steadily; but could they load them ten times as fast as they do, they would hardly be able to stop the work, so numerous are those engaged upon it."

"Yes we shall soon learn something of the quality of their artillery. The tower is strong enough to resist ordinary guns, but it will soon crumble under the blows of such enormous missiles. Never have I seen or heard in Europe of cannon of such size; but indeed, in this matter the Turks are far ahead of us, and have, ever since cannon were first cast, made them of much larger size than we in Europe have done. However, there is one comfort; they may destroy this fort, but they have still to cross the water, and this under the fire of the guns on the palace walls; when they once land, their great battery must cease firing, and we shall be able to meet them on equal terms in the breach. Fight as hard as they may, I think we can hold our own, especially as reinforcements can come down to us more quickly than they can be brought across the water."

The next morning, at daybreak, the deep boom of a gun announced to the city that the great battering cannon had begun their work. In the fort the sleeping knights sprang to their feet at the concussion that seemed to shake it to its centre. They would have rushed to the walls, but Caretto at once issued orders that no one should show himself on the battlements unless under special orders.

"There is nothing whatever to be done until the Turks have breached the wall, and are ready to advance to attack us. Every sword will be needed when that hour comes, and each man owes it to the Order to run no useless risk, until the hour when he is required to do his share of the fighting."

The time required to reload the great cannon was considerable, but at regular intervals they hurled their heavy missiles against the wall, the distance being so short that every ball struck it. After some twenty shots had been fired, Caretto, accompanied by Gervaise, went out by a small gate on the eastern side of the tower, and made their way round by the foot of the wall to see what effect the shots had produced on the solid masonry.

Caretto shook his head.

"It is as I feared," he said. "No stones ever quarried by man could long resist such tremendous blows. In some places, you see, the stones are starred and cracked, in others the shock seems to have pulverised the spot where it struck; but, worse, still, the whole face of the wall is shaken. There are cracks between the stones, and some of these are partly bulged out and partly driven in. It may take some time before a breach is effected, but sooner or later the wall will surely be demolished."

"I will go up and make my report to the grand master."

"Do so, Gervaise. I almost wonder that he has not himself come down to see how the wall is resisting."

Gervaise, on reaching the palace, heard that D'Aubusson was at present engaged in examining no less a person than Maître Georges, the right hand of Paleologus, who had soon after daybreak presented himself before the wall on the other side of the town, declaring that he had left the Turkish service, and craving to be admitted. News had been sent at once to D'Aubusson, who despatched two of the senior knights, with orders to admit him and receive him with all honour. This had been done, and the grand master, with some of his council, were now closeted with the new-comer. Several of the knights were gathered in the courtyard, discussing the event. There was no question that if the renegade came in good faith, his defection would be a serious blow to the assailants, and that his well-known skill and experience would greatly benefit the defenders.

"For my part," Sir John Boswell, who formed one of the detachment which the English *langue*, as well as all the others, contributed to form the garrison of the palace said, "I would have hung the fellow up by the neck over the gateway, and he should never have set foot within the walls. Think you that a man who has denied his faith and taken service with his enemies is to be trusted, whatever oaths he may take?"

"You must remember, Boswell," another said, "that hitherto Georges has not fought against Christians, but has served Mahomet in his wars with other infidels. I am not saying a word in defence of his having become a renegade; yet even a renegade may have some sort of heart, and now that he has been called upon to fight against Christians he may well have repented of his faults, and determined to sacrifice his position and prospects rather than aid in the attack on the city."

"We shall see. As for me, I regard a renegade as the most contemptible of wretches, and have no belief that they have either a heart or conscience."

When Maître Georges came out from the palace, laughing and talking with the two knights who had entered with him, it was evident that he was well pleased with his reception by the grand master, who had assigned to him a suite of apartments in the guest-house. In reality, however, D'Aubusson had no doubt that his object was a treacherous one, and that, like Demetrius, who had come under the pretence of bringing about a truce, his object was to find out the weak points and to supply the Turks with information. Georges had, in his conversation with him, laid great stress on the strength of the Turkish army, the excellent quality of the troops, and the enormous battering train that had been prepared. But every word he spoke but added to the grand master's suspicions; for if the man considered that the capture of the city was morally certain, it would be simply throwing away his life to enter it as a deserter.

The grand master was, however, too politic to betray any doubt of Georges' sincerity. Were he treated as a traitor, Paleologus might find another agent to do the work. It was, therefore, better to feign a belief in his story, to obtain all the information possible from him, and at the same time to prevent his gaining any knowledge of affairs that would be of the slightest use to the Turks. Instructions were therefore given to the two knights that, while Georges was to be treated with all courtesy, he was to be strictly watched, though in such a manner that he should be in ignorance of it, and that, whenever he turned his steps in the direction of those parts of the defences where fresh works had been recently added and preparations made of which it was desirable the Turks should be kept in ignorance, he was to be met, as if by accident, by one of the knights told off for the purpose, and his steps diverted in another direction.

Georges soon made himself popular among many of the knights, who had no suspicions of his real character. He was a man of exceptional figure, tall, strong, splendidly proportioned, with a handsome face and gallant bearing. He was extremely well informed on all subjects, had travelled widely, had seen many adventures, was full of anecdote, and among the younger knights, therefore, he was soon regarded as a charming companion. His very popularity among them aided D'Aubusson's plans, as Georges was generally the centre of a group of listeners, and so had but few opportunities of getting away quietly to obtain the information he sought. Gervaise delivered his report to the grand master.

"I am free now," D'Aubusson said, "and will accompany you to St. Nicholas. I have been detained by the coming of this man Georges. He is a clever knave, and, I doubt not, has come as a spy. However, I have taken measures that he shall learn nothing that can harm us. No lives have been lost at the tower, I hope?"

"No, sir; Caretto has forbidden any to show themselves on the walls."

"He has done well. This is no time for rash exposure, and where there is naught to be gained, it is a grave fault to run risks."

On arriving at the end of the mole, D'Aubusson, accompanied by Caretto, made an investigation of the effect of the Turks' fire.

"'Tis worse than I expected," he said. "When we laid out our fortifications the thought that such guns as these would be used against them never entered our minds. Against ordinary artillery the walls would stand a long battering; but it is clear that we shall have to depend more upon our swords than upon our walls for our defence. Fortunately, although the Turks have indeed chosen the spot where our walls are most open to the assaults of their battery, they have to cross the water to attack the breach when it is made, and will have to fight under heavy disadvantage."

"Tresham was last night saying to me, that it seemed to him it would not be a difficult matter for one who spoke Turkish well, to issue at night on the other side of the town, and to make his way round to the battery, disguised of course as a Turkish soldier, and then, mixing with the artillery-men, to drive a spike into one of the touch-holes. He said that he would gladly volunteer for the task."

D'Aubusson shook his head decidedly. "It would be too dangerous; and even were a spike driven in, the Turks would have no great difficulty in extracting it, for the tubes are so big that a man might crawl in and drive the spike up from the inside. Moreover, could one or more of the guns be disabled permanently, others would be brought down and set in their place, so that nothing would be gained but a very short delay, which would be of no advantage to us, and certainly would in no way justify the risking of the life of so distinguished a young knight."

A KNIGHT OF THE WHITE CROSS

The bombardment of St. Nicholas continued for some days. A breach was fast forming in the wall, and a slope composed of the fallen rubbish extended from the front of the breach to the water's edge. The grand master was frequently on the spot, and as this was at present the sole object of attack, the garrison was strengthened by as many knights as could be sheltered within its walls. At night the shattered masonry that had fallen inside was carried out, and with it a new work thrown up across the mole, to strengthen the defence on that side, should the enemy land between the town and the fort. Small batteries were planted wherever they could sweep the approaches to the breach, and planks studded with nails were sunk in the shallow water of the harbour, to impede the progress of those who might attempt to swim or wade across. For the time, therefore, the functions of Gervaise were in abeyance, and he laboured with the rest of the garrison at the defences.

At daybreak on the 9th of June, a great number of vessels and boats, crowded with soldiers, bore down on St. Nicholas. As they approached, every gun on the fortifications that could be brought to bear upon them opened fire; but in a dense mass they advanced. Some made their way to the rocks and landed the soldiers there; others got alongside the mole; but the majority grounded in the shallow water of the harbour, and the troops, leaping out, waded to the foot of the breach. On its crest D'Aubusson himself had taken up his station. Beside him stood Caretto, and around them the most distinguished knights of the Order. With wild shouts the Turks rushed up the breach, and swarmed thickly up the ruined masonry until, at its summit, they encountered the steel-clad line of the defenders. For hours the terrible struggle continued. As fast as the head of the Turkish column broke and melted away against the obstacle they tried in vain to penetrate, fresh reinforcements took the place of those who had fallen, and in point of valour and devotion the Moslem showed himself a worthy antagonist of the Christian. It was not only at the breach that the conflict raged. At other points

362

With wild shouts the Turks swarmed up the ruined masonry.

the Turks, well provided with ladders, fixed them against the walls, and desperately strove to obtain a footing there. From the breach clouds of dust rose from under the feet of the combatants, mingling with the smoke of the cannon on the ramparts, the fort, and Turkish ships, and at times entirely hid from the sight of the anxious spectators on the walls of the town and fortress, and of the still more numerous throng of Turks on St. Stephen's Hill, the terrible struggle that continued without a moment's intermission.

The combatants now fought in comparative silence. The knights, exhausted and worn out by their long efforts beneath the blazing sun, still showed an unbroken front; but it was only occasionally that the battle-cry of the Order rose in the air, as a fresh body of assailants climbed up the corpse-strewn breach. The yell of the Moslems rose less frequently; they sacrificed their lives as freely and devotedly as those who led the first onset had done; but as the hours wore on, the assurance of victory died out, and a doubt as to whether it was possible to break through the line of their terrible foes gained ground. D'Aubusson himself, although, in spite of the remonstrances of the knights, always in the thickest of the fray, was yet ever watchful, and quickly perceived where the defenders were hotly pressed, and where support was most needed. Gervaise fought by his side, so that, when necessary, he could carry his orders to a little body of knights, drawn up in reserve, and despatch them to any point where aid was needed.

The cannon still continued their fire on both sides. A fragment of one of the stone balls from a basilisk struck off D'Aubusson's helmet. He selected another from among the fallen knights, and resumed his place in the line. Still the contest showed no signs of terminating. The Turkish galleys ever brought up reinforcements, while the defenders grew fewer, and more exhausted. During a momentary pause, while a fresh body of Turks were landing, Gervaise said to the grand master,—

THE FORT OF ST. NICHOLAS

"If you will give me leave, sir, I will go out at the watergate, swim up the inner harbour, and in a very short time turn a few of the craft lying there into fire-ships, and tow them out with a couple of galleys. At any rate, we can fire all these craft that have grounded, and create a panic among the others."

"Well thought of, Gervaise! I will write an order on one of my tablets. Do you take my place for a minute."

Withdrawing behind the line, the grand master sat down on a fragment of stone, and, drawing a tablet from a pouch in his girdle, he wrote on it,—

"In all things carry out the instructions of Sir Gervaise Tresham: he is acting by my orders and authority, and has full power in all respects."

He handed the slip of parchment to Gervaise, who hurried to the water-gate in the inner harbour, threw off his helmet and armour, issued out at the gate, and plunged into the sea. He swam out some distance, in order to avoid the missiles of the Turks, who were trying to scale the wall from the mole, and then directed his course to St. Michael's, which guarded the inner entrance to the fort. He had fastened the parchment in his hair, and as some of the garrison of the tower, noticing his approach, came down to assist him, he handed it to them and was at once taken to the commander of St. Michael, answering as he went the anxious questions as to how matters stood at the breach.

"Aid is sorely needed. The Turks have gained no foot of ground as yet, but many of the knights are killed and most of the others utterly exhausted with heat and labour. Unless aid reaches them speedily, the tower, with all its defenders, will be lost."

The instant the commander knew what was required, he bade six of the knights embark with Gervaise in a boat moored behind the tower, and row up the harbour to the spot where the shipping was all massed together, protected by the high ground of the fortress from the Turkish fire. Gervaise waved his hand, as he neared the end of the harbour, to the officer on the walls, and while the six knights who were with him ran off to tell the master of the galleys to prepare two of them to leave the port instantly, Gervaise explained to the officer in charge of the wall at that point the plan that he was charged to carry out, and asked for twenty knights to assist him.

"It will leave us very weak along here," the officer said. "Then let me have ten, and send for another ten from other parts of the wall. Here is the grand master's order, giving me full power and authority, and it is all-important that no single moment shall be wasted."

"You shall have twenty of mine," the officer said, " and I will draw ten from the *langue* next to us to fill their places."

In a few minutes the quay was a scene of bustle and activity. Gervaise picked out ten of the smallest vessels; the knights went among the other ships, seized all goods and stores that would be useful as combustibles, and compelled the crews to carry them on board the craft chosen as fire-ships. Then barrels were broken open, old sails and faggots saturated with oil and pitch, and in little more than a quarter of an hour after his arrival, Gervaise had the satisfaction of seeing that the ten boats were all filled with combustibles, and ready to be set on fire. He now called for volunteers from the sailors, and a number of them at once came forward, including many of the captains. He placed one of these in command of each fire-ship, and gave him four of the sailors.

"The galleys will tow you out," he said, "and take you close to the enemy's ships. We shall range you five abreast, and when I give the word, the one at the end of the line will steer for the nearest Turk, and, with oars and poles, get alongside. The captain will then light the train of powder in the hold, throw the torch among the straw, and see that, if possible, the men fasten her to the Turk; but if this cannot be done, it is not essential, for in the confusion the enemy will not be able to get out of the way of the fire-ship as it drives down against her. At the last moment you will take to your boats and row back here. We will protect you from the assaults of any of the Turkish ships."

THE FORT OF ST. NICHOLAS

Having made sure that all the captains understood the orders, Gervaise took command of one of the galleys, the senior knight going on board the other. The ten fire-ships were now poled out until five were ranged abreast behind each craft; Gervaise requested the commander of the other galley to lie off the point of St. Nicholas until he had got rid of his five fire-ships, then to advance and launch his craft against the Turks. The smoke of the guns lay so heavy on the water, and the combatants were so intent upon the struggle at the breach, that Gervaise steered his galley into the midst of the Turkish vessels laden with troops ready to disembark, without attracting any notice; then, standing upon the taffrail, he signalled to the two outside boats to throw off their ropes and make for the Turkish ship nearest to them. This they did, and it was not until a sheet of flame rose alongside, that the enemy awoke to the sense of danger.

The other three fire-ships were almost immediately cast off. Two of them were equally successful, but the Turks managed to thrust off the third. She drifted, however, through the shipping, and presently brought up alongside one of the vessels fast aground. With but ten knights, Gervaise could not attack one of the larger vessels, crowded with troops; but there were many fishing-boats that had been pressed into the service, and against one of these Gervaise ordered the men to steer the galley. A shout to the rowers made them redouble their efforts. A yell of dismay arose from the Turkish troops as they saw the galley bearing down upon them, and frantic efforts were made to row out of her way. These were in vain, for her sharp prow struck them amidships, cutting the boat almost in two, and she sank like a stone, the galley, without a pause, making for another boat.

Looking back, Gervaise saw that his consort was already in the midst of the Turks, among whom the wildest confusion prevailed, each ship trying to extricate herself from the mass, upon which the batteries of the fortress now concentrated their efforts. Two fresh columns of flame had already shot up, and satisfied that all was going well,

Gervaise continued his attack upon the smaller craft, six of whom were overtaken and sunk. Three or four of the larger vessels endeavoured to lay themselves alongside the galley, but her speed was so superior to theirs that she easily evaded the attempts, and, sweeping round, rejoined the other galley which had just issued from among the Turks, who were already in full retreat. The defenders of St. Nicholas, re-animated by the sight of the discomfiture of the Turkish fleet, with a loud shout rushed down from the spot which they had held for so many hours, drove their assailants before them, and flung themselves upon the crowd assembled at the foot of the breach.

These had already suffered terribly from the fire of the batteries. Again and again they had striven to storm the mound of rubbish, and had each time been repulsed, with the loss of their bravest leaders. Seeing themselves abandoned by the ships, a panic seized them, and as the knights rushed down upon them they relinquished all thoughts of resistance, and dashed into the shallow water. Many were drowned in the attempt to swim across the deep channel in the middle, some succeeded, while others made their escape in the boats in which they had been brought ashore from the ships.

The struggle was over. The two galleys made for the breach, and the knights leapt out as soon as the boats grounded, and, wading ashore, joined the group that had so long and gallantly sustained the unequal fight. Fatigue, exhaustion, and wounds, were forgotten in the triumph of the moment, and they crowded round the grand master and Caretto, to whose joint exertions the success of the defence was so largely due.

"Do not thank me, comrades," D'Aubusson said. "No man has to-day fought better than the rest. Every knight has shown himself worthy of the fame of our Order. The meed of praise for our success is first due to Sir Gervaise Tresham. At the moment when I began to doubt whether we could much longer withstand the swarms of fresh foes who continued to pour against us, while we were overcome by heat and labour, Sir Gervaise, who had throughout been fighting at my side, offered to swim into the port, to fit out a dozen of the merchant craft there as fire-ships, and to tow them round into the midst of the Turkish vessels behind the two galleys that were lying ready for service. I remembered how he had before destroyed the corsair fleet at Sardinia with fire-ships, and the proposal seemed to me as an inspiration sent from Heaven, at this moment of our great peril. I wrote him an order, giving him full authority to act in my name, and in a time that seemed to me incredibly short I saw him round the point with the fire-ships in tow. You saw, as well as I did, how completely the plan was carried out. Ten or twelve of the Turkish ships are a mass of flames, and besides these I noted that the galley ran down and destroyed several smaller craft filled with soldiers. The panic in the ships spread to the troops on shore, and rendered the last part of our task an easy one. I say it from my heart that I consider it is to Sir Gervaise Tresham that we owe our success, and that, had it not been for his happy thought, the sun would have gone down on our dead bodies lying on the summit of the breach, and on the Turkish flag waving over the fort of St. Nicholas."

Until now none of the defenders of the breach had known how, what seemed to them an almost miraculous change in the fortune of the fight, had come about, and they thronged round Gervaise, shaking his hand, and many of them warmly embracing him, according to the custom of the time.

"It was but natural that the idea should occur to me," he said, "having before successfully encountered them with fire-ships; and as all on shore, and especially these knights, aided me with all their power, it took but a brief time to get the boats in readiness for burning. Much credit, too, is due to the merchant captains and sailors who volunteered to take charge of the fire-ships and to manœuver them alongside the Turks."

A KNIGHT OF THE WHITE CROSS

The grand master and the knights who had borne the brunt of the battle now retired along the mole to the town, bearing with them their most seriously wounded comrades, and assisting those whose wounds were less severe. The twenty knights who had manned the two galleys remained in the fort. Caretto continued in command, as, although he had suffered several wounds, he refused to relinquish his post. Gervaise, who had,—thanks partly to his skill with his weapons, but still more to the temper of the splendid suit of armour presented to him by Genoa,—escaped without a scratch, volunteered to remain with him until next morning, his principal motive for making the request being his desire to escape from further congratulations and praise for the success of his plan. After Caretto's wounds had been dressed by the knights, and he and Gervaise had partaken of some food and wine, which they greatly needed, Caretto was persuaded to lie down for a time, the knights promising to bring him word at once if they perceived any movement whatever on the part of the enemy. Gervaise remained with him, feeling, now the excitement was over, that he sorely needed rest after his exertions in the full heat of the summer sun.

"It has been a great day, Gervaise," Caretto said, "and I only hope that when again I go into battle with the infidel, I shall have you at hand to come forward at the critical moment with some master-stroke to secure victory. Claudia will be pleased indeed when she hears how the knight who bears her gage has again distinguished himself. She will look on the gay and idle young fops of Genoa with greater disdain than ever. Now you need not say anything in protest, the more so as I feel grievously weak, and disposed for sleep."

CHAPTER XXII
THE STRUGGLE AT THE BREACH

TWO hours later Caretto and Gervaise were roused by the arrival of a hundred knights in place of the previous garrison; these bore the news that the pasha had sent in a flag of truce to ask for an armistice until sundown, to enable him to carry off for burial the bodies of those who had fallen in the attack. The request had been willingly granted; but D'Aubusson had at the same time thought it well to send down a strong reinforcement to the garrison to prevent any attempt at treachery on the part of the Turks.

"I have seldom heard pleasanter news," Caretto said; "for just as I fell asleep I was wondering how we were to rid ourselves of the corpses of the infidels. By to-morrow the place would have become unbearable; and though, living, the Turks could not turn us out of the tower, they would when dead speedily have rid the place of us."

In half an hour a number of Moslem vessels were seen approaching. Caretto did not wish the Turks to imagine that he doubted their good faith, and while directing the main body of knights to remain in concealment near the breach, he placed two on sentry duty on the crest of the ruins, and, with four other knights and Gervaise, went down in complete armour to salute the officer in command of the burying party, as he landed from the boats. The ships anchored a short distance out, and a number of boats rowed from them to the shore. As the Turkish officer landed, Caretto saluted him, and said in Arabic,—

371

A KNIGHT OF THE WHITE CROSS

"I give you courteous greeting, Sir. When the cannon cease to sound and swords are sheathed, there is no longer animosity between brave men; and no braver than those whose bodies lie stretched there, breathed the air of heaven. If, sir, I and the knights with me do not uncover our heads, it is from no want of respect for the dead, but solely because we dare not stand bareheaded under the fierce rays of the sun."

The Turk answered with equal courtesy, complimenting the knights on their defence.

"Had I not seen it with my own eyes," he said, "I should have deemed it altogether impossible that so small a number of men could thus for hours have withstood the attacks of some of the best of the sultan's troops. Tales have come down to us from our fathers of the marvellous prowess of the knights of your Order, and how at Smyrna, at Acre, and elsewhere, they performed such feats of valour that their name is still used by Turkish mothers as a bugbear to frighten their children. But the stories have always seemed to me incredible; now I perceive they were true, and that the present members of the Order in no way fall short of the valour of their predecessors."

The knights remained with the Turkish commander and some of his officers while the work of collecting and carrying away the dead was performed, the conversation on their side being supported by Caretto and Gervaise. No less than seven hundred bodies were carried down to the boats, besides a great many wounded by the artillery fire. None were, however, found breathing among the great pile of dead at the upper part of the breach, for the axes and double-handed swords of the knights had, in most of the cases, cleft through turban and skull.

"This represents but part of our loss," the Turkish commander said sadly, as the last party came down with their burdens to the boats. "At least as many more must have perished in the sea, either in their endeavours to escape when all was lost, in the destruction of their vessels by fire, by the shot from your batteries, or by being run down by

372

your galleys. Ah, Sir Knight, if it had not been for the appearance of your fire-ships, methinks the matter might have ended differently."

"In that I altogether agree with you," Caretto said. "We were indeed, well-nigh spent, and must have soon succumbed had it not been that the fire-ships arrived to our rescue. You have a fair right to claim that the victory would have remained in your hands, had not those craft gone out and snatched it from you."

Then, with salutes on both sides, the Turks took their places in the boats, and the knights returned to the fort. As soon as darkness came on, a large body of slaves were marched down from the town, and, under the direction of the knights, laboured all night at the mound, removing great quantities of the fallen stones and rubbish in a line halfway up it, and piling them above so as to form a scarp across the mound that would need ladders to ascend. Another party worked at the top of the mound, and there built up a wall eight feet high. The work was completed by daylight, and the knights felt that they were now in a position to resist another attack, should Paleologus again send his troops to the assault.

The night had passed quietly. There was a sound of stir and movement in the Turkish battery, but nothing that would excite the suspicion of a large body of troops being in motion. When it became light it was seen that the Turkish ships had sailed away to their previous anchorage on the other side of the Island, and although at considerable intervals the great cannon hurled their missiles against the fort, it was evident that, for the time at least, the attack was not to be pressed at that point. A fresh body of slaves, however, came down from the town to relieve those who had been all night at work, and the repair of the defences was continued, and with greater neatness and method than had been possible in the darkness.

At eight o'clock the bells of St. John's Church gave notice that a solemn service of thanksgiving for the repulse of the enemy was about to be held. Notice had been sent down early to the tower, and all the knights who could be spared, without too greatly weakening the garrison, went up to attend it; the service was conducted with all the pomp and ceremony possible, and after it was over a great procession was formed to proceed to the shrine, where a picture of the Virgin held in special reverence by the Order was placed.

As it wound through the streets in splendid array, the grand master and officials in all their robes of state, the knights in full armour and the mantles of the Order, while the inhabitants in gala costume lined the streets, windows, and house-tops, the ladies waving scarves and scattering flowers down on the knights, the roar of great cannon on the south side of the city showed that the Turks had commenced the attack in another quarter. Without pausing, the procession continued its way, and it was not until the service in the chapel had been concluded that any steps were taken to ascertain the direction of the attack. As soon as it was over, the knights hastened to the walls. During the night the Turks had transported their great basilisks, with other large pieces of artillery, from the camp to the rising ground on the south side of the city, and had opened fire against the wall covering the Jews' quarter, and at the same time against the tower of St. Mary on the one hand and the Italian tower on the other.

From other commanding spots huge mortars were hurling great fragments of rock and other missiles broadcast into the town. The portion of the wall selected for the attack showed that the Turks had been well informed by their spies of the weak points of the defence. The wall behind which the Jews' quarter lay, was, to all appearance, of thick and solid masonry; but this was really of great age, having formed part of the original defences of the town, before the Order had established itself there. The masonry, therefore, was ill fitted to resist the huge balls hurled against it by the basilisks. The *langue* of Provence was in charge of this part of the wall, and, leaving them for the present to bear the brunt of the storm, the grand master sent the knights who could be spared, to assist the inhabitants to erect shelters against the storm of missiles falling in the town.

Sheds with sharply-sloping roofs, constructed of solid timber, were built against the inner side of the walls, and beneath these numbers of the inhabitants found refuge. The work was performed with great celerity by the inhabitants, aided by the gangs of slaves, and in two or three days the townspeople were all in shelter, either in these sheds, in the vaults of the churches, or in other strongly-constructed buildings.

Among the missiles hurled into the town were balls filled with Greek fire, but the houses being entirely built of stone, no conflagrations of importance were caused by them, as a band of knights was organised specially to watch for these bombs, and whenever one of them was seen to fall, they hurried from their look-out to the spot, with a gang of slaves carrying baskets of earth and buckets of water, and quenched the flames before they had made any great headway.

The roar of the bombardment was almost continuous, and was heard at islands distant from Rhodes, telling the inhabitants how the battle between the Christians and the Moslems was raging.

It was not long before the wall in the front of the Jews' quarter began to crumble, and it was soon evident that it must, ere many days, succumb to the storm of missiles hurled against it. D'Aubusson lost no time in making preparations to avert the danger. He ordered all the houses in rear of the wall to be levelled; a deep semi-circular ditch was then dug, and behind this a new wall, constructed of the stones and bricks from the houses destroyed, was built, and backed with an earthen rampart of great thickness and solidity.

The work was carried on with extraordinary rapidity. The grand master himself set the example, and, throwing aside his robes and armour, laboured with pick and shovel like the commonest labourer. This excited the people to the highest pitch of enthusiasm, and all classes threw themselves into the task. Knights and slaves, men, women, and children, and even the inmates of the convents and nunneries, aided in the work, and when at last the outer wall fell, and the Turks thought that success was at hand, the pasha saw with astonishment and dismay that entry to the city was still barred by a work as formidable as that which he had destroyed at an enormous expenditure of ammunition. There was now a short breathing time for the besieged; but the depression which the failure of their efforts excited among the Turks, was shortly dispelled by the arrival of a ship, with a despatch from Constantinople, in which the pasha was informed that the sultan himself was about to proceed to Rhodes with a reinforcement of a hundred thousand men, and a fresh park of artillery.

Paleologus had some doubts as to whether the report was true or was merely intended to stimulate him to new efforts for the speedy capture of the place. Knowing well that the grand master was the heart and soul of the defence, and that the failure of the assault was mainly due to his energy and ability, he determined to resort to the weapon so frequently in use in Eastern warfare—that of assassination. To this end he employed two men, one a Dalmatian, the other an Albanian; these presented themselves before the walls as deserters, and as there was no reason for suspecting their tale, they were admitted within the gates, and welcomed as having escaped from enforced service. They soon spread the tale of the speedy coming of the sultan with vast reinforcements, and as the pasha had on the previous day caused salutes to be fired, and other demonstrations to be made, the news was readily credited, and caused the greatest dismay among the defenders.

Some of the knights of the Italian and Spanish *langue*s believed the prospect of a successful defence against so enormous a force was absolutely hopeless, and determined to put pressure upon D'Aubusson to treat for surrender before it became too late. They opened negotiations with an Italian named Filelfo, one of D'Aubusson's secretaries, who undertook to lay their opinion before the grand master. D'Aubusson at once summoned the knights concerned in the matter before him. They found him with several members of the council.

"Sir Knights," he said, "I have heard from my secretary your opinions in the matter of a surrender, and since you are in such terror of the Moslem sultan, you have my full permission to leave the town; and, more than that, I will myself secure your safe departure, which might be imperilled if your comrades or even the inhabitants of the town came to learn that you had advocated surrender; but," he went on, changing his tone from that of sarcasm to sternness, "if you remain with us, see that the word surrender never again passes your lips, and be assured that, should you continue your intrigues, in that direction, you shall meet with the fate you so justly deserve."

Overwhelmed by the grand master's accusation and sternness, the Italian and Spanish knights threw themselves on their knees and implored him to grant them an early opportunity of retrieving their fault by battle with the infidel. Feeling that the lesson had been sufficiently severe, and that henceforth there would be no renewal of intrigues for a surrender, D'Aubusson forgave them, and promised them a place in the van when next the Moslems attacked. The incident was not without its advantage, for the two pretended deserters, believing that Filelfo, who had also fallen under the displeasure of the grand master, would be ready to join in the conspiracy against his life, approached him. Filelfo, who was greatly attached to D'Aubusson, saw by their manner that they wished to engage him in some intrigue, and, feigning great resentment and anger at his disgrace, led them on until they divulged the entire plot for D'Aubusson's assassination, and made brilliant offers to him if he would afford them facilities for carrying it out, producing, in proof of their power to do so, a letter of the pasha, authorising them to make such promises in his name.

A KNIGHT OF THE WHITE CROSS

Filelfo at once divulged the whole plot to D'Aubusson. The two men were immediately arrested, tried by the council, and sentenced to death. They were not, however, formally executed, for the populace, obtaining news of their treachery, broke in upon their guards, and tore them to pieces. Foiled in his attempt on the life of the grand master, the pasha prepared for a renewal of the attack, and it was not long before the knights on the look-out at the church of St. John perceived that the fort of St. Nicholas was again to be the scene of the attack. It was ere long discovered that a large number of men were busy some distance along the shore in building a long structure, that could only be intended for a floating bridge.

Among the sailors who had aided in the attack with the fire-ships were several men belonging to an English trader in the port. All who had done so had been handsomely rewarded for their conduct, and five of the Englishmen had afterwards gone to the English *auberge* and had asked to be enrolled for service against the Turks, as they were weary of remaining on board in idleness when there was work to be done. Their offer had been accepted, and they had, in common with all the sailors in the port, laboured at the construction of the inner wall. When that was completed, Sir John Boswell, under whose special charge they had been placed, said to Gervaise,—

"I think that I cannot do better than send these men down to St. Nicholas. It is probable that now the Turks see that they can do nothing at the new breach, they may try again there. Sailors are accustomed to night-watches, and there are many of our knights who are not used to such work, and can be better trusted to defend a breach than to keep a vigilant watch at night. Will you take these men down to Caretto, and tell him that he can sleep soundly if he has a couple of them on watch? One of them, Roger Jervis, who is the mate of their ship, can speak some Italian, and as he is in command of them, Caretto will find no trouble in making them understand him."

378

THE STRUGGLE AT THE BREACH

St. Nicholas had now been put into a fair state of defence, as a party had been kept steadily at work there. Gervaise had not been to the tower since the morning after the assault, and saw with satisfaction how much had been done to render it secure. He found that Caretto was fast recovering from his wounds.

"As it seems probable, Sir Fabricius," he said, after the first greetings to the knight, "that the Turks will favour you with another visit, I have brought you five watch-dogs. They are countrymen of mine, and were among those who navigated the fire-ships the other day. Sir John Boswell has sent them down; they are, of course, accustomed to keep watch at night. One of them is mate of their vessel, and will be in command of them; he speaks a little Italian, and so will understand any orders you may give him. I have been speaking to him as we came down; he will divide his men into two watches, and will himself be on guard all night. Will you assign them some quiet place where they can sleep in the daytime? They can erect a shelter with a piece of sail-cloth and a few bits of board, and they will, of course, be furnished with food."

"I shall be very glad to have them, for I am always restless at night, lest those on watch should close their eyes. You see, they have quite made up their minds that this fort will not be attacked again, and so are less inclined to be vigilant than they would be, did they think that an attack was impending."

Now that there was reason to believe that St. Nicholas might again be attacked, Gervaise was frequently there with orders or inquiries from the grand master. A number of vessels in the harbour were fitted up as fire-ships, so as to be in readiness when the attack came. He was about to start early one morning when he saw Roger Jervis coming up with a heavy anchor on his shoulder.

"Why, what are you bringing that up here for?" he asked. "Have you been diving; for I see your clothes are dripping with water?"

"Ay, ay, sir, I have been in the water, and that Italian commander told me to come straight up here to tell the grand master all about the story; and right glad am I to have met you, for I should have made but a poor fist of it alone; I don't know more of their lingo than just to talk a few words of it."

"Then you had better tell me the story before I take you in."

"Well, it was like this, Sir Knight: I had Hudson and Jeffreys posted upon the wall, and I thought I would take a turn down on the rocks, for it was a dark night, and you can see much farther when you are by the edge of the water than you can when you are at the mast-head. I sat there for an hour, and was thinking that it was about time to go up and turn out the other watch, when I saw something dark upon the water. It wasn't a ship, that was certain, and if it was a boat there wasn't any one in it; but it was too dark to make quite sure what it was. I watched it for a time, though I did not think much of the thing, taking it for a boat that had got adrift, or maybe a barrel from one of the Turkish ships. Presently I made out that it was a good bit nearer than when I first saw it.

"That puzzled me. There is no tide to speak of in these seas, and there was no wind moving about. I could make out now that it was a boat, though a very small one, but certainly there was no one rowing it. It looked a very strange craft, and as I saw by the way it was bearing that it would come ashore about five or six fathoms from where I was sitting, I slid quietly off the rock, put my sword down by me handy for action, and waited. Presently the boat came up alongside the rock, and a fellow stood up from behind the stern. I was glad to see him, for I had begun to think that there was witchcraft in the thing moving along by itself; but I can tell you I was savage with myself for not having guessed there was a man swimming behind and pushing it on.

"He stooped over the boat, and took something heavy out; then he felt about among the rocks under the water, and then laid the thing down there, and seemed to me to be settling it firm. I had half a mind to jump up and let fly at him, but then I thought it would be better to let him finish what he was doing, and go off with the idea that no one had seen him. So I kept hid until he started again. He waded a short way before he had to swim, and I could see that as he went he was paying out a rope over the stern. It was clear enough now what he had been up to: he had been fixing an anchor. What he did it for, or what use it could be to him, I could not say, but it was certain that he would not take all that trouble, with the chance of being knocked on the head, for nothing; so I waited for a bit till he had got out of sight, and over to the other side of the port.

"Then I got up and felt about, and, chancing to get my foot under the rope, went right over into the water. After that you may guess I was not long in finding the anchor. I unknotted the rope from it and carried it ashore; then it struck me that the Turks might take it into their heads to give a pull on it in the morning, and if they did; they would find out that their game, whatever it was, had been found out; so I got hold of a stone of about twenty pound weight, and fastened the rope's end round it. That was enough to prevent the rope getting slack and make them think that it was still fast to the anchor; but, of course, if they pulled hard on it it would come home directly. I went and reported the matter the first thing this morning to the governor. He seemed to think that it was important, and told me to bring the anchor up to the grand master, who would get one of the English knights to find out all about it; for he could not make out much of what I said."

"It is very important," Gervaise said, "and you behaved very wisely in the matter, and have rendered a great service by your discovery. I will take you in at once to the grand master."

Still bearing the anchor, the sailor followed Gervaise into an apartment where D'Aubusson was taking council with some of the senior knights.

"Pardon my interrupting your Highness," Gervaise said; "but the matter is so important that I knew you would listen to it, however occupied you were." And he then repeated the narrative of the sailor's discovery.

"This is indeed of the highest importance," D'Aubusson said, "and the knowledge that it gives us may enable us to defeat an attempt, that might otherwise have proved our ruin. You see, knights, it solves the question that we were just discussing. We agreed that this long floating bridge that they have been constructing, was intended to enable them to cross the outer port and again attack St. Nicholas; and yet it seemed to us that even by night our batteries would be able to keep up such a fire on the boats, towing the head of the bridge across, as to render it well-nigh impossible for them to get it over. Now you see what their plan is. With the aid of this rope, the end of which they think is firmly fixed on our side, they mean to haul the bridge across, and that so silently that they hope to be upon us almost before we have time to don our armour. We shall now be fully prepared, and need have no fear of the result."

There could now be little doubt that the attack would be made without loss of time, especially as the Turks believed that they could get their bridge across unseen. The fire-ships—which were altogether more formidable than those Gervaise had improvised—were ordered to be made ready for action. This being arranged, the admiral left the council at once, that no time should be lost in getting them in readiness. D'Aubusson then turned to the English sailor.

"You have rendered us a great service indeed by your vigilance, and showed great prudence by allowing the Turk to believe that he had accomplished his mission unsuspected. Had he thought he had been observed, some other plan would have been adopted. For so great a service it is meet that a great reward should be given."

THE STRUGGLE AT THE BREACH

He then took a bag from the hands of one of his secretaries, whom he had sent to fetch it, while they were discussing the matter of the fire-ships.

"Here are two hundred golden crowns," he added, handing the bag to the seaman. "With these you can either settle on shore, or can build a stout ship and pursue your calling. Should you do so, call her the St. Nicholas, in remembrance of the gratitude of the Order of St. John for your having saved that fort from the Turks."

Astonished and delighted at the reward, which represented a very large sum in those days, the sailor stammered his thanks, and added, "I hope to-night that if I again have charge of a fire-ship, I may be able to do more to prove to your Highness how grateful I am for the gift."

Throughout the day preparations for the defence of St. Nicholas went on unceasingly. Gangs of men, as usual, worked in the breach; but, as it was deemed advisable that there should be no outward show of activity that would lead the Turks to suspect that their design had been discovered, neither reinforcements of men nor munitions were sent along the mole; everything being taken out by boats, which, rowing closely along under the wall, were hidden from the view of the Turks. Barrels of Greek fire and pitch, cauldrons for heating the latter, a store of firewood, great balls of cotton steeped in oil and turpentine, sheaves of darts, spikes on short staves, that were, after darkness fell, to be thrust in among the fallen masonry to form a *cheaux-de-frise*—these, and all other matters that the ingenuity of the defenders could suggest, were landed at the water-gate of the fort, while the garrison was strengthened by the addition of a large number of knights. Stores of ammunition were collected in readiness at all the batteries that commanded the mouth of the outer port, and by sunset D'Aubusson felt that everything that was possible had been done to meet the impending storm.

At midnight the Turkish preparations were complete. The attack by the bridge was to be assisted by a large number of boats and other craft, and many armed galleys were also brought up to destroy or tow away the defenders' fire-ships. Paleologus himself was down by the shore directing the preparations. Some of his best troops were placed upon the floating bridge, and, when all was ready, the order was given to pull upon the rope. No sooner, however, did the strain come upon it than there was a jerk, the rope slackened, and it was at once evident that the anchor had been discovered and the well-laid plan disconcerted. Paleologus was furious, but, believing that the attack he had arranged would still be irresistible, he ordered a number of boats to take the bridge in tow, while a still larger force was to make a direct attack upon the breach. The movement was to be conducted as silently as possible until it was discovered, and then a dash forward was to be made.

It was two o'clock before the fresh arrangements were completed and the boats put out. They had gone but a short distance when the anxious watchers in St. Nicholas learnt by the dull, confused sound that came across the water, that the attack was, in spite of the failure of the plan to take the bridge silently across, to be persevered in. A cannon was at once fired to give notice to the other batteries to be in readiness, and as soon as the dark mass of boats was made out the guns of the fort opened a destructive fire upon them, and a moment later were seconded by those from the fortress; these, however, were at present being fired almost at random, as the Turkish boats could not be made out at that distance. Now that all need for concealment was at an end, the Turkish war-cry rose shrilly in the air, and the boatmen bent to their oars. The great cannon at St. Anthony's Church hurled their tremendous missiles at the tower, seconded by the fire of a number of other pieces that had in the darkness been brought down almost to the water's edge.

As before, the boats swept up to the foot of the breach, the Turks leaped out, and, undismayed by the storm of shot, climbed up to the assault. The short ladders that they had brought with them enabled them to surmount the escarpments so laboriously made, and with loud shouts of

THE STRUGGLE AT THE BREACH

"Allah!" they flung themselves upon the defenders on the crest of the breach. Here they were met by a line even more difficult to break through than before. The knights were ranged three deep; those in the front were armed with swords and battle-axes, while those in the other two lines thrust their spears out between the swordsmen, covering them with a hedge of steel points. Others in the rear brought up buckets of blazing pitch and Greek fire, and, advancing through gaps left for the purpose, hurled the buckets down into the struggling mass on the slope. There the fire not only carried death among the assailants, but the lurid flames enabled the batteries to direct their shot with terrible effect upon the breach, the crowded boats at its foot, and the bridge which was, with immense labour, presently got into position.

It was not long before fresh light was thrown upon the scene, as the fire-ships, issuing out from the inner harbour, burst into columns of flame, and, towed by boats, came into action. They were convoyed by the two galleys, each with a full complement of knights, and these soon became engaged in a fierce fight with the Turkish vessels that bore down to arrest the course of the fire-ships. The scene was indeed a terrible one, the roar of cannon, the shouts of the combatants, the screams of the poor wretches upon whom the terrible Greek fire fell, the clash of arms and the shouts and cries of the Turks as they pressed across the bridge, united in a din that thrilled with horror the spectators, both in the city and on St. Stephen's Hill.

Several of the Turkish galleys, in their efforts to arrest the approach of the fire-ships towards the bridge, became themselves involved in the flames; but they were so far successful that when daylight broke the bridge was still intact and the combat at the breach continued to rage with determination and fury on both sides. The Turks there were led by a brave young prince named Ibrahim, a near relative of the sultan, with whom he was a great favourite, and he was ever in the front line of the assailants, his splendid bravery animating the soldiers to continue their efforts. As the daylight broadened out, however, the light enabled the Christian gunners to aim with far greater accuracy than had before been possible, and, concentrating their fire upon the bridge, across which reinforcements continued to press to the support of the assailants, they succeeded in sinking so many of the boats that it was no longer passable.

Next they turned their fire upon the Turkish galleys, four, of which they sank. Shortly afterwards, a ball struck the gallant young leader of the Turks, who, although previously several times wounded, had continued to fight in the front line. He fell dead, and his followers, disheartened by his fall and by the destruction of the bridge, at once abandoned their efforts, and rushed down to the foot of the breach. The terrible scene enacted at the repulse of the previous attack was now repeated. The concentrated fire of the guns of the defenders carried destruction into the crowded mass. Some gained the boats that still remained uninjured, and rowed for the opposite shore; the greater number rushed into the water and strove to recross it either by swimming or by the aid of the debris of the shattered boats. Their total loss was greater even than that suffered by them in the first attack, between two and three thousand being either killed or drowned, among them a number of their best officers. The amount of spoil, in the form of rich jewels and costly gold ornaments, found on the bodies of the dead piled on the breach, was very great.

For three days after this terrible repulse the Turks were inactive, the pasha remaining shut up in his tent, refusing to see any one, or to issue orders. At the end of that time he roused himself from his stupor of grief and disappointment, and, abandoning the idea of any further attack upon the point that had cost him so dearly, he ordered the troops to move round and renew the attack upon the wall in front of the Jews' quarter, and commence the construction of a battery on the edge of the great ditch facing the retrenchment behind the breach before effected. The knights of Italy and Spain determined to seize the opportunity of retrieving the disgrace that had fallen upon them. At night they descended into the deep cutting, carrying across their ladders, and, silently mounting the opposite side, rushed with loud shouts into the unfinished battery. The Turks there, taken utterly by surprise, made but a slight resistance; a few were immediately cut down, and the rest fled panic-stricken.

The knights at once set the woodwork of the battery on fire, hurled the guns down into the ditch, and then returned triumphantly into the town, the dashing feat completely reinstating them in the good opinion of the grand master and their comrades.

The incident showed the pasha that he must neglect no precautions, and, accordingly, he commenced his works at a distance from the walls, and pushed his approaches regularly forward until he again established a battery on the site of that from which his troops had been so unceremoniously ejected. While forming the approaches, the workmen had been constantly harassed by the fire from the guns on the walls, suffering considerable loss of life; but their numerical superiority was so vast that the loss in no way affected the plans of the pasha.

As soon as the battery was completed, gangs of men, accustomed to mining operations, set to work in its rear to drive sloping passages downwards, opening into the face of the great cutting, and through these vast quantities of earth and stones were poured, so as to afford a passage across it, the depth being largely diminished by the great pile of rubbish that had already fallen from the breached wall. This novel mode of attack was altogether unexpected. The knights had regarded the fosse that had been cut at such an enormous expenditure of labour as forming an altogether impassable obstruction, and were dismayed at seeing the progress made in filling it up. D'Aubusson himself, full of resources as he was, saw that the defence was seriously threatened, unless some plan of meeting this unexpected danger could be devised.

A KNIGHT OF THE WHITE CROSS

He consulted Maître Georges; but the latter could make no suggestion; his only advice being the erection of a battery at a spot where it was almost self-evident that it could be of no utility whatever. Other circumstances combined to render the suspicions D'Aubusson had entertained of the good faith of the renegade almost a certainty. Georges was seized, tried, and put to torture, and under this owned that he had been sent into the town for the purpose of betraying it; and he was, the same day, hung in the great square. His guilt must always be considered as uncertain. There was no proof against him, save his own confession; and a confession extorted by torture is of no value whatever. There are certainly many good grounds for suspicion, but it is possible that Georges really repented his apostacy, and acted in good faith in deserting the standard of Paleologus. He was undoubtedly a man of altogether exceptional ability and acquirements, and even the knights who have written accounts of the siege do justice to the fascination of his manner and the charm of his conversation.

D'Aubusson now set to work in another direction to counteract the efforts of the Turks. He erected an immense wooden catapult, which threw huge pieces of rock into the midst of the Turkish works, crushing down the wooden screens erected to hide their approaches, breaking in the covered ways, and causing great loss of life among the besiegers. At the same time galleries were driven below the breach, opening into the ditch, where their exits were concealed by masses of rubbish. Through these strong working parties issued out at night, and carried away up the passages the rocks and other materials that the Turks had, during the day, brought, with immense labour, from a distance to the shoot. The materials so carried away were piled up behind the retrenchment, greatly adding to its thickness and strength.

For some days the Turks observed, to their astonishment, that the road they were constructing across the ditch was diminishing instead of increasing in bulk, and at length it became so evident that the garrison were in some way removing the materials, that the pasha determined to deliver the assault before the heap was so far diminished as to become impassable. His former defeats had, however, taught him that success could not be always calculated upon, however good its prospect might appear; and although he had no real hope that the defenders would yield, he sent a formal summons for them to do so. This was refused with disdain, and preparations were at once made for the assault.

The pasha promised to his soldiers the sack of the town and all the booty captured, and so assured were they of success that sacks were made to carry off the plunder. Stakes, on which the knights, when taken prisoners, were to be impaled, were prepared and sharpened, and each soldier carried a coil of rope with which to secure his captive.

Before ordering the assault, the way was prepared for it by a terrible fire from every siege gun of the Turks. This was kept up for twenty-four hours, and so tremendous was the effect that the knights were unable to remain on the ramparts. The Turkish troops moved into position for attack, their movements being covered by the roar of the guns, and soon after sunrise on the 22nd of July the signal was given, and at a number of different points the Turks rushed to the assault. All these attacks, save that on the breach, were merely feints, to distract the attention of the garrison, and to add to the confusion caused by this sudden and unexpected onslaught. The pasha's plans were well designed and carried out; the knights, unable to keep their places on the ramparts under the storm of missiles, had retired to shelter behind the walls. There was no thought of an instant assault, as they considered that this would not be delivered until the new wall behind the breach had been demolished.

Consequently, the rush of the Turks found the defenders altogether unprepared. Swarming across the mass of *débris* in the ditch, they ascended the breach without opposition, and their scaling ladders were placed against the new wall before the knights could hurry up to its defence. Even before the alarm was given in the town, the Turkish standard was waving on the parapet, and the Moslems were crowding on to the wall in vast numbers. The suddenness of the attack, the complete surprise, the sound of battle at various points around the walls, caused for a time confusion and dismay among the knights charged with the defence of the wall facing the breach. Roused by the uproar, the inhabitants of the town rushed up to their roofs to ascertain what was happening, and their cries of wild terror and alarm at seeing the Turkish banner on the walls added to the confusion. D'Aubusson sprang up from the couch, on which he had thrown himself in full armour, at the first sound of the alarm, and, sending off messages to all the *auberges* to summon every man to the defence, ran down into the town, followed by a small party of knights.

Rushing through the streets, now filled with half-dressed people wild with terror, he reached the foot of the wall, whose summit was crowded with the enemy, and saw in an instant that all was lost unless they could be driven thence without delay. The effect of his presence was instantaneous. The knights, hitherto confused and dismayed, rallied at once, and prepared for the desperate undertaking. The bank on the inside was almost perpendicular, and those charged with its defence had used two or three ladders for ascending to the rampart. These were at once seized and planted against the wall.

The position of the contending parties was now reversed; the Christians were the assailants, the Turks the defenders. D'Aubusson himself was the first to ascend. Covering his head with his shield, he mounted the rampart; but ere he could gain a footing on the top he was severely wounded and hurled backwards. Again he made the attempt, but was again wounded and thrown down. Once more he mounted, and this time made good his footing. A moment later, Gervaise, who had accompanied him from the palace, stood beside him. Animated with the same spirit as his leader, he threw himself recklessly against the Turks, using a short, heavy mace, which in a *mêlée* was far more useful than the long sword. Scimitars clashed upon his helmet and armour; but at every blow he struck a Turk fell, and for each foot he gained a knight sprang on to the wall and joined him. Each moment their number increased, and the war-cry of the Order rose louder and fiercer above the din. The very number of the Turks told against them. Crowded together as they were they could not use their weapons effectually, and, pressing fiercely upon them, the knights drove them back along the wall on either hand, hurling them down into the street or over the rampart. On so narrow a field of battle the advantage was all on the side of the knights, whose superior height and strength, and the protection afforded by their armour, rendered them almost invincible, nerved as they were with fury at the surprise that had overtaken them, and the knowledge that the fate of the city depended upon their efforts. After a quarter of an hour's desperate conflict the Turks were driven down the partial breach effected in the wall by the last bombardment, and the Christians were again the masters of their ramparts. Paleologus, however, hurried up reinforcements, headed by a band of janissaries, whose valour had decided many an obstinate conflict. Before ordering them to advance, he gave instructions to a company of men of approved valour to devote all their efforts to attacking D'Aubusson himself, whose mantle and rich armour rendered him a conspicuous object among the defenders of the breach. Advancing to the attack, the janissaries burst through the mass of Turks still continuing the conflict, and rushed up the breach. Then the chosen band, separating from the rest, flung themselves upon the grand master, the suddenness and fury of their attack isolating him and Gervaise from the knights around.

Surrounded as he was by foes, already suffering from two severe wounds and shaken by his falls from the ladder, the grand master yet made a valiant defence in front, while Gervaise, hurling his mace into the face of one of his assailants, and drawing his two-handed sword, covered him from the attack from behind. D'Aubusson received two more severe wounds, but still fought on. Gervaise, while in the act of cutting down an assailant, heard a shout of triumph from behind, and, looking round, he saw the grand master sinking to the ground from another wound. With a cry of grief and fury Gervaise sprang to him, receiving as he did so several blows on his armour and shield intended for the fallen knight, and, standing across him, showered his blows with such strength and swiftness that the janissaries shrank back before the sweep of the flashing steel. More than one who tried to spring into close quarters fell cleft to the chin, and, ere his assailants could combine for a general rush, a body of knights, who had just beaten off their assailants, fell upon the ranks of the janissaries with a force and fury there was no withstanding, and the chosen troops of the sultan for the first time broke and fled.

Excited almost to madness by the sight of their beloved master stretched bleeding on the ground, the knights dashed down the breach in eager pursuit. This action was decisive of the fate of the struggle. The panic among the janissaries at once spread, and the main body of troops, who had hitherto valiantly striven to regain the advantage snatched from them, now lost heart and fled in confusion. But their escape was barred by the great body of reinforcements pressing forward across the heap of rubbish that formed the breach over the deep ditch. Maddened by fear, the fugitives strove to cut a way through their friends. The whole of the defenders of the breach now fell upon the rear of the struggling mass, hewing them down almost without resistance, while the cannon from the walls and towers kept up an unceasing fire until the last survivors of what had become a massacre, succeeded in gaining their works beyond the ditch, and fled to their camp. From every gateway and postern the knights now poured out, and, gathering together, advanced to the attack of St. Stephen's Hill. They met with but a faint resistance. The greater portion of the disorganised troops had made no pause at their camp, but had continued their headlong flight to the harbour, where their ships were moored, Paleologus himself, heart-broken and despairing at his failure, sharing their flight. The camp, with all its rich booty and the great banner of the pasha, fell into the hands of the victors, who, satisfied with their success, and exhausted by their efforts, made no attempt to follow the flying foe, or to hinder their embarkation; for even now the Turks, enormously outnumbering them as they did, might be driven by despair to a resistance so desperate as once again to turn the tide of victory.

CHAPTER XXIII
THE REWARD OF VALOUR

GERVAISE knew nothing at the time of the final result of the battle, for as soon as the knights had burst through the circle of his opponents, he sank insensible on the body of the grand master. When he came to himself, he was lying on a bed in the hospital of the Order. As soon as he moved, Ralph Harcourt, who was, with other knights, occupied in tending the wounded, came to his bedside. "Thank God that you are conscious again, Gervaise! They told me that it was but faintness and loss of blood, and that none of your wounds were likely to prove mortal, and for the last twelve hours they have declared that you were asleep: but you looked so white that I could not but fear you would never wake again."

"How is the grand master?" Gervaise asked eagerly. Ralph shook his head.

"He is wounded sorely, Gervaise, and the leech declares that one at least of his wounds is mortal; still, I cannot bring myself to believe that so great a hero will be taken away in the moment of victory, after having done such marvels for the cause not only of the Order, but of all Christendom."

"Then you beat them back again from the breach?" Gervaise said.

"That was not all. They were in such confusion that we sallied out, captured their camp, with the pasha's banner and an enormous quantity of spoil, and pursued them to their harbour. Then we halted, fearing that they might in their desperation turn upon us, and, terribly weakened as

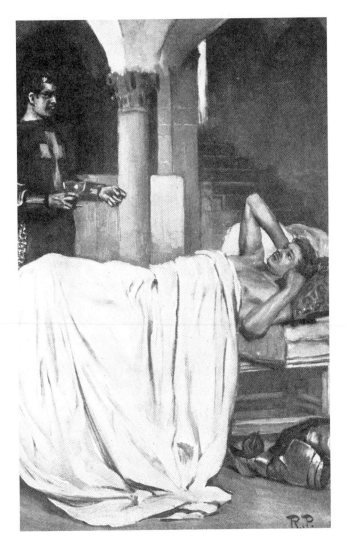

Sir Gervaise finds himself lying in the hospital of the Order.

we were by our losses, have again snatched the victory from our grasp. So we let them go on board their ships without interference, and this morning there is not a Turkish sail in sight. The inhabitants are well-nigh mad with joy. But elated as we are at our success, our gladness is sorely damped by the state of the grand master, and the loss of so many of our comrades, though, indeed, our *langue* has suffered less than any of the others, for the brunt of the attacks on St. Nicholas and the breach did not fall upon us, still we lost heavily when at last we hurried up to win back the wall from them."

"Who have fallen?" Gervaise asked.

"Among the principal knights are Thomas Ben, Henry Haler, Thomas Ploniton, John Vaquelin, Adam Tedbond, Henry Batasbi, and Henry Anlui. Marmaduke Lumley is dangerously wounded. Of the younger knights, some fifteen have been killed, and among them your old enemy Rivers. He died a coward's death, the only one, thank God, of all our *langue*. When the fray was thickest Sir John Boswell marked him crouching behind the parapet. He seized him by the gorget, and hauled him out, but his knees shook so that he could scarcely walk, and would have slunk back when released. Sir John raised his mace to slay him as a disgrace to the Order and our *langue*, when a ball from one of the Turkish cannon cut him well-nigh in half, so that he fell by the hands of the Turks, and not by the sword of one of the Order he had disgraced. Fortunately none, save half-a-dozen knights of our *langue*, saw the affair, and you may be sure we shall say nothing about it; and instead of Rivers' name going down to infamy, it will appear in the list of those who died in the defence of Rhodes."

"May God assoil his soul!" Gervaise said earnestly. "'Tis strange that one of gentle blood should have proved a coward. Had he remained at home, and turned courtier, instead of entering the Order, he might have died honoured, without any one ever coming to doubt his courage."

THE REWARD OF VALOUR

"He would have turned out bad whatever he was," Ralph said contemptuously; "for my part, I never saw a single good quality in him."

Long before Gervaise was out of hospital, the glad tidings that D'Aubusson would recover, in spite of the prognostications of the leech, spread joy through the city, and at about the same time that Gervaise left the hospital the grand master was able to sit up. Two or three days afterwards he sent for Gervaise.

"I owe my life to you, Sir Gervaise," he said, stretching out his thin, white hand to him as he entered. "You stood by me nobly till I fell, for, though unable to stand, I was not unconscious, and saw how you stood above me and kept the swarming Moslems at bay. No knight throughout the siege has rendered such great service as you have done. Since I have been lying unable to move, I have thought of many things; among them, that I had forgotten to give you the letters and presents that came for you after you sailed away. They are in that cabinet; please bring them to me. There," he said, as Gervaise brought a bulky parcel which the grand master opened, "this letter is from the Holy Father himself. That, as you may see from the arms on the seal, is from Florence. The others are from Pisa, Leghorn, and Naples. Rarely, Sir Gervaise, has any potentate or knight earned the thanks of so many great cities. These caskets accompanied them. Sit down and read your letters. They must be copied in our records."

Gervaise first opened the one from the Pope. It was written by his own hand, and expressed his thanks as a temporal sovereign for the great benefit to the commerce of his subjects by the destruction of the corsair fleet, and as the head of the Christian Church for the blow struck at the Moslems. The other three letters were alike in character, expressing the gratitude of the cities for their deliverance from the danger, and of their admiration for the action by which a fleet was destroyed with a single galley. Along with the letter from Pisa was a casket containing a heavy gold chain set with gems. Florence sent a casket containing a document bestowing upon him the freedom of the city, and an order upon the treasury for five thousand ducats that had been voted to him by the grand council of the Republic; while Ferdinand, King of Naples, bestowed on him the grand cross of the Order of St. Michael.

"The armour I had hung up in the armoury, where it has been carefully kept clean. I guessed what it was by the weight of the case when it came, and thought it best to open it, as it might have got spoilt by rust. It is a timely gift, Sir Gervaise, for the siege has layed havoc with the suit Genoa gave you; it is sorely battered, dinted, and broken, and, although you can doubtless get it repaired, if I were you I would keep it in its present state as a memorial—and there could be no prouder one—of the part you bore in the siege. I have seen Caretto this morning. He sails for Genoa to-morrow, where he will, I hope, soon recover his strength, for the wounds he received at St. Nicholas have healed but slowly. He said,"—and a momentary smile crossed the grand master's face—"that he thought a change might benefit you also, for he was sure that the air here had scarce recovered from the taint of blood. Therefore, here is a paper granting you three months' leave. His commandery is a pleasant one, and well situated on the slopes of the hills; and the fresh air will, doubtless, speedily set you up. I should like nothing better than a stay there myself, but there is much to do to repair the damages caused by the siege, and to place the city in a state of defence should the Turks again lay siege to it; and methinks Mahomet will not sit down quietly under the heavy reverse his troops have met with."

"But I should be glad to stay here to assist in the work, your Highness."

"There are plenty of knights to see to that," D'Aubusson replied, "and it will be long before you are fit for such work. No, I give my orders for you to proceed with Caretto to Genoa—unless, indeed, you would prefer to go to some other locality to recruit your strength."

THE REWARD OF VALOUR

"I would much rather go with Sir Fabricius, your Highness, than to any place where I have no acquaintances. I have a great esteem and respect for him."

"He is worthy of it; there is no nobler knight in the Order, and, had I fallen, none who could more confidently have been selected to fill my place. He has an equally high opinion of you, and spoke long and earnestly concerning you."

A fortnight later the ship carrying the two knights arrived at Genoa.

"I will go ashore at once, Gervaise," Caretto said. "I know not whether my cousin is in the city or on her estate; if the former, I will stay with her for a day or two before going off to my commandery, and of course you will also be her guest. I hope she will be here, for methinks we shall both need to refit our wardrobes before we are fit to appear in society."

"Certainly I shall," Gervaise agreed; "for, indeed, I find that my gala costume suffered a good deal during my long absence; and, moreover, although I have not increased in height, I have broadened out a good deal since I was here two years ago."

"Yes; you were a youth then, Gervaise, and now you are a man, and one of no ordinary strength and size. The sun of Tripoli, and your labours during the siege, have added some years to your appearance. You are, I think, little over twenty, but you look two or three years older. The change is even greater in your manner than in your appearance; you were then new to command, doubtful as to your own powers, and diffident with those older than yourself. Now for two years you have thought and acted for yourself, and have shown yourself capable of making a mark even among men like the knights of St. John, both in valour and in fitness to command. You saved St. Nicholas, you saved the life of the grand master; and in the order of the day he issued on the morning we left, granting you three months' leave for the recovery of your wounds, he took the opportunity of recording, in the name of the council and himself, their admiration for the services rendered by you during the siege, and his own gratitude for saving his life when he lay helpless and surrounded by the Moslems—a testimony of which any knight of Christendom might well feel proud."

It was three hours before Caretto returned to the ship.

"My cousin is at home, and will be delighted to see you. I am sorry that I have kept you waiting so long, but at present Genoa, and, indeed, all Europe, is agog at the news of the defeat of the Turks, and Italy especially sees clearly enough that, had Rhodes fallen, she would have been the next object of attack by Mahomet; therefore the ladies would not hear of my leaving them until I had told them something at least of the events of the siege, and also how it came about that you were there to share in the defence. I see that you are ready to land; therefore, let us be going at once. Most of the people will be taking their siesta at present, and we shall get through the streets without being mobbed; for I can assure you that the mantle of the Order is just at present in such high favour that I had a hard task to wend my way through the streets to my cousin's house."

On arriving at the palace of the Countess of Forli, Gervaise was surprised at the change that had taken place in the Lady Claudia. From what Caretto had said, he was prepared to find that she had grown out of her girlhood, and had altered much. She had, however, changed even more than he had expected, and had become, he thought, the fairest woman that he had ever seen. The countess greeted him with great cordiality; but Claudia came forward with a timidity that contrasted strangely with the outspoken frankness he remembered in the girl. For a time they all chatted together of the events of the siege, and of his captivity.

"The news that you had been captured threw quite a gloom over us, Sir Gervaise," the countess said. "We at first consoled ourselves with the thought that you would speedily be ransomed; but when months passed by, and we heard that all the efforts of the grand master had failed to discover where you had been taken, I should have lost all hope had it not been that my cousin had returned after an even longer captivity among the Moors. I am glad to hear that you did not suffer so many hardships as he did."

"I am in no way to be pitied, Countess," Gervaise said lightly. "I had a kind master for some months, and was treated as a friend rather than as a slave; afterwards, I had the good fortune to be made the head of the labourers at the buildings in the sultan's palace, and although I certainly worked with them, the labour was not greater than one could perform without distress, and I had naught to complain of as to my condition."

After talking for upwards of an hour, the countess told Caretto that she had several matters on which she needed his counsel, and retired with him to the next room of the suite opening from the apartment in which they had been sitting. For a minute or two the others sat silent, and then Claudia said,—

"You have changed much since I saw you last, Sir Gervaise. Then it seemed to me scarcely possible that you could have performed the feat of destroying the corsair fleet; now it is not so difficult to understand."

"I have widened out a bit, Lady Claudia. My moustache is really a moustache, and not a pretence at one; otherwise I don't feel that I have changed. The alteration in yourself is infinitely greater."

"I, too, have filled out," she said, with a smile. "I was a thin girl then—all corners and angles. No, I don' t want any compliments, of which, to tell you the truth, I am heartily sick. And so," she went on in a softer tone, "you have actually brought my gage home! Oh, Sir Gervaise,"—and her eyes filled with tears—"my cousin has told me! How could you have been so foolish as to remain voluntarily in captivity, that you might recover the gage a child had given you?"

"Not a child, Lady Claudia. A girl not yet a woman, I admit; yet it was not given in the spirit of a young girl, but in that of an earnest woman. I had taken a vow never to part with it, as you had pledged yourself to bestow no similar favour upon any other knight. I was confident that you would keep your vow; and although in any case, as a true knight, I was bound to preserve your gift, still more so was I bound by the thought of the manner in which you had presented it to me."

"But I could not have blamed you—I should never have dreamt of blaming you," she said earnestly, "for losing it as you did."

"I felt sure, Lady Claudia, that had it been absolutely beyond my power to regain it you would not have blamed me; but it was not beyond my power, and that being so had I been obliged to wait for ten years, instead of two, I would not have come back to you without it. Moreover, you must remember that I prized it beyond all things. I had often scoffed at knights of an order like ours wearing ladies' favours. I had always thought it absurd that we, pledged as we are, should thus declare ourselves admirers of one woman more than another. But this seemed to me a gage of another kind; it was too sacred to be shown or spoken of, and I only mentioned it to Caretto as he cross-questioned me as to why I refused the offer of ransom; and should not have done so then, had he not been present when it was bestowed. I regarded it not as a lightly-given favour, the result of a passing fancy by one who gave favours freely, but as a pledge of friendship and as a guerdon for what I had done, and therefore, more to be honoured than the gifts of a Republic freed from a passing danger. Had you then been what you are now, I might have been foolish enough to think of it in another light, regardless of the fact that you are a rich heiress of one of the noblest families in Italy, and I a knight with no possessions save my sword."

"Say not so, Sir Gervaise," she said impetuously. "Are you not a knight on whom Genoa and Florence have bestowed their citizenship, whom the Holy Father himself has thanked, who has been honoured by Pisa, and whom Ferdinand of Naples has created a Knight of the Grand Cross of St. Michael, whom the grand master has singled out for praise among all the valiant knights of the Order of St. John, who, as my cousin tells me, saved him and the fort he commanded from capture, and who stood alone over the fallen grand master, surrounded by a crowd of foes. How can you speak of yourself as a simple knight?"

Then she stopped, and sat silent for a minute, while a flush of colour mounted to her cheeks.

"Give me my gage again, Sir Gervaise," she said gently. In silence Gervaise removed it from his neck, wondering greatly what could be her intention. She turned it over and over in her hand.

"Sir Knight," she said, "this was of no great value in my eyes when I bestowed it upon you; it was a gage, and not a gift. Now it is to me of value beyond the richest gem on earth; it is a proof of the faith and loyalty of the knight I most esteem and honour, and so in giving it to you again, I part with it with a pang, for I have far greater reason to prize it than you can have. I gave it you before as a girl, proud that a knight who had gained such honour and applause should wear her favour, and without the thought that the trinket was a heart. I give it to you now as a woman, far prouder than before that you should wear her gage, and not blind to the meaning of the emblem."

Gervaise took her hand as she fastened it round his neck, and kissed it; then, still holding it, he said,—

"Do you know what you are doing, Claudia? You are raising hopes that I have never been presumptuous enough to cherish."

"I cannot help that," she said softly. "There is assuredly no presumption in the hope."

He paused a moment.

"You would not esteem me," he said, holding both her hands now, "were I false to my vows. I will return to Rhodes to-morrow, and ask the grand master to forward to the Pope and endorse my petition, that I may be released from my vows to the Order. I cannot think that he or the Holy Father will refuse my request. Then, when I am free, I can tell you how I love and honour you, and how, as I have in the past devoted my life to the Order, so I will in the future devote it, to your happiness."

The girl bowed her head.

"'Tis right it should be so," she said. "I have waited, feeling in my heart that the vow I had given would bind me for life, and I should be content to wait years longer if needs be. But I am bound by no vows, and can acknowledge that you have long been the lord of my life, and that so long as you wore the heart I had given you, so long would I listen to the wooing of no other."

"I fear that the Countess, your mother—" Gervaise began, but she interrupted him.

"You need not fear," she said. "My mother has long known, and knowing also that I am not given to change, has ceased to importune me to listen to other offers. Her sole objection was that you might never return from captivity. Now that you have come back with added honours, she will not only offer no objection, but will, I am sure, receive you gladly, especially as she knows that my cousin Sir Fabricius, for whom she has the greatest affection, holds you in such high esteem."

Six months later Gervaise again landed at Genoa, after having stayed at Rome for a few days on his way back. D'Aubusson had expressed no surprise at his return to Rhodes, or at the request he made.

"Caretto prepared me for this," he said, smiling, "when he asked me if you might accompany him to Genoa. The Order will be a loser, for you would assuredly have risen to the grand priorage of your *langue* some day. But we have no right to complain; you have done your duty and more, and I doubt not that should Mahomet again lay siege to Rhodes, we may count on your hastening here to aid us?"

"That assuredly you may, sir. Should danger threaten, my sword will be as much at the service of the Order as if I were still a member of it."

THE REWARD OF VALOUR

"I by no means disapprove," D'Aubusson went on, "of knights leaving us when they have performed their active service, for in civil life they sometimes have it in their power to render better service to the Order than if passing their lives in the quiet duties of a provincial commandery. It will be so in your case: the lady is a great heiress, and, as the possessor of wide lands, your influence in Northern Italy may be very valuable to us, and in case of need you will, like my brother De Monteuil, be able to bring a gathering of men-at-arms to our aid. Have no fear that the Pope will refuse to you a release from your vows. My recommendation alone would be sufficient; but as, moreover, he is himself under an obligation to you, he will do so without hesitation. Since you have been away, your friend Harcourt has been appointed a commander of a galley, and Sir John Boswell, being incapacitated by the grievous wounds he received during the siege, has accepted a rich commandery in England, and sailed but two days since to take up his charge. By the way, did you a reply to those letters expressing your thanks and explaining your long silence?"

"Yes, your Highness, I wrote the same evening you gave them to me."

"That is right. The money voted you by Florence will be useful to you now, and there is still a sum sent by your commandery owing to you by the treasury. I will give you an order for it. However rich an heiress a knight may win, 'tis pleasant for him to have money of his own; not that you will need it greatly, for, among the presents you have received, the jewels are valuable enough for a wedding gift to a princess."

Gervaise was well received at Rome, and the Pope, after reading the grand master's letter, and learning from him his reason for wishing to leave the Order, without hesitation granted him absolution from his vows. A few months later there was a grand wedding at the cathedral of Genoa, the doge and all the nobles of the Republic being present.

A KNIGHT OF THE WHITE CROSS

Ralph Harcourt and nine other young knights had accompanied Gervaise from Rhodes by the permission, and indeed at the suggestion, of the grand master, who was anxious to show that Gervaise had his full approval and countenance in leaving the Order. Caretto who had been appointed grand prior of Italy, had brought the knights from all the commanderies in the northern republics to do honour to the occasion, and the whole, in their rich armour and the mantles of the Order, made a distinguishing feature in the scene.

The defeat of the Turks created such enthusiasm throughout Europe that when the grand prior of England laid before the king letters he had received from the grand master and Sir John Kendall, speaking in the highest terms of the various great services Gervaise had rendered to the Order, Edward granted his request that the act of attainder against Sir Thomas Tresham and his descendants should be reversed and the estates restored to Gervaise. The latter made, with his wife, occasional journeys to England, staying a few months on his estates in Kent; and as soon as his second son became old enough, he sent him to England to be educated, and settled the estate upon him. He himself had but few pleasant memories of England; he had spent indeed but a very short time there before he entered the house of the Order in Clerkenwell, and that time had been marked by constant anxiety, and concluded with the loss of his father. The great estates that were now his in Italy demanded his full attention, and, as one of the most powerful nobles of Genoa, he had come to take a prominent part in the affairs of the Republic.

He was not called upon to fulfil his promise to aid in the defence of Rhodes, for the death of Mahomet just at the time when he was preparing a vast expedition against it, freed the Island for a long time from fear of an invasion. From time to time they received visits from Ralph Harcourt, who, after five years longer service at Rhodes, received a commandery in England. He held it a few years only, and then returned to the Island, where he obtained a high official appointment.

In 1489 Sir John Boswell became bailiff of the English *langue*, and Sir Fabricius Caretto was in 1513 elected grand master of the Order, and held the office eight years, dying in 1521.

When, in 1522, forty-two years after the first siege, Rhodes was again beleaguered, Gervaise, who had, on the death of the countess, become Count of Forli, raised a large body of men-at-arms, and sent them, under the command of his eldest son, to take part in the defence. His third son had, at the age of sixteen, entered the Order, and rose to high rank in it.

The defence, though even more obstinate and desperate than the first, was attended with less success, for after inflicting enormous losses upon the great army, commanded by the Sultan Solyman himself, the town was forced to yield; for although the Grand Master L'Isle Adam, and most of his nights, would have preferred to bury themselves beneath the ruins rather than yield, they were deterred from doing so, by the knowledge that it would have entailed the massacre of the whole of the inhabitants, who had throughout the siege fought valiantly in the defence of the town. Solyman had suffered such enormous losses that he was glad to grant favourable conditions, and the knights sailed away from the city they had held so long and with such honour, and afterwards established themselves in Malta, where they erected another stronghold, which in the end proved an even more valuable bulwark to Christendom than Rhodes had been. There were none who assisted more generously and largely, by gifts of money, in the establishment of the Order at Malta than Gervaise. His wife, while she lived, was as eager to aid in the cause as he was himself, holding that it was to the Order she owed her husband. And of all their wide possessions there were none so valued by them both, as the little coral heart set in pearls that she, as a girl, had given him, and he had so faithfully brought back to her.

THE END

PrestonSpeed Publications 51 Ridge Road Mill Hall, PA 17751
(570) 726-7844
www.prestonspeed.com

Historiae Dona Repertum

Other titles available from PrestonSpeed Publications

Books by G. A. Henty

For The Temple

The Dragon & The Raven

In Freedom's Cause

By Pike & Dyke

Beric The Briton

St. Barthlomew's Eve

With Lee in Virginia

By Right of Conquest

The Young Cartheginian

Winning His Spurs

Under Drake's Flag

The Cat of Bubastes

Wulf The Saxon

A Knight of the White Cross

St. George for England

With Wolfe in Canada

By England's Aid

The Dash for Khartoum

The Lion of the North

Won by the Sword

Preston/Speed Publications takes great pride in re-printing the complete works of G. A. Henty. New titles are regularly being released. Our editions contain the complete text along with all maps and/or illustrations. In order to ensure the most complete Henty editions, we review all previous releases for the most comprehensive version.